THE
JOURNEY
OF THE
PEACEKEEPER

THE
JOURNEY
OF THE
PEACEKEEPER

Forward

I was seventeen when I first became entangled in this Robin Hood world of my own creation. Seventeen when I dove into the realm of self-publishing with no idea what I was doing.

To those of you who might have read the original series, THANK YOU. I am forever astounded anyone takes interest in the stories I have to tell and immensely grateful for all of you. To those of you who have no idea what I'm talking about, let me explain …

When I started self-publishing I did so under the name Amanda Grace. The series I lovingly refer to as the OG Robin Hood series, five books in total, were all under that name. *Always in Shadow* was the second book that I ever published, when I was twenty-years-young.

Eventually I switched to writing under Mandi Grace, but left my old books behind me for several years. And then one day I decided to move all of my books under one name—and while doing so, revisit and rewrite the old ones to give them a more polished story and brand new covers. This is what you hold in your hand today.

Rewriting *Always in Shadow* and turning it into *The Journey of the Peacekeeper* was illuminating and rewarding in so many ways. The story I tell in this book is the one that I always meant to tell in the original version of this book—but it fell flat in *Always in Shadow*. Why, you might ask? Because the main character, Much, is very like myself. He's an enneagram 9, a peacekeeper and gentle soul. He doesn't always speak his mind (because why would anyone listen, his opinions hold no value), and that was also true of myself in many ways. I wanted to tell a story of transformation for Much in the book once known as *Always in Shadow*, but for anyone who read that version I'm sure you can see...he doesn't transform. He's still meek and afraid by the end of the book.

What I found in rewriting this book was that I myself have changed so much since I wrote the original. I have gone on my own transformation. I've grown confident in my convictions and I can speak my mind when I need to. I'm still a fairly quiet, gentle soul, but I don't have to be.

Finding out that I could give Much the story that he truly deserves simply because I have now lived the journey I wanted him to go on was beautiful for me. Rewriting Much's book was rediscovering myself as a young person and slowly guiding little me and little Much toward the confidence I knew we could both find (because I have). I feel so much more deeply connected to Much and his story now, and he holds my heart in a way he never did when I wrote *Always in Shadow*.

This new *Journey of the Peacekeeper* is twice as big, and given all that Much and I have gone through since its conception and now to its rebirth, I hope twice as good.

to the girl afraid to speak up

to Always in Shadow

Prologue

MARI-LU SKIPPED DOWN the dirt path, relishing the shades of orange and gold to her left beyond the rooftops of Wetherby as the sun set on this most glorious of birthdays. She had a bouquet of flowers in one hand, swinging wildly with every skip forward toward her house, and a wreath of more blossoms braided into her dark hair. Her blue eyes were dancing as she neared her home after spending time in the infamous meadow where the great Robin Hood and his band of outlaws had once lived.

Aunt Lucy was coming today.

Mari-Lu could hardly contain her excitement as her feet briskly danced down the old street. Wetherby was a simple village outside of the city of Nottingham—originally comprised of a few small houses of tenants of a manor nearby (as the villagers had been vassals to the lord who lived there) it had slowly grown into an independent village. With every year the village grew in size as more people built homes and added streets to their little corner of the world. Mari-Lu's father sometimes commented that Nottingham itself was going to envelop them at some point, bringing their little village into the city proper, but it hadn't happened yet. The city of Nottingham was expanding not only through the natural trade and growth of the world but also because of its connection to the legend of Robin Hood, as tourists from both within and far beyond England came to live near where Robin Hood had once walked.

As Mari-Lu turned the last corner toward her home—a house that had been in the family for at least four generations and built onto more times than even she knew—she caught sight of the reason for her eager anticipation.

Aunt Lucy was just at the door, talking with Mari-Lu's mother, so she quickened her steps—forgoing skipping in favor of an all-out run. Aunt Lucy had been away visiting Scotland for some weeks and had only just returned, and on this perfect day of all days, too!

Today was, after all, Mari-Lu's eighth birthday and she was feeling quite grown-up.

Aunt Lucy was undoubtedly the young girl's favorite relative. She was not, in fact, her aunt but rather her great-grandmother but Aunt Lucy had been called such by all the children around Nottingham— whether related to her or not—for nearly sixty years and Mari-Lu had adopted the name along with everyone else.

As Mari-Lu's feet carried her swiftly down the last stretch of the street, Aunt Lucy turned with a wide smile and opened her arms. Mari-Lu crashed into her and felt her great-grandmother's arms envelop her in a hug even as they both tilted precariously backwards for a moment before settling into a more stable sense of balance.

"Mari-Lu!" her mother scolded. "You could have knocked her over! You're lucky I was near enough to grab her shoulders."

"I'm alright." Aunt Lucy laughed, pulling back from the embrace to smile at Mari-Lu's mother, before turning to wink at Mari-Lu. "Happy birthday, young one."

Aunt Lucy bent and kissed Mari-Lu's cheek.

"Thank you! I'm eight today, you know."

"Oh I know," Aunt Lucy laughed.

Mari-Lu's mother, Marian, ushered the two of them inside, and Mari-Lu laced her fingers through Aunt Lucy's as they walked. The front room of their home was one of the original rooms of the house where the great Lady Marian—Mari-Lu's mother's grandmother by marriage—had grown up; within the small front room was a wooden table with chairs seated around it, a hearth to one side with more chairs pulled up to it, and several doors leading to other rooms, along with a staircase to the upper floors of the house.

"Did you bring me a gift?"

"Mari-Lu!" her mother scolded again, but Aunt Lucy only laughed.

Mari-Lu turned to Aunt Lucy with bright eyes. "Well?"

"I do have a gift for you." Aunt Lucy moved to a chair by the hearth. There wasn't a fire lit yet, as it was still early in the evening and the October days were still warm. "I am going to tell you another story, if you like."

"Oh, please do!" Mari-Lu clapped her hands and moved to kneel on the floor in front of Aunt Lucy, resting her arms across Aunt Lucy's knees, her chin sitting atop her hands. She loved a good story, and no one told a tale better than Aunt Lucy. It was why she was the keeper of the family histories, and why no one was trusted more with keeping the memories of Robin Hood and the rest of the gang of fearless rebels alive and well.

"Whose story do I get to hear now?"

"I want to tell you the story of one of the gentlest, kindest souls I have ever had the pleasure of knowing," Aunt Lucy replied.

"Who was that?"

"The one most known by people nowadays only as the great Robin Hood's faithful servant—but he was so much more than that! He was a hero, too, though he never knew it."

Mari-Lu smiled. "You mean Much, right? Tell me about him."

3

Aunt Lucy tucked a wisp of hair that had fallen from Mari-Lu's braid behind her ear, getting a faraway look in her eyes as she thought back to the adventures in Sherwood and beyond.

She had lived the adventures herself, and her memories still served her well, as she had never yet shied away from sharing her stories, recalling every detail much to Mari-Lu's delight. Aunt Lucy kept the memories of the famous gang of outlaws alive within the family itself, around Nottinghamshire, and far beyond the reaches of England to anyone who was willing to listen to her.

She had not only her memories and perspective on past events, but had been entrusted by the other members of the gang to carry on their stories, too. Mari-Lu hadn't been born when the rest of the gang was around, but she'd heard her mother talk about how some of them had sat down with Aunt Lucy and specifically shared their side of the story—their emotions, their struggles—so that no part of the history would be lost.

Mari-Lu had heard snippets of all Aunt Lucy's tales growing up, but it wasn't until a year ago that Aunt Lucy had finally sat down and told her the story of Sherwood—of Lady Marian, Robin Hood, and Aunt Lucy herself—from beginning to end. Yet even on that day she had hinted that there were other stories to be told, and Mari-Lu had eagerly waited for them.

"This is the perfect birthday present," Mari-Lu said softly, watching Aunt Lucy's misty eyes.

"I haven't even begun yet, child."

"I already know it's going to be wonderful."

"I think it will be," Aunt Lucy agreed. "But like many stories, it didn't start out that way. It began with a small baby being born prematurely, his poor young mother dying to give him life."

"Oh no," Mari-Lu groaned.

"Young Much was the son of a miller, but when his father had a terrible accident at the mill when the boy was only three years old, little Much was set adrift. He passed from relative to relative in his village—they all had their own mouths to feed and little money to spare on another child. Eventually, in desperate need of coin, they sold Much to an Earl from a distant city—Sir Edward, the Earl of Locksley…"

Chapter 1

MUCH FELT ANOTHER trickle of sweat slide down his brow as the heat from the sun bore down on him. The sharp *thwick* of a bow sounded and Much watched as Robin fired another arrow towards the target. They were in the grassy pasture between the manor house and the stables at Locksley estate, where Robin had set up the target made of wood and straw to practice his archery. He was a decent shot— certainly better than Much would ever be. They'd both begun lessons in weaponry at a young age, and now at fifteen Robin was proficient.

Robin grunted as he pulled another arrow from his quiver, his blue eyes flashing with determination. "I still can't quite get it."

"You hit the target," Much replied, hands on his hips as he watched Robin shoot again.

"I'd like to be able to hit the bull's eye every time though!" Robin pushed his blond hair out of his eyes and glared at the target as he pulled his arrow back until his bowstring was taut.

"So … that means we're not going inside any time soon?" Much's throat was dry, his tongue thick with thirst while his whole body felt oppressed by the heat of the sun. It was an unusually hot day.

"We're not going in until I can get this right," Robin replied, letting one arrow go and immediately grabbing another one.

Much wanted to sigh, but he did not. Though he and Robin were the same age, and in many ways Much felt they were brothers, he knew his place. It had, after all, been drilled into him his whole life.

Much remembered nothing of his life before living at the Locksley estate, growing up in the manor house alongside the Earl's young son Robin. He had vague memories of his first years in the manor house, sleeping in the nursery with Robin, sharing a nursemaid with the young lord. He could remember feeling at home, and growing to love Robin as a brother.

The most vivid of his early memories came when Much was five years old. Sir Edward had come up into the nursery while the boys were playing with carved wooden blocks—Robin trying to make a tower to reach the ceiling while Much built around it, strengthening the foundation—as their nursemaid sat in the corner, sewing and humming softly to herself.

The humming stopped and the servant girl was on her feet as the Earl came into the room. Robin glanced toward his father and grinned. "Do you see my high tower?"

"I see it." The Earl smiled at his son as he strode across the room and placed an affectionate hand on his son's head. Then he turned his gaze on Much.

"As it is nearly the end of the day, young Much, I am going to send Sarah up to help you move your things."

"Move my things?"

"Yes. You will be moving into the servant's quarters now that you are older and no longer in need of the nursery. My son will also be moving to a larger room."

"I like our room," Robin said, reaching on his tiptoes to put another block on his stack.

"Be that as it may," the Earl replied, "you will both be moving. Much, you will get a few weeks of lessons from Sarah and the other servants on what your duties will be moving forward."

"My duties?"

"Yes, child. You will be looking after my son as his manservant when you are older, and you will need to know how. It may take a year or two for you to become competent in your duties, and that is expected. I have older servants who will assist in the meantime and instruct you on how you will proceed."

"Will I still play with Robin?"

"Your task will not be 'playing' with Robin, but rather taking care of him. You are young now, but once you have learned you will be helping to ensure his clothes are clean and presentable before he wears them, make sure his horse is saddled when he needs it, make sure his food is always prepared on time—in short, anything that the young lord requires, his manservant will provide. Do you understand this?"

"So…we won't be playing?"

"Not always, no. Your childhood will come to a close as you take on your chores, but this is what I bought you for. You can be my son's companion and friend as far as you can, but you must never forget your place. He will inherit my estate—he will be the lord, the Earl of Locksley—and you are nothing more than his servant. Do not overstep."

"I'm a servant? Like Sarah?"

"Yes, precisely like Sarah," the Earl nodded. "You are not my son's equal, and now that you are old enough to understand this it is time for you to take your place in the household as such."

Much could hardly comprehend what any of the Earl's speech truly meant, but while his confusion swirled the Earl left and soon Sarah—a cook at the manor and the woman in charge of the rest of the servants—came to help both Much and Robin move to their respective rooms.

9

"But why do we have to be apart?" Much asked as Sarah tucked his few small sets of clothes into a bag.

"Because you were never truly together," Sarah said, giving his head a gentle pat. "He's a young lord, and you are his servant. It'll be alright, Much. You'll still see him every day; you'll get to play with him, grow up with him. You'll just have a few chores, too."

Much still didn't truly understand what the Earl or Sarah meant by saying he and Robin were not the same, but it didn't take long before he could comprehend and feel the difference.

Now, all these years later, Much knew that regardless of how uncomfortable he was in the heat of the day, until Robin said they could return to the manor he had to hold his tongue and simply stay at his master's side.

Robin nearly dropped the next arrow he grabbed and he cursed quietly, setting it down long enough to wipe his fingers, slick with sweat, across his trousers.

I think that's enough for one day.

Much didn't speak his thoughts. It wasn't his place to advise Robin, merely to look after him. If Robin stayed out long enough to be in danger of passing out from the heat and exertion then Much would intervene, but he'd already spoken up once about going inside so until he thought Robin might faint, Much was going to hold his tongue.

Robin shot two more arrows, grunting at both and looking entirely unsatisfied. Much bit his tongue, keeping a smooth and complacent look on his face throughout the ordeal. When Robin wanted his opinion, he would ask.

At any rate, the longer they spent at the archery range the less time they'd be in Wetherby. Not that Much disliked visiting the village of Wetherby and their friends there, but watching Robin attempt to flirt with Sir Godfrey's daughter Marian was not the most enjoyable way to spend an afternoon. How it compared to archery in sweltering heat, Much wasn't sure yet. At the end of the day he'd evaluate the good and bad of both and form his opinion—one he wasn't likely to share with anyone.

"It's too hot out here for all this," a cheery voice called. Much turned around to see Sarah moving toward them with two pewter cups in one hand and a pitcher in the other. Much moved forward to help her.

"I brought water," Sarah said as Much took the cups and held them up for Sarah to pour the water into. "Fresh from the spring, no less. I had Isaac run and fetch it for you both."

Much carried the cups to Robin, who gratefully set aside his bow and took one, guzzling the liquid. Sarah poured him more while Much finally put the refreshing liquid to his lips, closing his eyes as he savored the cool, clean water.

"You are a mess," Sarah chided, setting the pitcher at her feet and whipping a handkerchief out of her pocket, proceeding to wipe Robin's brow with it.

Robin grinned. "I'm trying to beat that target."

Sarah gave him a motherly frown and then turned to Much, gently wiping his face, too. "You should come to the kitchen, Much dear. Robin doesn't need you as he's quite capable of shooting those arrows without an audience."

Robin shrugged. "It won't be cooler in the kitchen where you're likely in the midst of preparing dinner … but you can go wherever you like, Much."

"See?" Sarah smiled at Much.

Much couldn't stop the delight from filling him at the thought of an afternoon with Sarah in the kitchens. It was a far better prospect than archery or Robin's flirting with Lady Marian.

Robin grabbed another arrow and shrugged again. "I'll be here a while."

"Are you certain you won't need anything?" Much asked, wanting to go with Sarah immediately but knowing his own desires and wants did not come before Robin's.

Robin lowered his bow, smiling at Much in a rather affectionate way that Much found condescending. "Always by my side, huh? Would you follow me even unto death?"

Much knew Robin was teasing, so he gave a mock bow. "Even unto death, my lord. I will do whatever you require."

Robin threw back his head and laughed. "Ah, Much, I would never ask such a thing of you. Go on, Sarah can probably put you to good use in the kitchen. And she's right, I don't need an audience."

"Don't stay out yourself for too long," Sarah said, grabbing Robin's shoulders and turning him toward her so she could study him. "I don't want you getting ill from the heat and exertion."

"I'm fine, Sarah." Robin bent and kissed her cheek. "Promise."

Sarah poured him another cup of water, watched as he drank it, and then seemed satisfied that he would be alright. Much walked with her back to the manor, though they left the water with Robin in case he desired more.

"What are you preparing for the meals today?" Much asked, and listened with delight as Sarah began to tell him what she had planned and how she could use his help.

When they reached the kitchens at the back of the manor house, Much moved to a table in the main kitchen area and started chopping the vegetables Sarah directed him to. He listened with pleasure to the cheerful chatter of the other cooks, as Sarah bustled about and bossed everyone around with her bubbly energy.

The kitchen was Much's favorite room in the house. Along one whole wall were shelves full of pots, pans, and other cooking utensils as well as various ingredients for food that Sarah and her underlings might use on a daily basis, and next to those shelves was the table where Robin and Much would always sit when they visited Sarah as children.

There were four doors on the opposite wall, leading to the larder—where raw meat, fresh milk, and other things in need of cooler air were kept; the scullery—where clean-up of dishes and laundry typically happened; the saucery—where the old saucer Matthew would do his work to create masterpieces for the Earl's dinners; and the wine cellar, which the Earl proudly boasted was as fine as the cellar in Nottingham castle itself.

Sarah's hearth—always filled with a roaring fire—and her clay oven were located along the far wall opposite the entrance to the main part of the house. Filling the center of the room was a long, wide table that was always crowded with food being prepared by various members of the kitchen staff. Much had never seen a larger table in his life—even the one in the dining room upstairs where the Earl ate was not as wide or long as the table used to prepare his meals.

The warmth of contentment spread through Much's chest as he took in the atmosphere of his sacred space. Sarah's bossy voice was easily heard about the chatter of the other servants. The smell of freshly baked bread wafted from the side of the kitchen where the clay oven was located; from the hearth drifted the delicious scent of the meat that one of the spit boys was slowly turning over and over above the fire. The sounds, smells, and sights had a nostalgic charm to Much. It was undoubtedly his favorite place to be.

Chapter 2

AS MUCH CHOPPED vegetables in the kitchen for Sarah, he thought back on those early years of learning how separate he truly was from Robin.

The servants quarters were located at the back of the manor house near the kitchens, and for a while Much had lived there, in a separate room from Robin. He'd wake early to the sounds of the kitchen staff preparing breakfast, which was soon followed by the delightful smells that always lured young Much out of bed and into the kitchens. Sarah would hoist him onto her hip and work around him, occasionally giving him bites of whatever she was cooking for breakfast as she worked.

But after a few years, when the separation in their rank and worth had been drilled into him by daily lessons with the Earl and learning how to care for Robin by the side of Isaac, Matthew, and other servants, Much was allowed to move into Robin's room at Robin's request. At that point, the visits to the kitchen came at Robin's bidding rather than Much's, and so he spent less time there than he would have liked.

He remembered the way he'd paused in the doorway and stared the first time Robin had led Much into the room they were to share.

"Come on!" Robin grinned, "Father gave me a new book for my birthday; an actual book. It's leather-bound and everything!"

Robin darted forward toward a shelf, but Much stayed rooted to the spot by the door.

The room was spacious, far bigger than the one Much had lived in for two years in the servants quarters—one which he'd shared with several of the other servants. This spacious room was filled with a large bed, a small table with a chair that served as a desk, and a large shelf covering one wall with various books, toys, and trinkets on it; the room had a large hearth on one side always filled with a roaring fire in winter months—the sort of thing that wouldn't be found in the servant rooms at the back of the manor.

Robin was flipping through the pages of his book at the small table while Much continued to stare from the doorway..

"It's in Latin, of course, which is impossible to read, but Father says I have to learn it. Latin, French, English...so many languages to learn to be a lord, he says. I have to be able to communicate at court with ambassadors and kings and who knows what all..." Robin trailed off and looked over at Much, still standing by the door. "What is it?"

Much shook himself and moved into Robin's room. "Nothing."

He wanted to tell Robin how in awe he was of this room, and of Robin's new book. Much loved reading; Sarah had taught him over the kitchen table—she'd often be kneading dough to make a loaf of bread, or stirring a pot of stew on the fire, as Much sat at the table nearby and she would painstakingly draw letters in the dust of flour on the table until he could recognize them, and then moved on to small words when she felt he was ready. To be given a whole book all for his own would be a dream.

But Much did not tell Robin any of his thoughts or feelings because Robin was his lord and he was a servant; they were not brothers.

Robin walked across the room and grabbed Much's hand, drawing him toward the small table. Robin set his book down, pushed Much into the chair, and then leaned against the table himself, leafing through the pages in the book.

"Isn't it marvelous? I knew you'd want to see it as soon as Father gave it to me."

Much tentatively reached out to touch the fragile paper, caressing it. "It is a beautiful book, though I can't understand a word of it."

Robin threw his head back in a laugh and then snapped the book shut. "Exactly! I've told Father I need you to take the language lessons with me so I can learn better. Sorry to make you do schooling on top of everything else, but I can't do it alone. I just can't. There's too much to learn."

Much felt a swell of warmth around his heart as Robin prattled on. He was going to get to learn—it was more than he could have ever hoped for, especially given his position in society.

Much's meager belongings were stashed under Robin's spacious bed, along with a smaller straw mattress to be pulled out at night for him. In the days that followed, the boys would rise early and spend their mornings in the kitchen with Sarah, and then spend several hours with the Earl as he instructed Robin in languages, diplomacy, history, horse-riding, and the use of a sword and bow.

They often had the afternoon to themselves and would play together at Locksley manor, or in Locksley village—and on the best afternoons they would cajole and convince either the Earl or one of the older servants to accompany them to the village of Wetherby nearby so they could play with their friends Marian and Mark.

Much shifted the knife in his hand, as he grabbed a nearby carrot from the stack of vegetables he was chopping for Sarah, letting his mind continue to wander through the memories of his childhood that this room had seen. Sarah had taught him to read here in the flour-dust on the table; she'd taught him to cook, too. He'd spent his happiest days in this room with Sarah, but more often than not he was always interrupted in his pleasure by the appearance of Robin wanting to drag him off on a wild adventure. Still, he'd enjoyed those, too.

Chapter 3

"ARE YOU NEARLY finished?" Sarah asked from across the kitchen. Eighteen-year-old Much looked down at the bread dough in his hands that he had been kneading.

"Nearly."

Much set the dough aside so it could rise, covering it in a small towel. He was working at the large table in the kitchen, and there were other servants around it as well putting together various pieces of the meals that Sarah had planned for the day. Sarah bustled about the kitchen in her bossy way, though with less energy than she once had; her hair had streaks of grey in it now, and Much wondered if she'd always looked so tired after a long day in the kitchen.

Much grabbed another batch of dough from nearby, removing the towel it had been under, giving the ball of dough a solid punch to release any air bubbles that might be inside. Then he shaped the dough in his hands, forming the semblance of a loaf as this set of dough had already finished its first rising.

"I've got another loaf ready for a second rise and then baking," Much called over the hum of the other conversations in the room. Sarah hurried over, taking the loaf and setting it on the small outcropping of stone over the hearth where it would sit for a few minutes before she transferred it to the clay oven.

"Much!" Robin's yell pierced the kitchen, though he wasn't yet visible. All of the servants in the kitchen paused what they were doing when they heard the call, glancing toward the door before turning back to their work.

Much braced himself for whatever grand scheme Robin had likely cooked up now, as Sarah placed a floury hand on his shoulder. "I do believe Master Robin is looking for you."

"So he is," Much sighed. He moved toward the doorway of the kitchen, jogging out just as Robin came racing in. They slammed into each other, Much stumbling backwards as Robin grabbed the wall to steady himself.

"So sorry, Much." Robin grabbed his arm and helped him find his balance. "That was entirely my fault."

"You were looking for me. Did you need something?"

"I have glorious news! The king has declared he is going to march in the Third Crusade! We're retaking Jerusalem from Saladin!"

"Who's Saladin?" Much asked.

"A man who took Jerusalem from the king who was ruling there…King Guy, I think. Doesn't matter; the politics aren't the point." Robin's eyes were bright with excitement and anticipation, and Much's heart sank to his toes as he waited for Robin to tell him the worst of his news.

"And this Crusade to retake Jerusalem is glorious news, because?" Sarah asked from across the kitchen.

The other servants glanced between Sarah and Robin—like Much they were not unused to seeing Sarah's casual interactions with the young lord, but unlike Much and Sarah they did not have such a personal connection to him and would therefore be less likely than even Much to openly speak their mind to him, so whenever Sarah did, it caught everyone's attention.

"Because I'm going!" Robin grinned, practically skipping across the kitchen to wrap Sarah in a hug. "We're going to war and it will be splendid."

Much doubted that a great deal.

"Oh, Master Robin." Sarah sighed. "I wish you wouldn't. You cannot mean that."

"I do mean it, Sarah. I will be a hero when I come home, I promise you that."

"Your father will not like it," Much offered as Robin let go of Sarah and she went back to work.

"My father does not have to approve of it, Much. I can do as I please."

"You are truly going to join the Crusades?" Sarah asked, glancing over her shoulder at Robin as she pulled a fresh loaf of bread from the oven.

"Of course. And Much is coming with me, so you needn't worry. He always looks after me."

Much bit his cheek to keep himself from saying anything to the contrary. He had no desire to fight in a war, but it was his duty to look after Robin and so he would.

When Robin told the Earl of his plan, the Earl forbade Robin from going, but Much knew that wasn't going to stop Robin. He had made up his mind, and Robin was too stubborn to give into anyone's advice or change his course of direction for any reason.

Robin waited a few days—until after Marian's birthday, wanting to spend the day with her in Wetherby—and then he quietly packed his bags.

Robin had heard of training taking place in London when all of the young men eager to join the Crusades had gathered there after the archbishop of Canterbury called on anyone willing to join the Holy Roman Emperor Frederick on his holy quest, but once the summons came from King Richard to cross the channel with him, the men eager for war or burning with religious zeal began to move in droves to the sea ports from Dartmouth to Dover, and so Robin intended to direct his steps toward the white cliffs.

The night Robin packed his bags, Much went to the kitchens to pack some provisions for them. It was a long trip to the city of Dover where they would be headed, and though they would likely take lodgings at taverns or abbeys along the way to Dover, Much wanted to be prepared.

He tried to keep his rustling about the dark kitchen to a minimum, but it wasn't long before Sarah crept in with a candle in her hand. "Much? What are you doing in here so late?"

"Robin and I are leaving, I'm afraid."

"Now? For the Crusades?" Sarah's eyes were wide. She moved forward quickly to wrap Much in a hug and then helped him gather his supplies. When Much was satisfied with his pack, he and Sarah left the manor and went to the stables together, where they met Robin.

The moon was shining brightly, and Robin carried a lantern with him as he entered the barn where the horses slept quietly.

"Have we already been found out?" Robin chuckled as Much and Sarah followed him into the barn. Much moved to wake and saddle a couple of horses while Sarah approached Robin.

"I may not be your mother," she said, pulling Robin into a hug, "but you will always be my little Robin and I will not let you sneak off without a goodbye."

Much watched the exchange from the corner of his eye as he finished saddling the horses.

"I love you so." Sarah's voice was strangled and shallow. "Please be careful."

22

Sarah took Robin's face in her hands and kissed his forehead.

"I will be careful. And besides, why are you so worried when I will have Much to look after me?"

Much led the horses toward Robin, who grabbed the reins of one while Sarah turned to Much, her eyes brimming with tears. "Oh, Much…"

Sarah placed a gentle hand on either side of his face. "Come home, son. I love you too well to lose you."

"We will come home, I promise you that. The Earl would certainly never forgive me if I lost Robin along the way."

Robin swung into his saddle. "Come on, you two, we can't have a prolonged emotional farewell for the rest of the night. I want to be gone before Father can stop us."

Sarah stepped back, letting her tears fall freely. "Come home, both of you. That's an order."

Robin grinned and bowed to her from atop his horse, and Much kissed her cheek before swinging into his own saddle. As the two of them trotted down the dirt path away from the manor and toward Locksley village, Robin glanced over at Much.

"You do not have to come."

"I could not let you go alone."

"You are so willing to follow me into battle?"

"I believe I once told you I would follow you unto death. Besides, this isn't just about my duty. Your father would insist I follow you anywhere, but more than that…I do love you as a brother, Robin. I can't let you go fight a war on your own."

Robin nodded, seemingly satisfied, and together they rode through the night toward some terrifying destiny that Much was reluctant to meet.

The journey across England was uneventful, and before too many days had elapsed they were nearing Dover.

Long before they entered the city, Much caught sight of the castle on the knoll overlooking the docks and the channel, a bridge connecting the outer wall of defense to the city below. Much took in the magnificent and formidable sight with awe.

Before long they'd passed through the city gate and the buildings around them began to obscure Much's sight of the castle.

As they rode along a busy street near the wharf, Robin viewed the signs of inns and taverns along the street while Much looked up in wonder at the striking castle on the hill overlooking the channel.

The castle stood valiantly on the top of the hill, and below it were the high walls of defense. Only a short distance further down the hill, there was another tall wall encircling both the hill and castle. From his vantage point by the docks, Much couldn't see the bridge that crossed into the city proper, but he was tempted to go look for it just to see the castle up close.

It was a far larger and more impressive looking castle than that of the castle in Nottingham where Sir Godfrey ruled as Sheriff. Much, Robin, and Sir Godfrey's two children—Marian and Mark—had played together in the Nottingham castle more times than Much could possibly count and had discovered all of its secrets.

The first time the group of friends had found a secret door in the kitchen, Much had been thoroughly amazed. *Why would anyone have a door that led into the wall?* But over time, the secret passages had become familiar as the four children played there every chance they got. It was exciting to wander in the darkness looking for new pathways. There were many twists and turns, and the doors that slid along the walls, rather than swinging inward, opened into many different rooms inside the castle…

Chapter 4

ROBIN SHOOK MUCH'S shoulder, breaking his reverie. "Hey. Are you still in there?"

Much glanced at his lifelong friend, standing on the street below where Much was still mounted on his horse. "I'm sorry, did you need something?"

"I've found us lodgings while you've been staring at that castle with your mouth hanging open." Robin grinned. He pointed to a building nearby, and Much quickly dismounted.

A young boy came running over. "I can stable your horse as I did for Master Robin!"

Much handed over the reins, letting the stable boy do his work as Robin pulled him toward the nearby establishment and led him inside.

The front room was wide, with a tall ceiling, and filled with many tables—most of which were full of various groups of young men, chatting and laughing and likely in town for the same reason as Much and Robin. There was also a counter along one side, behind which a young woman was hastily filling mugs of ale and mead at the request of the young men gathered at the bar. Behind her was a row of shelves, and a door that led into the kitchen. Various servers were running in and out of the kitchen, carrying platters of food to the ravenous young men scattered around the room.

"It's a bit full in here, but at least there was lodging," Robin called over the noise of the room. He pointed toward the stairs and Much followed him.

Once they were on the second floor, the noise from below became more muted, and after Robin had taken Much inside the room he'd procured and shut the door, the noise settled to a low hum below them, other than the occasional outburst of laughter that shook the floor beneath their feet.

The room Robin had taken Much into was small, furnished with a simple straw mattress; it had a hearth with a meager fire, and a small table off to one side.

Much moved to the window opposite the door and glanced down into the busy street where he could see seasoned and muscled sailors moving across gangways toward their various ships, hefting an assortment of crates and barrels to be stored there. They called to each other and laughed, seeming to find a great deal of amusement in watching the hordes of young men who wandered the street staring at ships and looking wide-eyed and out of place—rather as Much felt himself. There were grizzled soldiers on the street as well, overseeing some of the ships, or marching along the street on their own business with swords swinging at their sides and grim expressions on their faces.

Much turned away from the window, choosing to go in search of the stable boy so he could bring in the packs that held his and Robin's possessions and store them in the room where they would be staying. When that was through, Robin informed him he was going down to the docks to find them berths on a ship.

"The adventure is about to begin, my friend," Robin said with a wink. "I am eager for this journey."

He was gone in a moment, before Much had a chance to reply that he was not looking forward to this at all.

Much pulled a chair over to the window to watch the docks and keep an eye on Robin as best he could—though his line of sight was often blocked by piles of barrels and crates, tall sailors, and the boats themselves that crowded the harbor.

King Richard had wasted no time after his ascent to the throne in calling all willing men to the Cinque ports—five towns along the English Channel that kept ships at the ready to cross the channel at the king's bidding. Much had never left Nottinghamshire until this adventure, so the sight of the channel itself—the waves crashing against the shore in a never-ending rhythm—was a fascinating sight and he forgot he was meant to be keeping an eye on Robin.

The ships in the harbor were equally fascinating as Much had never seen one before. There were little fishing boats floating along beside ships nearly as big as the houses in Locksley village!

Robin returned after several hours empty-handed. There were a lot of young men eager to follow the king to the Holy Land, and the ships were filling up fast.

"I'll try again tomorrow," Robin said as the two of them went downstairs to the common room to order some supper and then retired to bed. Much slept on the floor wrapped in a blanket while Robin slumbered on the mattress nearby.

The next morning Robin and Much settled at the bar to order breakfast—the common room was not as full as it had been the night before, but there were a handful of soldiers, sailors, and lost young men like Much himself scattered about the room.

The harried young woman from the night before came walking over to Robin and Much to ask what they'd like to eat. Robin ordered breakfast, and Much bit the inside of his cheek.

As she moved through the door to the kitchen, a young man seated nearby spoke up.

"Are you joining the Crusades, like everyone else here in Dover?"

Robin and Much both turned to look at him. He was small in build, with sandy hair and disconsolate blue eyes that twisted Much's stomach when he met his gaze.

"Yes, we are," Robin answered his question. "I am Robin, son of the Earl of Locksley, and this is my faithful servant and dear friend Much."

"I am Allen of the Dale," the young man said, smiling slightly though it did not improve the downcast look in his eyes that unsettled Much. "I'm sailing on *The Barbara*. Which vessel do you sail with?"

"I have not arranged all those details," Robin replied. "We only arrived last night."

"Ah, well, if you'll allow me, I can help you. There's a few berths left on our ship. I hadn't realized until I arrived that the king had so many ships at the ready, and yet they're all being filled to the brim. Have you seen the harbor?"

The serving girl returned with plates of food for Much and Robin as Allen spoke.

"We have," Robin said. "It is quite the sight, especially considering how few boats of any size we've seen prior to this trip."

Robin glanced at Much. "Though I think my friend here is far more interested in the sight of the castle than the sight of the ships."

"It is rather an impressive castle your King Henry had constructed here," Allen said, referring to King Richard's late father.

"*My* King Henry?" Robin asked.

"Ours." Allen shoved a bite of food into his mouth before he spoke again. "Are you finished with your breakfast? We can head down to *The Barbara* and speak to the captain. You arrived in Dover just in time. We set sail in three days."

"Where to?" Robin asked.

"Along the coast of France, I believe, until we reach Marseille to meet up with King Philip's forces. Though I could be mistaken. I have only the rumors to go off of; no captains of the king's army have seen fit to discuss our strategies with me."

Robin chuckled at that. Once both Robin and Much had finished eating they walked with Allen down to the docks, and Allen led them to the ship called *The Barbara*.

Sailors and soldiers were moving about in the same busy manner that Much had seen the day before, and there were greenhorn young men leaning against barrels or sitting along the rails of docks watching the activity with keen interest.

Robin took a deep breath. "Do you smell the sea air, Much?"

Much wrinkled his nose. "It doesn't smell good."

Allen laughed. "You'll get used to it. I assume you haven't sailed before?"

"Never," Much replied.

"Neither have I. It should be an adventure."

"I have never fought either," Much added.

"Oh don't worry, Much!" Robin slung his arm around Much's shoulders. "We're both proficient with swords and bows."

"And I'm sure there will be training as we travel as well," Allen added. "The captain I have chosen to follow is convinced we're all lousy boys who need to be whipped into shape. He's impressively grumpy. You'll enjoy his personality, I'm sure."

Much bit his cheek as Robin and Allen continued to discuss the possibilities of training, and the glory awaiting them at the end of their

31

long journey. This journey, in Much's mind, could only end in death. He would kill people, or someone would kill him. Perhaps both, in the end. It was all far more serious than Robin was making it out to be, as he seemed to think it was all a grand game.

Allen pointed out *The Barbara*, and waved down a sailor to ask if the captain was nearby, but the sailor informed him the captain was on business in the city, making preparations for their departure. So instead, Allen went in search of the lord whose company of soldiers Allen had joined, and was now suggesting Much and Robin join as well.

They found the lord seated on a stone bench sitting outside one of the many taverns in the city. He was a middle aged man, probably around the Earl's age, with a wrinkled tan face and a greying beard. He frowned as Allen walked up to him.

"Sir Adam, may I introduce you to Robin of Locksley—son of the Earl of Locksley—and his servant Much? They desire to join our company."

Sir Adam studied Much and Robin, from their foreheads to their toes and then back up again. "Son of an earl, you say?"

"Yes, sir," Robin replied, his back straightening slightly.

"You could probably lead a company of your own, young Robin. Most noblemen in our ranks do, bringing their own soldiers from home, or picking up the strays who don't have a liege or lord to follow, such as this whelp," Sir Adam gestured toward Allen.

"I do not believe I have the experience necessary for that," Robin replied. "And I did not bring more than one man from home."

"Then by all means, you may join mine. Now if you don't mind…" Sir Adam waved them off casually, and Allen led them back down the street.

"Well, that's that I suppose," Allen said. "He'll let the captain know, no doubt, so you'll be given berths on the ship. And we sail in three days."

"Let the adventure begin," Robin grinned.

Within three days' time Much, Robin, and Allen were standing on the deck of *The Barbara*, watching the cliffs of Dover fade into the grey fog of the morning. It had been an interesting experience, stowing their belongings below deck in a room filled with hammocks—Robin was excited to sleep in one for the first time, though Much was less enthusiastic.

The worst part of the ship by far, however, was the constant rocking as the ship cut through the waves. The sailors mocked Much and the other lads who didn't have what they called 'sea legs' yet, and Robin laughed along with them every time he himself stumbled across the deck. Now, however, Much, Robin, and Allen were safely by the rail on the side of the deck which they could hold onto to maintain their balance.

"This is it, Much." Robin leaned against the boat's rail and took a deep breath, seeming to relish the moment. "Our adventure is beginning."

"Yes, Robin." Much bit his cheek.

"Isn't it splendid?"

Allen clapped Robin on the shoulder from his other side. "It is! Can you believe we are on our way to join the king? What a grand time we shall have."

Though his voice was as light as Robin's, Much could still see the darkness lingering in Allen's eyes whenever he met his gaze, and he didn't know what to make of it.

"We are going to war," Much spoke to Allen. "I do not believe 'grand time' is the best way to describe such a thing."

Allen laughed. "Don't be so grave, master Much."

"I am simply worried." Much grabbed the railing and leaned outward, toward England. "Shall we see this shore again, do you think?"

Robin raised an eyebrow. "Why would we not?"

"Casualties in war are not unheard of," Much replied, his voice dripping sarcasm before he could stop himself.

"Of course there are casualties, but we won't be among them."

Footsteps approached from behind the three of them, and they turned to see Sir Adam drawing near, fully undisturbed by the constant rocking of the deck as the ship moved through the waves.

"Robin of Locksley, I wish to speak with you. There is much you should learn, as a lord who ought to be leading your own men. You cannot spend your days in the laziness you are most likely accustomed to at home. Come with me, and I will show you how to lead. It is experience you say you lacked, after all."

Robin carefully let go of the rail. "Of course, Sir Adam. I am eager to learn."

Robin held his head high, undoubtedly feigning confidence as he walked with Sir Adam away from Much and Allen. Much watched them, his eyes never leaving Robin.

"You don't do anything without him, do you?" Allen asked.

"Why would I? He is my master, and everything I do is for him."

34

Chapter 5

MUCH LEANED AGAINST the rail, feeling the rise and fall of the boat cresting each wave. Robin was sitting on the deck at his feet, his back pressed against the side of the boat. The sun was shining on the water, and the white-tipped waves created a sort of dancing rhythm all around *The Barbara* that Much could not quite catch the music of.

On the left—or port, as Much had now learned to think of it—side the distant shores of Normandy lingered like a rain cloud on the horizon. On every side of *The Barbara* the other ships in the King's fleet sailed, all moving headlong toward whatever disaster might await them.

"So many men," Much commented quietly.

"You can't take Jerusalem from Saladin and his invaders with only a handful of men," Robin commented. "You can't do much of anything with only a handful of men."

Allen came sauntering over and plopped down on the deck beside Robin. He'd gotten command of his sea legs far better than Much in so short a span of time that they had been at sea. Much still stumbled over his own feet and consistently lost his balance both above and below deck. As often as he was able, Much would keep to the walls and rails of the ship to avoid looking like an idiot.

"I am tired already, and all we've done is sail," Allen sighed.

"We haven't even begun." Robin laughed, punching Allen's shoulder. "And I believe Sir Adam wishes to begin training every morning."

"Training?" Allen glanced about the deck of the ship and Much followed his gaze. There wasn't a great deal of space, and much of it

35

was filled with sailors, rigging, and pieces of the boat that Much did not understand or fathom the use for.

"Sir Adam wants to be sure everyone in his company can wield a sword to his satisfaction before we reach Marseille and the king sets us to actually using our skills."

"How far is Marseille?" Much asked.

"A long way, my friend," Allen laughed.

Robin was correct in his assumption that Sir Adam would begin training, for the next morning he called together the men and the crew to explain just that. Not everyone could be on deck at the same time and still leave room for sparring and training, so Sir Adam and the captain worked together to devise a schedule of sorts. Much, Robin, and Allen ended up on the earliest shift, which meant they would be waking at dawn for the remainder of their journey in order to train first with the other unlucky souls whose sleep was to be so interrupted.

One morning, as Much wiped the sweat from his brow, he broke apart from his training partner—Alaric—and took a deep breath. His sword was heavy in his hand, and his grip was made weaker as the hilt slipped in his hand slick with sweat.

"At least you stayed on your feet so far," Alaric said with a grin, watching Much struggle to wipe his palms on his trousers to rid them of sweat.

Much bit his cheek and raised his sword, ready for another attack. Alaric, however, lowered his sword. "I think we can call it a day. We've been at it the allotted hour and Sir Adam seems satisfied for the moment."

Much and Alaric both glanced toward the bow of the ship where Sir Adam sat glowering at the pairs of men sparring. The sounds of the men grunting and metal striking metal seemed to echo off the deck and across the water. Sir Adam made no move to stop those who were finishing their matches so Much lowered his sword as well.

Much appreciated Alaric's suggestion to stop for the morning, as his legs were wobbling beneath him from more than just the uneven movement from the waves beneath the ship. He stumbled toward the rail to lean his weight against it as he watched Robin and Allen sparring nearby.

Robin brought his sword smashing down onto Allen's, which he'd barely managed to raise in time to block Robin's blow. Allen's knees bent as his arm strained against the weight of Robin's attack, and then they both parted briefly, eyeing each other's defenses.

"Trying to kill me, Robin?" Allen asked, before he darted forward for an attack. With a flick of his wrist, Robin deflected the blow and with his free hand gave a solid punch to Allen's jaw.

Allen stepped back, lowering his sword and rubbing his face. "Ow."

"I didn't hit you that hard." Robin grinned, raising his sword until the tip was pressed against Allen's throat.

Allen shrugged. "You hit me hard enough. Either way, I think I have had enough for this morning. Unless Sir Adam the grump can stop me, I'm calling it quits." Allen gave a deep bow to Robin. "I concede, your lordship."

Allen sheathed his sword at his waist and then moved over to plop on the deck near where Much was standing at the rail. Robin followed.

"You're a better swordsmen than I, Robin," Allen sighed.

"I've had years of practice, but I haven't seen any real combat," Robin replied. "I'm the son of an earl, though, and I would be disgracing my father if I was not good at what I do. And anyway … I just can't bear not to be the best."

Much laughed before he could help himself. "That is very true."

"I think you'll come in handy." Allen grinned at Robin. "I doubt any Saracen could get through you."

"They won't even come close if I use my bow," Robin winked. "It's harder to showcase my brilliance in that respect on this boat, but just wait…"

"You keep praising your abilities with the bow and I'll expect nothing but perfection once I see you in action," Allen laughed. He reached a hand up to his jaw once more, wincing slightly.

"Oh come on, I didn't punch that hard." Robin reached over and pushed Allen's shoulder.

"Hey!" Allen shifted across the deck a bit to get out of reach. "That hurts, too, you know. Every muscle in my body hurts when we train. We've only begun this journey and already I am exhausted." Allen sighed, rubbing his shoulder. "This is going to be a long road…"

Sir Adam grunted as he walked near the group, glaring at Allen. "Longer than you know. Don't begin complaining yet. Save that for after you've been stuck in the Holy Land for more years than you care to count."

"Have you been before?" Robin asked.

"Of course," Sir Adam said. "I was a soldier in the Second Crusade."

Sir Adam continued on his way to greet the second hour of men training while those from the first set began to make their way below deck or to the rails to be out of the way. Much watched Sir Adam, with his grizzled face, scarred arms, and sour attitude as he began to instruct the next set of men.

He'd fought in the Second Crusade, and now here he was so many years later doing it all over again. Much wondered what could drive a person to such prolonged violence. He was here for Robin—to look after him, to keep him alive—but he did not have the passion for this war they were embarking on the way that Robin seemed to, and he would never be an experienced old soldier like Sir Adam; he'd almost rather die first than end up like that.

After a few weeks of sailing and training, Much was learning to hate the boat. There was no where to go, nothing to see or do apart from the training sessions. He wanted to walk on dry ground, wanted to see trees and hear birds singing. The sound of the waves crashing against the boat was growing annoying.

"I've been thinking." Robin's blue eyes held a faraway look as he, Much, and Allen swung in their hammocks below deck one day. The room was dimly lit, and the creaking of the boat around them filled the air.

"What have you been thinking?" Much asked.

"I've been thinking about home," Robin said. "About Sarah; her tearful farewell and how deeply she'll undoubtedly miss us. About my father, and how displeased he most likely was when he discovered we'd run away…"

"You ran away?" Allen asked.

Robin gave him a wry grin. "We did. Much didn't have a choice as I dragged him along on my adventure. Did you have the blessing of your family when you came to join the Crusades?"

Much watched with curiosity and concern as Allen's open expression shuttered instantly, the familiar unsettling darkness clouding his eyes.

"Not exactly."

39

"It's strange," Robin said, "we haven't been gone long and yet I already miss them; Sarah, Father … Marian."

"Who's Marian?" Allen asked.

"The daughter of the Sheriff of Nottingham," Much said. "A childhood friend of ours."

"And the woman I intend to marry when I return from the Crusades," Robin added with a grin. "She is remarkable."

Chapter 6

AFTER A FEW days of sailing along the continent, it became clear that *The Barbara* was the fastest ship in the fleet, outstripping all the others. Within a few days' time Much realized that they were practically sailing on their own, though the other ships' sails could sometimes be seen on the horizon past the stern. Consequently, they were the first to arrive in Marseille.

The captain of the ship brought them into port, and then Sir Adam arranged an inn for the company of soldiers to stay at while he sent messages to various nobles in order to inform King Richard and King Philip that the fleet was on its way.

Much, Robin, and Allen sat at a table in the back of the common room of the inn, watching the comings and goings of the others in their company, and various French individuals that they did not know. Robin had ordered a round of drinks for the three of them, and Allen was practically drowning himself in his.

"What comes next?" Much asked, seeing Sir Adam enter the common room and head straight for the stairs at the back of the room.

Robin shrugged as he leaned his chair back on two legs and rested his feet on the table. "The rest of our fleet arrives, and then King Richard and King Philip lead us to the Holy Land, I suppose."

Sir Adam came marching back down the stairs, surveyed the room, and then came toward their table with a determined stride.

"Young Robin, we have work to do."

"How so?" Robin sat up, his feet and chair legs hitting the floor with a resounding thud.

"King Richard is too impatient to wait for the rest of the fleet; he has a mission he wishes to accomplish immediately. We'll be setting sail once more."

"When?"

"As soon as the tide goes out. Come with me, we have men to find, a sea captain to rouse…"

"Work to be done." Robin nodded with a sigh. He pushed his half-drunk mug of ale towards Allen. "Finish this off, will you? I'll be back eventually."

Sir Adam and Robin left the tavern, and Allen picked up Robin's mug and began to guzzle his drink.

"You're going to get drunk," Much commented.

"That's the idea."

"We're apparently sailing tonight, and for the King of England himself, no less."

"I heard."

Much stood up from the table. "I'm going to make sure Robin's things are gathered and ready for our departure."

Allen said nothing, still tilting the mug to his lips, some of it spilling past his mouth to dribble down his chin.

Before too long, everyone in the company of soldiers was loaded back on the boat and the sailors were making preparations to sail while casting angry looks toward Sir Adam and the other high ranking officers who boarded the boat. With little to no fanfare, King Richard himself came aboard, but Much had been below deck at the time and hadn't caught a glimpse of him.

As the night crept toward dawn, Much sat atop a barrel pushed against one wall in the bunk room—a large room filled with hammocks hanging from the ceiling, and spare space filled with various crates and

42

barrels of food and weapons and other cargo. Allen and Robin were seated in a similar manner atop barrels along the wall, and Sir Adam and others swung in their hammocks nearby. Some were sleeping, some were not.

"What does the king wish to do in Sicily?" Much asked, having learned from Robin that that was their destination. "Why are we sailing there?"

"We're sailing there," Sir Adam grunted from his hammock nearby, "because last year William of Sicily died and was replaced by Tancred."

Much glanced at the frowning soldier, waiting for more explanation, but none came.

"Tancred imprisoned King Richard's sister Joan," Robin said. "We are going to Sicily to rescue her."

"It is foolishness," Sir Adam snorted. "The Crusaders in the Holy Land are dying and need our help, and we are stopping along the way to save a silly woman?"

"Wouldn't you take a detour to save your own sister, if you had one?" Robin asked. Much knew Robin would go to the ends of the earth to save the people he loved; he was a passionate man. Much wasn't sure how far he could go to save someone, but he appreciated that his king was apparently the sort of man to find his sister's plight more important than the war he was embarking on.

"Not when the fate of our army hung in the balance," Sir Adam replied, his expression grim. "We could return for Princess Joan on our way home, if she's so important. We need not delay our journey to Jerusalem."

"But that could be years away!" Robin said. "Anything could happen to her in that time. Do you have so little regard for women, Sir

43

Adam?"

"You have far too much regard for them," Sir Adam growled. "How many times have I heard you pining over the lass…what is her name? Marian? Wondering if she is waiting for you back home. I will tell you now, do not hope for it. Women are not worth the trouble."

Robin shook his head with a grin. "Clearly, you have never been in love."

For two months they sailed along the coast of Italy until they landed on Sicily, some miles north of the city of Messina. Much was asleep in his hammock when they came into harbor and was soon rudely awakened by Robin calling his name.

"Wake up!"

Much squinted up into Robin's face. "What?"

"We are on Sicily. The king is gathering all the men above deck."

Much sat up suddenly—too fast, for he whacked his forehead against Robin's nose.

"Sorry."

"You're forgiven," Robin laughed. "Now come on!"

"Why is King Richard gathering the company on deck?"

"He seems to be choosing men to go with him to rescue his sister, the princess. He was eyeing up soldiers when I came down to get you. Now hurry! I want to be chosen."

Much rolled out of his hammock, running his fingers through his ruffled hair as he followed Robin toward the ladder that would lead them above deck. Robin kept talking as they hurried along the ship.

"Most likely the king wants to take leaders; earls, barons, others of that nature. I have a good chance of being selected if we can get back on deck before he's done."

"There you are!" Allen threw up his hands in exasperation as Robin and Much joined him at the base of the ladder. "Come on, he's already talking to Sir Adam."

Much, Robin, and Allen hurried onto deck where most of the rest of the company were already gathered. It was not yet dawn, and the stars overhead were sparkling as they were only just beginning to wane. Even in the early light, Much was struck by the vibrant blue of the water and how it contrasted with the white beach nearby.

The king stood near the stern of the ship, speaking softly to the captain and to Sir Adam. He was younger than Much had expected, with dark hair that had only a few streaks of silver along his temples. His face was rugged and had sharp angles, but he did not seem as old as the Earl.

"Robin?" Much whispered as the three of them pushed into the line of soldiers nearest the king.

"What?"

"How old is our King?"

"Thirty-two," Robin glanced at Much with a chuckle. "Why?"

"No reason."

"How old is the Princess?" Allen asked.

"Twenty-four, I believe," Robin replied.

"Not so much older than we are," Much said. "And she was the Queen of Sicily before William died?"

"She was." Robin nodded.

Much could not imagine holding such power at so young an age. Robin was going to be the Earl someday, but his father still held the responsibility and prestige for now and Robin was free to do as he liked. Much couldn't imagine Robin as the Earl of Locksley; he was far too impulsive and wayward. How much power the princess had actually

45

held as the Queen of Sicily, Much didn't know, but if she was anything like Robin, Much had a hard time picturing it going well.

In another moment, Sir Adam turned and seemed to gesture in their direction. The king turned and when his piercing blue eyes met Much's grey ones for a brief moment, Much held his breath. King Richard moved on quickly and his gaze settled on Robin.

Soon enough Sir Adam and the king approached.

Much, Robin, and Allen bowed.

"You're Robin, son of the Earl of Locksley?" the king asked.

"Yes, Sire."

"I am told you are good with a bow and remarkable with a blade."

"I do my best."

"I have been informed you are better than most."

"I couldn't say, Sire."

Much was rather impressed with Robin's ability to feign humility.

"I would like you to come with me on the mission to rescue my sister."

"I would be honored, my King."

"Are these two companions of yours good fighters as well?"

"I would say so, Sire."

Sir Adam shook his head. "They have nowhere near Robin's skill, my lord, although Allen is a decent soldier. This one...I'm not so sure," Sir Adam gestured toward Much.

The king looked Allen over, and then turned to Much. "You do look too gentle to be on this ship, lad."

"I follow my master, Your Majesty, no matter where he leads."

"Ah, you are Robin of Locksley's servant then."

46

"He is my friend," Robin put in, "and he follows me as much from loyalty and love as from duty."

"All qualities I can admire." The king smiled, his skin crinkling around his eyes in a way that reminded Much of Sarah. "I will take the three of you."

The king turned and said something else to Sir Adam that Much didn't catch and then strode off to speak to other soldiers who caught his eye.

"Go get your weapons," Sir Adam snapped. "We'll be following the king to shore shortly."

Soon enough, the three of them were equipped with their weapons and leaving the boat as they followed the king and the other soldiers he had hand-picked onto the island, marching southward toward the town of Messina.

When they arrived, the city attempted to put up some resistance, but Sir Adam led the company in a brief skirmish and the inhabitants surrendered before a battle had even truly begun.

Much had seen no combat, having been at the rear of the company. Robin was disappointed in the skirmish, but Much was not; he had no desire to begin killing anyone.

As it turned out, many in the city had no qualms with King Richard coming to the island to rescue his sister—she was, apparently, a beloved queen.

The king chose a house to use as headquarters during their stay, and Sir Adam posted Much, Robin, and Allen outside the door to keep an eye on things. The sun had been up for several hours by that point and was shining down cheerfully on the three of them.

Allen leaned up against the door and then grinned. "I can hear them."

"Don't eavesdrop," Much said as Robin leaned forward with a, "What are they saying?"

"The king is sending a small group of soldiers to Tancred with a message."

"Who is he sending?"

Allen pressed his ear against the door and then shrugged. "I don't know."

The door opened a moment later, causing Allen to jump backwards as the king came out.

"Robin of Locksley!"

"Yes, Sire."

"I want you and your companions to deliver a message to King Tancred of Sicily. Come inside, and Sir Adam can show you on the map where his palace is located."

"Yes, Sire."

The king gestured them inside and the three of them followed him to a table with a map spread out across it. Sir Adam and several other nobles stood around the table. Sir Adam pointed out the palace, and then the king turned to Robin.

"You will go there today, deliver my message, and bring my sister back to me."

"Yes, Sire," Robin said.

"You will tell him that I demand the release of my sister Joan, and that I require her full dowry to be paid back to me."

"Yes, Sire."

"Stop saying that," King Richard chuckled. "It's rather annoying. The least you do is change it up a little bit. 'Your Majesty' works just as well, or 'King Richard' or anything other than 'yes, Sire, yes, Sire' over and over. I'll lose my patience."

"My apologies, King Richard," Robin replied, a hint of a smirk forming about his mouth.

In a short while, Much, Robin, and Allen were on their way out of the city of Messina and headed for Tancred's residence. The day was pleasantly warm, the sun shining down on them as they walked through the unfamiliar country.

Much's eyes darted every which way, trying to take it all in. Every time they crested a hill he could see the vibrant blue and green of the sea below, and all around him were bushes of vivid flowers and collections of cacti. The road to Tancred's palace was the most beautiful Much had ever seen.

Chapter 7

AFTER A FEW hours of walking, they came in sight of the palace. It was a large stone structure, with many towers and high turreted walls surrounding it. As they neared the front gate, two guards moved forward to intercept them with swords drawn.

"What do you want? No further, or you won't be waking up tomorrow!"

Much was grateful for his years spent learning alongside Robin, for the soldiers called out in Latin. Beside him, however, Allen looked thoroughly confused.

Robin stepped forward and bowed, speaking to them in Latin as well. "We bring a message from King Richard of England for King Tancred of Sicily."

"He dares to speak to our king after taking Messina with no provocation?"

"He believes there was a good reason to attack your city, but I must give the message to the king and not his guards."

The guards grunted, seemed to consider for a moment, and then called for the gates to be opened. They led Much, Robin, and Allen inside and through several passages before they stopped in front of a door and one of the guards knocked loudly.

The door creaked open and he was admitted, while the other guard stood outside with Much, Robin, and Allen. Much held his breath, surreptitiously trying to wipe his sweaty palm along his trousers to dry it. The wait seemed to last an eternity.

It wasn't long, however, before the first guard returned. "He will see you."

The doors swung inward and they were admitted into the throne room. It was a long, spacious room with a ceiling set so high above them that Much had to crane his neck to look up at it. The walls on either side of the room were made of long windows reaching from floor to ceiling and letting in the bright sunlight. Much could see the distant sea on the horizon, glimmering its brilliant shades of turquoise.

King Tancred sat on a throne on a raised dais with guards on either side of him.

Robin bowed, and Allen and Much followed suit.

"Your Majesty—"

"Did I ask you to speak?" King Tancred turned to Robin with a frown. They were both speaking Latin, and Much glanced at Allen to see if he could follow the conversation. Given the way his brows pinched together, it seemed unlikely.

"Your king has upset me greatly, taking Messina with no provocation," King Tancred said.

"You are no angrier with him than he is with you," Robin replied. "If I have my politics straight, you were not meant to rule this throne at all. William of Sicily appointed his aunt Constance as his heir before his death—you took the throne with no provocation, and imprisoned Sicily's beloved Queen Joan, who happens to also be the beloved sister of King Richard of England. My king is put out with you."

King Tancred leaned forward, his eyes icy with menace. "I can do what I like with my subjects."

"Not when it concerns the sister of my king."

Much was impressed with Robin's quick responses, and the way he stood before King Tancred—back straight, eyes forward, every bit the lord his father raised him to be. Much had a hard time not

52

cowering before King Tancred's anger, or moving closer to Robin to hide behind him.

"My king demands you release Joan to us, and pay back her dowry in full."

King Tancred shook his head. "Impossible."

"I would advise you not to upset our king further."

"What can he do to me?"

"A great deal, I imagine. You saw how easily we took Messina. If you refuse to release Joan and pay back her dowry, then our stay at Messina is likely to be lengthy, and you may find Englishmen storming your other cities as well, Your Majesty."

"I will not agree to your king's demands. Tell him that, and nothing more. Guards," Tancred waved a hand to the soldiers who had led them inside. "Take them away."

The three of them were rather rudely escorted back outside.

"Now what?" Allen asked. "I take it things did not go well, though I understood very little of it."

"Now we return to King Richard and explain that King Tancred has refused to meet his demands." Robin shrugged. "It went better than it might have, honestly. We could have been imprisoned or worse."

The walk back to Messina was a quiet one.

When they gathered before King Richard, Sir Adam, and the other advisors to the king to relate their news later that evening upon their return to Messina, King Richard was furious. He slammed his fist down on the table, and Much involuntarily took a step backwards.

"Refused me?" King Richard growled. "We'll show him. We'll take his castle this very day!"

King Richard and Sir Adam began to gather the soldiers and issue orders, and in no time at all they were marching toward King Tancred's castle.

King Tancred did not put up a fight. When he saw the army coming, he immediately surrendered leaving Robin once again disappointed in the lack of a real fight to prove himself. With his castle seized and King Richard threatening to take over the entire island, King Tancred finally relented and sent some of his servants to begin collecting enough money to pay back Joan's dowry.

"Where is my sister?" King Richard demanded in English, grabbing Tancred by the neck of his shirt and shoving him against the wall in the throne room. Much, Robin, and Allen were standing nearby, ready to be of use though the King's Royal Guard was surrounding him already.

"She is in the dungeon. I can send someone for her," Tancred replied, his own English perfectly good, leaving Much to wonder if his use of Latin before had simply been a power move.

"I'll send my own men," King Richard said. He turned to his Royal Guard, instructing them to bring Joan to him safely. As they left the room, King Richard looked over his shoulder. "Robin of Locksley!"

"Yes, Sire?"

"I've sent my personal guard to the dungeons to bring Joan to me, and you and your two companions will act as my guard until they return."

"Yes, Sire."

"Don't start that again," King Richard snapped, before turning back to Tancred with a vicious gleam in his eye.

Robin chuckled. "Forgive me, Your Majesty."

"You're forgiven, of course," King Richard said as he glanced at Robin and a hint of a smile played about his mouth. "I simply hate repetition."

"I am beginning to notice that, Sire."

Much didn't understand how Robin could feel so relaxed and at ease with King Richard. He was *the king* and here Robin was, speaking to him as easily as he would to his father. Teasing him and laughing with him as easily as he might do with Allen.

"Richard?"

Everyone turned toward the sound of a woman's voice, and Much's heart froze in his chest. A beautiful woman stood in the doorway in a flowing white dress, with her dark curls spilling around her shoulders, her blue eyes unsure and afraid.

"Joan!" King Richard dropped his grip on Tancred and moved swiftly across the throne room toward his sister. Joan ran to meet his embrace, throwing her arms around his shoulders.

"You came for me?"

"Of course I came for you! Look how much you've grown!" King Richard set her down and stepped back to look at her. "The last time I saw you, you were twelve years old and setting sail for Sicily, small and frightened. Look at you now; you're a beautiful young woman."

With Joan in tow, and the money to compensate for her dowry carried in carts, King Richard and his army retreated back to the sea. Before their departure from Sicily, however, the rest of the fleet from England arrived, as well as King Philip's forces.

Along with them came a boat carrying King Richard's mother —Eleanor of Aquitaine—and a young noblewoman named Berengaria of Navarre.

Sir Adam was with the king when he greeted the two women as they came off the boat, and Much, Robin, and Allen were there at the king's request. After embracing his mother and the young lady, King Richard turned toward the rest of them.

"Robin of Locksley, come meet my mother."

Robin moved forward as Eleanor glanced at her son. "Who are these fine young men, Richard?"

"Robin of Locksley, son of the Earl of Locksley. He has been entertaining company on our journey and I think you would enjoy knowing him. This is his servant Much, and Allen is a young soldier in my army. Robin of Locksley happens to be one of the best archers in my army, or so I've been told."

"Ah, is he indeed?"

"I would not boast as much as that, Your Majesty," Robin bowed to Queen Eleanor. "But I do shoot well."

"I haven't truly seen him in action yet," King Richard admitted, and then turned to the young woman to introduce her as well. "This is my bride-to-be, Berengaria of Navarre."

"But aren't you betrothed to—" Robin stopped, and Much shot him a look of dismay that he ignored as he continued. "It is an honor to meet you, my lady."

Berengaria laughed, her eyes dancing. "Oh, he was betrothed, Robin of Locksley. You are not mistaken."

"But I am breaking it off," King Richard said, wrapping an arm around Berengaria's waist. "So that I can marry my beautiful Berengaria."

They were soon dismissed from the group as the king, his mother, bride-to-be, and Sir Adam moved off on their own.

"He was betrothed to someone else?" Much asked as he watched the group walking away.

"Yes," Robin replied.

"I'm not sure Berengaria is beautiful enough to warrant breaking off another political marriage," Allen said. "Who was he engaged to before?"

"King Philip's sister, I believe," Robin replied. "Princess Alys. I imagine there will be some tension there … especially as we travel together to the Holy Land."

"Doesn't seem wise," Allen shrugged.

"Perhaps not, but did you see the way they looked at each other? If I was engaged to Princess Alys, I'd break it off in a heartbeat just to have Marian look at me like that. Love will make a man do almost anything." Robin grinned, his eyes getting a faraway look in them. "Someday you'll understand."

Allen's jovial expression shuttered all of a sudden and he shrugged. "Perhaps. Should we return to our quarters until we are summoned again?"

Without waiting for an answer, Allen began moving away from the docks at the harbor and toward the tavern where they were staying. Much watched him go, curious what Robin had said that he'd found so off-putting. Was the idea of falling love so distressing?

Chapter 8

KING RICHARD AND King Philip soon had their respective fleets sailing again—this time toward the Holy Land—while Queen Eleanor returned to her home. Joan and Berengaria had stayed with King Richard, and he'd put them both on *The Barbara* saying Robin of Locksley would entertain and take care of them.

As they sailed away from Sicily, Much leaned against the rail beside Robin who was speaking to the two noble ladies.

"So, Robin of Locksley, why does my fiance think so highly of you?" Berengaria asked with a laugh.

Sir Adam moved across the deck to lean against the rail on the other side of Berengaria and Joan as Allen joined the group and leaned in beside Much, and they made one long line of fascinating individuals watching the blue waves and the dark clouds in the sky as they talked.

"I do not know, my lady," Robin said.

"Please, Robin, just call me Berengaria."

"I doubt that would be proper," Robin said with a grin.

"Perhaps not, but I am not so much older than you are, and you are trying to make me feel ancient by comparison. I wish you would stop."

Robin laughed. "It is not about your age, my lady. And surely you are used to such deference."

"It bores me to no end." Berengaria sighed dramatically.

Joan threw back her head with a laugh, her dark curls shaking. "It isn't such a bad thing. I enjoy the bows and curtsies, the admiration, love, fealty, and flattery and all the rest of it."

"Ah, but you, Joan, were a Queen. I am just Berengaria."

"You will not be 'just Berengaria' for long," Robin said. "You are going to be the Queen of England. As such, I doubt I should speak to you as I would to a commoner, or as an equal. You will soon be my queen."

Berengaria laughed. "What foolishness! I am only human, as you are, why should we treat each other as though one were higher than the other? Much, does he treat you like a servant?"

"I *am* his servant, my lady."

"Yes, but does he treat you like one? No! I have seen the two of you together over the last few days. He treats you as a friend. Why can it not be the same for me?"

"Ah," Robin laughed, "But you see, even though I treat Much as a friend, he still treats me as his master. So you may treat me as a friend and I will continue to view you as above my station."

Berengaria sighed. "I shall never win."

"Of course not," Allen laughed, joining in the banter. "I have been traveling with Robin for many months and I assure you he doesn't lose arguments."

Sir Adam spoke up from the other end of the group, and Much could hear the disapproval in his voice, "I have traveled with him for the same amount of time, Allen, and what you say is true. Young Robin has too high an opinion of himself."

"Surely not," Joan laughed. "He seems humble enough, not allowing Berengaria the right to be treated as an equal."

"He says he must not treat our Lady Berengaria as an equal," Sir Adam replied, "and it is this that you mistake for humility. Yet even as he says this, he teases her as though she were not his queen-to-be."

"I am glad he does," Berengaria said. "You're too much of a bore, Sir Adam, and a cranky bore at that."

Much thought Sir Adam might snap back at her for that, but he said nothing.

Two days after they set sail from Sicily, the dark clouds finally caught up with them and *The Barbara* and other ships in the fleet were embroiled in a violent storm. The rain came down in torrents and great waves crashed over the side of the boat, the wind howling around them.

When the skies had opened up and let loose their fury, Much, Allen, and Robin had been on deck. Shouts from the captain of the boat insisted only his sailors remain above deck so Much and his friends ran for the ladder to go below deck.

The deck was already slick from the rain and the waves that began to crest over the railing, causing Much to slip and slide along the way to the ladder, his usual clumsiness from his lack of sea legs compounded because of the storm. The wooden deck seemed to buck and bounce beneath him with a violence intent on throwing him down.

Allen reached the ladder first and began to go below, and Much turned to let Robin go past him. Robin, however, had stopped following and had turned back.

"Robin!"

"Much, stay below!" Robin shouted over his shoulder as he darted across the deck. The rain struck Much's face as though it were pelting him with sharp needles as he watched Robin running through the torrential downpour toward the bow of the ship.

And then Much saw why.

Joan was there, clinging to the rail with white knuckles as she was inching her way along the side of the ship. The wind slapped against Much's face as he watched Robin running toward her.

Over the wind and rain came the sound of Joan's frightened voice calling out, "Robin!"

61

Robin reached her, grabbing her hand, but before they could go far a dark wave swept over the rail Joan had been clinging to, knocking them both off of their feet as it pushed across the deck, soaking any sailors and soldiers in its path.

Much darted forward, unsure what he could do to help but knowing he couldn't leave Robin in this predicament alone.

The deck pitched and heaved beneath him and Much stumbled to his knees as another wave crashed over the boat, sending Robin and Joan toward the rail.

As Much struggled to his feet, wiping rain from his eyes, he saw Robin grab Joan's arm as yet another wave crashed over the rail and swept toward them. Much lunged forward, grabbing Robin's arm and holding on with all he was worth as the wave swept all three of them over the side of the boat.

Much's grip slipped and he plunged into the icy water. For a moment all was darkness and cold as he thrashed in the turmoil of the waves, and then his head broke the surface and he gasped for air, hearing shouts above him.

"Man overboard!"

Much struggled to stay afloat, kicking his legs and waving his arms around. He'd never had to learn to swim properly in Nottinghamshire, and even if he had, the violent waves in the storm would have been difficult to overcome.

Above him, Much caught a glimpse of Robin clinging to the rail, hanging outside the boat with Joan wrapped tightly in his other arm and Allen's face peering over the side of the boat, his reaching for the princess.

In another moment, Much's head was below water and the force of the wave flipped him upside down and he tumbled through the darkness.

Much twisted and turned, trying to find his bearings, his lungs burning in his chest. Everything in the water was darkness, he couldn't see which way was up as the pressure of the rising and falling water pushed him around.

His lungs ignited in his chest, the pressure building until he could no longer help but open his lips and gasp for air. Salty sea water rushed into his mouth and Much began to choke, his body spasming. As he jerked around, his head crested the waves and he heard the muted sounds of shouting.

His throat was burning as he coughed up sea water even as he felt rough hands grab him, tying a rope around him. A moment later he swung dizzily through the air and his stomach recoiled, throwing up more sea water and whatever else had been in his stomach as the sailors were hauling him back on board the ship.

The sailors who'd leapt in to save him dropped him on the wooden deck and Much leaned over, coughing up more sea water.

The rain pelted his back and the wind was still howling around the ship as the waves tossed the boat forward and back in rough movements that caused Much to throw up again.

As his vomiting came to an end, he felt himself being pulled to his feet and then found himself in the firm embrace of Robin.

"Are you alright? Come on, we need to dry you off."

Robin pulled Much across the wet deck as another wave crashed over the side of the ship and swept loose cargo overboard.

Much's hands were shaking as he slipped down the ladder

below deck. His throat and lungs were on fire in a way he'd never felt before and he was colder than he'd ever been in his life.

"What were you possibly thinking, Much?" Robin asked as he ushered Much into the room where all the hammocks hung. Sir Adam and Allen were there and both turned toward Much and Robin as they entered.

"Y-you were g-going over-b-board," Much spluttered in answer to Robin's question, as his teeth began to chatter.

"And you thought jumping over the ship's side was going to help?" Robin snapped, grabbing a blanket from a hammock nearby and wrapping it around Much's shoulders.

"I c-couldn't just w-watch."

"Oh, Much." Robin's arms wrapped around him again, his voice as hoarse as Much's despite the fact he hadn't been the one who swallowed half the Mediterranean sea.

When Robin pulled back from the hug, Much rubbed his hands up and down his arms trying to warm himself up. The ship's pitching to and fro because of the storm seemed almost worse from below deck, and Much leaned against the wall for balance.

"How is Princess Joan?"

"As wet as anything, but unharmed," Allen answered Much's question.

"How are you, Robin?" Much eyed him suspiciously. He was soaked through, his hair dripping, his clothes sopping wet, and though he tried to hide it he was shivering from the cold almost as bad as Much was.

"I am perfectly fine," Robin said, stripping off his shirt and moving toward his pack to get a new one. "Don't try anything so rash again. The whole time I was clinging to that rail with Joan in my arms, every bone in my body was telling me to let go and dive in after you."

"Why?" Much tilted his head to one side as he watched Robin getting changed into dryer clothes. Why would he want to risk his life for Much?

"To save you, of course," Robin replied. "I couldn't live without you."

Allen groaned, plopping into his hammock, "Oh, shut up, both of you! Why do you have to be so emotional? You're brothers in spirit, you love each other, we get it. Move on."

Robin laughed. "Someday, Allen, you will have a best friend and then you will understand."

Sir Adam grunted from his own hammock, seemingly unimpressed with the conversation around him.

Robin moved toward Much and pulled the blanket from his shoulders. "Come on, you have to be in dry clothes, too."

Much swatted Robin's hands away and began to pull off his soaked clothes. It was one thing for Robin to say he wished to save Much, it was quite another for his master to help him dress.

"I had a best friend." Allen's voice was so soft that Much barely heard him over the creaking of the boat and the muffled yells of the sailors on deck.

"Then you should already understand," Robin said, watching Much until he was satisfied that Much was dry enough, and then pulling himself into his own hammock near Allen's.

"I do understand, Robin…" Allen sighed, his hand briefly covering his face before he continued. "My friend is dead. They're all dead. I'm alone in the world."

"You've lost everyone?" Much asked, suddenly thinking the darkness behind Allen's eyes made a great deal of sense.

"I lost everyone." Allen closed his eyes as he turned his face away from them.

"I'm sorry."

"I don't need the two of you to feel sorry for me," Allen snapped.

Robin rolled out of his hammock and moved toward Allen, putting a hand on his shoulder. "You may have no one of your own back home, but you have us."

"Robin, there's no need—"

"Nonsense," Robin said, giving Allen a wink and a grin. "I could do with another brother."

"Thank you," Allen said as Robin returned to his hammock and Much struggled to climb into his own in spite of the pitching boat.

Sir Adam rolled away from the three of them with a grunt and a frown, and Much wondered if he had his own tragic story he wasn't telling.

Much pulled his blanket close, shivering in his hammock as he listened to the creaking boat, and felt the hammock beneath him swinging wildly from the uneven movement of the rough waves.

Robin had been overwhelmed at the thought of losing him, and Much didn't know what to make of that emotion. Robin had always treated him as a friend, in ways that the Earl never would, but he was still a noble and Much was nothing. A deep sense of gratitude and love flared in Much's chest as he thought about his young master. Allen was right; they *were* brothers.

Chapter 9

MUCH DRIFTED INTO sleep despite the storm outside. What felt like the very next instant, but was in truth several hours later, Much felt the world spin around him as he fell to the floor—his head hit the wood with a resounding crack—and a body landed on top of him with a thump.

"What was that?" Robin struggled to sit up off of Much, rubbing his elbow.

Much sat up, his hand on his forehead. "Did we hit something?"

"Are you alright, Much?" Allen asked with a hint of a laugh in his voice.

"I think so. Are you?"

Allen shrugged from where he was also sitting on the floor. "No broken bones. Should we go see what happened to throw us out of hammocks?"

"Do you think the storm has passed?" Much asked.

"I doubt it," Robin said. "Can't you feel the rough waves? We may have hit a reef or something."

Much followed Robin and everyone else as they scurried above deck to see what was going on. The sky was still full of dark clouds, but they were no longer pouring rain. The sea was roiling around *The Barbara* and several other ships that had run aground on a reef, just as Robin had said.

One ship was broken to pieces, large chunks of wood being driven back to the sea as men clung to driftwood and thrashed in the water calling for help.

On the deck of *The Barbara,* Much watched for a second as the sailors, wet and tired from the storm, ran about listening to the captain's shouted orders as they tried to find a way to break from the reef without breaking the hull.

The sailors were scurrying about, pulling on ropes, shouting to each other, clambering up the masts, and leaning over the side of the ship to get a better view of how stuck they might be. Sir Adam was shouting his own orders to the soldiers who had, like Allen and his friends, made their way on deck. An effort was being made to lend aid to the drowning men of the wrecked boat.

"Where are we?" Much asked as he, Robin, and Allen moved to one side of the boat to be out of the way and wait for orders. He could see an island just off the starboard bow, and what appeared to be people on the beach.

"I'm not sure," Robin replied, watching the chaos of the sailors around them.

"Get your weapons!" Sir Adam's shout carried over the rest of the noise above deck.

"What is it?" Much asked.

"Soldiers," Robin hissed, pointing toward the island.

"We've run aground." Sir Adam came toward them. "There's a boat of soldiers headed our way, more coming behind no doubt. The captain thinks we're on Cyprus, but he isn't sure. He got turned around in the weather, the idiot."

"How do we know the coming soldiers mean us harm?" Much asked.

"We don't," Sir Adam grunted. "But you don't know they mean peace either, so get below deck and get your sword, soldier!"

68

Much, Robin, and Allen hurried below to fetch their weapons, along with the rest of the company before hurrying back on deck.

Much could see several boats that had put off from the island now, full of soldiers and headed toward *The Barbara* and the other boats that were grounded.

In another moment, archers from the boats had shot toward them and Much ducked under the rail out of sight as the arrows found purchase on deck or in the bodies of fellow soldiers and sailors on board.

Robin grabbed an arrow of his own, holding his bow aloft and taking aim. Allen stood beside him shooting as well. The first of their arrows sailed harmlessly into the water or struck the wood of the boats coming toward them.

"It's the wind," Allen groaned.

"You just have to compensate," Robin grunted beside him, taking aim again, though he seemed to be pointing his arrow slightly to the left of the approaching boats. As he let the arrow fly, it shifted in the wind and struck an approaching soldier, who fell into the icy water with the arrow protruding from his heart.

Robin turned to Allen with a grin. "See?"

"Show off."

Much gripped his sword tightly, hoping Robin and the other archers would keep him from having to take part in the battle. He didn't think he was capable of actually killing anyone.

Still, despite Robin and the other soldiers on *The Barbara* doing their utmost to stop them, the boats reached the reef where their ship had run aground and the soldiers below began to throw grappling hooks and swing on deck.

Bows were soon discarded and swords brought out. Much dodged and parried, always on the defensive. Robin and Allen stayed near him, the three of them in a relatively tight circle as they fought off the soldiers, but it was no use. They were soon outnumbered, and one by one King Richard's soldiers aboard *The Barbara* began to fall to the deck around Much with blood spurting from vicious wounds.

The fight didn't last long. Sir Adam soon had a sword to his throat and was ordered to surrender. He grunted the order to lower their weapons, and Much was more than happy to comply, dropping his sword to the deck. Robin was slower to obey, but he did it while still glaring at the enemy.

Soon the soldiers from the island were tying the survivors up and lining them along one side of the deck, while others went below and brought up any remaining cargo that hadn't been swept away or ruined from the storm, including Joan's dowry and Joan and Berengaria themselves.

Robin took half a step forward when he saw the two ladies being dragged above deck, but three soldiers from the island immediately pointed their swords in his direction and he settled back against the side of the ship beside Much.

Soon everyone from *The Barbara* was being loaded into boats and brought to the island. It was indeed Cyprus, they discovered, as they were brought to the castle of one Isaac of Cyprus and thrown into his dungeon.

As luck would have it, Much, Robin, and Allen ended up in the same cell. It was a small, square stone room with one tiny window set high in the back wall, and a large wooden door leading to the rest of the dungeon.

Days began to pass. Guards would bring them meals, but otherwise they saw and heard from no one. Robin spent most of his time banging on the door or attempting to kick it down. Much sat in one corner of the cell, watching Robin with wide and terrified eyes.

"Banging against that door is not going to knock it down," Allen commented quietly as Robin heaved his shoulder into the door again.

"We have to get out! It is our duty to rescue Joan and Berengaria!"

"We can't do anything," Allen insisted, seating himself beside Much. "We're stuck in here."

Robin rubbed his shoulder and sighed, moving toward them and sinking to the floor on the other side of Much. "We have to try."

"Good luck with that. You've been banging against that door for over a week and nothing has happened."

"Perhaps the king will come," Much said. "He will come and rescue us and the princesses."

Robin groaned at the mention of the king, putting his head in his hands. "I have failed him."

"We were sorely outnumbered, weak from the storm…you can hardly blame yourself."

"He told them I would take care of them."

"And you did! You rescued Joan from being thrown overboard and drowning in that storm."

"And now she's captured…" Robin shook his head. "And so is Berengaria."

"And so are we," Allen said. "Don't paint it too black, Robin. It's not as though we left them to fend for themselves when Isaac of Cyprus attacked. We're all in the same predicament."

As Robin and Allen continued their discussion, Much realized he could hear the sounds of many footsteps in the hallway outside their cell.

"I feel responsible," Robin replied. "And we don't know that we're in the same predicament. We don't know where they are being held or what's being done to them."

The sound of people outside was growing louder, and Much glanced between Robin and Allen, though neither seemed to have noticed.

"We weren't the only soldiers on *The Barbara* or the other boats run aground. Everyone was captured; in a way we're all responsible for failing to protect Joan and Berengaria."

"You are not making me feel better."

"Listen!" Much said, finally breaking into the conversation. Robin and Allen quieted. "Someone is outside."

A moment later they heard a key in the lock, and all three of them rose to their feet as the door of their prison swung inward and King Richard stood in the doorway.

"Your Majesty!" Robin bowed.

"Now what are you doing in prison, Robin?" the king asked with a laugh.

"I'm so sorry, Sire—"

"Never mind, Robin of Locksley, I was only teasing. I've heard all about it from Berengaria and Joan, not to mention from Isaac himself. He's trying hard to appease me after capturing my sister and fiance."

"Surely he will not go unpunished, Your Majesty?" Robin asked as the king led the three of them out of the cell. There were more of the king's soldiers in the hallway, opening other cells and releasing the rest of the prisoners, including Sir Adam.

"Of course he will not go unpunished, Robin of Locksley. He saw an opportunity to take my ships when they blew off course, and I now see one to capture his island and claim it for England. I will dedicate it to Berengaria, I think. How does that sound? But come, if we are going to capture this island you will all need your weapons."

It appeared the rest of King Richard's fleet, and that of King Philip, had landed safely at Crete to wait out the storm while *The Barbara* and several others had been blown off course to Cyprus. Once the storm had passed, both kings had brought the rest of the armies to Cyprus to free the prisoners and punish the ruler of Cyprus, Isaac. It did not take long before the combined armies swept through the small island and Isaac surrendered.

The king was so pleased with his success that he did not only dedicate the island to Berengaria, but he also married her. It was a simple affair, and was soon over.

As the soldiers dispersed from the gathering, and Isaac of Cyprus and other nobles were dismissed, King Richard stood on the hilltop where the ceremony had taken place with Berengaria, calling Much, Robin, Allen, and Sir Adam over to speak with them.

"You are quite the soldier, Robin," the king said without preamble.

"Thank you, Your Majesty. And congratulations to both of you," Robin bowed first to Berengaria, and then to the King.

Berengaria grinned at him, her arm linked firmly through her husband's.

"I have a mind to promote you to my personal guard, you and your two companions," King Richard said. "Berengaria agrees it would be an excellent idea."

"I do indeed," Berengaria said.

"Allen is an excellent soldier as well as you," King Richard continued, "from what I've seen and heard, anyway, and I know that young Much would not want to leave your side."

"I would not wish to leave his side either." Robin smiled at Much before turning back to the king. "But our company…?"

"Sir Adam will continue to lead his company as he has been," the King said. "You will be my Royal Guard."

Sir Adam cleared his throat, seemingly wanting to say something, but the king ignored him.

"Isn't there usually more to such a promotion than…" Robin shrugged. "I don't know, this all feels very rushed, Your Majesty."

"Believe me, we have considered it," Berengaria laughed. "And if you need fanfare, I'm sure we can provide it."

"Being in the King's Guard is quite an honor and I do not think I am worthy of it," Robin said.

"Foolishness," King Richard laughed. "I think you are perfect. And do something for me, will you? Just call me Richard."

"Your Majesty!"

"When we are not surrounded by commoners, of course. And perhaps you should not be so informal among most nobles, but…I am only human and I would prefer it."

"But you are my king!"

"You do not call my sister by any formal title. She is simply Joan to you. Well, I am simply Richard."

"Your Majesty—"

"Robin, if I have to order you, as your king, to call me Richard, I will do so."

Robin grinned. "I hardly think that will be necessary."

Sir Adam cleared his throat again, and this time the king turned toward him. "What do you need, Sir Adam?"

"Richard, I—"

"I do not remember giving you permission to address me so informally." The king frowned.

"Forgive me, Your Majesty." Sir Adam shot a glare toward Robin. "But I do not understand why you would appoint young Robin to your personal guard. Let alone Much, the servant. He is not—"

"I do not care what you think of 'young Robin' or his servant," the king said firmly. "I have formed my own opinions."

"You used to care for mine."

"Well I do not care for it now. Be off with you."

Sir Adam glared at Robin, but turned silently and stalked off.

Berengaria laughed gaily. "What a grump of the first order."

"Now, Robin," King Richard said. "As my personal guard I expect you to accompany me and your new queen to our quarters and ensure we are not interrupted for the remainder of the day."

Robin grinned. "Whatever you say, Richard."

Chapter 10

AFTER A COUPLE more months of sailing, the combined fleets of King Richard and King Philip finally made it to their destination—the port city of Acre off the coast of Palestine.

Acre was a strong and fortified city on the coast, garrisoned by a large force of Muslims who—at the time of King Richard and King Philip arriving—were besieged by a force of Crusaders commanded by King Guy of Jerusalem. King Guy's forces were themselves surrounded and besieged by Saladin's army, and it was into this chaos that Much, Robin, and Allen were soon thrust.

They sailed into the beach rather than the port itself, as the city was not under Crusader control. As they were hurrying ashore, Saladin's troops attempted to mount an attack, his archers firing on the landing boats as they came up the beach. But the Crusading army already camped outside the city fended them off until those from King Richard's and King Philip's armies could come ashore who were going to do so; the rest of the fleet fought with Saladin's ships that were in the water, trying to take control or break the siege from the sea.

As the soldiers gathered along the beach and moved inward, Much, Robin, and Allen stayed beside the king.

For several days they stood by him as he directed camp to be set up and gave orders to his generals to attack Saladin and strengthen King Guy's defenses, but because King Richard did not fight, the three of them saw no combat either. Much was relieved, more than willing to stand outside the king's tent as he met with his generals, keeping an eye out for suspicious behavior but partaking in no violence himself.

Robin, however, was restless.

"I didn't join the Crusades to stand by and watch!"

"Our job now is to protect the King of England," Allen replied. "It's noble enough."

"Who is going to hurt Richard while we're this far from the enemy?" Robin put his hands on his hips, surveying the wide fields in front of them where soldiers, tents, and horses spread out before the city of Acre. At the moment, there was a skirmish far to the left—a few hundred of Saladin's men being beaten back by King Philip's forces. Most of the field had been taken already, Saladin's land forces being pushed further and further from the city walls where the Crusaders had made camp. It would not be long before Acre was seized.

"I'm glad we're not in the fighting," Much said.

Robin shook his head in exasperation, but wrapped his arm affectionately around Much's shoulders. "Of course you are."

Between King Richard, King Philip, and then the arrival of Duke Leopold of Austria with forces of his own, the Crusaders swelled King Guy's forces to an overwhelming number. After some skirmishes, Saladin wisely withdrew his army and let the Crusaders besiege Acre without contest.

The siege was no more interesting than the brief skirmishes with Saladin's army; Much, Robin, and Allen stayed near the king as he directed his troops from the rear.

When the city itself was taken, King Richard had his standard put up to fly over the wall of the city. King Philip, and Duke Leopold of Austria, did the same. The Crusading army then made camp in the fields that had so recently been covered in the wounded and dying.

Saladin's army had retreated, the resistance in the city had surrendered or been killed, and the Crusaders now had a moment of respite—though Robin felt they hardly needed it.

One afternoon Much, Robin, and Allen were sitting together on the hard earth outside the King's tent, watching soldiers moving about the camp around them. One lifting a flask to his lips, two of them laughing nearby, a few of them sparring in the distance. Everyone was relaxed, waiting for whatever would come next without the slightest concern. High over the city walls flew the standards of King Richard and King Philip.

"Robin?"

"What, Much?"

"What happened to Duke Leopold of Austria's flag? It was flying beside the others yesterday."

"King Richard pulled it down."

"Why?"

"Because he did not believe Leopold, as a duke, had the right to fly his standard beside those of kings. He was rather upset by it."

"Which is absurd," Allen said. "Our king can be somewhat pompous, but not in all things. He speaks to you as a friend and wants you to call him Richard, but 'oh no, the Duke of Austria dares fly his flag by mine.'" Allen rolled his eyes.

"It is unwise, too," Robin said. "It's true, Much, so don't give me that look. He is alienating the Duke of Austria. There are rumors he was so affronted by the removal of his flag and the disrespect of our king that he may return home and not continue on the Crusades at all. It weakens our army."

Much thought all of the politics were ridiculous. The king didn't want his flag flown by a duke's, the duke didn't want his flag taken down, and such petty concerns now created tension in the camp and part of their forces were leaving? Absurd.

The king soon appeared at the flap of his tent, calling for Robin.

"Yes, Your Majesty?" Robin sprung to his feet.

"I have been receiving disturbing news from England for several months now. Letters from those loyal to me in England, and from my mother as well. My brother is doing things that I do not appreciate, trying to seize power in my absence. I saw no reason to burden you with such details as they did not concern you. My brother is trying to seize control of England and in doing so is murdering many nobles who are loyal to me."

"I am sorry to hear it, Sire."

"I am afraid I am now telling you of the troubles in England because I have news that does, in fact, concern you. Your father was one of those nobles, Robin. Your father has been killed for his loyalty to myself."

Much felt a jolt of pain run through him and he glanced at Robin, watching his blue eyes darken and a frown mar his usually jovial face.

"I am sorry, Robin," King Richard continued, "You are the Earl of Locksley now."

The king soon returned to his tent and Robin sank slowly to the ground. Much touched his arm. "I am sorry, master."

Robin started slightly. "Much…why did you call me that?"

"I am your servant, and you are now the Earl of Locksley."

"I'm Robin…" Robin looked up at him with tears welling in the deep sadness of his eyes, and Much regretted his part in upsetting his friend.

"I am sorry. I meant nothing by it." He slipped his arm around Robin's shoulders in what he hoped was a comforting manner.

An ache was growing in Much's chest as tears pricked his eyes. The Earl had never been particularly kind to Much, but he was still the only father Much could remember, and for his part, Much loved him.

"Allen?" Robin looked over toward him, anguish written all over his face.

"Yes, Robin?"

"We are in the same position now," Robin glanced at Much. "We three are all orphans now and we only have each other."

"Orphaned brothers-in-arms," Allen responded grimly.

"Precisely. We must stick together, we three."

The days passed in relative calm, camping outside Acre as King Philip and King Richard established their control and planned for their next move on the long journey to retake Jerusalem. King Guy of Jerusalem was eager for the Crusaders to march that direction and take his city back from the Muslim forces and Saladin's army that had taken the city from him in the first place.

The days were spent watching over the king's tent or following him to various meetings, and nights were spent sleeping on the rough ground outside of his tent, taking turns keeping watch every few hours. Things fell into an almost boring routine.

Robin didn't speak of his father's death, but Much knew it affected him. He was not quite his usual cheerful self, and there was a lingering shadow in his eyes to match Allen's now—although Allen's darkness seemed to Much to run far deeper.

One night, as Much sat awake on watch, King Philip visited King Richard's tent. Much remained outside, sitting between Robin and Allen who were both sound asleep.

The camp and the city of Acre were both still and calm as most people were slumbering. There was little sound in the camp, apart from a few low voices of guards on watch or the gentle crackling of their small fires. In the far distance, Much could hear the faint sounds of the sea breaking against the shore.

Soon, however, the calm was broken by raised voices in the tent behind him.

"I cannot believe you broke the engagement with my sister—"

"It is over and done with, Philip! There is nothing to discuss—"

"I will not stand for this affront against Alys!"

Allen stirred beside Much, rubbing his eyes and sitting up. "How long have they been arguing?"

"A little while. King Philip is upset."

"About his sister it seems."

"I will not stay after all this!" they heard King Philip shout.

"Then you will dishonor your kingdom! To abandon the Crusades—"

"I'll leave a few thousand soldiers," King Philip hissed. "My honor is intact. It is yours that is in need of mending. You are on your own, Richard."

King Philip swept out of the tent after that. Allen sighed. "You'd better wake Robin. He'll want to know."

Much shook Robin awake and informed him that King Philip would likely be leaving soon.

"Leaving? When?"

"As soon as he can, I suppose. He mentioned leaving soldiers for the fight in order to not go back on his word and retain some honor, but...he's angry and he's leaving."

"And once again, our army is weakened." Robin sighed, shoving a hand through his hair. "We haven't even begun yet, and already two high ranking nobility have abandoned us."

"We apparently have a rather contentious king," Allen said with a wry grin.

With Leopold and Philip gone, King Richard was now the undisputed leader of the entire Christian army, and he soon saw fit to leave Acre behind and march his men toward the city of Jaffa.

Before they left, however, he called Robin, Much, and Allen into his tent.

"I would like your advice, Robin."

"I doubt I could have an opinion worth sharing, Sire."

King Richard raised an eyebrow at him, leaning against the table set up in his tent as he watched Robin with an amused expression on his face.

"Er...Richard," Robin corrected himself with a laugh.

"We are marching on Jaffa because I think it is necessary to take the city. It will be the perfect place to stage our march toward Jerusalem."

"And?"

"And what of it?" King Richard gestured toward the map on the table in front of him, which Robin bent and inspected.

"Why would you need the approval of a simple earl, and a very young one at that?" Robin asked.

"I value your opinion."

"Well I think your plan is perfectly sound, Sire."

Before leaving Acre, the king left Berengaria and his sister Joan in the care of a garrison of soldiers they were leaving in the city where they could safely stay until the Crusades ended.

Along the road to Jaffa, the army was regularly attacked by swarms of archers on horseback who would ride in, shoot a few arrows, and then gallop away.

The first time this happened, Allen smirked. "What good do they think that will do? Kill a couple soldiers at a time?"

But the Saracens persisted in this line of attack as the army marched toward Jaffa. They were in and out of range so swiftly that very few of the Saracens died, but each day more were added to the number of deceased in the Crusading army.

"It's effective," Robin grunted, watching the horses of the Saracens disappear over the horizon once more. "You have to give them that."

Allen sighed. "It is. And it is annoying."

"To say the least," Robin replied.

Sometimes King Richard would order a company to give chase, sometimes they would simply ignore the archers as though they were nothing more than pesky flies. They did more damage than flies would have done though, killing more men every time.

On one particular day when the list of the dead was gathered for the evening, Much and his companions learned that their old commander Sir Adam had been among those shot down.

Chapter 11

A FEW DAYS later, as Much trudged along beside Robin and Allen, he watched the sun sinking into the Mediterranean sea to his right, the reflection of the golds and oranges setting the blue sea aflame. It was beautiful.

The army was still a fair distance from Jaffa—the next town they would be passing through on their way was Arsuf. They hadn't entered any towns along the road, merely paused long enough to ensure they weren't under Saladin's control and Much assumed the same would happen tonight when they reached Arsuf.

Much looked forward again, past the king on his horse, and squinted at the horizon ahead of them where he saw movement.

"Robin, what is that?" Much pointed.

"I don't know," Robin replied, his own eyes narrowing as he peered into the distance. "It could be soldiers."

"That's what I thought."

"Your Majesty!" Robin strode forward to walk beside the king's horse and inform him of the potential threat on the horizon. King Richard pulled his horse to a stop, calling for his commanders and captains and preparing to arrange the army to meet whatever threat was headed their way.

They were still a great distance from the army that was approaching from the south, and it took another day of marching before they were able to make out the individuals among the army and the standards flying over the approaching enemy.

As King Richard's forces advanced, it became clear that it was, indeed, Saladin's army they were about to face off against. In the distance the rooftops of Arsuf were visible as the sun shone down brilliantly from the west, lighting the field that would soon be stained with red.

King Richard sent the archers forward first, which included Robin and Allen, and Much was given the sole responsibility of staying at the king's side and keeping him safe. It wasn't a hard job as King Richard commanded from the rear during this battle in a similar fashion to how he'd staged the siege of Acre.

From his vantage point beside the king, Much could see the arrows flying between both armies and saw the Saracens falling like the grain in the fields outside Locksley during harvest season. Saladin's army continued to press forward, however, and when they breached the line of archers, swords were drawn on both sides.

Much could feel his heart pounding in his chest, beating out a rhythm like a hurried drumbeat as he watched the battle before him. He was standing beside the king, holding the reins of the king's horse which he'd been given after King Richard dismounted. Messengers were running back and forth from the king atop the hill to the captains in the thick of the battle as King Richard played with the human lives before him as one might play with the game pieces of a chess board.

"Do not look so concerned," King Richard glanced in Much's direction. "The Saracens are falling by the hundreds. We may take losses, but they are taking more."

Much kept his eyes on the fighting, unable to look away.

Robin and Allen were down there somewhere in the midst of the bloody chaos and whatever else he thought of the violence in general, Much could not stand the thought of either of them not coming through the battle.

He bit his lip, scanning the leather-bound, iron-clad, and even the armor-less soldiers from both armies, trying to find a familiar shock of blond hair, but he was too far from the battle, and the fighting too chaotic—with both armies intermingling and merging together—for Much to make out anyone specific.

The day stretched onward, and Much's heart grew weary of watching men die.

It was an enormous relief when Saladin's army retreated and King Richard called for his dead to be buried and wounded to be looked after. Much stayed at the king's side as he spoke with his commanders and plans were made for the wounded, and for taking the city of Arsuf now that Saladin's army was moving away.

Much's grip on the reins of the king's horse became slick with sweat as he waited with bated breath for any sign of his brothers.

Messengers were still scurrying from the king to various places on the field now littered with bodies as preparations were being set in motion for dealing with the injured and dead, taking the city of Arsuf, and settling in for the night.

In another moment, Robin and Allen pushed through the men hurrying this way and that around the king, and Much felt the tension in his shoulders instantly relax. Robin and Allen were both coated in sweat, and the darkness hovering around Allen seemed to have deepened, but they both appeared unhurt.

"Robin of Locksley," King Richard greeted him with a smile as he and Allen approached. "Made it through alright?"

"We did, Sire."

"I am glad of it. More than one of my commanders praised your archery to me after the battle. I'd be sorry to lose such talent so early in the war."

"If that is the only reason you'd miss me, Sire, I'll take it," Robin grinned with a bow. The king laughed, and Much felt a flash of jealousy; it wasn't a familiar emotion, but watching Robin be so easy with a man so far above him in station gave Much a longing to have the courage to do the same.

He could not, however, be so free with Robin or any other noble. He was nothing; a servant. The difference lay there, Much decided. Robin was nobility, and nobility could speak to royalty on friendly terms with easy, familiar manners. Servants and slaves could not do the same, nor should they wish it.

When the wounded had been cared for and the dead buried, the journey continued southward. Within a few more days of marching they finally arrived at the city of Jaffa.

Taking the city was easy enough given the large numbers of King Richard's army and the lack of Saladin's forces to protect it. For nearly a hundred years the city had been under the rule of the kings of Jerusalem, and King Guy was pleased to take it back from Saladin's intruders.

King Richard took up residence in a house within the city, and Much, Robin, and Allen stayed there as well—keeping watch over his door at night, and staying by his side during the day as he planned with his advisors and commanders for the march to Jerusalem, and potential attacks on Saladin's forces depending on where the Saracens went next.

One day, as they stood guard outside the king's chamber, he called Robin inside to speak with him. Allen unashamedly leaned against the door to listen, but it was unnecessary; the sounds of their voices carried and Much could hear the conversation clearly despite not attempting to eavesdrop as Allen was.

"The victory at Arsuf was encouraging," King Richard said.

"Yes, it was," Robin replied.

"But our army is unfortunately dwindling, both due to losses in battle as well as some desertion. I was not expecting to have to deal with such a problem to such an extent as I have. We are on a noble quest, that ought to be enough to give men the motivation to remain true to our purpose. I need your advice."

"About anything specific?"

"We could still take Jerusalem with this army, perhaps, but it becomes a more difficult prospect with every lost soldier; the more desertion we face, the more challenging taking the city will be. This is only made worse by the knowledge that most of my men wish to return to their homes in Europe as soon as we conquer Jerusalem. I do not feel I could command them to stay here in the Holy Land indefinitely, but how will we hold Jerusalem after we leave?"

Allen crossed his arms as he leaned against the door, glancing at Much. Much held his peace; his opinion on the politics and the war had no bearing on what the king would choose to do.

"You think Saladin will lead his Muslim forces to take it back as soon as we're gone."

"I do. Unless I kill him, so they have no one to rally behind."

"So what is your plan? Find Saladin before taking Jerusalem?"

"I do not know. I do not think we should take Jerusalem only to have it fall again."

"I agree with that."

"There is the possibility of beginning negotiations with Saladin, to see if we cannot come up with a peaceable solution to our problems."

"I see nothing wrong with that either, assuming the treaty ends with Jerusalem returned to King Guy and the Saracen control given back to us."

"Thank you, Robin. That is all."

As soon as the door creaked open, Allen pulled away from it and feigned nonchalance, but once Robin had shut it behind him, Allen punched his arm.

"Look at that! King Richard seeks out our brother for advice!"

Robin laughed and shook his head, but Allen wasn't done. "I can't believe I am friends with the man that the King of England goes to for advice. A year ago I had never seen the king in person."

Robin snorted. "It isn't that impressive, Allen. Stop making more of it than this deserves."

Much disagreed with Robin, of course. It *was* rather impressive to know that his childhood friend was respected and sought after by the King of England.

In the following weeks, the king sent messengers to Saladin's army and received messengers in return. Negotiations for peace had begun.

Chapter 12

ONE DAY, THE king decided to give Much, Robin, and Allen a day of rest and called for his original Royal Guard to spend the day with him.

"Tired of our company?" Robin had teased, which the king had merely laughed at as he waved them off.

Allen suggested he wanted to spend the time alone, and soon wandered away from Robin and Much.

"I wonder what that was about," Robin said, slinging his arm around Much's shoulder as he watched Allen walk away. "Where shall we spend our afternoon of leisure?"

"Your wish is my command."

"Now don't be like that."

Robin led the way down the street, the stone buildings of the city encroaching on either side of the narrow street—one long line of stone, with the only break in the line the crossing streets. The port city itself was built on a high ridge, with a broad view of the sea and coastline below it.

Suddenly from behind them a fair voice shouted out Robin's name. Much swung around even as Robin turned to see who was calling for him.

Princess Joan was coming along the street behind them, her dark curls framing her beautiful face and her blue eyes flashing.

"Joan!" Robin stood stunned for a moment before he moved forward to meet her, and Much followed along behind him. "What are you doing here?"

"You left us at Acre and I chased you down to tell you what I thought of that."

"That was the king's decision, not mine," Robin laughed.

"Whoever decided it, I don't care. We were left behind. So Berengaria and I hired, cajoled, and threatened men until we had our own guard to protect us and we came down here to Jaffa to be with my dear brother."

"That was not wise, my lady. You could have been hurt or even killed along the road—many of our soldiers were."

"But we weren't," Joan said. "Much, dear, how are you?"

Much felt his heart leap in his chest and the blood rush to his face to be addressed by the princess. "Very well, my lady."

"Good. Been rescuing Robin a great deal, I imagine."

"He does not need to be rescued, my lady."

"Well I seem to recall you trying to save him anyway, during that storm on *The Barbara*."

Robin laughed, playfully elbowing Much. "He didn't rescue me; he threw himself overboard."

Joan threw back her head and laughed, her dark curls shaking around her face. "True! But it is the thought that counts, or so I have been told. And, Robin, dear, you really should not be so concerned for my safety, or that of Berengaria. We are intelligent women, capable of taking care of ourselves."

"As you say." Robin bowed.

"And anyway, we did hire men to guard us. More than that, we hired a woman, too."

"A woman!" Robin raised an eyebrow.

"Don't look like that. Men!" Joan rolled her eyes, tossing her hair over her shoulder. "You don't believe in women at all, do you? I'll have you know, that girl was our greatest protector. She is also a healer, saving the men who nearly died protecting us. She, on the other hand,

92

never received a scratch in any of the encounters with bandits and Saracens. She is remarkable!"

"I am sorry if I sounded incredulous," Robin said. "I have not known many fighting women before."

"Neither have I," Joan acquiesced. "But I know one now, and she is splendid. I told my brother he needs to make her a part of his Royal Guard with you; she would be the perfect addition."

"I don't know about that."

"Oh come on, you must meet her before you make such a decision." Joan grabbed Robin's arm and pulled him along the street back toward the house where the king had taken up residence, and Much followed along behind them.

"See, there she is now!" Joan pointed up the street.

Much followed Joan's pointing finger to where a young person was standing beside King Richard and Queen Berengaria.

The queen was speaking urgently and waving her hands around while King Richard silently listened to her, an amused expression on his face. The king's guards were a few feet behind the king, watching the exchange.

The young woman standing beside the king and queen appeared to be a native of Palestine and not a European. Her hair was cut short, however, and she wore similar clothes to that which Much was wearing. If Joan hadn't said she was a girl, Much could easily have assumed she was simply a young boy. Not ugly, by any means—pretty, actually, for a boy—but not so obviously and beautifully female as Princess Joan herself.

"She found it safer to pretend to be a man," Joan was saying to Robin as they approached the group. "Don't say anything about it; and don't mention she is a 'her.' She is still pretending to be a man, and of course Berengaria and I know the truth and so does Richard. And you do, too, but no one else must know."

"You might have mentioned that sooner," Robin said. "But Joan…is she an Arab?"

"Yes. I don't know her story, to be honest, she isn't very talkative. Come on, I have to introduce you."

Joan dragged Robin over and Much waited outside the gathered circle of royalty and nobility.

"Joan!" King Richard shook his head at her. "I wondered where you'd wandered off to. You never should have come; can you even begin to comprehend the danger that could have befallen you and my wife? I'm sick with worry thinking about it."

"You clearly don't need to worry, brother. We arrived safe and sound. We aren't in any more danger here than we were *left alone* at Acre."

King Richard looked unconvinced. The young woman stood silently watching the exchange, her dark eyes full of emotions that Much couldn't read.

"Regardless, my love, it is done now," Queen Berengaria said. "Robin, please help me convince my dear husband to take on this young fighter. They are remarkable, I swear."

"She–er–he–uh…." Robin stuttered for a moment and found his composure. "I have heard good things about this fighter."

King Richard laughed at Robin's obvious discomfort and confusion. "As have I, but that doesn't change the fact that she is a woman. This will not end well."

"Richard!" Joan crossed her arms, her lower lip falling into a pout. "No one knows she's a woman, and no one ever will if you will shut up about it."

"How can you be sure no one will discover the truth?"

"They haven't figured it out yet," Queen Berengaria said.

"I will leave if I am a problem to you." The young woman spoke for the first time since Much and Robin had joined the group. She had a deeper voice than Much had expected—rich and deep and beautiful. "I do not need your protection, King Richard; I simply wished to fight alongside your men."

"Why?" King Richard eyed her suspiciously. "You are a Saracen, are you not? Perhaps you are a spy for Saladin."

"If by that you mean I am Muslim, then no. I am not. I was trained by the Saracen army, yes, but I have never fought for them and I do not share their faith. I have, however, fought alongside the Crusaders for several years."

"Why?"

"Because I am a disciple of Christ and I will not take up a sword against the Crusaders."

"So you joined them."

"We have a common belief in our Savior; I do not see why we cannot work together despite our different backgrounds."

"I am not sure we all—" the king cut off whatever he'd been about to say, and studied the young woman again.

"I have no love of Saladin," the young woman offered quietly, a bitterness and pain running through her voice now.

The king frowned. "I will agree to take you on. You will remain a part of my guard alongside Robin and the others—not only to appease my wife, but to keep you safe as well. I will not have you mingling with just anyone in this army. You are safe with Robin and his companions; they are noble and honorable men."

"I appreciate the sentiment, Your Majesty," the young woman said.

"Of course. Now I have things to attend to so I will leave you in Robin's care."

The king turned and went inside the house, and Queen Berengaria went with him, as Joan grinned at her brother's retreating back.

"That worked magnificently. I knew he would allow her to join you."

"I am not sure this is wise," Robin said, eyeing the woman skeptically.

"You do not think I can fight?" The woman smiled at Robin, her eyes dancing with laughter. "That is alright, because it is true. I do not fight as well as some, but I can manage."

"This is Robin," Joan said. "I've told you about him. The Earl of Locksley."

"So you have," the woman agreed.

"This is his servant Much, and the other member of the King's Guard is Allen, though I don't see him here."

"I'm not sure where he is at the moment," Robin said. "He's wandered off."

"It is a pleasure to meet you, Robin, Much." the young woman bowed her head slightly in greeting.

"And your name is?" Robin asked.

The young woman sighed, looking off to the side for a moment, the laughter in her eyes replaced with a deep sorrow. "I cannot say. I do not wish to be known by my childhood name, the memories are too painful to me. Yet I have yet to choose a name to answer to now."

"What do people call you in general?"

"Nothing."

"They must call you something!" Robin insisted. "What has Joan been calling you?"

"Some people refer to me as 'the Saracen.'"

"The Saracen, huh?"

"You may call me that if you wish."

"I suppose I'll have to if you'll give me no other name," Robin said. "But I'm sure we can do better than that."

Chapter 13

WHEN ALLEN WAS introduced to the Saracen later that day, he was incredulous. The group gathered in Robin's room as the 'day off' that the king had given them was not yet over. Robin and Allen lounged on chairs near the window, while Much sat on the floor at Robin's feet and the Saracen sat cross-legged against the wall under the window.

"Why do you want to fight anyway?" Allen asked. "You're a girl."

"Do not say that so loud," Robin said, glancing toward the door and then to the open window. "We don't want that getting around to the men."

"But she *is* a girl!" Allen insisted.

"No," the Saracen laughed, turning her keen gaze on Allen. "I am not a girl. I am a *woman*. I am nearly twenty years old."

"That's certainly older than we are," Robin said. "All three of us are eighteen."

"Triplets?" the Saracen laughed.

"We aren't actually related," Much said.

"But we are brothers-in-arms," Robin said.

"I know." The Saracen smiled. "I can see the attachment between you already; bound together by loyalty and love."

"Loyalty and love," Allen repeated, "That ought to be our mantra, Robin."

Robin laughed. "It does have a nice ring to it."

After the Saracen joined their group, the next few weeks were spent in relative peace. The king continued to send and receive messages from Saladin as negotiations for peace continued. His Royal

99

Guard, now consisting of four, stood outside the rooms where he met with his advisors and ambassadors from the Saracen armies, and they watched over his room when he retired to sleep, but for the most part there was little of interest to shake up the monotony of their time.

Robin and Allen had a great many questions for the Saracen, but though she was not shy and would converse with them easily, she kept quiet about her past and said little about herself at all.

One day as the four of them stood outside the king's door, the king popped his head out to inform them he had decided to give Joan as a wife to Saladin's brother. It was his opinion that such a gift would appease Saladin himself so that the rest of the terms of the treaty could be in the Crusaders' favor. Much was given the unfortunate task of finding Joan to inform her and bring her to speak with her brother.

Much moved slowly down the hallway away from the king before trudging up the stairs toward the room where Princess Joan was lodged. From the things he'd been hearing since the rescue on Sicily, it seemed she'd had a happy marriage with William of Sicily the first time she'd been used as a political tool; but from what Much knew of Joan, she wasn't likely to appreciate her brother using her in such a fashion again.

When he reached her room, Much waited a full minute outside her door before he had the courage to knock. She opened the door before he'd finished, a smile lighting her face.

"Much! Did you need something?"

"I have a message from the king, my lady."

"And my brother couldn't be bothered to walk upstairs and tell me? What is it?"

"He wishes to inform you…that is, he's going to offer you as a bride to Saladin's brother as part of his negotiation of the treaty between the two warring factions."

"He is doing what?!" The smile left Joan's face and color flooded her checks as her eyes began to flash.

"He is offering you—"

"I heard what you said!"

"I am sorry, my lady."

"This is not your fault. I do, however, have a few things to say to my brother." Joan pushed past Much and stomped down the stairs.

Much wanted to call after her not to be hasty, not to anger the king, but he kept his mouth shut. If she had wanted his opinion or advice she would have asked for it.

Much followed after her quietly; before he'd reached the king's door he could hear her raised voice.

"If you think you can use me as a bargaining chip, I certainly have the right to give you an earful of my opinion on the matter!"

"Let's move away," Robin said as Much joined him, Allen, and the Saracen outside the door.

"I do not think moving will help," Allen said. "Joan is already raising her voice; no doubt they will soon have a shouting match."

"I agree with Robin," the Saracen said firmly. "It would not be kind to eavesdrop."

As they moved away from the door and down the hallway a tad, Much glanced over his shoulder. What would come of this argument?

"Joan will not harm the king," the Saracen said softly, placing a hand on his shoulder. "Do not fear, Much."

"It is the king's anger that concerns me."

101

"He won't hurt Joan," Robin said with a laugh. "Her will is as strong as his, and anyway, he adores her."

Joan and the king argued for quite some time, but King Richard wouldn't change his mind. Word was sent to Saladin later that day and soon the peace offering was accepted and plans were set in motion for a royal wedding.

Days passed and more messages passed between King Richard and Saladin as they prepared for the wedding of their siblings.

One day, Much stood at his post as usual, his lower back aching from the stiffness of his stance, when Joan came tramping down the stairs from her room.

Allen lounged against the door behind which the king was conducting his business as Joan linked her arm through Robin's and pulled him away his post.

"Come now, Robin, I need someone to entertain me during my last days as a free woman, before my brother so kindly shackles me to Saladin's brother."

"I am on duty, my lady," Robin replied.

Joan sighed heavily, laying her head against Robin's shoulder. She turned her head slightly, letting her hair fall across her face, but it wasn't enough to hide the tears Much saw escaping her beautiful eyes.

Much wished there was a way he could reach out to Joan and comfort her, but he was only a servant and she was a princess.

"I must have entertainment before I am a slave," Joan said in a surprisingly chipper voice as she lifted her head from Robin's shoulder, briskly wiping the tears from her cheeks. "Come on, humor me."

Robin and Allen began to tell outlandish jokes, while the Saracen stood quietly beside Much and watched the three of them with her keen dark eyes.

In the days since the news of her political engagement, Joan had brooded about the town, dragging Robin away from his duties as often as the king would allow so she could vent her frustrations to him. Robin politely listened, and Much was sure he would do what he could to make Joan laugh and bring a smile back to her face. But Robin would not give Joan the one thing Much knew she wanted from him. Joan was falling in love with Robin. To Robin's credit, at least in Much's estimation, he remained forever faithful to Marian.

A week or so later, rumors ran through the camp that officials of the church had come all the way from Rome just to speak to the king. These rumors proved true for soon they were approaching the king's rooms and Robin let them in while Much, Allen, and the Saracen kept watch.

Angry voices soon issued from beyond the closed door.

"We should not be listening," the Saracen said. "This does not concern us."

"I am sorry, Saracen," Robin replied. "But I want to know what is going to happen to both Joan and the king."

The furious shouting continued, both from the king and from the church officials threatening excommunication if he married Joan off to a Muslim—peace treaty or no peace treaty.

Allen glanced toward the Saracen. "No offense to you, I'm sure."

The Saracen turned her sharp gaze on Allen. "I am not a Muslim, Allen of the Dale. I am a disciple of Christ."

"Fair enough," Allen shrugged. "Makes no difference to me."

The church officials from Rome and the king had several more heated discussions in the days that followed, but in the end Joan was free. The king rescinded his offer to marry her to Saladin's brother.

The king summoned Robin into his chamber after he'd made the decision and messengers had gone to and from Saladin as the change to the peace treaty was discussed. Much stood outside the door with Allen and the Saracen trying not to eavesdrop, though Robin had left the door open and they could hear every word.

Allen, of course, was unashamedly leaning toward the open door while Much did his utmost to refrain from giving him reproving looks.

"Saladin is asking too much from me; I feel we need to teach him who is in charge here," the king spoke to Robin. "We are only suing for peace for the good of the people, not because we couldn't demolish him in an all-out war."

"Whatever you think, Sire."

"That's Richard to you."

"Right."

"I have decided we are going to move out from Jaffa and march on Ascalon. That city was demolished by Saladin and his forces not too long ago, and I feel we could spend time rebuilding it, at least in part."

"As you wish, Sire."

"Why so formal, Robin?"

"It is habit."

"A habit you fall into more often when you are upset with me, I think. What is your true opinion of marching to Ascalon?"

"You said you wanted to intimidate Saladin, yes? And rebuilding Ascalon will prove to Saladin, what exactly?"

"That he cannot destroy cities and lives without recourse."

"And yet," the Saracen spoke softly beside Much, "we do the same here. Destroying cities and lives without recourse."

104

Chapter 14

MUCH KEPT PACE beside the Saracen while Robin and Allen chatted amiably as they walked behind the king on the long march to the city of Ascalon. They had left Jaffa early that morning as the sky had been filled with purples and pinks of varying shades, the air clean and fresh. Much's spirits had lifted, his mind refreshed and clear—more so than it had been since the Crusades began, he thought.

His good mood was not to last.

The road they marched along cut through two hills, and as they wound their way through them a volley of arrows flew from either side of the road.

It was an ambush!

The arrows cascaded into the marching soldiers, some piercing shoulders, necks, legs. Men fell to the ground lifeless or screaming in pain as others reached instinctively for their weapons and spun toward the archers who'd dared attack their caravan.

Much pulled his sword from the sheath at his waist and spun to put his back to the king. The Saracen and Allen did the same, forming a small circle around him while Robin whipped his bow from his back and set an arrow to the string, searching for a target along the hilltops. He didn't have to wait long, as the enemy came charging down both hills, pouring into the ranks of soldiers congested in the road.

As battle broke out around him, Much did his best to drown out the screams of the dying and wounded men.

A soldier came toward him, sword raised, and Much instinctively blocked the blade with his own. He parried, he struck, he tried to keep any enemy soldiers from coming near the king, as was his duty.

In the heat of the battle, he soon found himself several feet away from his companions. Much glanced over his shoulder to gauge how easily he might traverse the battlefield to get back to Robin when he saw a sword bearing down on his friend.

Robin's back was to the blade arcing toward him, and Much darted forward, shoving men from both sides of the battle aside as he tried to get to Robin, but he was too far.

"Robin!"

Much watched in horror as the sword sliced its way through Robin's side and he collapsed to his knees, blood pouring from his torso. Much struggled toward him, raising his sword to block the attack of a nearby opponent. He felt frustration and panicking rising, constricting his airway, as he was forced to pause his advance toward Robin and focus on the enemy at hand.

From the corner of his eye, he saw the Saracen dart toward Robin, standing over him and keeping the blades of other soldiers away from him. Her movements were swift and fluid, making Much think of dancing more than fighting.

As Much plunged his sword into his own opponent and took off running for Robin again, jumping over corpses on his way, he watched as Robin slumped onto the road and the Saracen quickly knelt at his side.

"Allen!" The Saracen's voice carried over the din of battle. "Watch my back!"

"On it!"

Allen moved to stand beside the Saracen as she knelt over Robin, and then Much caught sight of the king—alone and unprotected, surrounded by enemy soldiers. With his companions occupied around Robin, Much was the only member of the Royal Guard who could defend him.

Much sent Robin one last glance, his heart leaping to his throat, and then wrenched himself away from his friend and ran for the king.

As a blade swung toward King Richard, Much lunged forward to block it, pushing the soldier aside and moving to stand shoulder to shoulder with his king.

"Much," the king grunted.

"Sire."

They moved around each other, the king with grace and dignity, his sword moving with power and precision as he cut down his enemies —and Much, less graceful and more bumbling but still getting the job done.

In the midst of the fighting, he couldn't stop his eyes from wandering toward Robin now and again. When he did, he caught glimpses of the Saracen kneeling over Robin, her eyes closed and her mouth moving in some prayer or whispered word that Much could not hear from his distance and the cacophony of sound rising from the battle around him. His next glance their way, he saw the Saracen whip out a small pouch from her belt and begin applying something to Robin's side.

The moment the fighting began to die down and the skirmish appeared relatively over, but for a few soldiers farther along the road and nowhere near the king, Much ran for Robin.

Robin was sitting up, leaning heavily against Allen as the Saracen continued to apply some sort of salve to his wounds.

Much knelt down, his wide eyes taking in the blood, the salve, and Robin's relaxed grin.

"I am fine, Much. The Saracen has cleaned my wound. It isn't so bad."

"You will be weak," the Saracen put in, "and in pain for some days, I imagine. This was not a small cut."

"But I will live, thanks to you."

"The wound is not so deep," the Saracen shrugged, wiping the remnant of the salve from her hands on her trousers before putting her pouch back on her belt. "Perhaps you would not have died from it at all."

"But I was incapable of protecting myself either way, and would have died at the hands of those soldiers if you had not been there. You were magnificent! I've never seen anyone fight like that before; you are quite the warrior, Saracen."

"Thank you, Robin." She spoke softly and calmly as always, but Much could see the shimmer in her eyes and the emotions emanating from deep within. She portrayed herself to be calm waters, but Much could see the undertow.

"I cannot continue to call you by no name," Robin said suddenly, his usual grin lighting his face. "You have become a friend in the last month, and now you have saved my life."

"What would you call me?"

"Warrior," Robin said with a wink.

Allen snorted, shaking his head as he playfully whacked Robin's shoulder. "That is not a name."

"Dustin, then," Robin said. "It means the same."

"That does not seem very feminine."

"You seem very opinionated about a name that isn't yours," Robin replied, elbowing Allen as he leaned against him for support.

"Dusty," Much said, then immediately bit his lip. He hadn't meant to say that out loud. It was too late now, all three of his friends were looking at him expectantly. "Call her Dusty."

"Dusty…" the Saracen whispered, seeming to feel the sound of it, the weight of it on her tongue. She smiled at Much. "I like it."

"Dusty; the warrior, healer, and friend of mine," Robin said. "I like it, too."

"Dusty it is then," Allen said. "It will be nice to actually have a name for you now, instead of always calling you 'the Saracen' when we speak to and about you."

Once the dead from the battle had been buried and the wounded had been cared for, the army continued on its way to the city of Ascalon.

Upon arriving in Ascalon, the king set out rebuilding the citadel there. The king, of course, did none of the actual work and therefore neither did his Royal Guard. Much, Robin, Allen, and Dusty stayed near the king as he met with his advisors to plan for the future of the war with Saladin. The ceasefire that had been in place while they were in Jaffa crafting a peace treaty was now over, and what came next occupied the king's mind a great deal. Any hope Much might have harbored about going back to England and away from the war anytime soon was quashed in the king's new fervor.

The king's overabundant passion soon led him to change his mind about taking Jerusalem directly, and he soon marched his army in that direction.

They had not been marching long before inclement weather overtook them. Much trudged along the road, every footfall sounding with a squelch and every step requiring he wrench his foot out of the mud once more. The rain pelted down on him from the sky as he followed after the king and Robin, with Allen and Dusty on either side.

After the rain came days of fog, where Much could not see his own hand in front of his face if he held his arm out at length. The fog itself was inconvenient, but the bone-shivering cold that came with it was almost unbearable. Much kept opening and closing his hands to keep feeling in his fingers as they lumbered along the road.

"Robin, can you see anything?" Much asked as they trudged forward in spite of the weather, the king determined to reach Jerusalem.

"Not particularly, but at least it is better than the rain."

"Hardly," Allen interjected. "I can't feel anything—I've gone numb. Except for my nose, of course, which stings considerably."

"It is not as bad as all that," Dusty laughed. "A little water, a little cold. It will not kill us."

"It's more than *a little* water," Allen whined. "It rained for seven days straight!"

"Robin!" the king's voice carried through the fog in front of them and Robin strode forward, almost disappearing from Much's view.

"Yes?"

"We will stop at the city of Beit Nuba tonight to take shelter. Pass the word through the ranks."

"At least we won't be camping again in this weather," Allen said as Robin walked past them toward the captain leading the company directly behind them in order to pass along the king's command.

"Being inside will be a blessing," Dusty agreed.

For some days the soldiers of the Crusaders' army shivered miserably in tents set up outside Beit Nuba while the king and his guard gathered inside a house on the edge of town. The rain continued, and soon it began to hail each day as well.

One day, Much stood near the window of the room where he, his companions, and the king were currently located on the upper level of a house near the edge of Beit Nuba. The room was dark, due to the weather outside, lit only by the light of the fireplace and a few candles —all of which sent shadows dancing along the walls. The king and Robin were bent over a table at one end of the room, discussing what their next move might be. Allen watched them from a short distance, standing over the fire to keep warm.

Dusty was sitting in one corner of the room, leafing through the herbs she carried on her belt and used for healing. She'd taken to assisting more than just Robin when wounds were present in the army, and after all the rain and cold, she'd started mixing teas in order to keep people healthy despite the weather they marched through every day. It wasn't much; her supplies were depleted and Much wasn't sure where she planned to get more.

Still, as Much watched the people in the room about their various business, he felt a warmth spreading through him that had nothing to do with the fire nearby. The only person he still felt was a great distance from himself—and therefore had less to do with his current warm feeling—was the king himself.

Much turned back to the window to watch the weather as he contemplated how he'd ended up here. Fighting in the Crusades, which was madness enough, and now trusted by the very King of England. Of course, Robin held that trust far more than the rest of them, but even so. They were all here, in this room with the king, and he was relaxed and at ease as though he was among friends.

It was beyond comprehension.

"It's hailing again," Much commented from beside the window, pulling his cloak tighter around him as the warm feeling passed and his body remembered just how cold it truly was.

"So it is," Dusty replied.

"I am glad we are not forced to march in this weather," Much said.

"Yet we cannot stay in Beit Nuba forever," Allen sighed. "I wish a decision would be made. Either we move forward toward Jerusalem or we go somewhere else. Sitting here doing nothing is beginning to irk me."

"I wish we would move on as well," Dusty said. "Less because I am irked and more because I fear what you and Robin might do when pushed past the point of boredom."

There was a twinkle in her dark eyes when she said this, and Allen grinned in response. "We wouldn't do anything too drastic."

"You might," Much laughed.

Allen laughed heartily, and it made Much feel that warmth again. Somehow, he felt *almost* on equal footing with his friends. Robin had always been a brother to him in some fashion, but now Allen filled that role as well, and Dusty was the sister he'd never had.

The king, of course, was still the king, and he was still deliberating over his map. Much doubted he would ever feel as at ease with the king as Robin did, but he did not think that was such a bad thing. He was, after all, just a servant. Even feeling so about Robin and Allen was a stretch given their noble blood.

In the end, the king decided to delay the march to the city of Jerusalem because of the inclement weather and the effect it had on morale as well as the health of his army, and returned his men to the city of Ascalon instead.

On the first warm day in a good long while, Much found himself sitting atop a high stone wall that had recently been constructed around the citadel that King Richard had overseen the construction of.

From his vantage point, Much could see that a great deal of the original city had truly been demolished by Saladin in his attempt to sabotage any strategic ports and cities of the Crusaders. Whole sections of the town were filled with only broken stone buildings and the burnt husks of any wooden structures that might have once stood.

King Richard's citadel was the only part of Ascalon that didn't look like a disaster—though much of it was still undergoing construction. Beyond the sorry looking remains of Ascalon was the Mediterranean sea, sparkling a deep blue—the beauty of the sea only served to make the brokenness of the city that much more obvious, at least to Much's eye.

Robin hoisted himself up onto the wall beside Much and draped his arm casually across his knee. Much glanced at him, studying the lines on his face and the tan that had overtaken his skin since they had left England.

"It is your birthday, Robin."

"I know."

Much turned back to the sea. They hadn't discussed it, but it was heavy on Much's mind. If they had been at home—and the Earl had still been alive—there would have been a feast and celebration at Locksley manor to commemorate the birth of the young lord. Marian and Mark would have come with their father Sir Godfrey, along with many other nobles. Much would likely have had the day off of attending to Robin in order to help Sarah in the kitchens as extravagant meals were prepared for the young master.

113

Instead, they were here. Sitting atop a newly constructed wall overlooking the remains of a broken city—both of their hearts and minds occupied with darker thoughts than they would have been at a Locksley celebration a year ago.

"It's been a long year," Much said.

"We've only been traveling with the king for about ten months … but I agree, it has been long."

"I never imagined we would be doing the things we've been doing or seeing the places that we have seen, not in all my years."

"Oh, I could definitely imagine it. I often dreamed of the amazing feats we might accomplish someday."

"Did you dream you would be an advisor and friend to the very King of England? I never thought I would so much as meet him face to face."

Robin laughed. "I did not imagine I would be his friend, but I am glad that we came on this adventure and that things have turned out as they have. I enjoy the king's friendship. And that of the queen, and Joan. Hers, especially, means a great deal."

Much bit his cheek. He wanted to tell Robin to be more careful with Joan; she was falling in love and Robin was undoubtedly going to break her heart—he'd never had eyes for anyone other than Marian.

Robin glanced his direction and Much quickly turned his gaze on the sea once more.

"What are you thinking?"

"Nothing."

"Much."

"Just that it is so strange to think I know such royalty. I am only a simple servant, after all."

"You are much more than that. You are a member of the King's Guard to Richard the Lion-Heart himself, you have turned into quite the warrior, and you are a fiercely loyal friend of mine. I am more grateful than you will ever know that you agreed to follow me to the Crusades. I could not have faced all that we have faced alone, without you."

"You still would have met Allen in Dover and had a friend on this journey even if I had not come. And you would have met Dusty at Jaffa and found a second friend."

"And yet neither Allen nor Dusty could ever mean to me what you do."

Much didn't have a response for that, but he felt the weight of the warmth of his love spreading through his chest yet again. He could almost, if he closed his eyes as he listened to Robin saying such things, remember what it had felt like when he'd first moved to Locksley and had lived in the nursery with Robin. Back when they had truly been equals and brothers, before the Earl had seen fit to put Much in his place. It was a vague, abstract sort of memory, those years as brothers, but sometimes when Robin would say something like he just had, Much could *feel* the memory of brotherhood and he craved that feeling.

In truth, there were no words for the love that he held for his master, but he could easily pinpoint the desire for that distance—that rank—to no longer exist between them.

And yet how could it not? Even with the Earl gone, Much still felt his disapproval so far from England and beyond the grave. Every time he laughed with Robin, or teased Allen, he could feel the Earl frowning at him, telling him to mind his place and remember he was no more than a servant.

"You, my friend, look far too serious."

115

Much glanced at Robin, giving him half a smile. "I was merely lost in thought."

Thoughts that he could never share with Robin, or anyone for that matter.

Chapter 15

ONE DAY, ROBIN was called into the king's chambers with his other advisors as they made plans, and Much waited outside the door with Allen and Dusty. The citadel of Ascalon was nearly complete, the skirmishes between King Richard's army and that of Saladin's forces frequent but not monumental, and King Richard was itching to do *something* to turn the tide in his favor.

Allen leaned up against the door and Dusty swatted his arm. "Stop eavesdropping."

"I'd like to know what's happening next."

"Robin will tell us when he comes out," Dusty replied, her glare enough to cause Much to shrink back from her though her ire was not directed toward him.

Allen ignored her and pressed his ear to the wooden door. Dusty crossed her arms but said nothing further. In another moment, however, the door swung open and Robin stood there grinning.

"The king says you can break for lunch, he's going to call for other guards to stand at your post while you eat."

Much could see over Robin's shoulder into the room beyond, where the king was looking toward the group at the door with what looked like an affectionate—if exasperated—look.

"I think he knows you like to eavesdrop," Much said.

Allen shrugged. "Lunch it is, I guess."

Robin returned to the room with the king after assigning new soldiers to the post outside the door, while Much, Allen, and Dusty gathered a meager lunch—provisions were always relatively scarce in the army, made worse when they weren't near a thriving city—and moved outside to find a place to sit and eat in the sunshine. They'd soon settled atop a wall overlooking the sea.

"It's hardly fair Robin is trusted and we are not," Allen commented. "Besides, the king knows he's just going to come tell us what's happening anyway."

"It's possible they do discuss private matters that Robin does not disclose to you," Dusty replied.

It wasn't long before Robin came striding down the street below them and cheerfully pulled himself up onto the wall beside Much.

"I have news."

"Good news or bad news?" Allen asked.

"Just news. We're marching again. Apparently Saladin has captured another city that was under European rule and is now most definitely not, and he wants it back."

"What city?" Much asked. "And how long of a march will it be?"

"It's a city called Darum," Robin replied and Much heard Dusty's sharp intake of breath.

"We are marching to Darum?" Dusty's dark eyes were roiling with emotions that Much could not name, her voice shaking slightly as she spoke.

"That is what the king has decided," Robin said.

"We're capturing Darum."

"Releasing it from Saladin's capture, but yes."

"I cannot go."

Allen was cheerfully eating his lunch, but Much was staring at Dusty. She drew her legs up underneath herself, seeming to shrink somewhat. Dusty, though soft-spoken, had always impressed Much with

118

her strength. She was always confident and sure of herself and what she believed, but now her hands were shaking from whatever emotion she was feeling.

"Why can't you go to Darum?" Much asked, reaching out his hand and laying it gently on her arm.

"I cannot," Dusty repeated, her voice strong despite her physical shaking. She was determined, if nothing else.

"Dusty, what is wrong?" Robin asked, leaning around Much to get a better view of her.

Dusty looked between Much and Robin, then glanced toward Allen who had stopped eating and was watching the exchange silently. There were tears glimmering in her dark eyes as her lower lip trembled.

"It is…Darum is where I come from. The city of my birth."

"You don't want to fight against your own city?" Allen asked, his own voice full of the darkness and pain that Much so often saw in his eyes. "It is only Saladin we are after, is it not? It is possible we won't destroy the town itself or its inhabitants."

"Like there wasn't a massacre at Acre?" Dusty snapped. "But no, it is not that I don't wish to fight my own city. The people of Darum are mostly descendants of the Crusaders from the First and Second Crusades, or like myself have both European and Arab blood in their line. The connections the people of Darum have to England, France, Germany—the Holy Roman Empire as a whole—are strong. That is likely why Saladin keeps attacking that city. Those who are left will not fight against the Crusaders."

"Those who are left?" Robin asked.

"Saladin captured my city when I was eighteen," Dusty said. "He destroyed the politically strong there, devastating the city and the

119

people. So many families' lives were destroyed as he dismantled the power of the Crusaders there."

"That's when you lost your own family," Robin said.

"Yes."

The single word seemed to hang in the air over the group, heavy and dark. Much couldn't remember his own family—the parents who had died and left him an orphan. His only understanding of family came from Robin, Sarah, and the Earl. He couldn't comprehend her grief on the basis of experience, but he could easily imagine the despair he would feel if he ever lost Robin, and the grief that would overwhelm him if anything happened to Sarah.

"I am so sorry," Robin said.

"So am I," Dusty replied. "But I cannot go back to Darum. I couldn't … I haven't been back there since…"

"I understand, but we cannot leave you behind."

"I do not see why not," Dusty said. "I only joined up with your army provisionally, given Joan's insistence. And I do appreciate the friendship the four of us have found together, but I can't go back. I won't. I don't have any allegiance to King Richard; I am not one of his subjects. I don't have to go. I won't."

Much shifted his hand off of Dusty's arm and wrapped his fingers around hers, giving them a gentle squeeze. "Perhaps going back will help you finally face your grief."

Dusty closed her eyes, a frown forming on her lips as tears slipped down her cheeks. After a moment, she opened her eyes and nodded, giving Much's hand a tight squeeze. "You are right. I will pray for the strength to return to Darum and face my past. Perhaps it will be good for me."

"I thought you were a Saracen," Allen commented, causing Much, Robin, and Dusty to turn and look at him.

"What?"

"We all thought you were a Saracen, that's why we called you that before you had the name Dusty. But you said the inhabitants of your city were mostly descendants of the earlier Crusades."

"Yes, they were. I myself am a child of both descendants of the European Crusaders and also native Palestinians. I was never a Muslim, as Saladin and most of his soldiers are, but when he attacked my city I hid my identity—dressed like a man, let them recruit me as a soldier and sympathizer. I lived with what you call Saracens—and then at the first opportunity I joined the Crusading army."

"To get back at Saladin."

"I do not often agree with the decisions of King Richard and those in charge—I do not feel the same fervor that they do in terms of who should live and rule in the Holy Land. Uprooting the people who live here or forcing them to abide by your customs and religions is not the way of life that I would wish to pursue. I wish there was *peace*. But Saladin himself? He destroyed my people, my city, my family. You are fighting him, and that is enough for me for now."

"Dusty, I am so sorry that this happened to you," Robin said. "It's only been, what? Two years? I understand on some level the grief that you feel, and the anger. My own father was murdered by those seizing power in England during King Richard's current absence. I don't know the details—I haven't gone home yet, I don't know what all happened—but I understand."

"It is alright," Dusty said, straightening her shoulders as her voice grew in confidence. The Dusty Much knew and loved was returning, the shattered shell of a grieving woman retreating into the

121

background once more. "Do not fret over me. I have been well looked after by the Lord, and now I have you three whom I have come to count on as my second family."

"I would be proud to call you my sister," Robin replied.

"Thank you."

Much didn't know what to say. He wanted to comfort Dusty, but what could he do or say that Robin could not do better?

He felt a burning in the back of his throat and knew that if he spoke up now he would undoubtedly burst into tears. His friends had all had such difficult lives—Allen had lost his family before the Crusades, Dusty had lost hers. Robin had lost his mother at a young age and now he'd recently lost his father to dubious circumstances. Yet in spite of all their losses and pain, they had a family again—the four of them. They were bound together in a deep way that Much was certain most families could not boast.

The march to Darum was long. As they traveled, Much kept a close eye on Dusty. She did not show any more signs of breaking apart emotionally as she had when she'd first heard they were traveling to her home, but she did grow progressively more reserved the closer they drew to Darum. She was not a particularly outspoken woman to begin with, but Much could see the difference.

One fine day, as they marched along the dust-covered road and hard-packed earth, the sun shining down from above in a hot and heavy way, Dusty seemed particularly distracted.

The king was in front of Much, with Robin and Allen on either side of him, engaging in easy conversation with the former. Dusty and Much walked behind, and they were meant to be keeping an eye out for any threats to the king. Yet Much's concern was the threat to Dusty's peace of mind.

She was watching the fields and orchards beside the road as they walked, her eyes an even darker shade than usual. Her expression was almost grim.

Much didn't know what to say, but he stepped closer to her and lightly bumped his shoulder against hers just so she would know that she wasn't alone. Dusty flashed him a sad smile, and then returned to her reveries.

When the city—and Saladin's forces stationed there—came into view, the general chaos of preparation began and Much could no longer watch Dusty as he had been.

The king was issuing orders to his captains, the companies of soldiers were rearranging themselves to prepare to meet Saladin's forces, and Much's duty to protect the king took precedence, to his chagrin. He would have preferred to talk with Dusty and comfort her in any way that he could rather than prepare to fight a battle he had no interest in fighting. But the army moved resolutely forward and the battle commenced whether he liked it or not.

The king had changed his tune from the earliest days in the Crusade—there was no commanding from the rear now. King Richard was a ferocious warrior and he lived for the battles, wanting to lead from the front and be in the thick of things and so Much and his three friends were there, too. Protecting the king, and doing their utmost not to get themselves killed in the process.

What any of the rest of them thought of the violence, Much didn't know. He suspected it didn't bother Robin, though he imagined Dusty had a more reverent and solemn approach to what they did. Much himself was more than a little horrified.

As the battle commenced with archery, Robin was among the first in the initial action, but soon enough it came to swordplay, as it

123

always did. Much kept beside the king as Saracens descended on them, gripping his sword with a sweaty palm.

An opponent rushed toward the king and Much darted in front of him, blocking the enemy blade and then striking. His sword arced through the air with an efficiency he'd never imagined it would, cutting down one man after another who approached the king, until it was dripping crimson. Much's stomach flipped at the sight, but he kept his head and did not double over and throw up on the spot, no matter how much he might wish to do so.

Saladin's forces retreated for a time, and a rough camp was made for the night, but they were back at it again in the morning. For five days the tide of the battle ebbed and flowed, and Much's sword painted the ground in crimson hues.

Eventually, however, Saladin removed himself from Darum, fleeing the city with the remainder of his forces.

As the king marched down a street in the city with Much and his companions at his side, he was thoughtful. "There are few left in this city who were not a part of Saladin's forces. What has become of the city's population?"

"They were killed, Sire," Dusty said.

"Ah. That is unfortunate."

"Yes, it is." Her eyes remained directed firmly on the toes of her boots rather than at the king or at the surrounding city.

Some of the city was still standing, but there were portions of it that were little more than charred remains as though from a massive fire, and there were many stone buildings that had been torn down and stood in crumbled ruins. Much did not blame her for not wanting to look at it.

"I do feel invigorated from this victory," King Richard said, surveying their surroundings with his hands on his hips. "I believe we should try to march on Jerusalem once more. It was only bad weather that deterred us the last time, and the weather is fair now. And more than that, we have Saladin and his army on the run."

King Richard's army began to make camp in and around the city of Darum—most of which was an eerie ghost town since so few of the inhabitants remained. The king retired to his chamber to sleep after his long five days of battle, and Allen and Robin took up the first watch at his door.

This left Much without responsibilities. He stood in the hallway outside the King's room unsure whether he should stay by Robin's side or go to bed. He was exhausted and heartsick and a bed sounded enticing.

Suddenly he heard a soft voice just behind him. "Much?"

"Dusty?"

"I…can you come with me?"

The expression on her face was enough to break Much's heart, let alone the history and grief he knew accompanied it.

"Where are you going? I will gladly come with you if that is what you desire."

"I want to go home. I need…" Dusty looked up at him, her eyes shining with unshed tears. "I need support."

"Should I grab Robin?" Much asked, glancing down the hallway to where Robin and Allen were chatting and laughing together outside the king's door.

"No, Much. I want your support if you are willing to lend it."

"Oh."

Dusty began walking down the hallway and toward the front door and Much followed. He fell in step beside her as she exited the house King Richard had commandeered to be his quarters and began walking slowly down the street. Dusty was quiet, walking with determined steps but not saying a word and Much simply followed her.

As they passed from that street into another, and then into a slightly more open area of the town Dusty began to point things out in a soft whisper.

"That is where the marketplace was. I played there often as a child, especially at the milk stand. I loved to play with the goats."

"Did your father have goats?"

"No. My father…" Dusty hesitated, coming to a full stop. Much stood beside her, watching the tears form in her dark eyes and then fall gently down her cheeks. He reached out and took her hand.

"My father picked dates, outside the city walls. He worked in the orchards."

Dusty started walking again and Much followed along beside her, still holding her hand. Soon she was pointing again, her voice still hushed as she spoke.

"That was the home of a woman named Daniyah. She was my mother's dearest friend and she, more than anyone else, taught me about the Scriptures, about Christ."

Dusty kept walking past the house in question, more tears finding there way down her cheeks as she turned down another street.

The buildings around them grew less and less stable as they traveled into the district of the city filled with the most rubble that used to be stone homes, and the charred remains of all wooden structures.

Dusty's steps slowed further, her feet almost dragging through the dirt.

126

"There." Dusty stopped, her hand lifting to point into the distance. "At the end of the street. That is where I lived."

Much looked at the pile of rubble, stones that had once been walls and roof were now collapsed in on themselves and broken into chunks.

"When Saladin came with his army he did not destroy much of the city, but he did destroy this corner of town. My parents were killed."

"I am sorry." Much gripped her hand.

Dusty stared at the pile of rubble as a few more tears wandered down her cheeks. "So am I."

"Did you have brothers or sisters?"

Dusty was quiet for a moment, and then whispered, "No. It was only me and my parents."

"Were you close?"

"Very."

Much hesitated, unsure what he should do. His heart ached for this woman who'd become a sister in so short an amount of time that he'd known her. But what could he do or say to assuage the pain of losing her family? He half wished Robin could have been there to help her, but she'd asked for Much specifically.

Much let go of her hand and wrapped his arm around her shoulder. Dusty leaned her head against him and wept for a time. Much could feel a knot in his chest and tears in his eyes and he did not fight it, letting himself cry with her.

When she'd calmed down a bit, she spoke again, "Thank you."

"For what?"

"For being my friend. You care, and that touches my heart."

"We all care for you, Dusty."

"You were right, you know. Coming back here … it is facilitating healing in a way I didn't know was possible. I didn't grieve before, not like I should have. I ran. Partly in survival; I had to stay alive. But also because I couldn't face the truth."

Dusty took a shuddering deep breath and Much simply waited.

"It was easier to fight to deceive Saladin's army, to pretend to be a man and lose my past and my identity altogether, than to face the pain. I turned to my Comforter to just keep breathing, keep putting one foot in front of the other but I didn't face it, not truly."

"It's a lot to face."

Dusty straightened her shoulders, turning to Much. There were still tears in her eyes, but her expression was already more peaceful and accepting than it had been prior to their walk.

"Thank you. I am grateful God led me to you, and Robin and Allen. He has blessed me with a second family and I am glad of it."

Chapter 16

AS SOON AS King Richard and the other leaders of the Crusading army were ready, they did as the king had hoped and used their momentum from the victory at Darum to march toward Jerusalem. This time, they did indeed come in sight of the city, but before they could lay siege to it, the various rulers and nobles once more began to bicker.

Within a few days of the standstill, the king summoned his Royal Guard into his room to vent. The fact that he wished to speak to Robin did not surprise Much, but that he, Allen, and Dusty were invited as well shocked him. When had he been included in so great an honor?

Much and his friends gathered around the king in his tent. The army's encampment spread out along the horizon and off in the distance beyond the tents, they could see the city of Jerusalem shining on the hill.

The king ran a hand through his beard which had been growing ever more scruffy and full since Much had first met him. He looked tired and flustered.

"What precisely is the matter?" Robin asked. "Why the stall in our march toward the city?"

"I have been in dispute with the Duke of Burgundy, the leader of the largest French contingent of our army. Since King Philip abandoned us at Acre all that time ago, the Duke has been commanding the few troops he left behind to 'keep his word' when he packed the rest of his soldiers up and went home."

"And what have you and the Duke of Burgundy been arguing over?"

"Whether or not to march on Jerusalem."

129

"I thought that had already been decided," Robin said, his eyebrows shooting towards his hairline.

"And we marched all the way here," Much added, and then instantly recoiled. How could he dare speak to the king so casually?

"Sire," Much hastily added. "I mean…what changed your mind, Your Majesty?"

"I have decided it is not a wise decision. I was correct in my initial reluctance. If we take the city, we will not be able to hold it. I believe we should march down toward Egypt instead, and invade that territory. We could weaken Saladin's power that way, given that is where he is from and where much of his power is drawn from originally."

"Cutting off his support does seem wise," Robin agreed.

"Once we weaken him—take his seat of power, ensure he has nowhere to run and fewer allies to turn to—we could force him to relinquish Jerusalem to us. Staying here, marching on the city, would mean a lengthy siege and even if we took the city, Saladin would simply amass his army and strength and come take it back. Rather than play tug-of-war, we should be rid of Saladin himself."

"The Duke does not agree with you?" Robin asked.

"No. He believes that a direct attack on the city is the best course of action, despite the tug-of-war that will follow.

"We did come all the way here," Allen pointed out.

"I do not believe attacking the city will accomplish anything in the long run," the king replied. "I simply refuse to do so."

"You refuse?" Robin asked. "Wasn't this your idea? What does the Duke say?"

"He has refused to march to Egypt with me. I cannot take Egypt alone, and he cannot take the city of Jerusalem without me. We are at an impasse."

"Surely some arrangement could be made," Robin said. "A compromise?"

"I have said I will accompany his attack on Jerusalem but I will not lead the army. I would only go as a simple soldier. So I will not command my men to lay siege to the city, I will not give them direction to attack at all. The Duke of Burgundy would have to do so."

"The entire army will not answer to the Duke," Robin said. "They won't follow anyone but you."

"I know." The king's expression was decidedly smug.

"So what will we do?" Much asked.

"If we cannot agree on a course of action, the next step would be negotiating peace with Saladin," the king sighed. "There is nothing else to be done. Either we attack the city as a unified whole—which I refuse to do—or we march to Egypt, which the Duke refuses to do."

"You're going to call for a ceasefire and negotiate peace simply because you cannot find a way to agree with the nobles who lead this army with you?" Robin shook his head. "I suppose there are worse reasons to end a war. But you didn't accomplish what you set out to do."

"Perhaps not. Jerusalem may be lost to us for now, but much of the kingdom has been restored to Guy of Jerusalem, and he can set up his capital in Acre for now."

"Until Saladin roots him out."

"Which he will not do because we are negotiating a peace treaty."

"I suppose that's it then," Robin shrugged.

131

The king sighed and then gave a firm nod. "I suppose it is."

The army soon retreated back to the coast to the city of Jaffa and negotiations with Saladin began once more. With the end of the war presumably close at hand, King Richard sent his wife and sister Joan back home.

The day they packed up and boarded a ship at Jaffa to sail for Europe and make their way to Aquitaine where the Queen Mother was living, Joan had thrown herself into Robin's arms for a last hug and cheerfully kissed Allen and Much on the cheek, before giving a much longer and more affectionate farewell to Dusty and her brother the king.

After the departure of Joan, there was little of interest to interrupt the days of the King's Guard. They stayed beside King Richard as he moved around town and spoke to various nobility and royalty, they watched as he dictated messages to send to Saladin and received messages in return, and they stood watch outside his door when he met privately with his advisors—which often included Robin.

One day, Much stood near the harbor as the king was making preparations to load his army into a fleet of ships and send them home again. Peace was not yet secured, but the king felt it was close.

The Mediterranean sea sparkled and danced with brilliant hues of blue and green and Much could feel the tension of the years of fighting leaking from his shoulders. He would be going home soon; back to Nottingham and Locksley, back to the days when his biggest concern was how long Robin would spend flirting with Marian.

The sounds of shouts and running feet soon broke his reverie. The king noticed the commotion as well, and he—along with Robin, Dusty, and Allen who were all nearby—turned to see what the fuss was about. Soon a couple soldiers came running across the docks from the city toward the king.

"Your Majesty! Saladin is coming!"

"I did not know to expect him," the king said. "Though perhaps meeting in person will move things along swifter than our missives have been able to."

"No, Your Majesty, you don't understand. Saladin is coming with his army. They are mounting an attack on the city walls even now!"

"What?!"

The king's hand went instinctively to his sword hilt at his waist. "Show me."

The king began to stride after the soldiers who had brought the news as they hurried back into the city and along the streets toward the outer wall. Much, and his friends kept pace with the king.

"What is Saladin thinking, with peace so near?" Dusty asked.

"He has been reluctant to relinquish his power," the king replied. "This must be his last ditch effort to assert control so that he can demand a surrender—with terms to his liking, because we would have no negotiating leverage—rather than a peace treaty."

When the king reached the city walls, it became clear that there were, indeed, Saracens trying to breach the city gates and archers shooting down any Crusading soldiers who were unlucky enough to show their heads above the wall.

The king strode along the wall in search of his commanders and began issuing orders. Robin and Allen were sent to join the Crusading archers atop the wall to deter any of Saladin's forces from continuing with their efforts to breach the city.

Much and Dusty stayed at the king's side as he issued orders and surveyed the battlefield. His keen eyes were darting around the

133

violence below, and Much was sure he was formulating a strategy of some sort.

It wasn't long before the king was in motion once more. As his archers and a few companies of soldiers kept Saladin's forces at bay along the walls, the king selected a few more companies of soldiers to follow him outside the city wall on the opposite side of Jaffa. Much and Dusty stayed at his side, as was their duty, and so Much soon found himself sneaking around the city at the king's side, preparing to flank Saladin's forces.

Within minutes, Much was in the thick of the fighting as King Richard sliced his way through the enemy. The groans of the dying men filled the air, surrounding Much with the horror he so wanted to escape.

He stayed at the king's side with Dusty beside him, cutting and slicing at anyone within reach and trying to keep the space around King Richard clear. Unfortunately, King Richard seemed determined to stay in the thickest part of the fighting.

Before Much could grow discouraged, however, the skirmish was over. Wounded and dead men from both sides lay scattered across the land in front of the city walls and Dusty and the other healers set to work while the king angrily gathered the remaining leaders of the Saracen forces together to execute them.

Negotiations with Saladin began once again, and this time they came to an end; a treaty was signed.

"What was the final outcome of the treaty?" Much asked as Robin joined him, Allen, and Dusty in the hall outside the king's chambers a few days after the battle. Robin had been privy to the final dealings of the treaty with Saladin as he was now one of King Richard's most trusted friends.

"Jerusalem remains under Saracen control, but unarmed pilgrims and traders of other faiths and political views will be allowed to visit the city with no harm coming to them." Robin shoved a hand through his hair, shrugging. "Other than the city of Jerusalem and a few surrounding areas, most of the 'Kingdom of Jerusalem' has been returned to Guy's control."

"But we did not do what we set out to do," Allen said.

"Neither side is completely satisfied with this treaty, I think," Robin said. "But it is what it is, for now at least. Until someone decides there needs to be a fourth Crusade."

"Do you think they will?" Much asked, his heart sinking.

"Not any time soon. The monetary drain on the treasuries of the royals in Europe, and the lives lost in this war that would potentially have no end—neither side being overwhelmingly larger in number, and every other battle being won by the opposite side—if we did not come to a compromise in this treaty, the Third Crusade might never end."

"So it's done," Much said.

"Yes, I believe it is."

"And we can finally return home." Much sighed, letting the relief wash over him. He didn't have to fight anymore. He didn't have to kill anyone.

"I don't have a home to return to," Dusty said.

"You're coming with us." Robin grinned, throwing his arm around Dusty's shoulders. "You and Allen both are more than welcome in our home."

"Thank you," Dusty said. "I would be glad of that."

"So would I," Allen agreed. "You three are all the family that I have."

It was not long after the peace was finally agreed to that King Richard and his Crusading soldiers were, at last, loading onto the fleet of ships that had arrived to take them all back to their various homes in Europe.

As Much stood above deck on the vessel the king had chosen for himself, Robin came and leaned against the railing beside him.

"We're going home," Robin said.

"Yes."

"This has been quite the adventure, but I am ready for peace and quiet."

"So am I."

"I'll finally see Marian again! Do you think she missed me at all?"

"I am sure she did."

"Don't expect too much peace and quiet," Allen said, sauntering over and leaning against the ship's rail beside Robin as the ship finally put off from the port and made its way over the gentle waves out to sea —the city of Jaffa becoming smaller and smaller as they sailed away from the shore.

"The king has heard more reports from England in the last few weeks as negotiations were coming to a close." Allen glanced at Robin and then toward the shoreline they were leaving behind. "Prince John is up to no good, and it will likely take at least a few months after our arrival to clear things up."

"Perhaps the king will have a busy few months, but I imagine there will be little for us to do after we arrive home," Robin replied. "Except to marry Marian, of course. That will take up my time."

"I am eager to meet this Marian," Allen laughed. "You speak so highly of her."

"She is perfect, Allen. Absolutely perfect."

"And yet you so often doubt if she loves you or is waiting for you back in England ... why is that?"

"I don't know," Robin said. He shoved a hand through his blond hair, looking rather sheepish. "It's just sometimes ... I can't tell with Marian. She's stubborn. And though I would like to say that I know without a doubt that she loves me ... she's never actually said as much."

"She loves you," Much said. "I am sure of it, even if you are not."

Dusty joined the group, standing beside Much and watching the coastline grow ever more distant. There were tears glistening on her lower lashes, though none fell from her eyes.

"What is England like?"

"Beautiful," Robin replied. "You will love it, Dusty. It's lovely, it's green. We will live in peace and I promise you, you will not have so many hardships as you have had here. You will have a good life."

"I am not afraid of hardships," Dusty replied. "They do much to strengthen one's character."

"Have you ever left Palestine before?" Much asked, watching Dusty's solemn expression as she stared at the retreating coastline.

"No."

"I hadn't left England before coming on this adventure with Robin. It was surprisingly unsettling to wonder if I'd ever return."

"I know I will not return ... but there is nothing to return to." Dusty turned toward Much and smiled in spite of her tears. "But I have much to look forward to, a bright future ahead, so I will not regret leaving my past behind."

They had not sailed far from the Holy Land before the entire fleet was caught in another storm.

137

Much was beginning to believe sailing was the most dangerous way to travel. The ship rocked violently back and forth as he huddled below deck with his friends—no one, thankfully, went overboard this time.

Hours passed in the relative darkness, with nothing but the creaking of the boat, the shouts of sailors overhead, and the shrieking of the wind to keep them company. It was difficult to remain balanced as the boat pitched first this way and then that, and more than one soldier below deck ended up banging elbows and heads against the walls and the floor—and some, including Dusty, were soon retching any contents from their stomach—but eventually the storm began to clear. When it did, Much and the others hurried above deck.

The deck was still rolling in a most unnatural way as the waves —still not entirely calm—buffeted the boat. The dark clouds in the sky were floating past and giving way to the blue sky as morning dawned.

Much grabbed the rail along the side of the boat to steady himself as the deck continued to rise and fall at a rapid and uneven pace.

"Not enjoying this, Much?" Robin asked, laughing as he strode confidently along the deck in spite of the rolling.

"No. I will be glad when we finally reach home and I can be free of sailing for the rest of my life."

"I'm not sure how soon that will be. We seem to have been separated from the fleet in that storm."

Much looked over the side of the boat, but saw no other ships nearby. "How does this keep happening to us?"

"At least we're with the king this time. It won't be like when we were thrown in prison on Cyprus."

138

Allen came hurrying over with Dusty, who looked more than a little green around the edges.

"We're off course, according to the captain and the king," Allen said. "We're heading for the nearest port, which they think is Corfu. I don't know what the plan is once we get there."

"I hope it isn't a long stop. I am eager to be home," Much said.

"So am I," Robin agreed. "I need to see Marian's face again. I swear the closer we get to returning home to England, the more desperate I become just to see her smile, to hear her laugh. Do you suppose she missed us terribly?"

"I am sure she missed you."

"I hope so."

Much sighed, biting his cheek. He did not understand Robin's doubts in regard to Marian, and though he would never dare tell Robin how he presently felt—he was getting annoyed with Robin's constant questioning if Marian missed him.

When land came in sight, the captain declared they were indeed sailing for the island of Corfu. Once their battered and bruised ship docked, the king made arrangements to stay at an inn for the night with his four guards while the captain of the ship and the sailors made their own arrangements for repairs to the hull, mast, sails, and everything else that had been harmed in the storm.

As Much and his companions gathered outside the door of the king's room, Robin informed them of the king's desire not to sail all the way to England.

"I don't blame him," Much said, easing to the floor beside the king's door as the others sat down as well. "With all the storms we've encountered, I wouldn't want to sail."

"We have to sail," Allen said, sitting against the wall opposite Much, with Dusty beside him. "Unless we're staying on the island of Corfu for the rest of our lives."

"We will sail," Robin said. "But we go alone, the five of us, and we make straight for Aquileia on the coast of Italy—not far from here—and we'll travel by land from there."

"We're going home on foot?" Much asked.

"Why?" Allen asked.

"We're going home undercover," Robin said. "The king doesn't wish to continue sailing, but traveling with a large force by land will attract attention."

"The king has made many enemies," Dusty said. "He fell out with King Philip, he insulted the Duke of Austria, he alienated the Holy Roman Emperor with his attempt to marry Joan to Saladin's brother, he fought with the Duke of Burgundy…"

"In other words," Robin said. "The only safe way home if we go by land is to go undercover. We'll be going through the lands of some of those royals and nobles that the king has angered in the past. And sailing wouldn't be easy even without the storms—Corsairs infest the North African coast, and France is barred by King Philip"

"So…we go on foot," Much sighed.

Chapter 17

ROBIN ACQUIRED PASSAGE on a ship for the five of them the next day, and then King Richard gathered them all in his room before departure. It was a simple space, like every other room Much had seen in the inn—a small bed, a small table, a small fire place in one wall.

King Richard crossed his arms, eyeing the group before him. "Robin is not the only one who will speak to me informally. Every formal title has to end; I am only Richard."

"That is wise," Allen said. "We wouldn't want to give away who you are. No more 'Your Majesty's to you."

"Precisely," the king nodded.

"Of course, Richard," Dusty said, her tone casual and nonchalant. "It is important that your identity remain secret as we travel through your enemy's territory."

Much stared at Dusty, convinced he'd never be able to talk to the King of England in so easy a way.

"Robin, you will have to have a long talk with Much about this," the king said, his eyes dancing merrily. Much glanced between the king and Robin; could they read his thoughts?

"With me, Sire?"

"Exactly."

"I imagine this will be a challenge for our dear Much," Robin laughed.

"He's the king and I am a humble servant, how could I ever—"

"You will have to find a way," the king said firmly. "I am only Richard."

Much nodded. He understood the logic behind it, and understood it would be keeping the king safe. But what would the Earl have thought if he saw Much calling the King of England by his first name as though they were friends and equals?

"This is a necessity," the king said. "We must get home without being attacked. In order to stay safe, no one can know who I am. Just remember that and I'm sure you'll be fine—if you call me Richard you are, in fact, protecting your king."

"Yes, Si—uh, Richard."

Sailing from Corfu to the coast of Italy was simple enough. They stashed their more flashy clothes—any of the king's clothes with his sigil, anything with the Crusader cross, and the like—in their packs and donned the most ordinary outfits they had, though they kept their weapons on them. They boarded the boat Robin had procured berths on with no difficulty, and the passage across the Mediterranean was calm.

They spent one night at Aquileia, and then the long march home began. As they walked along the green countryside late in the afternoon on their first day out from Aquileia, Robin fell into step beside Much. Allen and the king were just ahead of them, and Dusty walked behind.

"The first thing I'm doing when we get home is going to Wetherby and asking Marian to marry me."

"I assumed you would."

Robin grinned, throwing his arm around Much's shoulders. "And the first thing you'll do when we get back to England is…?"

"Go to the kitchens and cook with Sarah."

"Who is Sarah?" Allen asked, glancing over his shoulder at them. "Is she Much's equivalent to Robin's Marian?"

Much laughed. "No."

Robin snorted as he tried not to laugh too hard and then said. "No! Sarah is one of my servants. She's the head cook at Locksley manor and is at least twice Much's age, perhaps more."

"Ah, I was mistaken then," Allen chuckled.

"Do you enjoy cooking, Much?" Dusty piped up from behind.

"Yes. I do. And cooking with Sarah, specifically, means the world to me. She's…well, to put it simply, she's the only mother I've ever known."

"What sorts of things do you like to cook?" King Richard asked.

Much looked at the king, who'd slowed his walk ahead of them so he could turn and ask his question. "Uh…"

King Richard sighed. "You don't need to be afraid of me."

"I enjoy cooking most anything, Sire."

"Much!" Robin and the king both scolded simultaneously and Much cringed.

"Sorry. Slip of the tongue," Much said.

"You have to be careful," King Richard said with a sigh before he began walking again. "Robin, what did you do to your servant that he thinks so little of himself?"

"He is right beside you," Dusty said, a bit of a reproach in her voice. She moved forward to walk beside Much, glaring at the king. "I doubt Robin did anything to bring this humbleness and shyness about."

"I agree," Robin said. "I've always felt he was my brother more than my servant."

Much knew exactly who had drilled his humility into him, but he wasn't going to upset Robin by diminishing the memory of the father he'd loved so well.

143

"I think part of it is his God-given nature," Dusty said, smiling at Much. "You are a sweet man."

"Thank you," Much said. He wasn't convinced she was wrong —he had always been less assertive than Robin, even before the Earl had made it necessary—but he knew there was more to it than his personality.

When the king felt they had traveled enough for one day, they took shelter at the first town they came to. Robin was sent to procure them rooms at a tavern, and they were soon sleeping soundly, exhausted from their exertion. When the sun rose, they were on their way again, and their travel continued in that manner for days.

One night, Much lay curled in his bed beside Robin's, images of home filling his mind. He could see Sarah smiling, her eyes dancing as she bustled about the kitchen giving orders to her underlings. He could feel the warmth of her embrace, see the love glimmering in her eyes when she looked at him. He missed his mother, not caring that he was not hers by birth. He knew the bond between them was as real as any other parent and child.

Much rolled over and sighed. They were headed home, and for that he should be excited, but already they'd met with one disaster. Who was to say how many more might befall them along the journey? Much had the sinking suspicion they weren't going to make it back to England at all.

When it became clear to Much that his mind was too active to let him sleep, he exited the room he shared with Robin, silently sneaking down the stairs and across the common room of the tavern where they were staying, and out into the chill air of a late autumn night.

144

He sat down on the front steps, and peered up at the sky. The stars shone brilliantly and the moon lit the village where they were staying. The street was empty and silent, every house dark.

"Much?"

Much turned around and by the light of the moon could see Dusty seating herself beside him.

"Why are you up so late?"

"Me?" Dusty asked. "I could not sleep; I heard movements, like those of a mouse, and came to investigate."

"I am not a mouse."

"You could have fooled me. What is bothering you?"

"Nothing. I am merely thinking."

"So late at night? What are you thinking about?"

Much kept his gaze upward towards the moon, hesitating.

As far as Much knew, there was not a social hierarchy separating them the way there always would be with Robin. And, too, Dusty had already opened up and been vulnerable with him in Darum in a way that he knew she hadn't with Robin and Allen; it created a sort of bridge between them, at least in Much's mind, and for the first time, he realized he wasn't afraid of being honest with his friend.

As he turned toward Dusty—relaxed, and with no sound of the Earl hissing in his ear—he wished briefly that he could feel so at ease with Robin.

"I was thinking of home. I am eager to return to Locksley. I want to see the manor, to smell the garden, to see Sarah ... yet it will all be strange without the Earl."

"Did you know Robin's father well?"

"Not exactly ... I was merely a servant in his household."

"And yet I feel he was more than that to you."

145

Much nodded. "My earliest memories at Locksley … it felt like Robin and I were brothers. The earliest impressions I have of the Earl are that of a father. That soon changed, however."

"How long has it been since he died?"

"A year or so."

Dusty didn't respond, and Much turned toward her, suddenly realizing she must be thinking of her own family. He reached over and slipped his hand in hers.

"Will it be hard for you?"

"Will what be hard?"

"Seeing all of us return to our homes and our families, when you don't have either to return to?"

"No, Much. I have become content with where God has placed me in life. You helped me with that, actually," Dusty smiled at him. "Besides, you *are* my family now. Where you and Robin go, there will be my home. I believe a person's home is where they find comfort, with those they love … where they keep their heart."

"Mine is at Locksley with Sarah and Robin."

"I know." Dusty laughed, the sound light and airy.

For a time they lapsed into silence, enjoying the stillness of the night and the brilliance of the stars above them.

"Dusty?"

"Yes?"

"How do you heal people?"

"With herbs and prayer."

"I know that; I have watched you do it. It's … amazing. I can't comprehend it. I watched a sword slice through Robin, and then the next time I saw him, you had healed him up and he was talking and fine. Injured still, but … fine."

"It is God's gift."

"You healed so many while we were in the Holy Land."

"I merely helped where I could."

Much glanced at her. He felt a kinship with her humility, though she deserved higher praise than he ever would.

"Could you teach me?"

Dusty smiled, her eyes alight. "I can show you the herbs I use and how to mix them. But not tonight. We need rest. We have a long journey ahead of us."

"Assuming we make it to England at all."

"Why would you say that?"

"I don't know ... I just have a bad feeling about our trip. We've already been thrown off course and forced to travel by foot across land —undercover no less—instead of sailing safely home."

"Things will play out how they are meant to be. You cannot stop them, and worrying about it will only make you anxious."

"I can't help it."

"Just pray for God's guidance as you travel through life."

"Does he answer your prayers?" Much looked intently at his friend. He'd never given a great deal of thought to God—despite spending years fighting in a 'holy war' driven by the faith of the Holy Roman Emperor. He had only fought in the Crusades because of Robin. Yet now he was curious—Dusty claimed her abilities to heal came directly from a higher source, and if that was true, Much wanted to know.

"Sometimes His answers are not what I would like to hear, but He always answers. He loves His children dearly."

"Does he?"

"Don't you know? Don't you claim to be a Christian? Isn't that why you went on the Crusade, to retake Jerusalem for the glory of your religion?" Dusty did not seem impressed with the idea of conquering Jerusalem for such a reason, but though her voice was laced with anger, her words remained straightforward.

"Robin came for war and glory."

"And you merely followed Robin, as you always do."

"Yes."

"Do you know the Lord at all then, as He so wants to be known by you?"

"Probably not. I certainly don't share the kind of faith you do."

"Can I tell you about Him?"

"If you'd like to."

"I would like nothing better."

Dusty took a few minutes to gather her thoughts, and Much simply sat in silence beside her, waiting.

Eventually, she spoke again, "When I was young, I was full of curiosity and questions. Annoyingly so. I grew up in a city filled with Christians and Muslims alike, and I hounded adults and childhood friends from both faiths with my questions. I hungered for the truth."

Dusty shifted her position on the step beside him, staring up at the night sky. "What I found from one faith was the expectation to be perfect, and if I did not live up to Allah's standards then I would perish. 'To those who disbelieve and do wrong, surely Allah *will not* forgive them or lead them to any path.' It left me feeling worthless; I wanted to do good, to be a good person, but I could never attain that kind of righteousness."

Much couldn't imagine Dusty not being good—she was undoubtedly the best person he knew.

148

"The books of religious text that my Muslim teachers would read with me told me that if I didn't attain that high standard, I would go to hell. I was left in fear and confusion, knowing I couldn't attain it but terrified of not trying because who wants to burn in hell?"

Dusty's gaze dropped from the stars to Much's face, and the intensity of her keen eyes as they bored into him unnerved him.

"My teachers tried to comfort me with things like 'They whose balances are heavy will be blessed, but they whose balances are light will lose their soul and abide in hell forever.' It was not remotely comforting to the little girl who wanted to do right but knew she could never live up to perfection. I was being told that if I didn't do the impossible, I would go to hell. That was it. That was the only reality. But what I found in the other faith was only grace."

Dusty smiled, the intensity in her eyes melting into pools of light, soft and full of love. "My mother's dearest friend was the most patient person in my life, letting me bring all my doubts and questions to her without ever judging me for them."

As Dusty described her friend Daniyah, Much thought of Sarah —the only mother he'd ever known. He could talk to her about anything and she would never fault him for it.

"She showed me the difference between the salvation through works of one faith, versus the gracious gift of the other. 'But God demonstrates His own love toward us in that while we were still sinners, Christ died for us.' He didn't wait for us to be perfect—He knew we never would be. So He made a way for us to draw near to Him regardless of our imperfection. *While we were sinners*, He forgave us. Not after we'd worked hard to become perfect did He then deliberate over our deeds, both good and bad, and decide whether or not to be forgiving based on how the scales balanced."

"I can see why you'd be drawn to the Christian God then."

"To be fully transparent, there were phrases to be found in the texts of my Muslim teachers that spoke of God's forgiveness and mercy, too. But they also rely on works as much as Allah's grace for salvation —'to those who believe *and do deeds of righteousness* has Allah promised forgiveness.' 'O you who believe! If you are careful of your duty to Allah he will grant you distinction.'"

Dusty shook her head, her expression sorrowful. "They had a piece of the truth, but it was coupled with the idea that we are born good and perfect, not sinful, and I knew from my own experience— from my heart—that I was neither good nor perfect. Also the idea that salvation was about more than just God's grace saddened me; their idea that it also required something from me in the form of good deeds. Their teachings left me in fear because I knew that as I made mistakes I would constantly be in need of repentance, and if I didn't repent I would be punished eternally in hell-fire. It was a vicious cycle."

Dusty's eyes flashed as she spoke, her hands starting to wave about as though she couldn't contain her passion. Much had never seen her so animated. "What if I genuinely sought after God, and then made a mistake, and then died immediately after sinning? I hadn't had time to repent. What then? Trust a vague idea that maybe Allah would forgive me because the rest of my deeds outweighed this one big mistake I'd made?"

Much hadn't studied either religion that Dusty was now lecturing him on, but he was fascinated by her enthusiasm. He'd never seen Dusty so vivacious before.

"With Jesus, it is not vague. It is straight-forward and factual. He took the punishment of all sin, once for everyone—it's over and done with. All I have to do is accept His gift of salvation and freedom and my place at His side for all eternity is secured. With one faith, there was no way to know for certain if my good deeds would outweigh my bad and therefore *earn* grace from a God they claim is so forgiving, but with the other I was told I was loved and forgiven because He chose to do so long before I ever thought to seek Him at all."

Dusty smiled, the lines in her face softening once more as her eyes brightened. "I can rest in His grace knowing it is sure, rather than the arbitrary grace of an Allah who may or may not forgive me depending on how sincerely I may or may not repent or how many good deeds I may or may not do that may or may not outweigh my bad ones. You see my point? So that is how I came to know the Lord."

Dusty took a deep breath, seeming to take a moment to think before she spoke again. "It is not always the same for everyone—don't get me wrong, Jesus and what He did for us is exactly the same, but sometimes we face different questions and doubts and He gently guides us to the truth in a way that suits our own needs. For you, for example, I think you need to hear that you have inherent value because you are a Child of God. You are not less than."

Much shifted uncomfortably as Dusty's sharp gaze bored into him. She wasn't wrong; his sense of self-worth was where his greatest insecurities lay.

To Dusty he simply said, "I have never given a great deal of thought to any faith; I certainly don't have the same questions as you did. I don't need to compare and contrast religions in a desperate search for the truth."

Dusty chuckled softly, folding her hands in her lap and looking abnormally self-conscious. "I was searching for a different truth—that I didn't have to be perfect to be loved and forgiven. You, on the other

151

hand, while you may need to hear that truth as well, your soul is longing for something else—namely, that you have value. Yes?"

Much shrugged. "I suppose."

"Robin's father is the one who convinced you that you are less than, isn't that right?"

"He made sure I knew the difference between the son of an earl and the son of nobody significant."

"And yet both the noble man and the servant are the same in the eyes of God. Both are made in His image, both are His creation. Both are seeking love, acceptance, significance—the things that make up our identities and where we measure our worth. God offers all of them— love, acceptance, significance—to His children in a way that no human could. Robin's love will inevitably fail you, his acceptance will fail you. The significance that he may lend you—if he lends you any—will not last. But God can give you all this, and more securely—eternally— offering an undying love that will never change, accepting you exactly as you are and never wavering in His grace."

"You are so confident in what you believe."

"God has never been unfaithful to me; not once. His promises, both spoken to my heart and those found directly in Scripture, have always been fulfilled."

"I am envious of the assurance you have in your faith in God. And I do … I do wish I could be confident that I am…enough."

"You are, because He says you are. You are, because He made you to be. You are, because He is willing to forgive you and clothe you in His own righteousness and make you more than you could ever be on your own. That connection that you seek, the desire to be on equal footing with someone and not seen as 'just a servant', the ability to open up and be vulnerable with a friend without the fear of 'forgetting your place' is all found in God."

"But isn't it more terrifying to overstep the Creator of everything versus offend a nobleman like the Earl? He's … I mean, He's God."

"Yes, He is. And He is absolutely deserving of reverence and fear, of worship. But He gave up His glory willingly to meet you exactly where you are, Much."

I love you.

Much's head jerked toward Dusty, but she hadn't said anything. The gentle whisper seemed to come from inside himself.

I love you.

That was it; that was all it said. But it said it with a firmness and power that Much could not deny. His palms began to sweat and he closed his eyes. Was it possible he had imagined it?

I love you.

No, it was definitely there. Someone was speaking to him and it terrified him. As his heart began to pound, Much felt a peace and gentleness wrapping around him.

I love you.

There was no judgment in it, no expectation in it. Just simple truth.

"I'm sorry, was this all too much?" Dusty asked. Much opened his eyes to see Dusty watching him with a concerned expression. "I get passionate, I know I do. I am sorry if I have overwhelmed you."

"No. You didn't. It's interesting. The idea that I could be valuable simply because God says so is intriguing. I want that."

You have value because I say that you do. You are mine.

Much took a slow shuddering breath, trying to focus on Dusty and not the strange whispers caressing his aching heart.

"God created all of us to desire community, connection," Dusty said. "But the only place we can find true connection is with Him. Robin will not sustain you, Sarah will never be enough to assuage the longing for true acceptance and love that can only be found in Jesus."

Long into the night, the two of them continued to talk. The moon drifted across the sky and toward the horizon, and the sun was announcing its imminent arrival with an array of vibrant colors across the sky when the two of them finally returned to their beds that night.

Much slipped underneath the simple blanket, pulling it to his shoulders and letting all the words from the conversation with Dusty spin around his mind. Her digging into the differences between her faith and that of the Muslims she'd grown up with blew around in a chaotic manner, mixed with the idea that God would view him in any light other than worthless, and then that voice. Oh, that voice.

It was still there, whispering over him, speaking of love and acceptance and grace. Much couldn't comprehend it.

"I don't know you," Much whispered.

But I know you.

"I'm no one, I'm not worth your attention."

You are my son. I created you and I love you.

Suddenly Much was thinking about the Earl, about all the times Much had longed for Robin's father to reach out to him the way he did for Robin. He remembered every heart-wrenching moment he'd seen the Earl playfully ruffle Robin's hair, every time his hand had stroked Robin's face, every time his arms had surrounded Robin in an embrace.

You are my son. I love you.

154

Much could feel, not exactly physical arms surrounding him, but an embrace of warmth and love unlike anything he'd ever experienced before, even from Sarah.

"I am just a servant."

I love you.

"I don't matter…"

You matter to me.

Much could feel himself fighting against the embrace so full of tenderness and affection and suddenly wondered why he was struggling so hard.

So he let go.

Much sank into the peace and love surrounding him, overpowering him. His eyes filled with tears as he felt so clearly that he —Much the miller's son, who was just a servant in the house of Locksley and nothing more—was someone whom God would take pleasure in knowing. He could feel it with certainty.

You are my delight and my joy. You are my son.

Much let the tears soak his pillow as he wept, though he tried to stifle his sobs so as not to wake Robin. He doubted Robin would understand what he was feeling just now.

As morning crept ever closer, Much continued to relish in the feeling of being wanted, valued, and called worthy as the still small voice continued to caress his wounded heart until he eventually fell asleep.

Chapter 18

THE NEXT MORNING came far too soon, and as the group gathered in the common room to partake of breakfast, Much could barely keep his eyes open. Dusty, on the other hand, seemed annoyingly alert, saying a cheerful good morning to Much, Robin, Allen, and the king, and then proceeding to open a sunny conversation with the servant who brought over a plate of food for her.

Robin and the king were discussing their route for the day in low voices, presumably trying not to draw the attention of the tavern keeper or the servants who bustled in and out of the kitchen, bringing food to the various travelers who were seated at tables around the room. Allen had his elbow propped on the table with his chin resting in his hand, his eyes blinking slowly. He looked about as awake as Much felt.

Soon enough they had eaten breakfast and they were on the road again, walking along the Austrian countryside following the king and Robin, who'd planned their route for the day. Much usually fell into step beside Robin as they traveled, but today he left him as he drifted to the back of the line to walk beside Dusty.

"How are you not tired?" Much asked as he fell into step beside her.

"I feel quite invigorated from our conversation yesterday, I must confess."

"The conversation was certainly interesting, but I am still incredibly tired."

Dusty laughed. "It might also be that I am used to getting little sleep and my body learned to adjust long ago."

They walked in silence for a time as Much tried to put into words everything he was feeling. That small voice was absent so far today, but the feeling of acceptance and peace still wrapped him in the warm embrace of the Father.

"I probably should not have kept you up so late," Dusty said. "I know I can get so passionate about the Lord it can be hard to shut up about it..."

"I enjoyed our conversation. And honestly, I do have more questions."

"I would be happy to answer them."

Much glanced forward where Robin and Allen were flanking the king, all three of them lost in a conversation of their own.

"Take your time, Much. These questions—whatever they are— are likely the most important you'll ever ask. Finding the truth of who God is, is a powerful thing, and vitally important both for our lives here on earth and for the fate of our eternity in heaven or hell. But you should know that God does not shy away from our questions and doubts. He welcomes them, in fact, so that He can have the chance to prove Himself worthy. Because He is. Always worthy."

"I cannot get over how confident and assured you are when you speak of your faith, or about God."

"He has never failed me."

"Does He ever ... speak to you?"

"All the time! When I read Scripture, He has so much to show me."

"But does He ever talk to you ... I wouldn't say verbally, but..."

Dusty grinned, looking at Much intently. "Yes." Her voice held so much conviction and strength and it continued to astound Much. "He does speak directly to me sometimes. It's not always a voice that I can hear with my ears, but my heart hears it."

Much nodded. That sounded like what he had experienced the night before.

Dusty held Much's gaze for a moment. "Did He speak to you?"

"I think … maybe."

"What did He say?"

Much hesitated, his gaze drifting to the mountains looming in the distance, and then to the sprigs of purple and white flowers growing close to the road. With anyone else, he might have felt uneasy relating the things he thought he'd heard in the middle of the night, but he knew Dusty would not judge him or think him crazy. "That I am His son, and He values me."

"Both statements are true."

Much nodded, trying to imagine how he could put into words the way that he felt, the way that the acceptance and love of God seemed to envelop him last night and lingered still.

"You said you had questions?"

"I can almost feel the fatherhood of God, and it is overwhelming and wonderful. But you touched on more than just His affection yesterday … you spoke of Christ and what He'd done, but I'm not entirely sure I understand what that was."

"Well, it starts with the fact that God is holy and perfect and good. Do you believe that?"

"I guess. I can't imagine Him being anything less if He's God."

"Exactly. And then He created this strange and beautiful world, and He created us. Humans. His children. At the beginning there was communion between God and man, until man sinned."

"Which means what, precisely?"

159

"Anything that we do or say that breaks His laws. It can be as extreme as murder or as simple as lying. It's our angry thoughts and our envious words. Anything that isn't good and perfect and true is apart from God. He cannot be near the ugliness and the horror of our sin and darkness. If we don't take the significance of sin, and our sinful nature as humans, seriously then we cannot truly appreciate what Christ did when He died to save us from those very sins."

"That makes sense."

"God is so serious about sin that His response is wrath. 'The wages of sin is death' that's what Scripture tells us. We cannot live with God if we are in open rebellion against Him, because He is a just and righteous God. He cannot let wrongdoing go without punishment."

Dusty was once more growing enthusiastic, her eyes alight as her hands began to gesture almost of their own accord. Much found it fascinating to watch. She was generally a quiet observer and had little to add to conversation, but now that she'd opened up about her faith, she couldn't seem to stop talking.

"This is where the Muslim faith I studied as a child begins to differ from the truth of Christ, both in the knowledge that we are, indeed, sinful people who deserve separation from God and eternal damnation, and also that we cannot do anything to assuage God's wrath. We do wrong, and He punishes. We can't 'be good enough' to ever change the fact that we are guilty. Our bad deeds will forever outweigh the good ones. Scripture even says that 'all of our righteous deeds are as filthy rags' because it's never going to be enough compared to the pure goodness of God. Our salvation is not through any acts that we might perform. God could have left us in our punishment—separation from Him eternally, but He *chose* something different because of His great love for us."

160

"Why didn't He simply accept us into His grace then, why the need for Christ to die?"

"Because He is a just and righteous God. There has to be punishment for sin, that doesn't change because of his love. Wrongdoing deserves correction. What He did was not remove consequences for wrongdoing, but rather take those consequences upon Himself so that justice would still be upheld, but mercy and grace would be present as well."

Dusty grinned at Much, her eyes dancing. "He didn't have to save us, but He chose to do so in the only way possible while still maintaining punishment for sin. He carried the punishment so that we wouldn't have to. Only He could be that Savior for us—if anyone else had died, claiming to do so to free all men from sin, it wouldn't have done any good. But Jesus—being God—lived a perfect life here on earth, entirely free from sin, and therefore He alone was able to make that sacrifice. And it didn't end there—He rose from the dead victorious, powerful enough to bring us with Him to life eternal. *That* is why Christ is our only hope for salvation."

Much let everything Dusty was saying settle into his mind. It was a lot to consider—the justice and the mercy of God both being present and undeniable. And through it all, that still small voice.

I love you.

Much glanced toward the deep blue sky, where thick white clouds floated lazily along whatever path the wind would take them down. He thought about his resentment—deep and mostly unacknowledged—toward the Earl, toward Robin, toward society at large that told him he was less than they were. His anger, his frustrations. He thought about all the times he'd lied and been deceitful,

161

about everything that he might have done throughout his life that would have been in opposition to God's perfect law.

And then he considered that little voice whispering grace and love across his heart and he knew without a shadow of a doubt that what Dusty said was the truth.

Much smiled. "It is strange to say this ... but I feel at peace in a way I never have before."

Dusty's face lit up, a rare and wide smile stretching across her cheeks as her eyes twinkled with merriment. "Do you? I am so glad!"

"I do believe what you're saying—what God says. I don't understand it all ... but I believe Him."

"That is the most wonderful thing I've heard you say."

"I feel ... confident," Much said, and it was true. He knew in that moment that his faith was as sure as Dusty's—He could trust his heavenly Father and He would never fail him. And through that knowledge, and the truth that he was held in high esteem by his Father, he began to feel that he did, indeed, have worth beyond what the Earl had ever been able to see.

Chapter 19

AS AUTUMN BLED into winter, the air turned cold and the rain began to come. It reminded Much of their march toward Jerusalem when they'd been waylaid by foul weather. When the rain turned to snow, King Richard chose to stop their traveling until the spring.

"We cannot stay in one place for too long for fear of drawing attention to ourselves," the king said one night as they settled into their rooms at an inn, the snow falling heavily outside and covering the world in white. "So we will live in this village for a handful of weeks and then travel a short distance to another nearby, and so forth. I do not wish to travel great distances in this weather, but I also know we cannot stay in one spot for long."

Robin agreed that the king's plan was wise, and so from then on that is what they did. They would find lodgings in a village for a few weeks, and then move on a few miles to another town and live there for a few more weeks. Their goal, as they moved along the villages, was to eventually land in Saxony. The Duke of Saxony—Henry the Lion—was King Richard's brother-in-law, and King Richard felt it would be safest to spend their winter months there if they could reach Saxony without being caught by any enemies.

As they traveled, Much often found himself pulling Dusty aside to discuss more about God and Scripture, and she seemed more than happy to oblige him.

In one of the villages where they stayed for a handful of weeks, Robin had managed to procure a chess set which he then carried with him for the rest of their journey. As the snow fell outside, the group would gather in one of their rooms, circled up by the hearth to feel the heat of the fire as Robin and the king played an intense game of chess—and occasionally Allen would try his hand at beating Robin as well.

Sometimes Dusty and Much would watch their games, sometimes they would retreat to a corner of their own to discuss Much's blossoming faith and Dusty would answer all his questions regarding Scripture. Dusty also began to teach him the different healing properties of the herbs and spices she used, and how to apply them to various wounds, as Much had expressed interest in that as well.

In every village the group entered there was plenty of gossip in the tavern common rooms about the politics of the world. The end of the Crusades was discussed—whether it had been right to go or not in the first place, and whether or not the end was satisfactory—and also the chaos in England. Rumors abounded that the country was in shambles because the king had abandoned England for his Crusade, and Prince John was ruining things.

They were only rumors and wild speculation, of course, but coupled with the reports that the king had been receiving while still in the Holy Land, it was disheartening. Robin and the king both continued to feel that a few months was all that would be required once they were home to bring everything under order and peace once more, but Much wasn't convinced.

The winter months passed slowly and the group never made it to Saxony, but eventually warmth returned to the air.

"We still have a long way to go," the king said as they set out. The short distances they'd traveled over the winter were going to be a thing of the past as the king was eager to pick up the pace.

Their travels were slow and the king was frustrated by the pace, though it was self-imposed. He didn't want the people they encountered in the various villages where they stayed to be suspicious of five travelers no one knew who seemed to be running from something, so they moved more slowly than they might have otherwise. Never staying long enough to arouse too much attention, but not fleeing either.

Much began to feel more hopeful about their eventual arrival home. Nothing had waylaid them since their long march began, and now he was beginning to have the same sort of faith and confidence in all things working together for good that Dusty had—and, therefore, felt on a deep level that even if something were to occur, God would still have their best interest at heart and would look out for them. Much could see that He had been doing so all along, even when Much didn't know to look for the signs of His faithfulness—He was there.

One day, the king sent Much ahead to procure rooms for the night at the village they were approaching. He generally sent Robin, or even Allen, but Much felt more than up to the task.

He entered the village, nodding a greeting to the various people who were in the street going about their business. He scouted out several inns along the edges of the town, stopping a passerby to ask which they felt was the most reputable.

"Staying long?" the man asked, his English overshadowed by a deep accent.

"A few days, probably, before we pass on."

"Where are you traveling to?"

"Wherever my master leads."

"That's vague enough," the man chuckled. Then he pointed out the tavern he'd recommend and moved on as Much entered the establishment and spoke with the tavern keeper to procure rooms for his party. It all went off relatively smoothly, and Much confidently returned to his party on the outskirts of the village.

They moved into the village together and Much led them toward the tavern, where the king stopped with his hands on his hips to give the building a once-over.

"I believe you've found us a good place, Much. I wasn't sure our mouse could manage the mission, but you did."

"Thank you, Sire," Much said, biting his cheek against the comments he wished to speak against the condescension the king was clearly displaying. It had once been easy to ignore people's comments —a simple bite of the cheek would remind him to keep his place. But now that he was beginning to know his own value as a person loved and chosen by God, it became more difficult to take people's comments in stride. He knew now that he did deserve to be treated better than that.

"Much!" Robin's reproachful voice brought Much out of his reverie. "How many times do we have to tell you?"

Robin was glancing about the street at the villagers walking past on business of their own, and Much suddenly realized he must have addressed the king formally once more.

"I am sorry, it was the slip of the tongue."

"You have to stop doing that."

King Richard placed a hand on Robin's arm. "Let us move inside. We don't need to draw more attention with this argument than his off-hand comment would have on its own."

A glance along the street suggested to Much that no one was paying their little group any attention, but they hurried inside nonetheless and moved to their rooms for privacy. As soon as they were alone, Allen turned toward Much with flashing eyes.

"You have to stop doing that. Pay more attention to what you say."

"I do try," Much replied. "It's an old habit and hard to break."

166

"Don't continue to scold him, Allen," the king sighed. "He means well."

"Thank you, Your Ma—"

"Much!" Robin and Allen both threw up their hands in exasperation as the king chuckled. Much sighed.

"Sorry. Perhaps I should stop trying to talk to the king at all."

"You mean to Richard," Allen replied with a roll of his eyes. "He's just Richard. Come on, maybe you need to practice. Repeat after me: Richard."

It was Much's turn to roll his eyes. "Thank you for the assistance, but I think I can manage."

"Clearly you can't."

"Allen!" Dusty cut in, "That's enough."

"We will not stay long in this village," the king said. "The people of…where are we?"

"Scheifling," Robin said.

"Yes, Scheifling. They may or may not have noticed Much's slip, but I wouldn't want to risk staying if they did. We'll leave in the morning. Someone might have heard our mouse calling me 'sire' and I don't want to deal with the consequences if they did."

Early the next morning, they set out from the tavern. There were few people in the street so early in the morning—they'd left without so much as a breakfast from the tavern for the king was eager to be one their way—and those who were up and about paid little attention to the group heading out of town.

As they passed the last house and left the village behind, Much could feel tension easing in his shoulders. He hadn't wanted to admit it, but he'd been on edge since the moment he'd made his mistake yesterday and he was glad to be away from any potential danger.

167

As soon as he thought it, he heard the sounds of hoofbeats coming along the road behind him.

The king glanced over his shoulder and then stopped walking. "This does not look good."

Much turned to see who was following after them and saw a company of soldiers on horseback hurrying down the road from the village they had just exited.

Robin and Allen drew their swords immediately, moving instinctively in front of King Richard.

"There are twenty-seven of them," Allen said. "We're outnumbered by a large margin."

"Doesn't matter," Robin replied. "We defend the king regardless."

"Robin." The king spoke quietly, but there was a firm note to his voice. "There is no need to die here. We will see what they want."

Much's heart sank into his toes as the men galloped up to them and soon had their small group surrounded.

"King Richard the Lion-Heart," the leader of the group called out. "You have been a hard man to find since your disappearance after the end of the Crusade. There is no need to hide your identity any longer. We have orders to arrest you and bring you to Durnstein castle."

"Who gave you such an order?" Robin demanded, his sword still gripped tightly in his hand. The soldiers around them were all armed as well, and every sword and spear was pointed directly toward the five of them.

"We come by order of Duke Leopold of Austria, who is most displeased with the King of England."

"You cannot arrest a Crusader," Dusty said. "It's an affront to the church of the Holy Roman Emperor, is it not?"

"We'll see about that," the man scoffed.

There wasn't much of a fight. Robin clearly wanted to defend the king, but he told him to put away his weapon. With the king surrendering, there was nothing more to be done. Robin reluctantly released his weapon to the soldiers, who took everyone's swords, bows, and daggers and then bound their hands behind their back and began to lead them down the road.

During the long march to Durnstein castle, the scoffing and scorning of their captors sank deep into Much's heart and mind. This was his fault.

It was a week before they arrived at Durnstein castle, where they were promptly thrown into a cell in the dungeon. The long hallway on a lower level of the castle was lined with rooms that were used as cells, and it was into one of these that they were all escorted.

The cell was roughly six feet across both ways, with stone walls on three sides, along with a dirt floor and an iron gate to shut them in.

Much sat against the back wall of the cell, glancing around at the confines of their prison, and then at each of his companions in turn.

"I am sorry."

"There's nothing to be done about it now," Robin sighed from where he stood by the bars of the cell, glaring at the guards at the far end of the dungeon.

Allen crossed his arms. "He could have listened to us in the first place and just called the king 'Richard' like everyone else."

"Leave him be." Dusty glared at Allen. "You've made mistakes, too."

"It's not my fault we're in this prison!"

"Maybe this is where God wants us to be for now, have you thought about that?"

For a moment, silence greeted her question, and then the king tilted his head to one side as he regarded her. "God? What does he have to do with us being thrown into prison?"

"I believe God is in control of everything that happens to us," Dusty said. "So He has a lot to do with us being thrown into prison. Maybe there is something for us to learn here, maybe He wants us to witness to the prison guards and spread His love here, maybe something far worse would have befallen us if we'd continued on our journey and He is protecting us from whatever it might have been. There are endless possibilities. Maybe whatever this experience turns out to be will strengthen our character in some fashion, or draw us closer in our relationship to the Father." Dusty glanced toward Much and smiled. "Who knows?"

"What are you going on about?" Allen asked. "We're not Friars or monks or whatever."

"No, but we're Christians."

Robin shook his head. "Not like you are. You take everything far too seriously."

"Robin—"

"Not now, Dusty!" Robin shook his head. "We're stuck in a prison and really ought to be working on how to get out, not arguing over theology that doesn't matter."

"It does matter." Dusty frowned, a crease forming in her brow. "It matters more than anything else in this world. Your life depends upon it."

Allen rolled his eyes. "Now really, Dusty, don't be so melodramatic."

Dusty didn't say anything further, lowering her head. Allen might have thought she'd given up the argument in defeat, but Much could tell that she was, in fact, praying.

He wanted to come to her defense, and to the defense of the gospel she so firmly believed in. He shared that belief now, after all. She was right; it was the most important thing they could ever discuss. But Much was the reason they were all in this cell and he was sure none of them would be willing to hear him out. Not only was he a servant whose opinion should not matter to a nobleman, but now he was the cause of their distress as well.

Chapter 20

THE DAYS BEGAN to pass most unpleasantly. There was little space in the cell—during the day the five of them sat or stood around the edges, trying to stay out of each other's way as much as possible; at night there wasn't enough room for all of them to lay down comfortably, so they would crowd together—laying on their sides close together, or leaning against the cold stone walls and attempting to find rest in that position.

For the most part they were left on their own, their only view of other people coming from the front of the cell where there was an iron gate rather than a stone wall, and from there they could see the guards at the end of the hall. There did not appear to be anyone else in the various cells along the hallway, but Much imagined in a castle of this size the dungeon continued on for some time beyond what they could see, and there were undoubtedly other helpless prisoners rotting beneath the castle somewhere.

The light in the dungeon was dim at the best times, but not too dark for Much to notice a rat or two scurrying along the hallway now and again. The most interesting occurrence each day was the changing of the guards at the end of the hall, but they rarely spoke to the prisoners. Food was brought once or twice a day—maggoty bread, slimy water, nothing worth eating.

As the days bled together, Allen's anger at Much did not subside. He rarely spoke to him at all if he could help it. Given the cramped quarters, meager rations, and long boring hours stuck in the cell, Robin and the king became rather snappish as well and Much found himself the recipient of their pent up energy and frustration more often than not.

He didn't blame them. He'd gotten them all stuck in this place, it was his fault. They could abuse him if they desired; taking it quietly was the least he could do to make amends for the predicament he'd gotten them into.

One night, Much sat in one of the back corners of the cell, keeping himself as out of the way as possible while the king, Dusty, and Allen stretched out to sleep—as much as one could—along the floor. Robin shifted carefully along the wall in the dim light until he reached Much's side, and then sat beside him.

"We're in an interesting dilemma," Robin said quietly as Allen began to snore.

"I'm sorry." Much meant it. He'd been an idiot to give away the king after so many warnings to watch his tongue, and now that they were stuck in this prison, he felt the weight of his guilt crushing down on him like the weight of Durnstein castle upon the dungeon.

"You cannot continue to blame yourself, Much. What's done is done."

"I truly am sorry. I never intended to get us thrown in this prison, and if there was some way that I could get us out, I would."

"I know. You don't have to apologize. Though I feel that I owe you an apology."

"For what?"

"For not being a good friend to you these last few weeks."

"How so?"

"I have taken out my frustration on you; being locked up is not sitting well with me. But you deserve more from me than to be insulted and belittled."

174

"I forgive you, Robin."

"I'm sure you do, because you're a saint, but I am sorry for it all the same.

To fill their hours, Dusty began to sit with Much and tell him more about the herbs and spices she used for healing. She did not have any on her anymore—given that they were searched and their pockets emptied when they were thrown in the cell—so she no longer had a visual aid when teaching him, but Much was more than happy to simply listen to her talk about her work. She was knowledgeable, and a gentle and patient teacher, and Much already knew she was proficient as well because he'd seen her healing in action.

One day, when their rations were brought and they each studied the moldy bread trying to decide just how hungry they were, Allen heaved his toward Much. The green hunk of bread hit Much across the face.

"You can have my portion of that rot," Allen hissed, crossing his arms. "It's your fault we're here."

"Allen!" Dusty chided.

Much felt a flash of annoyance and nearly glared at Allen. Robin was right; he did deserve better than to be treated the way that he had been since they'd been locked in this cell. But Allen was right, too —it was Much's fault they were here.

The king sighed heavily, looking about at the group. "This is no one's fault but my own. We are here, not because Much misspoke, but because I alienated Duke Leopold at Acre. If the Duke was not angry with me, he would not have seen fit to throw us in prison as we crossed his lands."

"It matters not," Dusty said, "Nothing can be done about it now. Laying blame is not helping anyone."

175

Allen huffed loudly from the corner of the cell where he was sitting, but he said nothing. Much winced at his frustrated exhale of breath and on reflex opened his mouth to apologize. Robin cuffed his shoulder in an affectionate way and shook his head, silencing the apology before it left Much's mouth.

Life continued on in the same manner for some weeks, nothing of interest happening during the day except the changing of the guards at the end of the hall, the occasional scurrying of rats, and Allen's perpetual frustration with Much.

Soon, however, a new development began to spice up their dull existence. The Duke of Austria began to visit the prison cell every day or two to ridicule King Richard. The two would hiss and snarl at each other through the iron gate while Much crept into the back corner of the cell. Robin and Allen had no qualms jumping into the fray, shouting their own insults toward the Duke.

Dusty never joined the argument, and Much certainly did not. The only interesting thing Much learned from these encounters was that the Duke was holding them for ransom and hoping to drain England dry or let the king rot in his dungeon.

One night, after they'd been imprisoned for nearly two full months, Much sat in his corner of the cell listening to the gentle snoring of his companions. The king, Robin, and Dusty were sound asleep. Allen kept shifting his position on the dirt floor, which led Much to believe he was still awake. The light within the cell was as dim as it always was, but Much could make out the shadowy lump that was Allen, rolling first one way and then another in the small amount of space allotted to him.

That day, Allen hadn't spoken a single word to Much, but that was better than the days he ranted and threw bread at him. Much still felt the weight of his guilt bearing down on him.

Robin would likely never see Marian again—she'd never know how he died, either. She'd probably assume he died fighting in the Crusades when the truth was that he slowly rotted away in a prison cell.

Allen shifted again, and Much glanced toward the shadow of his form on the floor.

"Allen?"

For a moment there was silence, and then Allen sighed. "What do you need?"

"You know I am sorry I got us into this mess."

Allen was quiet, and Much bit his lip. The confidence that had been growing in him while they were traveling—particularly after his encounter with Jesus—had been shriveling in this prison cell. Who was he to assume he had value to add to anyone's life? After all, the best he could manage was getting his whole crew thrown into prison.

Allen sighed again, and then he spoke softly into the darkness, "Our companions are right, Much. I suppose this was bound to happen. We were surrounded by enemies and our swift traveling could easily have been suspicious at some point."

Much didn't respond. The vague idea that it could have happened anyway did nothing to assuage his guilt—*maybe* it could have happened that way, but it didn't. Much caused this disaster.

"I know I've been ignoring you and tearing into you by turns, and I am sorry."

Much felt a jolt of surprise run through him. Allen was apologizing?

177

"I should not be treating you like this. I have been—I *am*—upset by what has happened. I do not wish to be in prison, I don't want the king in prison. I don't want to die here. But I cannot continue to hold it against you. You are sometimes a foolish little mouse, indeed, but you are a good-natured one and don't mean any harm."

Much was growing to hate the nickname Dusty had given him. When Dusty said it, there was no malice in it, but ever since the rest of the group had picked up on it Much felt every ounce of their condescension deep in his bones every time he heard it.

"Let's put it behind us, Much. We should devote our energies to finding a way out of this prison rather than arguing among ourselves, after all."

"Do you think we can?"

"If we work together, we will find a way. We survived the Crusades…and if a mouse like you can make it through the war unscathed, anything is possible."

Much bit down hard on his cheek, the metallic taste of his own blood filling his mouth.

Chapter 21

THE DAYS CONTINUED to pass in relative boredom. The group could not live in such close quarters—never having relief from one another's company—without a few arguments arising between them, but for the most part they would sit on the dirt floor of their cell and do nothing.

When the Duke visited to gloat, Robin and Allen got their only entertainment for the week as they and the king traded insults with him, but Much did not enjoy or partake in that activity.

Much's only enjoyment came from Dusty continuing to teach him—she began to write out Scriptures using her finger to carve letters into the dirt floor as she told him more about the faith that they shared.

At first she'd written in Arabic, which had gotten Robin's attention and he'd begged to learn to speak her native language. Dusty agreed to Robin's request and so to pass the long boring hours in the cell she began to teach everyone. Yet when speaking of Scripture with Much she switched to writing in English.

Much had great difficulty comprehending Dusty's Arabic lessons, but Robin seemed to have a keen mind for it. At any rate, it was something to do and even the king joined in to be free of boredom for a few hours.

The summer came and went in this fashion, with everyone in the cell attending to Dusty's lessons on Arabic and her faith—most were far less interested in the latter, but Much enjoyed everything she had to say.

Late in the year—after one of the many snarling matches between the Duke and the residents of the cell had ended and he'd left them in peace—Robin threw himself onto the floor of the cell in a most dramatic fashion and groaned.

"I give up!"

"On what?" the king asked.

"Everything. We'll never get out."

"Nonsense," the king replied. "The Duke has said he's holding us for ransom, has he not? I believe he is capable of doing something so treacherous as hold a king for ransom. And if he is, my people will pay."

"But your brother is running your kingdom, remember?" Robin said. "Even if you have forgotten, I can still hear the voices of those who spoke of the terrible things that were happening in England by the hand of Prince John. I still recall the day you informed me your brother was most likely involved in the murder of my own father!"

"I have not forgotten all the reports," King Richard said. "But I do believe the people will pay the ransom. Even if they will not, my mother Queen Eleanor will see to it that we are released. My sister Joan will be equally anxious to get you out of prison."

Winter came, but there was little change to their situation except the temperature of their cell. The cool stone walls grew colder and Much spent most of his days shivering between Robin and Dusty. As the air grew colder—enough that they could often see their own breath in the air in front of them—the five of them took to huddling close together to share what little body heat they possessed.

"I have never been so cold before!" Allen complained one day.

"Surely you remember those days in the Holy Land when the rain was never ending?" Dusty asked with a laugh. "I thought you would never stop complaining about the cold then."

"I forgot about that." Allen gave Dusty a wry grin and Much could tell she'd broken the sour mood. "You are right. That was just as miserable."

"I think this is worse," Robin said. "Because we can't do anything. We're just stuck in prison, freezing to death."

"It is not quite that dramatic, Robin," King Richard laughed.

"So you're not so cold you're too stiff to move?" Allen asked. "I'm frozen solid."

"As am I," Robin nodded firmly to Much's left, though the way he shifted his sitting position as he said so belied his words.

"It is cold, I don't deny that," King Richard said. "But I refuse to freeze to death."

Allen rolled his eyes. "You are like Robin, Sire. You prefer to blatantly lie to make yourself look good."

"What?" King Richard turned his raised eyebrows toward Robin.

Robin shrugged. "I don't know what he's talking about."

Allen reached around Dusty and Much to whack Robin's arm, hitting both in the process. "Yes, you do! You would never complain about anything on our travels to impress Sir Adam and anyone else watching. I'm sure Much remembers."

"I remember you calling Robin a liar," Much replied.

King Richard threw back his head with a laugh. "You've offended the mouse, Allen."

Allen shrugged. "You can't say anything against Robin, true or otherwise, without offending the mouse."

Much bit his cheek. He hated that nickname and he was tempted to say as much, or to start giving them all annoying pet names of his own. But he held his tongue, as he always did. God might find value in him because He created him, but on earth he was still a nobody whose opinion mattered to no one but himself, and perhaps Dusty.

Winter passed away, and with the dawning of spring came a new determination from Allen and Robin to find a way out of the dungeons. Robin felt their knowledge of the schedule of the changing of the guards at the door might be useful, and Allen suggested they dig through the back wall.

"It is out of the line of sight of the guards," Allen whispered, his eyes darting toward the iron gate and the hallway of cells beyond it. "We can see them, and they us, only when we're up at the front of the cell.

"But it would take so long," Dusty replied. "And when our meals are brought, and when the Duke visits, we'll be found out."

A few more weeks passed as Allen, Robin, and Dusty debated possible solutions. Much did not offer any wild schemes to try and escape the dungeons. He wished there was a solution so he could absolve some of his guilt by freeing his companions, but he could see no way out of this situation that didn't end with them being caught and probably killed.

The air was still cold, and Much wondered if the world above was covered in snow. The king developed a cough, but Dusty laid her hands on him and prayed for him and his illness passed. Even without her herbs there was healing in her fingertips and Much was forced to confront the idea that the God he was slowly getting to know was powerful and could work miracles.

One day as his companions carried on their hushed conversations, dreaming of wild escapes, Much leaned against the back wall of the cell in the corner he so often found himself in. The stones gave way slightly against his shoulder and he straightened, turning to look at the wall.

In the dim light of the cell it looked the same as always, but when he reached out to touch it his fingers sank into the soft soil in the cracks around the stone. It wasn't deep, hardly enough to even need to wipe the remains off his hand onto his trousers, but enough that'd he'd noticed.

As fascinating as the wet wall was, Much turned around, leaning against it as usual and watching his companions. What was a little more mud on his back? His clothes were filthy. He reeked, as did his companions, and the cell in general. They were not given the decency of a lavatory, after all, and they had been in this place for months.

When she wasn't joining in planning for a hopeful escape, Dusty continued to teach Arabic to the group. She would often use her finger to draw in the dirt of the floor to show them the words she was saying, but this did little to enlighten Much. The little squiggles and lines she drew on the floor were fascinating, but Much could make no sense of them even with her patient help. Robin and Allen, however, seemed to take to it easier than he. The king listened to the lessons with mild interest, but the longer they sat in the cell the more downcast he became and the less interested he was in any conversation happening around him.

One night, Much saw Dusty studying the back wall of the cell, and then motion to Robin and Allen. With significant glances and hand gestures she seemed to be pointing out the mud seeping through the cracks.

Allen reached out and wiped his hand across the stones, taking a glob of mud with him.

183

"It's the moisture," Dusty whispered. "It must have snowed through the winter, and given way to rain now that it's spring. It's softening the earth."

"So we *can* dig." Allen grinned, wiping the mud from his hand across his trousers.

Much felt a flash of annoyance toward himself and then a sharp jealousy. He'd noticed the softening of the back wall days before, but now that Dusty was pointing it out his chance to prove himself worthy once more was gone. Why hadn't he thought of Allen's escape plan when he'd first noticed the wall?

"But we're so far beneath the castle," Robin said, wiping his own hand slowly across the back wall. "If we dig…we'll have miles, perhaps, to dig to the top. Where will all that dirt go? It won't fit in this cell. Once it spills out, the guards will notice."

"They'll notice before that, when they bring food and see us digging along the back wall." Dusty said.

"But we can try," Allen said. "It's something; it's all we've got."

Robin shrugged. "We can certainly try."

Much shifted closer to the wall, running his own hand through the mud. There was a great deal more of it than when he'd first noticed the change. "We cannot be too deep if the moisture on the surface is affecting this wall."

"It is odd," Robin agreed. "I guess we'll find out how far we have to go once we start digging. Allen's right; it's our only shot. I'm not so sure it will work, but we have to try something."

So every night the group began to work on the back wall, loosening a few stones to pull from the wall in order to use them as digging tools before carving into the muddied earth of the wall. They

184

picked a low section of the wall, one they could easily sit in front of and cover whenever food was brought to the cell.

The king watched with little interest, slumped against one of the cold stone walls.

They worked for several days, until their haphazard carving tools cut through the wall, Robin's hand disappearing for a moment before he pulled it back.

He glanced at Allen, and then the two of them began digging with a vengeance, pushing the earth as much as digging it out until there was a hole large enough for Robin to shove his head through.

His muffled voice came drifting back through the wall.

Allen whacked his arm. "What?"

Robin pulled his muddied head back into the cell. "There's a hallway of sorts, a tunnel."

"A tunnel? That is definitely our way out."

"Why is there a tunnel by the dungeons?" Much asked.

"Castles have plenty of secrets," Robin said, winking at Much. "Ours certainly does, if you recall."

Much couldn't argue with that.

"We have to be quick," Dusty said. "We have to carve a big enough hole to fit through, get everyone out, and then get far enough away that we won't be caught once the guards bring our food, realize what's happened, and come after us."

"It's risky, but we can do it," Robin said. "We'll be fast." He immediately started digging again.

Much fell asleep watching Allen and Robin furiously dig at the hole in the dim light. He awoke to Dusty shaking him. "We need to go."

"Go?"

"To England! Wake up."

Much squinted around the cell. Robin and Allen were speaking quietly to each other in one corner, near the hole. The king sat across from them, slumped against his wall, with a slight frown on his face.

"Robin?"

"Yes, Sire?"

"Your plan is risky."

"We know that, Richard."

"And you know that if you are caught—which is likely—you will undoubtedly be killed by the Duke."

"We are well aware, but we have to get out."

"I am no good to England dead, Robin. I cannot come with you."

"Richard!"

"No, do not try to argue with me. I cannot take the risk."

"It is dangerous," Dusty said. "Perhaps if we wait, the ransom will be paid."

Allen crossed his arms. "I refuse to be too afraid to do this. I will not stay in this prison."

"Robin is no use to England—or Marian—dead either," Dusty said. "If we stay, we have no risk of being killed by the Duke."

"Just of dying from the cold, the lack of nourishing food, the fact we haven't seen the sun in who knows how long," Allen began to tick reasons off of the fingers of one hand.

Much listened to his four companions as they continued to debate whether or not they should go, and whether or not the king should stay behind.

Much knew he would go wherever Robin did. His own opinion on the pros and cons of the options laid before them hardly mattered, as evidenced by the fact that none of his friends turned to him to ask for his thoughts on the matter.

Finally, the king said, "You have to go, Robin. We heard many terrible reports about what is happening in England. I believe my people are suffering. But I cannot leave here and risk it. I will wait for the ransom. Yet I cannot leave my people to their fate, whatever it is. You have to go."

"Richard—"

"No, Robin. Do not try to change my mind. Just go. I'm entrusting England to you. Keep my people safe."

Robin hesitated, but a loud guffaw from one of the guards stationed at the end of the hall set everyone's hearts racing, and Allen immediately pushed through the hole that had been created in the back of the cell.

Much looked to Robin, as did the king. Robin slowly reached out to clasp the king's hand. "I will look after England. I promise, I will."

"I trust you."

"And I will see to it that your ransom is paid as swiftly as I can."

"Go, Robin! You are needed in England."

Robin squeezed through the small opening after Allen, and then Much followed suit. Last of all came Dusty.

"We have to hurry," Dusty said as she straightened. The dim light from the cell drifted through the hole, but it did not illuminate much of the tunnel they had entered. "Who knows how soon the guards will notice what has transpired."

"Where are we?" Much wondered aloud.

"In a passageway in the castle?" Robin shrugged. "The wall is clearly the back of our cell, the whole tunnel seems to be encased in dirt…there's no stone work on the walls or floor that I can see or touch."

"Where does it lead is a better question," Dusty said.

"We will find out when we follow it," Robin replied. He took the lead, and Much walked close behind him, reaching forward to put his hand on Robin's shoulder. Dusty's hand came to rest on his own shoulder, and he imagined Allen must have done the same to her.

Much wondered what Robin's plan would be if the tunnel led to a dead end, or if it opened into a populated area where there would be soldiers nearby. The entire plan seemed only half thought out and haphazardly thrown together, but they were rather desperate, after all, and it seemed their only chance.

Moving through the darkness of the tunnel reminded Much of wandering through the secret passages within Nottingham castle. The major difference, however, was that every dark hallway and every crack in the cool stone walls of the castle in Nottingham were familiar and he could always orient himself and know where he was. The dirt of the tunnel they traversed was just…dirt. Unfamiliar, eerily quiet, with no way to know where it would eventually lead.

Every once in a while they passed openings where the tunnel branched off in other directions. The darkness never changed, but the change in the air—and sometimes even the hint of movement in the air—alerted Much to the change. Robin kept moving along the straight path, however, and so everyone else followed his lead.

A few more minutes of wandering blindly into the passageway and Much could see a light glimmering in the distance. As they drew closer to it, the tunnel slowly began to become visible around them in the same sort of dim light that the cell had been provided with for all the months they'd been trapped in Durnstein castle. Much could see the dirt floor, walls, and ceiling. He could see Robin in front of him, walking confidently down the unfamiliar tunnel.

Slowly, the light grew brighter until they reached the end of the tunnel where torches were hanging in sconces along the wall. Passages branched off in several directions, most of them lit with torches, and here the dirt floor gave way to a stone pavement.

"I think we've come to the portion of these tunnels people use," Dusty commented.

"For what purpose though?" Allen asked.

"Back home, where Much and I are from, there's a castle that is filled with secret passages," Robin said. "They were originally built for the nobility to have ways to escape if their fortress was overrun. I imagine these hold a similar purpose for the Duke."

"Which way do we go?" Much asked.

Robin shrugged and started walking, throwing his hands to either side. "I'm sure this leads somewhere."

As Robin began walking down one of the hallways with a stone floor, Much hurried after him. It wasn't long before Dusty and Allen fell in line as well.

The passage sloped gently upward, and before long it stopped at a door. Robin paused, glanced silently at his companions, and raised a finger to his lips. Then he tried the handle.

It was unlocked.

Slowly, Robin pushed the door inward and Much held his breath. They were entirely unarmed, malnourished, and in need of a nap. They would be hard pressed to win a fight if they surprised guards on the other side of the door.

Robin glanced past the door as he slid it open, and then he visibly relaxed. He glanced over his shoulder long enough to wink at Much and then slipped inside the room. Much immediately followed.

Past the door was a small room with no furnishings, smaller than the cell they'd been kept in. Robin was already at the other side of the room pushing open another door. That one led into a hallway. It was wide, well-lit, with a stone floor and many wooden doors on both walls at various intervals.

"I think we're in the actual castle," Dusty whispered.

Robin nodded, putting a hand to his lips again. He began moving down the hallway, and the others followed after him.   They had no clear idea where they were going, and certainly no knowledge of the layout of the castle, but Robin led them through corridor after corridor. Judging by the grey light of dawn creeping through the windows they passed, it was quite early in the morning. Thankfully, that meant most of the castle was still asleep. They met few individuals as they traveled, and those they did see, they saw from a distance—at the end of hallways or in rooms with doors slightly ajar.

It wasn't too difficult for the group to keep out of sight until they found a door out to the courtyard of the castle. From there they sneaked their way along the edge of the courtyard near the wall, keeping out of sight—hopefully—of any soldiers that might be on lookout or patrol. There was a guard house at the gate, which Much felt could pose a problem, but Robin seemed undeterred.

When they reached the guard house, Robin ducked low to avoid windows, and slowly crept along the ground. He raised himself slightly, peeked in the nearest window, and then grinned and glanced back toward Much and the others who were anxiously waiting by the wall.

190

Robin mimed sleeping gestures toward them, still grinning, and then stood up and sprinted past the guardhouse. Much took a deep breath, trying to still his racing heart, and then took off running after Robin. Allen and Dusty followed, and the group ran as fast as they could away from Durnstein.

Once they were several miles from the castle, Robin led them toward an outcropping of trees and they finally stopped running.

Much collapsed onto the ground wheezing, his hand holding his side where he'd developed a stitch.

"What's…the…plan…" Allen panted as he sank to the ground beside Much.

"We have no money, no food," Dusty glanced around at the group. "We're weak and malnourished. What *is* the plan, Robin?"

"We go home."

"Yes, that much is obvious. But how do you plan to do that?"

"Very carefully," Robin said. He looked around at the trees and then shrugged. "We press forward. Maybe we can get work in a village in exchange for food and lodging, and then we keep traveling onward."

"And if we get arrested because the Duke sends people after us?" Dusty raised an eyebrow. "Or if we get arrested because the village we beg for work in doesn't take kindly to vagabonds dressed in refuse-covered rags?"

"We'll deal with the situations as they arise," Robin said. "As it stands right now…we can sit in this bit of trees until we starve to death, we can go back to the castle and turn ourselves in, or we can press forward. I vote for the latter."

191

Chapter 22

THE GROUP TRUDGED across the countryside—knolls of tall grass rising and falling between lakes of shimmering blue in the distance and even further away tall mountains—for a few hours until they came in sight of a town. It was larger than some villages that were merely a collection of buildings with a street or two that they'd skirted around—this town had several streets, shops, and even a small wall around a portion of it, but it was by no means as populated as a city like Nottingham.

The group paused while still a distance from the town and Robin stared at it with his hands on his hips. They were not yet traveling by an actual road, simply cutting across the grassy fields and hills to avoid detection.

"Do we go in?" Allen asked.

"We reek," Robin replied with a frown. "Dusty was right; we'll be no better than street scum to anyone of prestige. We'll get thrown out."

"It is always possible there will be people of compassion," Dusty said. "If there is an abbey or monastery we could start there."

Much surveyed the view before them—the town, nestled up against a grassy knoll looking inviting and menacing at the same time; the surrounding countryside full of green grass, a few trees. Judging by the placement of the tree line off to the right, it was possible there was a stream in that direction. They could possibly try and bathe and look a bit more presentable before going into town. It was too far of a walk to get to the lake on the horizon and they weren't headed that direction anyway.

His traveling companions were also surveying the countryside and the town, probably all debating what the next course of action should be.

"Let's go in," Robin said at last. "We can't just stand here all day."

He set off toward the road to the left of them that led into the town, and Dusty and Allen immediately followed. Much glanced toward the treeline to his right for a moment, and then followed after Robin.

As they entered the town by the road, several people who were going about their business turned to stare at the group. Robin moved to speak to them, but they all turned and hurried along.

"We're disgusting and look ridiculous." Allen sighed, scratching his beard.

A tall man, muscular, with a sword at his hip soon approached them.

"What is your business here?" he asked in German. Much's brain scrambled for a moment, trying to place the words. He wasn't quite as familiar with the language as he was with French.

"We are Crusaders merely trying to return home," Robin said.

The man eyed each of them in turn, his eyebrows rising as he undoubtedly took in the dirt, refuse, and tattered clothing hanging off of their thin frames.

"I speak the truth," Robin said. "I would be more than happy to supply you with dates, names, facts of our travels, battles, and the like. If you hand me a bow I can prove my prowess with the weapon."

"I am not about to arm vagabonds who came wandering into my town smelling like they've been sleeping in horse manure."

"I have no other proof to offer you," Robin said. "We have had some unfortunate adventures on our journey home, and we are penniless, weaponless, and rather disgusting, as you can see and smell no doubt."

"Where is home for you?"

"England."

"Ah." The man nodded thoughtfully. "Rumor has it the Duke is holding your king hostage somewhere and demanding ransom for him."

"So they say," Robin replied. "Many of your people have been more than happy to mistreat us on the Duke's behalf. I was hoping you would be different, and would respect Crusaders for the work that we have recently done and the horrors we endured during the war."

"*If* you are Crusaders," the man said, suddenly switching to speaking in French. "That remains to be determined. In any event, I am Isenbern, the younger son of Count Jodok. I have charge over this town and the surrounding lands, and I do respect the Crusaders, if that is indeed who you are."

"What can we do to assure you of our honesty?" Robin asked.

Isenbern studied him for a moment, his nose wrinkling. "I'm not taking you into my home just yet, so I'll ask questions here. What is your name?"

"I am Robin, Earl of Locksley," Robin replied. "This is my..." Robin glanced toward Much and his brows drew together for a moment. "My servant Much, my traveling companions, Allen and Dusty."

Isenbern nodded slowly, crossing his arms.

"Much and I met Allen in the city of Dover, just before we set out on the Crusades. We traveled to Sicily, Cyprus, and eventually to Acre where we joined the fight in the Holy Land."

195

Isenbern seemed reluctant still, but he uncrossed his arms and turned and began walking down the street. Robin walked beside him—though Isenbern kept a distance between them, likely due to Robin's stench—and Much and the others followed behind.

Much listened as Robin—with Allen's help—began to tell the tales of their time in Palestine. They told the stories with a relish, polishing them into heroic feats of arms though Much felt they were nothing of the sort.

When they reached a large manor on the end of a street, Isenbern paused. "I would like to continue this discussion once you are…less disgusting. I'll send my servant out who can take you through the servant quarters to get you washed up, and then you can join me in the house proper."

Isenbern disappeared inside the front door.

"This is going easier than I thought it might," Robin said with a satisfied grin.

"Assuming he does send his servant for us, and assuming he doesn't decide to kill us once we're inside," Allen said, "and assuming —"

"Okay, okay," Robin held up his hands. "Be alert, of course. Though without weapons I suppose there's only so much we can do if he is going to try and have us killed."

A young man exited the house a moment later, wrinkling his nose as he drew close to them. "You are far worse than he described," he said. Then he waved for them to follow him and began walking around the manor.

Much and the others dutifully followed him to the back of the house and through a simple door. He led them down a narrow hallway and then into a small room with a wooden tub.

"There. It's got fresh water. If it needs changing after each of you, fine. Knock on the door. I've got Bernhard boiling more water as we speak. Christoph will be waiting for the knock and get Bernhard and the water for you. There's clothes," the young man gestured toward a table near the wooden tub that had four sets of clothes laid out side by side. "Once you're relatively clean and dressed, I'll take you to the master."

"Thank you, uh...your name?" Robin asked.

"Friedrich. My father has run of the household, and I will once he's dead." And with that, Friedrich left the room and pulled the door shut behind him.

"Pleasant fellow," Allen commented.

"I'll wait outside," Dusty said, glancing at the tub and then at Much and the others.

"Oh, Dusty, we can wait," Robin replied. "You go first. Come on." Robin grabbed Allen with one hand and Much with the other and dragged them toward the door. "Let us know when you're through."

In the hall stood another young person around their age, presumably Christoph.

"Are you already in need of fresh water?" he asked.

"No," Robin replied. "We just decided to bathe in more privacy."

They only waited in the hall with Christoph for a few minutes before Dusty appeared at the door. Her skin was clean, the stench was gone, and her dark hair had gentle waves that Much had never seen before. He'd always seen her hair cut short when clean, and in the prison it was long but so dirty and stringy that he hadn't seen it in its glory. He rather liked it.

"Who's next?" Dusty asked. "Also, I need my hair cut."

"We need a shave, too," Robin commented, rubbing his chin. Robin turned to Christoph, "Could you help with that?"

Christoph glanced between Robin and Dusty, his eyes widening. "Uh, yeah, I can get a shaving kit…and, uh…sorry, my lady," Christoph awkwardly bowed to Dusty. "I didn't…I mean…Friedrich said there were four men…"

Dusty smiled. "Yes, that is rather the point."

Christoph stared a moment longer before he started, shook himself, and moved off down the hall, presumably in search of the shaving kit and some implement to cut Dusty's hair.

They each began to take a turn in the bath—with Bernhard bringing fresh water between each bath, and Christoph returning with shears for Dusty and a small knife for shaving the unwanted beards—and when it came to Much's turn he sank into the heated water with a relish. His aching muscles relaxed in the heat, and the grime of the Crusades, traveling, and imprisonment all began to wash from his skin. It took some scrubbing to get all of it off, but it was a relief to see the color of his skin was still there underneath all the dirt once it began to come free.

Once they were all clean, shaved, and Dusty's hair was cropped short once more, Christoph fetched Friedrich who in turn led them through several corridors away from the servants' part of the house and into the nobility portion. The rooms were wider, ceilings higher, and furniture far more ornate in this part of the manor—none of which surprised Much. He'd spent his whole life walking between the servants' half of a manor and the noble half.

Friedrich led them into a wide room with a large hearth, with several chairs pulled around it—wooden chairs with pillows piled in them to make them more comfortable, as well as a low settee. There was a wooden desk on one side of the room, and several bookcases along the walls. Lord Isenbern was sitting by the low fire—far smaller than it could have been given the proportion of the hearth as a whole.

"Ah, I can almost see the Earl in you," he said to Robin as they entered the room. "Come, sit."

He waved to the chairs by the fire, and they all sat down.

"I have been informed one of your number is, in fact, a girl. I apologize, my lady, for your treatment in this house thus far."

Dusty shook her head. "I am used to far worse, Lord Isenbern. And I am not a lady—my parents were no more nobility than Much's, but I appreciate your concern. As it is, we have found it safer on our travels to let the world believe I am not a woman, so if you would be so kind as to keep our secret…"

Isenbern dipped his head. "As you wish, my lady." Then turning to Robin, "Now, tell me about your travel and battles during the Crusade."

Robin and Allen delighted Lord Isenbern with their tales for some time, and as they talked, more of his servants appeared bringing platters of food along with a small wooden table upon which the food was placed.

The moment the smell of the fresh bread hit his nose, Much's mouth filled with saliva. The boiled beef with the minced apples and some sort of sharp sauce that Much did not recognize delighted his taste buds so long deprived of proper food. His stomach appreciated a full meal, too, of course, but Much was more concerned with the taste than the nourishment. He was almost convinced he'd never tasted anything quite as delicious as that first meal Lord Isenbern fed them as Robin and Allen entertained him with their war stories.

"You have convinced me to let you show off your skill," Isenbern said at last. "I wish to see your archery."

He sent for Friedrich, and informed him to bring a bow and meet them outside, and then Isenbern led them to the back of the manor where the sloping hillside provided a grassy enclosed area for them.

A bow was brought, and Lord Isenbern pointed out various targets for Robin—all of which he hit.

"You are as good as you say," Lord Isenbern conceded. "And you speak and hold yourself with the authority of someone well-bred. I am inclined to believe your story, despite your lack of proof."

"I appreciate that," Robin said.

"You can stay here to rest and recuperate," Lord Isenbern said.

"We may need to work here," Robin replied, "as we will need to accrue funds for our further travels."

"I'm sure something can be arranged," Lord Isenbern agreed.

They stayed with Lord Isenbern for several weeks—Robin, Allen, and Much joining the ranks of the town's guards who patrolled along the outer wall of the city to watch for intruders. Dusty helped the sick among the townspeople and earned the most affection of all of them.

Once they'd earned enough from Lord Isenbern's generosity, they set off on their travels again equipped this time with money, clean clothes, and freshly commissioned and purchased weapons of their choice from the town's blacksmith.

At the next village. it was easier to convince the people that they were, indeed, soldiers returning from the Crusades because they were no longer covered in their own refuse and emaciated from lack of proper food. Even so, they traveled at a snail's pace it seemed to Much, who was growing ever more eager to be home and for the whole long adventure to be over and done with.

Chapter 23

TWO MONTHS OF traveling from village to village, using their funds from Lord Isenbern, and they finally made it to the coast. Robin paid for their berths aboard a ship, and they sailed across the channel to England.

As soon as the familiar white cliffs of Dover came into sight, Much felt his throat constrict. He leaned against the railing of the boat, his eyes glued to the English shore as his vision clouded with tears. The sun was shining, there was a light breeze in the air pushing puffy white clouds across the sky, and everything seemed far too perfect. Much was waiting for a disaster to strike as they drew into the harbor, but all appeared well.

Dusty stood beside him at the ship's edge, watching England come ever closer.

"You are nearly home now," Dusty said.

"Yes. I will be glad to return to Locksley for some well deserved peace and quiet."

"It will be pleasant to finally have some calm. And yet…it has been so long since my life has resembled anything close to calm, I am not sure I will know how to live."

"We were pretty calm in that prison, I suppose…"

Dusty laughed, a rare and heartwarming sight, and Much felt his composure return as his tears gave way to lighter feelings.

The moment they disembarked from the ship and set foot on the docks at Dover, Much felt transported to nearly three years ago when he'd first caught sight of the fortress on the hill, and seen the channel and ships for the first time in his life. If he never set foot on another boat again he wouldn't be upset by it.

Robin hurried them toward the tavern they had used for lodging before they left on the Crusades. The barkeep surprisingly remembered them—Much couldn't imagine how, given there had been many young men passing through eager to join the Crusades, and they'd only stayed a few days, and it had now been years since they'd left…but somehow, he knew them as soon as they wandered into the common room and up to the counter to ask for food and lodgings.

There were only a couple people in the common room—the difference between a tavern filled with soldiers eager to follow the king, and one filled with its normal customers. The proprietor soon brought them food at the counter, though it was meager fare compared to how they'd been dining abroad after Lord Isenbern had got them on their feet again. Just a simple loaf of bread and a small chunk of cheese.

"Sorry I don't have real meat as yet, but I can fry a few fish if you need it," he said.

"Why the meager fare?" Robin asked, taking a bite out of the bread.

The innkeeper filled their mugs of ale and spoke softly, "It is Prince John and his men. He has replaced almost every sheriff in England with ruthless men of his own. The taxes are unbearably high and we all suffer for it."

"Surely there is justice somewhere," Allen said.

The innkeeper glanced nervously over his shoulder at the other customers in the room. "If you can't pay the taxes, you'll be hung."

"Surely not!" Much gasped.

"If things continue as they are," the innkeeper said, "the Prince will have no more subjects left to tax."

"Is no one doing anything about it?" Robin asked.

"There are some who fight it, but they never live long. Here at the coast…you'll find more people leaving England as coming here. People are trying to get away from Prince John's ruthless reign."

"We are hoping for a speedy return to our home in Nottingham," Robin said. "Could you direct me to the nearest livery where I can procure horses?"

"Horses?" The innkeeper raised his eyebrows. "Where have you been that you think there are horses to be found?"

"Not in England, clearly," Robin replied. "Listen, it's been a long few years. I am sorry for your troubles, and I aim to do what I can about them for King Richard's sake. Don't worry about the horses, but if you can spare us some provisions for our travel that would be much appreciated."

"I don't have much," the man said. "But I can gather a bit for you, I suppose. Being Crusaders, and all…"

"Thank you."

They finished their meal quietly, and then Robin made arrangements for their provisions to take along on their journey in the morning.

When they retired to their rooms for the night, Robin pulled Much into his room.

"I need to talk to you for a moment."

"Is something the matter?"

"Not at all."

Robin stood in front of the small hearth where a few logs were beginning to crackle merrily to keep away the chill of the evening breeze off the water. Much seated himself on the small bed pushed up against the wall, watching Robin and waiting.

Robin rubbed his hand along his chin and then gave Much a lopsided grin. "I've been thinking about this for a while…for years really, since the Crusades began and our adventures started. I don't think of you as my servant, Much. You are my brother."

"I know."

"I'm not sure you do, as you still answer my every beck and call. But the point I'm making is that I don't want you to be my servant. I appreciate how you look out for me, but I want you to do such as my equal."

"Meaning what?"

"Meaning, I guess I'm relieving you of your duties to me. You are free, to go where you choose, when you choose. Get a job elsewhere, or buy some land and start a manor of your own…whatever you want to do, Much. You're free."

Free.

Free from what, exactly? Assisting Robin and looking after him? He loved him, he'd do that anyway. Free from living at Locksley? Locksley was his home! He had no desire to be anywhere else. As long as he was with Robin and Sarah—assuming she bustled about the kitchen as per usual despite their three year absence—he would have all that he needed.

Much realized Robin was watching him, so he offered a smile. "Thank you."

"I want us to be brothers, truthfully brothers," Robin said. "You owe me nothing. I am not your master."

"I understand, and I appreciate the gesture. If you aren't opposed to it, I would still prefer to live at Locksley…"

"Of course! Locksley is your home for as long as you want it to be."

Much was sure he wasn't reacting as Robin had expected or hoped, but he didn't know how to feel. With nothing else to say, he soon returned to his own room to sleep for the night. Before long it was morning once more and the group set off for home. Much thought the world looked precisely as it had when he was a servant, and he felt the same, too. Nothing had changed. Yet it seemed to make Robin feel better not to be called master, so Much was okay with the new arrangement.

He wanted to be treated as an equal, too. He'd desired to be valued for who he was and not looked down upon, but somehow Robin's gesture didn't feel like he'd expected or wanted equality to feel.

Chapter 24

THEIR TRAVEL HOME was slow as they were on foot, and everywhere they went on their journey home they found the same poverty—people were starving. They also began to witness the cruelty of the soldiers who worked for sheriffs put in place by Prince John—beating people on the streets of the cities they passed through, dragging unfortunate souls from their homes to the prisons in their shires. They passed more than one rotting corpse—both young and old people alike—hanging in the towns they passed, left up as a warning to those who would dream of defying Prince John and his underlings.

Even with those threats and dire warnings however, reports and rumors of the rebellions in various shires and of 'the men of the night' who were secretly fighting back against Prince John and his Sheriffs began to reach them as they traveled.

As they settled around a wooden table in a dimly lit common room in an abbey in the town of Chetham not far from their home shire, Much caught wind of the conversation of a man at a table nearby.

"She just shoved the pouch of coin into my hand and told me to run."

The man was talking to the tavern keeper, and in his lap was a small girl with her arms wrapped protectively around his neck.

"Sounds harrowing," the innkeeper said.

"She was amazing. She knocked him right out with the back of her blade—he didn't even see her coming."

"I wonder why we keep calling these heroes 'men of the night' when nearly as many tales of such exploits seem to include this woman."

"Do you get lots of such stories?" Robin asked, leaning his chair toward the table where the man was sitting.

The man turned to stare at Robin, and the innkeeper went quiet.

"We're no friends of Prince John, I can promise you that," Robin assured them. "We've been away from England for some time, and we're headed home to Nottingham. We've been shocked by the state of affairs here since our arrival, but the rumors of rebellions bring us some hope."

"You are going to the worst and best place in England," the innkeeper said. "Nottingham has the most ruthless of Prince John's servants—Sir Guy of Gisbourne. He's one you don't want to cross. And yet…the rebellion against him and the Sheriff there is the most successful so far, according to rumor. No one's been caught or killed yet."

"The rebellion against the Sheriff?" Much asked. "It is not Sir Godfrey, is it?"

"I wouldn't know," the innkeeper replied.

"I imagine not," Robin said. "Prince John has been assigning his own lackeys to the positions of power throughout England. Sir Godfrey was likely deposed. I doubt he would spend time with this Gisbourne fellow who is said to be so bad. In any case, it is good to hear that our shire is being looked after. I am afraid of what I will find upon our return home."

"These 'men of the night,'" Dusty said, "we hear them spoken of so often…why have those in Nottingham not been killed as so many others have been?"

"They are more secretive," the innkeeper replied. "So far as we can tell, they've been working in hiding, never showing their faces. No one knows who they are…but they always seem to know what the

Sheriff there is planning before he does it—even when he only speaks with his most trusted friend Gisbourne. At least, that's what folks say. I've had people from Nottingham pass through here before, saying they were fleeing after these folks saved them from an unlawful execution or some such, gave them some coin and sent them on their way…"

"It is good to hear," Robin said. "Thank you for trusting us with your confidence." Robin gave a nod to the man with the daughter in his lap, before ordering some food from the innkeeper.

After their food was brought and they were left in peace once more, Robin leaned forward. "You should know before we continue that I am hopeful of finding and joining these 'men of the night' in Nottingham, if we can."

"It does seem the most efficient way of making a difference for the people right now," Dusty said. "At least until the king eventually comes home. The next question will be how we are to raise funds for the ransom to get him home."

"I am not sure about that yet," Robin said. "But I am beginning to have a plan. If the people in Nottingham really do know every scheme of the Sheriff there before his plots are carried out, it is likely they are using the secrets of Nottingham castle to spy on him."

"Secrets of the castle?" Allen asked.

"There are many passageways, a bit like those we found under Durnstein castle," Much said.

"If the 'men of the night' are using those passages, that can only mean Marian is helping them!" Robin grinned.

"Marian?" Allen asked. "How do you figure?"

"It is just what she would do. She'd never stand by and watch all this suffering silently. I'm sure she would feel compelled to do *something*. I wonder if Mark is one of the 'men of the night' and that is how they remain undercover."

"It is possible," Much said.

"When we get home we'll have to go to Wetherby before we head to Locksley village."

Along with the rumors of the 'men of the night' that followed them, the closer they got to Nottingham, the more stories of a mysterious person known as the Hooded Rescuer began to reach their ears.

One day as they stopped to eat a meager lunch on the side of the road, Allen plopped down beside Robin. He'd gone into town to see if there was news and had just returned.

"Everyone has been talking about the Hooded Rescuer's exploits, but that's about it."

"I wonder who it is," Much said.

"And how he fits in with the 'men of the night' we've heard so much about," Robin said.

Another two weeks of travel, and Much and Robin were finally looking on a familiar sight. The tree line that sprouted along their right was their beloved Sherwood Forest, and soon they were crossing the stream where they had played as children with Marian and Mark.

Much could almost smell Sarah's kitchen, almost feel her strong arms wrapping around him. His throat constricted as his heart squeezed inside his chest. They were so close to home.

"Hurry, my friends," Robin said. "We must go to Wetherby! I cannot wait another moment to see Marian!"

Much's heart sank as they turned their direction toward the city of Nottingham and the village of Wetherby a few miles outside the city walls. He couldn't help but glance toward the south where Locksley village and the manor lay, though they were too far distant to see yet.

As soon as they entered the village of Wetherby, Robin marched swiftly down the well-worn street toward Sir Godfrey's house.

Standing outside the house restringing a bow was Marian. Her dark hair, her determined posture; it was all the same as it had been three years ago. Much glanced at Robin, who had stopped walking altogether and was merely watching her silently.

Dusty and Allen came to a halt as well, and joined Much in staring at Robin as he took in the sight of Marian. Suddenly his eyes began to dance and he darted forward.

As Marian laid her bow against the wall of the house, Robin scooped her up from behind, grabbing her waist and spinning her through the air. Allen started laughing quietly beside Much.

"Did you miss me, Marian darling?" Robin asked as Much walked toward them.

Robin set Marian on the ground and she looked up at him silently. He took her hand and clasped it to his heart just as the door of the house opened and a young man leaned against the door frame.

"Who's this?" the newcomer asked.

Robin dropped Marian's hand and muttered something that Much couldn't hear. Whatever he said made Marian smirk as she said, "Will Scarlett, this is Robin of Locksley."

"The Earl?" the stranger asked.

Robin bowed stiffly to the young man named Will. "One and the same." Then he turned back to Marian. "I was sorry to hear of my father's death. I wish I could have been here."

"We were sorry for it, too. And you *should* have been here. Your father's death was one of the first things that spurred me into action."

Much could see a darkness and pain behind Marian's eyes as she spoke to Robin that had never been there before.

"Ah," Robin grinned. "I wanted to speak to you about that. My comrades and I have heard tales of this Hooded Rescuer and the 'men of the night' in Nottinghamshire who seem to know the Sheriff's every move."

Robin gestured toward Much, Allen, and Dusty."You remember Much, Marian? This is Allen, a brother in arms."

Robin gestured toward Allen and he moved forward.

"It is a pleasure to meet you, Lady Marian. We've heard a great deal about you." Allen glanced at Robin and winked.

Robin shoved Allen aside, and then placed a hand on Dusty's shoulder. "And this is Dusty, our master healer."

Marian moved forward and Much suddenly found her arms around his neck. "It's good to see you."

For a moment Much stood still, shocked by her embrace. Then his arms settled around her as he returned the hug. "You, as well, Lady Marian."

He had not expected such a welcome and as she pulled away he was tempted to shake his head to clear it. Had Marian just hugged him? He had not thought she would even notice he was gone. Robin, of course, she was expected to miss. But Much?

Robin turned back to Marian as she pulled out of the unexpected hug. "Now, about these rumors."

"Rumors?" Marian asked.

"Even when he only tells his most trusted servant Sir Guy of Gisbourne in the darkest chambers of the castle, rumors say these mysterious heroes still know what the Sheriff and Gisbourne are planning and stop them. Now I know perfectly well how one might obtain such secret information, and I also know only a few people know of the castle's secrets. Two of those people have been away from England, which to my knowledge leaves you, Mark, and your father. Have you been helping them?"

"Helping us?" Will laughed from the doorway. "She's one of us. You, sir, are addressing the leader of these 'men of the night'."

"Truly?" Robin asked. Much could hear the surprise in his voice, but somehow it didn't shock Much. Marian had always been bossy, even when they were young children. The fact that she'd be leading the rebellion in Nottingham was perfectly natural.

"Truly," Marian replied to Robin. "You doubt I could do such a thing? It wasn't as though there was anyone else around to take care of the suffering people."

"Well it is a surprise," Robin said, "but not so shocking. You've always been a protector. Who is the Hooded Rescuer then, or do you and your companion," he gestured toward Will, "take turns under the mask?"

"No, that's Mark."

"Remarkable," Robin grinned. "Where is your father?"

"In custody, as he has been for a year. I've only been able to see him for the briefest moments when spying in the castle. Mark hasn't seen him at all. My father is ill, Robin."

Suddenly the darkness in her eyes began to make sense to Much.

"I am sorry," Robin frowned. "One of my friends has great knowledge of healing, as I said. Dusty's remarkable."

"I'm afraid the Sheriff isn't inclined to let my father have visitors of any nature, let alone physicians." Marian glanced down the street and then said, "You've all been introduced to Will Scarlett, my right hand, now meet my brother—the famed Hooded Rescuer, and the last member of our crew, Little John." Marian gestured behind her and Much noticed Mark coming down the dirt path that constituted a road in Wetherby. He walked beside a tall, muscular man of impressive size, and both carried parcels covered in cloth—what they contained, Much could only guess.

As they approached the group outside Marian's home, Robin's eyes widened. "Little John? Why didn't you name him Mountain John?"

"We thought about it," Mark grinned as he drew near, setting aside his parcels, and then running forward to hug Much.

Much felt a surge of affection for Sir Godfrey's children that he'd never quite felt before. Both had embraced him as an old friend— and so he was, but to be treated as an equal and of value was still not something he was entirely used to.

"Where have you been off to Mark?" Robin asked as he received his own hug.

"Nottingham. We went to Marcus to collect some weapons we commissioned."

"Marcus?"

"Don't you remember him?" Marian asked. "Of course you don't. You never notice anyone but yourself."

"Marian!" Robin laughed, though Much could tell he was offended by her comment.

"What? Marcus is one of the blacksmith's in Nottingham. We used to play at his house as children if you recall."

"I do remember, I just couldn't place the name at first."

Marian shrugged. "It doesn't matter. Are you in a hurry to return to Locksley or can you stay for dinner?"

"We can definitely stay for dinner."

Robin re-introduced Dusty and Allen to Mark and Little John and then Marian ushered everyone inside the house. It was precisely as Much had remembered it—the small front room with a hearth along one wall and a simple table with chairs around it; there were doors that led to bedrooms and the small kitchen on each wall.

The group had a merry dinner that night, catching up on the three years they had missed in each other's lives. Robin was most intrigued by Will's account of their camp in Sherwood.

"We couldn't stay with Marian and Mark here in Wetherby without drawing suspicion," Will said. "The same held true for Nottingham. We were both already outlawed in our home shires, and once we came here and began helping Marian's crew, it was too dangerous for the group for us to remain in the open. We risked exposing everyone. We do visit, as often as we can, for we have plenty of information to pass along between us as we plan our various exploits. But we live in Sherwood Forest."

"There ought to be a way," Robin sat thinking, "...if we learn the secrets of Sherwood Forest the way we did of the castle, and make camp deep in its heart..."

"What are you thinking, Robin?" Marian asked.

"He's thinking," Dusty answered in his stead, "he'll help you set up a more stable camp in Sherwood."

Much caught the sharp look Marian sent Dusty's way, but he didn't think she or anyone else seemed to notice it.

"Many caravans pass through the Sherwood road," Dusty continued, "carrying the taxes supposedly collected for the king's ransom. The Sheriff here seems to have Prince John's ear and his favor, for most of the taxes seem to gather here and line his pockets before being shipped to London. If we knew the forest well enough, we might be able to way-lay the caravans, relieve them of their unjust shipments, and escape into the thick of the woods where no one could track us."

"We'd be a flash in the night," Robin said. "They wouldn't know what hit them."

"You must let me come with you," Mark said. "I can help! I'd love to be a part of the Sherwood gang."

"I do not know, Mark…"

Much remembered how Mark had begged to come on the Crusades with them, and Robin had so swiftly refused him. Evidently Mark remembered, too.

"You cannot now say that I am too young," Mark laughed. "I have been fighting the Sheriff's men without you."

"You seem to already have a crew here," Allen said. "Would you abandon them?"

"Wouldn't it be better if we all worked together?" Mark replied. "We know Nottingham, we know the Sheriff. If you set up camp with Will and Little John and start raiding caravans, we can work in tandem to the benefit of the people of England."

"That's a decision for our leader, isn't it?" Will said, giving Mark a sharp glance.

"He's right," Marian said. "I appreciate the loyalty, Will, but we might as well join forces. It's no different than when you and Little John came to join Mark and I."

"I will return to Locksley," Robin said. "I might be able to assist as the Earl of Locksley as much as raiding the caravans."

"So you stay in Locksley, Marian in Wetherby, and the rest of us live in the forest?" Allen sighed. "I was so looking forward to an extended stay on an actual bed."

Much laughed, though his own heart was sinking. "Allen is the biggest complainer you will find in the king's army."

"I like beds!" Allen protested. "There's nothing wrong with that."

Much echoed that sentiment quietly. When would they truly be allowed to stop fighting and simply rest? There was some hope, however, that he could return to Locksley with Robin to keep up the facade of an ordinary nobleman—who would, of course, be in need of his trusted manservant—and therefore be home with Sarah rather than living in the forest with Allen, along with Marian's friends Will and Little John.

Chapter 25

IT WAS LATE that night when Robin finally led Much, Dusty, and Allen toward Locksley. The moon was obscured by clouds, and it was a relatively dark walk but Much knew the roads as well as the secret passages within the castle and had no fear traversing them in the dark. This was home.

Before too long, lights in windows appeared, and they were passing through the village of Locksley. Every step was bringing him closer to home, closer to Sarah, closer to the memories of the Earl who was now dead.

Once they passed through the village they followed the winding road to the manor itself. Lights glimmered in a few windows, but for the most part it appeared dark, the shadow of the house looming up in the darkness in front of them.

"Nice house," Allen commented, his voice breaking the silence between them.

Robin chuckled as he moved forward to knock. Nothing seemed to happen at first, so he pounded his fist with more gusto.
Soon enough, the door was swung open and old Matthew stood there.

"Who goes there?"

"Your master," Robin said, stepping forward and pushing past Matthew into the front room. It was lit by a fire in the hearth, and Much took in the sight of the familiar room with clouded vision as his tears returned.

"Master Robin!" Matthew bowed. "You're home!"

"I am, indeed. I'll need my room ready for the night, as well as three guest bedrooms for my companions here. By the way, Much no longer works for me. He's a free man, so treat him as such."

Matthew glanced toward Much with a quizzical look and Much lowered his eyes to look at the tips of his boots.

"Let us know when the rooms are ready for us," Robin said. "We'll be in the kitchen, assuming that's where Sarah is."

"I imagine she is, sir," Matthew replied.

Robin hurried through the house and Much followed, his heart fluttering in his chest. He hastily wiped his tears from his eyes, wanting to see Sarah clearly.

As soon as he hit the doorway of the kitchen, he was overwhelmed by the smells that wafted toward him, and then he saw her. She was seated at a small table to one side of the kitchen—one where Much and Robin had so often eaten breakfast as children—her silver hair shining in the light of the fire.

"Sarah!" Robin darted forward. She turned and her face lit up.

"Master Robin! You're home!" She rose from the table, wrapping her arms around Robin as he flung his own around her neck. "Oh, child…I will never let you go."

"You'll have to. Much will want a hug."

Sarah pulled back from Robin and looked behind him. Much's heart dropped to his toes for a moment, and then Sarah was pulling him into her firm embrace and he sank into it, letting the tension and frustration of the last few years melt into her warmth and solace.

"My boys came home." Sarah kissed his cheek as she pulled back from the embrace. "I wasn't sure you would. But you're so thin!"

"There wasn't always a lot to eat on our travels," Robin said. "But we did come home. And we brought friends." Robin gestured toward the doorway where Dusty and Allen were awkwardly waiting out the family reunion.

"Oh, guests," Sarah straightened. "I'll have Matthew see to rooms—"

"Already done," Robin kissed her cheek. "This is Allen of the Dale, and Dusty."

"Pleasure to meet you," Allen gave a little bow but Dusty moved forward and gave her a swift hug.

"I have heard a great deal about the woman who took it upon herself to love and raise two motherless boys as her own," Dusty said. "I am glad to finally meet you."

"You can't believe the things Robin says," Sarah replied. "He's been known to exaggerate."

"Whereas our dear humble Much only speaks truth," Dusty replied. "I have heard the report of your character from him."

Sarah ran her hand affectionately through Much's hair and he felt the blood rushing to his cheeks.

"I was so worried," Sarah said. "Worried my boys would never come home...and then Sir Edward died..."

"I was wondering about that," Robin said with a sigh. "We have heard rumors that his death was not...natural."

Sarah crossed her arms. "It most certainly wasn't. It was that wretched Prince John and his servants."

"Have they done any more harm to our household, Sarah?" Robin asked.

"No. But I don't like them. The Sheriff is a terrible man. He hangs people for the fun of it. He almost hung Sir Godfrey! But the outlaws were able to stop that. I can't imagine how, but we're all grateful for it. You know Sir Godfrey has always been a beloved sheriff of our shire, until the Prince deposed him and put his own wretched man in his place."

"Sir Godfrey was almost hung?" Robin asked. "I'd heard he was in prison?"

"He is now, but he was nearly hung before that. How he was rescued, I don't know. It had to have been the guardian angels of Nottingham, no doubt, but having no idea who they might be I haven't gotten the detailed story from anyone."

"You don't know who the 'men of the night' are, or the Hooded Rescuer?"

"No, Master Robin. I do not. But enough of serious talk, you all must be famished after your journey! Let me get you something cooked up right quick, and then you can head to bed."

Sarah bustled about the kitchen in a familiar and homey way, and Much immediately moved to work by her side, slicing a loaf of bread and pulling cheese from the larder as Sarah gathered meat and vegetables for a pie.

The four of them sat to eat with Sarah watching over them and putting more food before them every few minutes, convinced they weren't eating enough. Matthew soon returned to tell them rooms had been prepared, and before too long Much was sinking into the soft mattress of a bed in the noble half of the house, rather than retiring to sleep on the pallet under Robin's bed where he'd slept before the war. It was disconcerting in many ways to have a room to himself, but he was exhausted and sleep took him before he could consider the circumstance for too long.

The next day Will and Little John took Much, Robin, Allen, and Dusty to their camp in the woods to show them how they'd been living. It was no more than two roughly put-together tents—seemingly made out of any spare cloth that could be found—set up under the trees some distance from the main road that cut through Sherwood Forest. There was a burnt patch of grass and dirt where they had a fire occasionally, and that was about the extent of it.

"This is hardly an ideal spot to create a well established camp," Robin commented. "It's too close to the Sherwood road. If we set up a large, functional camp here, we'll be noticed. We need to go deeper into the woods."

Will shrugged. "We basically just sleep here. If we need to go deeper to suit your purposes, then so be it. Lead the way."

Soon Robin and Dusty were wandering through the forest with the rest of the group following behind them as they searched for a better place to house their growing number of outlaws.

"We have to become familiar with these woods," Robin said to the group. "Intimately familiar. We need to know these trees as well as we know our own names."

"We'll spend as much time as we can in the forest," Dusty said, "getting acquainted with it as we search out its secrets. If we know it better than those who might want to find or harm us, we will be able to hide effectively here in the trees."

"Much and I will return to Locksley and bring supplies to the camp as soon as we start building one," Robin said.

"We will need to build shelters of some sort—tents, or huts, or something," Dusty said.

"Yes, and we'll need food," Allen replied.

"We usually visit Marian and get supplies from her," Will said. "We visit every few days for that purpose, as well as to exchange information or plan rescues."

Robin shook his head. "We cannot continue to take supplies from Marian. The less we do through her, the better. I don't want her getting hurt."

"She's led us well this past year," Little John growled.

"Yes, I know," Robin replied. "But I'm here now, so she doesn't need to worry about it. She can gather information in the castle if she sees fit to do so, but there is no reason for us to expose her unnecessarily. We need to be careful."

"You are rather protective of her," Will commented.

"Yes, I am. She is the love of my life and I will not see her hurt or in trouble. I will do everything in my power to avoid it."

Much bit his cheek. Robin didn't give Marian enough credit— she'd been leading the famous 'men of the night' while they'd been away on the Crusades; clearly, she was capable of handling herself. Even so, Much understood the emotions behind Robin's sentiments, so he couldn't judge him too harshly.

As the days passed, the camp in Sherwood began to take shape. Everyone spent time in the forest learning how to get to the new camp without getting lost under the trees. Dusty and Marian began sewing an abundance of green and brown clothes for the gang to wear, with hoods and capes to match, so they would blend into their environment better.

Chapter 26

MARIAN SOON DISCOVERED there was a caravan of taxes headed through Sherwood on its way to Nottingham—where the Sheriff would undoubtedly line his pockets before he sent it on its way to Prince John.

When Marian had burst into camp to relate the news—which she'd heard while spying on the Sheriff from within the secret passages in Nottingham castle—Robin had been excited, and before long the group was planning their first ambush.

As everyone gathered in a circle to talk about what might be done to steal the treasure before it got to the Sheriff, Much stood to one side and watched. He wasn't entirely sure how he felt about this new outlaw venture they were embarking upon. What would be the point? To steal money to send to the Duke of Austria to ransom the king who hadn't wanted to come with them when they escaped? A king who alienated and upset so many nobles and made so many enemies on their travels that he was just as responsible for the time spent in prison as Much was for giving away his identity. How would bringing King Richard home truly help anyone?

And more to the point, would violence be the state of Much's existence forever? He certainly hoped not. Coming home was supposed to mean peace and quiet, cooking in the kitchen with Sarah and spending his days with happier activities than ambushing soldiers and killing more people.

Dusty knelt to pray for their safety before they left the camp to begin their ambush and Much silently joined her, though he didn't make the same outward display of kneeling. There was no need to draw attention to himself.

He hardly knew what to say at all, apart from asking for Robin and the rest of the group to remain safe. He wasn't sure he wanted to be a part of this at all, but here he was and it was too late to back out now.

Besides, if Robin was going to do this, Much had to. He couldn't let him face danger alone; it was his duty to protect Robin.

Soon, Much found himself pressed up against the trunk of a tree, a bow in his hand. Much could hear the laughter of the soldiers guarding the treasure as the creaking wheels of the carts and wagons drew closer.

His heart beat in a dull thudding rhythm in his chest as he fingered his bow and waited for Robin's signal. He had no desire to keep killing, but if this was what Robin was going to do, then so was Much.

Suddenly the sharp sound of a whistle pierced the air—Robin's signal! Much leaned around the tree, bow raised, and aimed for the nearest soldier. Arrows were flying from both sides of the road as the rest of the group shot from their own hiding places, and soldiers were falling to the ground off of carts and out of horses' saddles.

Much let his arrow fly into the fray, adjusting the aim slightly. It bit into the bark of a tree on the opposite side of the road.

Robin appeared from his hiding place, moving out into the road to take the halter of the only surviving soldier's horse. "I thank you for your generous donation to King Richard."

"You...you wouldn't dare," the soldier sputtered.

"Oh, but we would," Robin said.

Much moved from behind the tree and made for one of the wooden carts weighed down by chests presumably filled with the taxes extorted from the people of England.

Little John began pushing a cart off the road while Will and Dusty jumped up onto two other wagons, guiding the horses that pulled them off the road as well. Allen grabbed a loose chest that had rolled from one of the carts in the chaos, and followed after Much as he steered the mule pulling the cart he'd clambered onto away from the road and toward their camp. Mark followed along behind the lot of them, doing his best to cover the wheel tracks.

Much could still hear Robin's talking with the soldier over his shoulder, but he kept moving. The plan was to get everything away before reinforcements could arrive. Robin was going to let one soldier make it to Nottingham alive to let the Sheriff know he could no longer steal the taxes uncontested.

"Give my regards to the Sheriff!" Much heard Robin shout. He pulled the reins guiding the mule pulling his cart, causing him to slow to a stop as Robin came running through the trees.

"Hurry! We must get all of this back to the camp. Little John, as soon as that soldier is out of sight, head back and bury those soldiers we killed."

"I'll help," Dusty offered, jumping off of her wagon. Robin leaped up where she'd been sitting, grabbing the reins.

"Let's get this done quickly," Robin said.

Much urged his mule forward again, guiding him around trees and bushes and the worst of the undergrowth behind Robin, with Will following him.

Mark still came along behind them all to brush aside the deepest ruts of the wagon wheels to hopefully ensure no one could follow them to the camp.

The cart's wheels creaked and groaned as Much drove over the bumpy terrain and scraped over rocks along the ground, but though he was afraid the wheels would crack and break he did, in fact, make it back to the camp in one piece.

Will and Robin drove their wagons into the clearing as well, and before too long Dusty and Little John returned from burying the dead. Dusty insisted they pray to give thanks for their safety and success.

"Is that really necessary?" Allen rolled his eyes.

"You may not think so, but I do," Dusty replied.

Will shrugged. "I see no reason why we can't. Robin?"

"Whatever," Robin said. "I don't care.'

Much joined Dusty and Will as they knelt in the middle of the clearing. He was impressed by Dusty's ability to do what she believed to be right in spite of the mocking of Allen and the apathy of Robin. Such attitudes made Much uncomfortable to the point that if Dusty hadn't been there, he most definitely would not have been kneeling in the grass thanking the Lord for their safety.

"Now on to more important business," Allen said when Dusty rose from the ground. "What are we to do with the horses and wagons we've acquired?"

"We can take the carts apart," Will suggested, "and use the wood to begin building our huts."

"And we can give the horses to a deserving farmer or two in the area," Robin said.

"Why not keep them here?" Allen asked. "They could prove useful."

"We'd have to feed them," Will said. "I'm not sure we could manage taking care of horses while none of us are here—we're going to be busy spying on the Sheriff, saving innocent people from unlawful executions, and so forth. At least if things follow the sort of pattern we've been living by these past years under Marian's direction."

"I agree," Robin said. "It might prove more nuisance than help to have the horses here."

Will and Little John elected to work alongside Mark to find appropriate homes for the horses, and Dusty and Allen offered to help. Soon the whole group save Much and Robin had left the clearing, leading the animals away.

Robin glanced at the collection of chests they had removed from the carts, lifting the lid of one and staring down at the gold coins that glistened in the sunlight.

"What are you thinking Robin?"

"I am debating what can be done with the gold we've taken off the Sheriff's hands." Robin flipped open the lid of another chest. Jewels of various colors sparkled from the top of this one, and Much could see gold coins beneath them. "I want to free the king…but I suppose…"

"You suppose what?" Much asked, moving to stand beside Robin as he stared down at the treasure.

"I'm going to see Marian."

"Marian?"

"I need advice."

Much bit his cheek. Of course Robin wouldn't ask him for his opinion. He was just a servant, after all, free or not.

Chapter 27

ROBIN DID GO to visit Marian that night, and when he returned he came to sit beside Much where he was leaning against a tree and watching Will and Allen debate the best way to start a fire as they piled logs in the circle of stones that had been constructed for that use.

"Well, I discussed the treasure with Marian," Robin said as he plopped onto the grass.

"Oh?"

"We've decided we'll send a portion of the treasure to the king to pay off his ransom, and keep the rest to distribute to the people of England so that they can pay the outrageous taxes and have money for food and clothes and such."

"It does sound like a good plan." Though why Robin couldn't have had the same conversation with Much, he didn't know.

After that first raid, news of a 'Robin of the Hood' or 'Robin Hood' began to spread in Nottingham and the Sheriff issued a decree declaring him an outlaw, along with anyone in association with him.

"The Sheriff hasn't yet made the connection, but I imagine he will," Robin said one day. He and Much were sitting at the large oak table in the dining room of Locksley manor, enjoying one of Sarah's fine-cooked meals. They were perhaps not as extravagant as they might have been a few years ago, but Much didn't expect them to be given the state of things in England. No one was as well off as they might have been before the king left on his Crusade.

"You think he'll realize that you and this 'Robin Hood' character are one and the same."

"He'd be an idiot if he didn't figure it out," Robin sighed. "I shouldn't have given that soldier my name during our ambush. Anyway, it's too late now. We might need to be careful about when and where we appear in Nottingham so as not to draw attention to ourselves."

"Master?" A young servant boy appeared in the doorway, wringing his hands. "There is a man riding this way. It's…it's Sir Guy of Gisbourne." The boy shuddered as he said the name.

"Much, go see what he wants."

Much bit his cheek. It was natural for Robin to issue orders—he was an Earl, after all. And Much had been his servant his whole life. It may have been Robin's own idea to free Much, but it wasn't unnatural for him to fall back into his old patterns.

At least, that's what Much told himself as he left the dining room and headed for the front door of the manor.

As he stepped outside, he saw a young man riding through Locksley village toward the manor. He was dressed all in black, and from this distance Much could make little out apart from his black clothes, his black hair, and his black stallion which he rode with ease. Much didn't know how anyone could look so at home on the back of a horse, but Sir Guy of Gisbourne certainly did.

As he drew near, he dismounted and Much moved forward to grab the horse's reins for him. "Can I help you?"

"Who are you?" Sir Guy of Gisbourne barked, his dark eyes flashing.

Three words. That was all. And yet the way he said those three words sent them piercing through Much, straight to his bones. He was far more intimidating than facing down the entire Saracen army.

"My name is Much. I'm Robin of Locksley's servant."

Suddenly he heard Robin's voice behind him. "May I help you?"

Much felt the tension in him ease slightly as Robin stepped out of the house and moved toward Sir Guy of Gisbourne.

"You are Robin of Locksley?" Sir Guy of Gisbourne asked.

"Yes, I am. And who are you?"

"Sir Guy of Gisbourne."

"Ah. I've heard of you. Nothing good, of course."

Sir Guy of Gisbourne frowned, his dark eyes flashing again.

"What do you want?" Robin asked. "I really have a million things to do. I've been gone for several years. Maybe you've heard, the king is on a Crusade?"

"I heard he was in prison," Sir Guy of Gisbourne said.

"Yes, he is, which is one reason that I came home. But, as you may imagine, I have many things to put in order now that I am back. It will take some getting used to as well. I wasn't the Earl when I left England. My father died soon after my departure, but maybe you know more about that than I do."

"I know nothing of your father's death. I was not in Nottingham at the time. I don't doubt he deserved whatever he got."

Much's grip on the stallion's reins tightened. He hadn't always been overly fond of the Earl, but that was no way to speak of Robin's father. Much glanced toward Robin in time to see his shoulders tense.

"If you don't have a reason to be here," Robin's voice was filled with an icy tone that Much had not heard before. "I'll have to ask you to get off my property."

Sir Guy of Gisbourne didn't budge, glaring at Robin.

Robin stepped forward, his hand dropping to his side where his sword swung from his hip. "I meant that. Get. Off. My. Land."

"The Sheriff sent me here."

"For what purpose?"

"I...to..."

"That's what I thought," Robin took a step back, his shoulders relaxing somewhat. "Get out, will you? I have things to do. And your horse is eating my valuable grass. I might have to charge you for that."

Sir Guy of Gisbourne pulled a gold coin from his pocket and flipped it toward Robin. "Keep the change."

With that he snatched the reins from Much's hand, swung into his saddle, and rode back down the road the way that he had come.

Robin chuckled.

"What is so funny to you about that encounter?" Much asked, trying to ignore the knots that had formed in his stomach.

"Our unexpected guest amuses me," Robin said, flicking the gold coin in the air and catching it.

"I found him rather intimidating."

"He's ridiculous is what he is," Robin replied. "And he amuses me."

Robin glanced down the road as Sir Guy of Gisbourne rode out of sight beyond the houses in the village of Locksley.

"If the Sheriff sent him here to see if I met the description of the outlaw...we may have to leave."

"Leave?"

"Move to the camp with everyone else. We can't stay here openly if the Sheriff knows who we are. Until we're declared outlaws we can still use Locksley and the supplies here as much as we can, but we shouldn't stay for long periods of time. Not if the Sheriff knows or guesses who we are. Come along...let's go tell Sarah."

"Tell her what? That we're moving to the forest?"

"Exactly that," Robin said. "She deserves to know where we are."

Much couldn't argue with that, so he followed Robin through the house and down to the kitchen where Sarah was busy preparing so that everything would be set to make breakfast in the morning.

"Much and I are going to be moving to Sherwood," Robin said without preamble as he entered the kitchen.

Sarah looked up from where she was chopping vegetables at the large table in the middle of the room, a frown on her face.

"Why?"

"Because the people of England need help, and we're going to help them."

"By stealing gold?" Sarah asked, then she shook her head. "Whatever you see fit to do, Master Robin."

"We will still visit you," Robin said.

"You had better. Why are you wanting to join the outlaws?"

"Someone has to stand up against the Sheriff and his cronies. We've already begun to do so."

"Then you are Robin Hood, aren't you?" Sarah said. She set aside her knife and studied Robin closely.

"Robin Hood? Who's that?"

"Only the outlaw who stole the Sheriff's treasure and has since been declared a traitor to the crown."

"We're not traitors," Much said.

"We did steal that treasure though," Robin laughed.

Sarah moved around the table and pulled Robin into her arms. "Please be safe."

Then she turned to Much. "And you, too. Look after each other. I appreciate the sentiment, fighting against the Sheriff, but just…be safe. But how will you find the other outlaws? No one knows who they are, though they've been seen helping many people in Nottingham and the surrounding area these past years."

"We already know who they are," Robin said. "Do you not have any idea who they might be?"

"No," Sarah said.

"Well if you don't know, then I am not going to reveal their secrets."

"Just be safe, Master Robin."

"I will, Sarah. We both will. We survived the Crusades, you know. Nothing could be worse, I'm sure."

"You are not taking this seriously," Sarah chided.

"On the contrary, I am taking all of this very seriously," Robin replied. "King Richard himself asked me to take care of his people and I intend to do just that."

Chapter 28

ROBIN WAS SERIOUS about the move, and before the week was out he'd gathered some clothing, weapons, and food from Sarah's kitchen and moved himself to the camp in Sherwood. Much dutifully followed along behind him. The gang began to build huts in the clearing where they were setting up camp—using the wood from the stolen carts as Will had suggested, as well as cutting some wood from the plentiful forest that surrounded them.

Each member of the unlikely gang soon had a hut of their own, and another was built to store the stolen treasure—until they could send it to the king or distribute it among the people—along with the excess weapons they procured from Marcus the blacksmith who had been working alongside Marian, Mark, Little John, and Will for the three years that Much and Robin had been away from England.

Most of the huts in the meadow were merely large enough to sleep in and house a few small things, but Much suggested his hut be larger so he could build a simple kitchen into it with plenty of room for shelves to hold the food and cookery that they brought from Sarah's kitchen and bought at the marketplace in Nottingham, and Robin heartily agreed.

The fire ring with the logs pulled around it as benches was a short distance from Much's hut so that he could go back and forth between them easily when cooking meals for the gang. It was also the place where the gang gathered every evening to talk and share news from their various activities during the day. Slowly, the camp began to feel like a home more than a simple clearing in the forest.

Much was often lost among all the trees of Sherwood Forest, but he rarely went anywhere alone and therefore was never afraid of becoming truly lost. And with every trip to Nottingham or Wetherby and then back to the camp, the paths through the woods became more familiar and easier to tread.

One afternoon, Robin gathered the gang in the meadow, informing them they were going to have a day of training.

"Training for what?" Marian asked. "We can all use weapons."

"To varying degrees," Mark chuckled, elbowing Marian.

The sun was warm, the grass was green, the leaves of the trees around their camp were deep reds and vibrant yellows. It was a beautiful day and Much was glad to be spending it out of doors—regardless of whatever activities Robin had planned—rather than hiding in the cramped, cold, dark secret hallways of Nottingham castle, or planning an ambush and engaging in violent behavior.

"We need to be able to move through the forest without leaving a trace," Robin said. "No footprints, no discarded items, no broken twigs or such like. We can't leave a trail leading right back to the camp every time we raid the caravans of treasure."

"He has a point," Will said. "I don't think the Sheriff is in possession of any great trackers—unless Gisbourne is…which, now that I think about it, is entirely possible. He seems well-versed in almost everything. But anyway, the point is, the Sheriff didn't find the sad little camp that Little John and I were using before, so he probably won't find this one. But we should take every precaution either way."

"Apart from simply following our trail to the camp—which could be detrimental to our cause," Robin said, "a good tracker could be able to tell from signs left behind how many people traveled through, where they were headed, how far ahead they might be, even their

240

capability to defend themselves from an attack. If this Gisbourne, or anyone else working for the Sheriff, can do this we have to combat it by blending into the woods."

"Meaning what, exactly?" Little John asked.

"Footprints are the biggest thing. I had Mark try to erase our tracks after our first raid for a reason. So, when possible, stick to walking on hard-packed soil or rocks. Stay away from streams where the ground is softer and footprints more easily made. Please, for the love of everything, don't get mud on your shoes. Apart from footprints in the mud itself, you'll also carry it with you and leave a trail of it to follow."

"That seems easy enough to avoid," Marian said.

"If you want to, you can tie cloth to the bottoms of your boots —or leaves, even, if you want to—so you'll be less likely to leave obvious footprints."

"You want us to walk around with leaves stuck to our boots?" Allen asked. He crossed his arms and shook his head with a short laugh. "Isn't that a bit much?"

"Do you want to be found? Hanged for treason?" Robin crossed his own arms and glared at Allen. For his part, Allen merely shrugged.

"When moving as a group, we should walk in single file as often as we can," Robin continued his lecture. "Potentially eliminating the possibility of our pursuers knowing how many of us they are following. This can, however, lead to deeper and more obvious footprints, so be aware of that."

"So many rules," Allen rolled his eyes.

"Avoid areas with a lot of undergrowth—it's almost impossible not to alter plants and bushes if you're passing through them."

"We're living in a forest, Robin," Mark said. "There's only so many places we can be where there aren't plants and undergrowth beneath the trees."

"I get that…I'm just giving you an overview of things to look out for. Also, outside the forest, if we're walking through fields and tall grass, don't walk single file."

"Oh, now we don't walk single file?" Allen asked.

"In grass, if we all walk the same path it will mow down the grass and leave a clear and obvious path for pursuers to follow. Also, be careful around the trees here in Sherwood Forest. Don't break branches or scrape off bark if you can help it."

"Anything else, oh great leader?" Allen asked.

"Keep everything outside of this camp as clean as possible, don't leave anything behind. Keep it quiet, too, if you can help it. Our voices travel. And keep it dark as much as you can when traveling at night. A torch will be seen through the trees from a great distance away. And be mindful of things you wouldn't expect—like your very skin—that can reflect the moonlight. Cover up when you go out at night."

"Is that everything?" Will asked.

"Everything I'm lecturing about," Robin replied. "But now we're going to spend the day practicing."

"Practicing?" Mark asked.

"Yes. You're going to walk through Sherwood and try not to leave a trail. Let's get moving."

There were groans from Allen, Mark, and Little John, but Dusty, Will, and Marian followed after Robin without complaint as he strode out of camp.

Much followed along behind, trying to remember all of the wisdom Robin had just imparted. It was too much to recall after only hearing it once, but as the afternoon continued on and Robin continued his lecture every time he spotted a footprint or a broken twig or a bent blade of grass, it slowly began to sink into Much's mind—and he imagined everyone else's as well.

When that particular adventure was through—for now at least —Robin, Allen, Will, and Little John also began constructing traps to lay around the outskirts of the camp to discourage anyone from sneaking up on them if their hiding spot ever was discovered.

As the days passed, Robin and Will were often seen making new arrows while in the camp, and Dusty would spend many days gathering plants and herbs for her healing purposes, many of which she kept on her belt at all times in case she would need them. Much often joined her on her walks through the woods and she took up teaching him about healing once more, this time with the ability to actually show him the plants and roots she used and how to mix them together.

Chapter 29

MUCH LEANED AGAINST the windowsill of a tailor's shop in Nottingham Square. Down below him was the market place, but the booths had been shoved aside to make way for a gallows in the center of the Square. The Sheriff was hanging a man who, according to Marian, had committed to greater crime than intervening when Sir Guy of Gisbourne had been spotted beating a woman in the street. The woman had fled, but the young man had been arrested by Gisbourne, and was now being executed.

Marian had relayed the news to the gang, and they were in Nottingham Square, preparing to rescue him. The people of Nottingham had gathered, filling the space around the gallows. Robin had sent everyone to various locations around the Square, and Much had found himself in this tailor's shop, peering down on the proceedings from above, his bow in his hand.

His heart beat a panicked rhythm in his chest as he watched Gisbourne—dressed in black as he always was—roughly dragging the man toward the gallows and preparing to hang him.

Much raised his bow, settling his gaze on the rope that Gisbourne was tying around the man's neck. As Gisbourne tightened the noose, Much let his arrow fly; it sliced through the rope above Gisbourne's hand, effectively snapping it.

The rope drifted in the breeze as Gisbourne threw down the bit left in his hand, and shouted out orders to the Sheriff's soldiers nearby.

The rest of the gang began to fire their own arrows at the soldiers as Little John charged through the crowd to collect the man from the gallows and get him out of the scene.

Much snatched another arrow from his quiver and shot down a soldier chasing after Little John, and then another. More arrows from other members of the gang were cutting down the rest of the soldiers in the Square. Gisbourne was no where to be seen any longer.

Once Little John was out of sight, Much strapped his bow to his back and hurried out the back entrance of the shop—the door that entered into a street and not the Square itself—and hurried toward the nearest gate that would lead him out of Nottingham. His part in the rescue was finished, and now it was time to return to the camp in Sherwood and wait for everyone else.

It wasn't long before everyone, including Little John, made it back to camp. Little John relayed how he'd gotten the man out of Nottingham and sent him on his way away from the city with some of the gold the gang collected from the Sheriff. Everything appeared to have gone off without a hitch.

As the weeks passed, the gang fell into a rhythm. Much's most frequent occupation was spying inside the hidden passages in Nottingham castle with other members of the gang. The dark passages were a familiar comfort, despite being cold and pitch-black apart from the cracks and chinks in the walls where they could see into various rooms in the castle or slide open the secret doors.

Much never opened any of the doors—the point was not to get inside the castle proper, but to watch and listen. In this way the gang was able to keep an eye on the Sheriff and potentially stop any unlawful executions such as the most recent rescue, as well as confiscate the treasure passing through Nottingham on its way to Prince John. Robin and the gang always struck hard and fast when they'd ambush caravans of taxes passing through Sherwood, and there was little resistance.

On one particularly warm summer day, Much was rearranging the pots, pans, and other cutlery in his little kitchen when Allen dropped a chest of jewels onto the floor of the supply hut next door with a resounding thud. "Robin...we look wealthy."

Much stepped out of his kitchen and leaned around Allen to look at the supply hut. There were stacks of chests that were filled to the brim with gold and jewels, with piles of sacks sitting beside and on top of the chests, filled with more treasure as well. Spare weapons from Marcus were hanging on one wall, and Dusty had a stash of herbs and spices hanging to dry on the other wall.

"We do look rather wealthy," Much agreed.

"We need a lot," Robin said, stepping up between them and slinging his arms around both their shoulders. "We have an entire country to feed and clothe, not to mention we're paying off the ransom for the king. We need all the gold we can get."

"Allen!" Will's voice called from across the clearing and Much, Allen, and Robin turned around. Will was just entering the camp, his arms full with a rather heavy looking bundle covered in cloth.

"What is it?" Robin asked.

"I've got the rest of the supplies so Little John and Allen can finish building their forge."

"Forge!" Robin glanced between Allen and Will with a grin. "I didn't realize we were building a town here."

Allen shook his head. "We aren't. But you and Will are constantly making extra arrows and bows; Little John and I thought we'd craft a few swords and daggers, too."

"We have Marcus for that," Much said.

247

"True, but it could become dangerous at some point to keep smuggling weapons from Marcus," Allen replied. "Little John and I thought it best we be prepared in case of that emergency."

"That's not a bad idea," Robin said.

"We don't have an army to equip," Much said. "Why would we need so many weapons?"

"You never know," Allen said. "We might recruit some men for our gang. If we're saving the entire country, we will need some help. As Robin once said during our long adventures abroad, you can't do anything substantial with only a handful of men."

"Are we getting help, Robin?" Much asked.

Robin shrugged. "Who knows? But Allen is right; we are too small of a group to save all of England."

The meadow where they lived continued to take shape as huts were finished, the forge was built, and the place began to take on the feeling of a home despite being little more than a break in the thick forest of trees.

Every morning Much would rise before everyone else and begin preparing a meal for the gang to eat before Robin sent them all out on their various missions. It was one of the best parts of the day, when he could simply exist in peace and quiet, doing one of his favorite activities. It would have been nicer to have been doing it at Locksley manor with Sarah at his side, but it was the best he could get for now.

One morning, however, Robin and Mark were already awake when Much exited his hut and began gathering supplies to cook the breakfast meal. They were some yards away on the other side of the clearing, with bows in hand. Much felt a tightening under his eyes as he watched; Robin seemed to be instructing Mark in the use of his bow.

With a dry throat, Much knelt over the stone fire ring and began to fill it with logs from the freshly cut stack that was leaning against the side of his hut. Everyone in the gang took turns chopping wood to keep their stack full.

Much wasn't sure why he was so frustrated by the sight of Robin helping Mark. Maybe it was simply that Robin didn't often take the time to teach Much. But why would he? Much was a nobody, after all. Just a servant.

As Much lit his fire and continued to prepare breakfast, he did his best not to stare at Robin and Mark across the clearing. Robin could do what he pleased, it shouldn't bother him so much.

Once the smell of Much's frying eggs began to waft through the meadow, Robin and Mark came over to sample his food while other members of the gang began to poke their heads out of their huts and make their way over as well. Another busy day of spying on the Sheriff, possibly rescuing innocents from cruelty, and planning raids was about to begin. Life within the gang continued on...

One night when the gang gathered around the campfire under the bright starlight with the moon shining down on them, Robin shared a piece of news that worried Much.

"I was speaking with Marcus today in Nottingham," Robin said.

Much sat beside him on one of the benches pulled around the fire ring, and Marian sat on his other side. The rest of the gang was there as well, scattered around the make-shift benches.

"We have now been declared outlaws. Myself, Much, Allen, and Dusty have been named as wanted by the authorities. They have finally come to the conclusion that I am, indeed, Robin Hood and that everyone in affiliation with me will now be considered an outlaw and traitor to the crown."

There was a brief moment of silence and then Little John laughed, a deep gravelly sound that burst from within his chest. "It is about time you joined us."

"It is not funny," Will said, shaking his head. "Although I would never change what I have done, this is a serious business."

"What do we do now, Robin?" Much asked.

"The same as we have been doing. Nothing has changed. We will have to be more careful when we are in Nottingham and the other villages, of course, but none of the king's people would betray us. We only need to keep out of sight from the Sheriff's men, which I doubt will be difficult."

Dusty smiled at Much. "We will pray for our continued safety."

Allen rolled his eyes. "You do that; just don't expect the rest of us to join you."

Dusty sighed, but said nothing.

"What will happen to Locksley though?" Marian asked. "Now that you are officially an outlaw. Will the Sheriff confiscate your property? Put someone else in charge there?"

"I am not sure," Robin said. "I'm going to visit Sarah and keep her informed on what has transpired, and I'll keep an eye on Locksley to see what becomes of it."

Robin was soon no longer satisfied to raid only the Sheriff of Nottingham and stop his unfortunate hangings. Robin would catch wind of a beating or execution planned in a shire over, or even further away, and decided his gang should rescue those innocents as well. Much was all for saving people, and gladly went where Robin did. The gang was small, however, with only the eight of them, and the more they traveled outside of Nottinghamshire to help other people the harder their jobs became.

The rest of the month passed in frantic activity, with Marian constantly coming to the camp with news of one plot or another of the Sheriff's and the gang setting to work foiling the Sheriff's plans. Then there were the reports from the other shires and cities, which Robin would respond to by sending the gang out in groups of two or three to go rescue people elsewhere. These trips sometimes lasted several days or even a week as they tried to reach the whole kingdom.

Robin also began to send members of the gang traveling through England once a fortnight to deliver money to the people so they could pay taxes and buy food. Slowly the reputation of Robin Hood and his gang was born, and all of England was coming to rest their hope in Robin Hood to save them from their terrible fates under the leadership of Prince John.

Chapter 30

AS THE SUMMER turned to autumn, the famous Nottingham Fair soon approached. It had been one of Much's favorite times of the year growing up. Merchants from across the world would come and crowd Nottingham Square with their booths—selling jewelry, clothing, weapons; anything and everything imaginable. The food was Much's favorite part—the breads, the pies, the stews and meat that lent a savory flavor to the very air of Nottingham. The crowds of haggling people he could do without, but the food was worth it. There were also always performers to sing and dance and act and entertain the citizens of Nottingham along with the hordes of people who came to visit from around the world.

Much had almost forgotten about the magic of the Nottingham Fair while he and Robin had been away from England, but now that the time was drawing near once more and the merchants were traveling into Nottingham, his anticipation rose.

Much leaned against a stone building on the edge of Nottingham Square with Robin beside him, watching the crowds of people. The usual market in the Square was busier than it typically was as the incoming merchants from outside Nottinghamshire were setting up their booths and laying out new wares while more of Nottingham's citizens were perusing the market than would generally be found in there. Despite the heavy crowds, Much knew the Square would be even more full once the Fair was officially underway. This was just the appetizer.

The cheerful chattering in the Square quieted almost instantaneously as Sir Guy of Gisbourne marched into the market from one of the side streets that attached to the large open space. There were a handful of soldiers following him as he strode across the Square.

Much pressed his back into the stone wall behind him, trying to avert his gaze and not draw attention. He was, after all, an outlaw. Robin, however, stayed exactly where he was, glaring at Gisbourne as he went by.

Gisbourne did not engage in conversation with anyone, although most of the people in the crowd watched him storm past. Once he'd disappeared down another street, the usual hum of the busy Square returned.

"I wonder where he's off to," Much said.

Robin crossed his arms and scowled. Much studied his glowering face for a moment.

"Are you alright?"

"No." Robin's eyes were spitting fire and Much was tempted to step away from him. "He's interested in Marian."

"Who? Gisbourne?"

"Yes, Gisbourne. I've seen them talking in town before…the way he watches her…" Robin's scowl was intense.

"You know she loves you. You don't need to worry."

"He's a powerful man—rumors suggest there is no one better with a sword. He has an estate, far from Nottingham. He's risen in power and authority until he has Prince John's ear…if he wants Marian, he'll think he can do anything to get her. And if she does anything to upset him, he'll be hard to stop if he tries to harm her."

"Are you sure you aren't worrying unnecessarily?"

"Perhaps."

Later that night, however, Robin came storming into camp after a visit to Wetherby. When Allen asked what was bothering him, he was promptly barked at. Much, however, went to talk to him.

"Marian is going to the Fair with Gisbourne."

"Not because she likes him," Much tried to comfort Robin.

"She thinks she'll be able to pick up information about him and the Sheriff. I wish…" Robin sagged against a tree at the edge of the clearing, giving Much a rueful smile. "I should be the one to accompany her to the Fair."

"You can't go. You'll be killed if you're caught!"

"I know. But we sneak around Nottingham just fine…"

"Maybe she will find out something important."

"Maybe, but I doubt it. Tomorrow will simply be a waste of time…time spent with Gisbourne instead of with me."

"You're jealous." Much smiled.

Robin sighed. "Very."

Much went to sleep in his hut that night still amused by Robin's jealousy, but he was far less amused when Robin rudely shook him awake the next morning.

"Much! Get up."

"What is it?" Much glanced around, realizing he could barely see Robin at all in the relative darkness. "Is it even morning?"

"Just barely dawn," Robin replied. "Come on. We're going to Nottingham. I'm going to keep an eye on Marian."

"Robin!" Much sat up quickly and Robin pulled back. "If you draw attention to yourself you'll be caught and hung!"

"Getting caught is rather doubtful," Robin replied with a casual laugh. "Regardless, I can't leave Marian to Gisbourne."

"She can take care of herself. And we're outlaws…"

"I know, I know. We'll stay undercover."

"And you can't go yourself because…?"

"Too afraid to come with me?"

"Not at all. I'm just not sure you need me."

Robin had been in the process of backing out of Much's hut, but he paused in the doorway and stared at Much intently for a moment. "You have grown melancholy of late, Much. You must tell me what is bothering you. Why do you keep assuming that you are a burden to me?"

Much shrugged and looked at his hands, not sure he liked the fact that Robin could read him so well.

"Much."

"It doesn't matter."

"It matters to me," Robin replied, moving to sit on the edge of Much's bed. "Talk to me."

The command in his voice was undeniable, though Much doubted Robin realized it.

You only wish to seek advice from Marian rather than talking to me, you teach Mark archery and swordplay when you've never taken the time to do the same for me.

"You've been a bit abrupt of late, probably because of your emotions regarding Marian, and also the stress of living in the forest as a fugitive."

"I am sorry if I have been rude," Robin said. "Forgive me?"

"Always."

"Then come on! We need to get to Nottingham to keep an eye on Marian."

Much hurriedly got dressed, strapping his sword to his waist. He quickly fried some eggs and sausages so the rest of the gang would have something to eat as they woke up, which Dusty took over when she exited her tent.

"Headed to the Fair?" Dusty asked.

"Yes," Much said. "Robin is concerned for Marian's safety."

"You don't give her enough credit," Dusty told Robin.

"Perhaps not, but we need to get going regardless. Much?"

"I'm right behind you."

The walk through the forest and then down the road to Nottingham was a long and quiet one. Much bit his cheek, debating whether or not to talk to Robin about how he actually felt. He knew Robin would care, but *should* he?

When they arrived in Nottingham, they melted into the hordes of people crowding the streets. Robin kept his eyes peeled for Marian, though for most of the morning they did not see her or Gisbourne. They made sure to keep a distance from any of the Sheriff's soldiers, though the people of Nottingham knew they were there. More than one person shook Robin's hand to thank him for what the gang was doing to save people. And they would circle around Robin and Much if soldiers came too close, acting as though they were simply chatting while they formed protective walls blocking Robin and Much from the sight of the Sheriff's men.

When they finally caught sight of Marian, walking arm-in-arm with Gisbourne through the crowded Square, Robin began following them. He kept a distance from them to not draw attention, but he never let them out of his sight. Much stayed by his side.

The jostling, bustling crowds with their loud voices and louder laughter were more than he could wish for, but as Robin stalked Marian, Much was able to stop at a booth or two with wonderfully sweet and savory dishes and the food almost made the whole excursion worth it.

There were also the singers and dancers which he watched for a time while Robin eyed Marian who was speaking with Gisbourne as the two of them stopped to admire the entertainment.

Then there were the foot races and horse races set up in the fields outside Nottingham—the latter of which Gisbourne participated in and won. The day was busy and loud, but nothing of import seemed to happen to Marian. She was safe, she was in one piece, and she seemed more at ease than Much had seen her of late.

When they returned to camp that night, Robin was in a cheerful mood. He was even whistling a tune as the two of them strode into camp and toward the fire ring where the rest of the gang was already gathered.

"How was the Fair?" Will asked with a grin as they sat down around the crackling fire.

"Entertaining, as it always is," Robin said. "I always loved it as a child."

Truth be told, Robin had spent little time exploring or enjoying the Fair as a child. He'd been far more interested in playing with Marian in Nottingham castle, but Much kept that addendum to himself.

"Was Marian in any danger?" Allen asked, brushing his shoulder into Robin's with a laugh.

"She was in grave danger," Robin groaned rather dramatically. "That man has his eye on my Marian and I do not like it."

Allen and Little John both laughed at that.

"She'd never think of anyone but you, Robin," Much said.

"I know," Robin said. "Did you see the way she looked at him when he wasn't paying attention? I've never seen more disgust on her face."

"Does she ever look at you that way?" Allen asked, and Robin immediately whacked his arm.

"No, she doesn't. But I may have seen her glance in your direction with that look on her face."

Will threw back his head and laughed at that, and Allen gave Robin a grin.

"You wound me, Robin," Allen said. "I'll never forget this."

"You sound truly heartbroken." Robin rolled his eyes. "I'm sick with remorse."

Much watched the easy banter between Robin and Allen and felt his muscles tense. He *wanted* that, but he was never going to get it.

Chapter 31

MUCH STRETCHED HIS shoulders, trying to release the kink in his neck. He and Dusty had been seated outside her hut, bending over her array of dried plants as she prepared them for use, teaching Much as she did so.

She had a small pestle and mortar beside her to crush the plants she needed in powder, as well as several small bowls she was using to mix several different herbs and spices together before pouring the mixtures into vials and tiny pouches that she would then put into her storage or the larger pouch that she kept on her belt.

Much watched her nimble fingers work, only half listening as she explained the use of the plant in her hands.

They were the only two in the camp at the moment. Mark was in Nottingham, but most of the rest of the gang was spread far and wide across England at the moment.

Reports from other cities in England began to make their way to Nottingham as the people reached out through their friends and acquaintances, trying to get word to Robin Hood and his gang whenever they felt their lives were in danger.

Much rarely went along on these missions. Robin would divide the gang up and direct the group this way or that, but Much he always left in Nottingham. Mark usually stayed in Nottingham as well, continuing his work as the Hooded Rescuer and also, Much assumed, keeping an eye on his sister Marian.

Much could see why Robin would allow Mark the privilege of staying in Nottingham, but he didn't understand why Robin felt he himself was too inept to help with the missions to other cities in England.

"Much, you aren't listening to me."

"Sorry." Much focused his attention back on Dusty and let his bitterness over Robin's apparent neglect sink into the back of his mind. "I was lost in thought."

"I could tell. If you've had enough for the day, I will not be offended."

Much shook his head. "No. Keep going. I want to know this stuff; I'd love to be able to help people if I find someone hurt and you aren't nearby."

"I do think it would be good for everyone in the gang to have some knowledge of how to deal with situations that might arise. Here." Dusty handed him the mortar and pestle with some leaves in it. "Crush these. Perhaps if you're physically engaged in the work, your mind will stay on task."

Much dutifully set to work turning the leaves into powder as Dusty continued to explain the various uses of the plants as she sorted them.

As autumn gave way to winter, there was less for the gang to do. Fewer caravans traveled to Nottingham with treasure, and the Sheriff was in less of a hanging mood, so there were fewer rescues to be made. There were, however, plenty of people to feed and clothe, and the cold weather also brought more sickness to Nottingham and the rest of England, so Dusty was fairly busy with her healing work while the rest of the gang spent most of their time shivering in camp or in the cold, stone, secret passageways of Nottingham castle.

Marcus the blacksmith procured horses for the gang to use at their leisure—which he kept in Nottingham—that made traveling beyond Nottingham easier in the winter months so the gang could continue to take food and money to the rest of England.

When Dusty wasn't busy healing the sick, she picked up her Arabic lessons with Robin, Allen, and Much once more, and Will eagerly joined the group, and slowly the winter months gave way to spring once more.

One evening Robin knocked on Much's hut and then stuck his head inside. "Are you awake?"

"Yes."

Robin leaned against the door frame. "I've let everyone know their destinations for this week. Most will be leaving bright and early in the morning, but you will be staying in Nottingham with Mark."

"Of course."

Robin started to leave and then hesitated, giving Much a sharp look. Much tried to look perfectly complacent, and he thought he must have succeeded because Robin gave him a smile and reached over to squeeze his shoulder.

"You shouldn't be offended when I leave you in Nottingham, Much."

"I'm not offended."

"I can see that you are, but you needn't be. I leave you here because I trust you, and I need someone I can count on keeping an eye on the Sheriff while I am gone."

"That is why Mark and Marian are here—"

"Mark and Marian do a fine job, but they are young and both are less experienced than we are. More than that, you know Marian is dear to my heart. I entrust them to you, Much. Had I not expressed that? I worry less knowing you are here."

Much studied Robin in the growing darkness of the twilight. Did he mean it? He seemed perfectly sincere. "I had not realized...I will do my best."

"I know you will; you always do."

Summer was fast approaching, and Robin continued to send the gang out in various directions to assist the people of England beyond Nottingham. Such travels became easier as the roads cleared and the weather brightened.

One day, as the gang was sitting around the campfire in the early hours of the morning, the clearing lit by the soft grey light of dawn and filled with crisp clean air, Robin was once more handing out orders.

"Much, Marian will need more food to hand out in Nottingham."

Much nodded.

Robin turned to Little John. "Little John, Allen, you're going northward until you hit Scotland, and then coming back south again. Take a full chest or two of our gathered treasury—you never know how much you'll need to pass along to the people, depending on how desperate they are. Dusty and Will, you'll do the same but heading southward."

"Of course, Robin," Dusty said.

"Mark, you're coming with me this time," Robin said. "We're going to London to help the residents there. Now come on, everyone, we all have work to do to prepare. Marcus will have the horses ready for our travels at his house. We'll meet back at camp in a fortnight or thereabouts; some of us may be on the road longer than others. Travel swiftly and safely, my friends."

The gang disbanded from the fireside, and Much went to the storage hut to grab a bit of coin before heading through the forest toward the road to Nottingham.

The walk to Nottingham was uneventful. As Much approached the gates to the city he pulled his hooded cloak up over his head despite the fair weather and fell in line behind a farmer driving a wagon of produce into the gate. The Sheriff kept a few guards at the gate to watch for suspicious behavior, but they rarely stopped the average citizen so as long as the members of Robin Hood's gang could slip in without drawing attention to themselves there was little chance of getting caught at the gate.

Once within the city walls, Much moved toward Nottingham Square and the market there. There were always booths set up around the Square—though not nearly as many as during the Fair—and all along the edges of the Square were shops for tailors, blacksmiths, fletchers, and just about everything under the sun.

Much went to the baker first to buy bread—the easiest thing for Marian to carry and hand out to the needy. The shop smelled delightful, but Much wished he could have gone to Sarah. No one made a better loaf of bread than she did. Much did not wish to draw attention to Locksley, however, so he had decided not to try and sneak into the village or the manor to speak to Sarah and take food from her. She was safe as long as no one knew how closely connected to Robin Hood she truly was.

After the baker's, Much went to a stand in the Square to get fruits and vegetables as well. He always used the same sellers, trusting that they wouldn't rat him out since they hadn't yet.

When he felt he'd purchased enough that Marian could help the needy, but not too much to draw the attention of the Sheriff's men or

Gisbourne on himself as he walked the streets with a basket full of food, Much made his way out of Nottingham and toward the village of Wetherby.

He made straight for Marian's home once he arrived in the village. He saw her down the street at Widow Mary's house and so waited patiently at her door until she finished her conversation and moved toward him.

"Much! What brings you to Wetherby?"

"I'm to keep you supplied with food, Lady Marian, for the next few weeks."

"Ah, Robin and Mark are off then?" Marian led Much into her house and took the food from him, storing it in her kitchen.

"Everyone is preparing for departure this morning, my lady. Did Mark not come to say farewell?"

"We said our goodbyes last night before he retired to the camp," Marian replied. "You've had a busy morning, do you want to sit down? I can get you a glass of water, or something?"

"No thank you, my lady. I should get back to Nottingham and take up post in the Square, watching for any suspicious behavior from Gisbourne or the Sheriff's men."

"Of course. I'll come with you. I just passed out the last of my stores this morning, so I don't need to make the rounds with food today. I'll use what you've brought me tomorrow. Hold on...just let me grab my dagger."

Marian was soon armed with a jeweled dagger in her belt, and the two of them set off for Nottingham once more.

"How is your weapons training coming along?" Much asked.

"Not as well as I would like. I wish I had more of an affinity for it; I'd like to be able to defend myself and others efficiently should the need arise."

"Robin says you do remarkably well."

"Does he? He doesn't say that to me. He tells me all the things I'm doing wrong."

When they reached the gates to the city proper, Much's eyes darted toward the Sheriff's men, his fingers twitching at his side.

"No one ever stops me," Marian said softly, drawing Much's arm through her own. "I'm the highest ranking noble in Nottingham, next to the Sheriff and Gisbourne. No one will question you if you walk beside me."

Marian was right; the Sheriff's men barely gave them a passing glance. They moved through the streets with ease and once they came to the Square they found a place near the edge where they could sit and keep an eye on the activity around them.

"So…what else does Robin say about me?" Marian asked, her eyes wandering over the crowd of people rather than looking at Much.

"I beg your pardon?"

"You said he praises my progress in training? He doesn't say anything of the sort to me directly, so I was wondering if perhaps that was true of other topics as well."

Much shifted on the cobblestone beside Marian, glancing around the Square.

"Now don't be uncomfortable, Much dear. It was a simple enough question. Does he talk about me at all?"

"Often, my lady."

"Don't 'my lady' me, Much. We've been friends since we were babies."

"Forgive me, but you said yourself you're the highest ranking noble in Nottingham."

"And you're a free man, unless Robin lied about releasing you from his service."

"That doesn't make me noble."

"You know you've always been our equal, Much. Even before Robin freed you, he viewed you as his brother."

"I know." Much bit his lip, looking anywhere but at Marian. It was impossible to try and explain his emotions to her. He wanted to be Robin's brother and equal, and he was grateful Robin tried to see him that way. And yet he still felt less than in many ways.

Have you forgotten so quickly, my son?

Much's sharp intake of air caught Marian's attention.   "What? What did you see?"

"Nothing. I was...thinking."

"About what?" Marian studied his profile as Much resolutely kept his gaze on a hanging sign across the Square advertising the bakery he'd visited earlier that morning.

"Robin, I guess."

"And thinking about Robin startled you?" Marian's voice sounded entirely unconvinced and Much sighed.

"Kind of. He's...Robin, you know. And I'm just Much."

"You really need to get over this belief in your inferiority. Robin doesn't see you that way; neither do I. We're a family, you know...the four of us. It was always you and Robin and Mark and I against the world growing up. It didn't matter that you weren't noble like the rest of us."

"It didn't matter to you, perhaps." Much could barely keep the bitterness from bleeding into his voice. Given the way Marian's gaze softened, he must not have succeeded as well as he would have liked.

"Do you still worry about the things Sir Edward used to say? I know he was Robin's father, and my father's best friend…and I loved him, too. But he wasn't right to suggest you were somehow less worthy, Much. You're not."

Much leaned back against the rough wood of the building behind them and glanced toward the sky to see fat, fluffy, white clouds drifting overhead. "Speaking of your father…how is he doing?"

"I can hardly tell, since I can't visit him often." Marian sighed. "But from the view I can get from the secret passage that runs by the dungeons…I'd say he's not doing well."

"I am sorry for it."

"So am I."

"I thought Gisbourne was helping with that?"

Marian nodded. "Yes, he did bring a physician to see my father. And occasionally he'll accompany me down to the dungeons and let me visit my father, but it's not as often as I'd like. And I'd prefer to go without an escort if I could."

"Still, Gisbourne's interest in you is certainly beneficial in some ways."

"It is…much to Robin's chagrin, I'm sure."

Much chuckled at that. "He doesn't love Gisbourne for it, that's for sure."

Chapter 32

THE WEEKS CONTINUED to pass in relative peace—the gang traveled far and wide, bringing money to the poorest of England, buying and distributing food to those in need. The Sheriff of Nottingham attempted to hang people who angered him and was foiled again and again by Robin Hood's gang.

The Sheriff grew tired of the raids on his caravans of treasure, however, and attempted to outsmart the gang—which was difficult to do considering they walked the very walls of his castle, though he did not know it.

A caravan of collected taxes was set to travel through a town to the south of Nottingham rather than come through Sherwood to Nottingham as usual, and when the gang learned of it they headed that direction.

It wasn't often that Robin brought Much along on such adventures outside the city, but he wanted all hands on deck for this one.

"We'll hit the ambush as we always do," Robin said as he stood on the road, surveying the foliage around it. "There's less cover than in the forest, but we can manage with the ditch here at the curve in the road, and there's enough bushes over there to make something work."

"Similar set up as always?" Will asked.

"It hasn't failed us yet," Robin replied. "You and Allen go over there," Robin said as he began pointing to various spots off the road and calling out names of the gang to assign them to a hiding spot.

Much had never felt more like a highwayman robbing innocent passersby than he did as he crouched along the steep bank beside the curve in the road, a few scrubby bushes hiding him from sight—at least until the caravan came around the bend, but by then he wouldn't need to remain hidden.

They'd ridden the horses Marcus kept at the ready for them to the village of Leicester, and stabled them there with a few families who were loyal to Robin Hood and his cause—as many of the people of England were—and then made their way to this bend in the road on foot. Despite not being in the forest, the strategy of their ambush seemed relatively routine, and Much wasn't too stressed as he studied the road beyond his hiding place.

The distant sounds of cart wheels creaking under the weight of chests filled with gold soon reached Much's ears, and he tightened his grip on his bow, waiting for Robin's whistle.

Much kept his gaze on the portion of the road that he could see —nearly level with his face, and obscured only slightly by the bush he was crouched beside. In another moment, he could see the wheels rolling along the dirt path, and then Robin's whistle pierced the air.

Much rolled down the embankment and into a crouch, whipping an arrow out of his quiver and putting it to his bow in the same swift motion. He wasn't nearly as adept as Robin was at this sort of thing, but he managed to keep his feet and find a target before the soldiers guarding the caravan were aware of him. His arrow sprouted in one soldier's chest as the rest of the gang hit their own marks.

Much stood, putting another arrow to his string and surveying the chaos that was overtaking the caravan—soldiers dying, others reaching for swords or firing their own arrows back toward the gang, while still others tried to spur their horses forward to get themselves and the treasure out of reach.

Robin's arrows followed those who attempted to flee, striking down first one and then another. Much's eyes danced through the confusion to find another target, and when he'd settled on a particular soldier he let his arrow fly, grabbing another almost immediately as he once more began to scan the skirmish laid out on the road.

A small shriek soon rent the air and Much lowered his bow, searching for the source of the sound. The fighting seemed to pause all around the road.

A soldier came climbing up the embankment on the opposite side of the road from Much, dragging a small child with him. He held a knife to the child's throat, and Much could see a thin line of blood already trickling down the small boy's neck.

Robin stepped into the road, arrow trained on the soldier.

"You let the boy go, and I might let you live."

"If you fire at me, this boy dies with me."

"My arrows fly faster than the muscles in your wrist could twitch."

"Try me."

Robin glared at the soldier. Much dropped his bow to the ground, and noticed most of the gang were lowering their own bows and blades, though they eyed the surviving soldiers around them warily.

"I and my surviving comrades are taking this treasure into town. We're keeping this little play-actor with us. Wanted to be a part of Robin Hood's band of outlaws? He gets treated like one. If you don't let us go, I kill him. If you follow us or attack us on our route, I kill him. The Sheriff of Nottingham will likely kill him once we arrive safely, but who's to say? Maybe he'll be lenient, despite him being caught fraternizing with Robin Hood in the middle of an act of treason."

"He's just a kid," Dusty called out from further down the road. "Let him be, please."

"You can have one of us," Will offered. "Let the child go."

Much winced as the knife cut deeper into the child and the boy cried out in pain as more blood trickled down to the collar of his shirt.

Robin still had his arrow nocked to his bowstring, aimed at the soldier. Much could see how tense the muscles of his shoulders and arms were, how taut he held his arms, how tightly he gripped the bow.

The soldier began moving, keeping the boy in front of him and between himself and Robin, the knife still firmly pressed in place. He called out orders to the other surviving soldiers to start leading the horses pulling the carts down the road. They slowly moved to do so, and the gang simply let them, all eyes joining Much's as they watched Robin.

He kept his bow aloft, but he didn't fire, and he didn't say anything else as he watched the boy being dragged down the road, knife to his throat.

Much moved to stand beside him as the carts began to wheel by. "What do we do?"

"If we attack the other soldiers, he'll kill that boy," Robin hissed, finally lowering his bow as the last cart passed them. The soldiers had lashed the reins of the horses who no longer had masters to drive them to the back of the other carts so that every bit of the Sheriff and Prince John's money went with them and there was nothing for the gang to scavenge.

"Robin?" Dusty stepped up on his other side.

"I don't know." Robin flung his bow across the road and ran a hand through his hair with a groan. "I don't know!"

The others gathered around.

"We can take 'em," Little John growled. "Get the jump on him."

"He's not going to let that kid go," Will said. "If we try another ambush or attack, he'll slit the kid's throat."

"If we let him take that child back to the Sheriff, the Sheriff will not be kind to him," Dusty said. "He'll never see his family again. We have to save him."

"We're going to save him." Robin sighed, kicking the road and causing a puff of dust to float above his boot for a moment. "I don't know how, but we're getting that kid back to his family, and we're getting the Sheriff's treasure. Just let me think…"

Robin began to march down the road, and Much walked down the embankment to collect Robin's discarded bow.

As they walked toward the nearby village, a man came running toward them.

"Robin Hood!"

"We know." Robin sighed.

"You've heard? You have to return to Nottingham at once!" The young man ran up to them, his breathing labored and his eyes wild. "The Sheriff is hanging six children!"

"Hanging children?" Much asked.

Robin grabbed the man's shoulders. "Six? Now?"

"Lady Marian sent word, she's trying to reach you. It may be too late already!"

"When is the Sheriff hanging the children?" Will asked.

"*Why* might be the better question," Dusty said.

"At dawn," the villager replied. "Or so said the message from Lady Marian."

"We're too far from Nottingham to arrive before dawn," Little John commented.

"Oh no, the children…" Dusty turned aside, kneeling on the road. Much was sure she was praying.

"We have to go," Allen said. "We can't let six kids hang."

"We can't get there in time to help," Little John said.

"And we have a kid here who needs help," Robin said. "If we run off to Nottingham, who knows what becomes of that little boy?"

"But six kids are being hung!" Allen began to pace. "We can't let that happen."

"We can't do anything," Little John repeated.

"If we hurry we might make it by morning!" Allen said. "Not if we stand here arguing, of course, but if we leave and we don't stop all night…we might make it."

"But that still leaves the question of our own hostage kid," Robin said. "He's our priority. Marian and Marcus can figure out something for the Nottingham kids."

"What if they don't?" Allen asked.

"What if we leave to save them and our kid is killed instead?" Robin replied.

"Saving six over one…if it's down to math, Robin…"

"It's never down to math!" Will snapped. "All seven of the children in question matter. All seven lives are valuable. But Little John is right, it's not about saving the six or saving the one. It's about possibly, *maybe*, potentially being able to arrive in time to do something for the six but most likely failing to get there in time, or to do something for the one we have right in front of us."

Robin sighed, his fingers curling into fists. Much held his breath. He didn't know what the right answer was in this situation, he didn't feel qualified to offer his opinion because he didn't have one. Both situations broke his heart.

"We find a way to save our kid," Robin said. "We save the kid, get the treasure, and then make haste for Nottingham."

"We'll be too late," Allen said, crossing his arms.

"We'll likely be too late for the Nottingham kids either way," Robin replied. "We don't have to be late for the kid who's only a few miles down the road. Now let's move! We need to catch up to that caravan and make a plan."

Chapter 33

A FEW HOURS later, Much was riding Marcus' borrowed horse, crashing through the tall grass following Robin. The gang wasn't riding on the road where they would easily be seen by the caravan, rather they were swinging wide to both sides, miles from the road itself.

Once they caught up, the plan was to move closer to scope out where the child was. Once Robin got a good idea where the kid was and how likely it was that he could kill the soldier who'd kidnapped him without harming the boy himself, the second stage of the plan would fall into motion.

Robin's plan depended on where the kid was located with the soldiers. If the soldier who'd grabbed him still had him close by, Robin planned to shoot the soldier and then the rest of the gang would break into the ambush raid they usually did while Robin grabbed the kid and headed toward safety. If the kid was just tied up and discarded in a cart, the gang would ride ahead—their horses were faster than the carts laden with treasure—and plot another ambush without waiting until Robin had separated the kid from his kidnapper. However, Robin was still going to run straight for the boy and get him out of the way of the fighting in the case of the full-on ambush.

It was reckless. If the gang were going to be close enough to be able to see the caravan in order to know when they'd caught up and could get closer to it on either side, the caravan of surviving soldiers would no doubt see them, too, and kill the kid immediately. The thought turned Much's stomach.

Still, there was little else for them to do.

Much caught sight of the dust in the distance, forward and to his left. No doubt the sign of the carts driving along the road. His muscles tightened as his heart skipped a beat, his feet slipping from the stirrups as his limbs involuntarily jerked toward his chest, his knees squeezing the horse's side and urging it into a gallop that he did not intend.

"Easy, boy!" Much cried, but it was too late. The sudden movement beneath him sent Much sliding to the left, not entirely out of the saddle but far enough to be hanging uncomfortably. He felt several pokes just behind his ear and turned to see several arrows bouncing out of his quiver at his shoulder and falling to the ground as he raced forward. His fearful reaction had set the horse running, and with a sinking heart Much realized his own horse's reaction had also set off the horses of Robin and Mark beside him, all of the animals surging forward in a violent burst of speed.

Much tangled his fingers through the horse's mane in a desperate attempt to keep his balance as the wind whipped through his hair and he struggled to get his feet securely into the stirrups once more.

"Steer clear of the road," Robin shouted over the sounds of their horses' pounding hooves. "There's an outcropping of trees up there, do you see it? Don't move to the road until you can move into the trees and out of sight."

Much hoped someone in the other group—Allen, Dusty, Will, and Little John—on the opposite side of the road would also come to the conclusion that the trees were the best place to move closer to the caravan and get a look at the kid. If the ambush only happened on one side of the road it would be less efficient, but there was no way to communicate their plans now that they were in motion.

Much's gaze shifted between the trees and the dust of the caravan as they continued their race forward. Eventually Robin banked left toward the trees and Much followed him. Within minutes Much, Robin, and Mark were under the trees and pulling their mounts to a walk.

Robin swung from his saddle and hastily threw the reins around a tree trunk. "Come on, let's get to the road before the caravan comes through!" He whipped his bow off of his back and ran forward, and Much hurriedly dismounted while Mark did the same. Together they pulled their own weapons and ran after Robin.

In a few minutes they were approaching the road. Much moved toward a tree and leaned against it on the northern side, knowing the caravan was approaching from the south. He gripped his bow in his hand, peeking around the tree. He could already see the caravan drawing closer. They hadn't reached the trees yet, but it would only be a few more minutes.

Much glanced to the other side of the road, wondering if the rest of the gang would be coming soon.

He pulled an arrow from his quiver, briefly lamenting the shrinking number of them. They'd left their last ambush in such a rush they hadn't collected their arrows or buried the dead, and then he'd lost a few more when he'd nearly fallen off his horse.

The first cart with a soldier sitting proudly at its front guiding the horse pulling it with a firm hand entered the outcropping of the trees. Counting the soldiers on the slow moving carts, Much's heart sank. Somewhere between the first ambush and now, the original surviving soldiers had apparently gathered reinforcements. There were at least twenty men with weapons drawn riding atop and walking beside the carts of treasure.

281

Movement across the road caught Much's attention and he saw Little John failing to blend into his surroundings as he gripped his quarter staff and glared at the road. The rest of the gang had arrived in time after all.

Much tried to ignore his sweaty hands and his pounding heart, but it was difficult. He hadn't felt this unnerved leading into one of their ambushes since the very beginning. It had been so routine lately, but today was a disaster of epic proportions.

And all the while, six children were about to be hanged in Nottingham…

As the first cart drew near to Much's position, he tried to locate the small boy but couldn't see him. In another moment, Robin's whistle pierced the air and Much sent his first arrow soaring straight toward the soldier leading the first cart.

Little John ran into the road with a shout of anger and a raised quarter staff while Robin ran for a cart further down the line where Much could now see the small boy bound and gagged, but at least he didn't have a knife to his throat. Much, Dusty, and Will let more arrows fly while Allen and Mark joined the fray with swords drawn.

Much drew arrow after arrow, searching the chaos for a target without harming his own friends and dropping one soldier after another. He saw Robin dart off the road and back toward the trees with the kid in his arms and felt some of the tension in his shoulders release.

"We've got the kid!" Little John shouted. "Do we stay for the treasure?"

The soldiers nearest him were bearing down on him with swords raised, but Little John used his brute strength to shove them aside, knocking more than one unconscious with a thwack from his thick wooden staff.

"We have six kids in Nottingham to deal with!" Dusty shouted from her position on the other side of the road.

"And we have treasure right here!" Little John called back.

Much wondered what the soldiers they were fighting would make of their conversation, but he joined the shouting match anyway. "I vote we leave the treasure and race for Nottingham! We could be too late as it is, why waste time?"

"I agree!" Will's voice called from the trees on the other side of the road.

Soldiers began to surge toward the sides of the road where Much, Will, and Dusty had remained, firing their arrows.

"We have to go now!" Dusty yelled.

"Get a move on!" Robin's voice suddenly joined the yelling.

Much slid the arrow in his hand back into his quiver and swung around, darting through the trees back toward the horses. Given the sounds of boots crashing through the underbrush behind him, he was sure there were soldiers following.

Much felt some measure of relief when his horse came into view. He bolted forward, swinging himself up into the saddle. His momentum was too much, however, and he slid right across the saddle and nearly fell down the other side of the horse. Robin was already mounted, the kid sitting in his lap, and Mark hurriedly mounted as well.

The soldiers ran towards them, but Much and his friends spurred their horses onward and raced northward, breaking through the treeline and running toward the road that would lead them back to Nottingham.

"They're on foot and dragging carts," Robin called as the rest of the gang raced toward them from the other side of the road. Much quickly counted heads and then realized Robin was glancing around doing the same. "The soldiers will be slow. Even if they unhitch the carts to use the horses to give chase, that will take time. We have a head start, let's get to Sherwood as fast as we can."

"Sherwood or Nottingham?" Dusty asked as they continued their sprint down the road, their horses kicking up dust with every hoofbeat.

"Wetherby," Robin called, spurring his horse into a faster gait. "If Marian isn't there, we'll go to Nottingham to see if we're too late, and then convene at the camp."

Much leaned forward over his horse, urging him to move faster. They had hours of travel ahead of them—a full night's worth—before they'd be back in Nottingham, and Little John was right; they might not make it in time at all.

What if they arrived in Nottingham to find six small bodies swinging from gallows constructed in Nottingham Square? Much shuddered at the thought as his stomach revolted and he nearly retched right on the neck of his horse.

Even if they'd left right away rather than chasing down the caravan and fighting to save the other boy—who still rode with Robin —they might not have made it to Nottingham in time to save the children. But Much couldn't help wondering if they could have, maybe, perhaps the innocent children swinging with snapped necks could have been avoided...

Chapter 34

THEY RODE THROUGH the night and into the early hours of the morning. The tension in Much's shoulders grew with every passing hour. When Wetherby came into view, he chewed on his lower lip, not wanting to hear the news Marian would have for them. But Marian was not at her home.

Robin patted his horse's neck gently and glanced at the rest of the group still mounted. Everyone—the horses especially—was breathing heavily.

"We can't all ride into Nottingham in this state; we'll draw attention. I'll go and see if there's bodies swinging in Nottingham Square. Meet me back at the camp. Take little James with you."

"We'll wait to hear the news," Dusty said. "We'll meet you on the road between Nottingham and Sherwood."

Robin nodded. "Alright. I'll see you soon."

Robin handed the reins of his horse to Much. The kid, James, still sat in Robin's saddle, and he looked more than a little overwhelmed by the ordeal he'd been through. His eyes were wide, and his face tear-stained as he watched all of them silently.

Dusty led the group away from the village of Wetherby and toward the main road that led out of Nottingham, keeping out of sight of the city. The sun was rising over Sherwood forest, dousing the land in shimmering light and painting the sky with hues of purple and pink. It was a stark contrast to the darkness Much felt brewing in his chest.

"We're too late."

"Don't say that, Much," Allen snapped. "We don't know what happened."

"The children were to be hanged at dawn," Little John sighed. "It's past dawn, and we weren't here. Much is right. We're too late."

Much glanced at young James, who was crying softly on the horse beside him. "It's alright, James. You're safe."

"And we'll get you home soon," Dusty said, guiding her horse over so she could reach out and brush the child's tears away. "Just as soon as we get all this sorted, we'll get you back to your parents. Don't worry."

"Robin's coming!" Mark said, causing everyone to turn and look down the road. Robin was, indeed, approaching.

"The kids?" Dusty asked, her voice wavering with the emotions Much was also feeling.

"No executions. Marcus doesn't know what went down specifically, but the kids aren't dead. The Sheriff hanged some of his soldiers this morning; they're still swinging in Nottingham Square."

"The soldiers are, but the kids aren't?" Will asked.

Robin shrugged, pulling himself into his saddle behind James. "That's what I saw and what Marcus confirmed. I didn't see Marian. If she's not in Wetherby or Nottingham, she's probably at the camp. Let's go see what she has to say."

When the gang rode into camp, Marian was sitting at the fire ring. She looked up as they came into the clearing, and then ran over to Robin and threw herself into his arms as he dismounted.

"Robin! So much has happened, I don't even know where to begin!"

"Start with the children," Robin said, helping James off of his horse as Much and the others also dismounted and gathered around Marian.

"The Sheriff was going to hang six kids because he was angry with their parents. You were all gone, and I didn't know what to do. I tried to talk to Gisbourne; I asked him to let them go, but he refused."

"Of course he did," Robin said. "What did you expect?"

"Wait, Robin, I wasn't finished," Marian crossed her arms. "When I went to the Square, fully expecting to see the children hanging, the Sheriff was hanging his guards instead. From his angry ranting, I managed to make out that the children had escaped and he was hanging the guards who were keeping watch over them."

"I did see the dead soldiers," Robin said.

"But what about the children," Dusty interjected. "What happened? Where are they?"

"Sir Guy—Gisbourne—came to see me late last night. He told me he'd taken the children from custody and brought them to the edge of Sherwood. He didn't know what to do with them so he asked me to bring them to you. He figured you could keep the children safe here, and Robin…" Marian bit her lip.

"What?" Robin asked even as Dusty and Will exclaimed "The children are here?"

"Gisbourne proposed after he rescued the children…"

"He what?!" Robin's eyebrows hit his hairline. Will dropped the bow he'd been holding and Little John starting chuckling and then choked as he tried to cover his laughter. Much was so shocked he could scarcely breathe for a moment.

"Gisbourne proposed?" Robin asked as the initial shock of Marian's pronouncement dissipated.

"Yes," Marian said.

"And you said?"

287

"No! Obviously, I said no. Really, Robin, why would you ask that? Sir Guy of Gisbourne is a wretched, cruel man. Why would I marry him?"

"I'm relieved you feel that way."

"I was worried after I refused him that he'd take the children back and go through with the Sheriff's plan to hang them...but he didn't."

"I'm rather surprised at that, but I'm glad. And of course we'll keep the children! They're here now?" Robin asked as the group moved toward the fireplace and seated themselves on the logs circled around it. James sat between Much and Robin, watching the conversation unfold with wide, confused eyes.

"Yes, they're sleeping in the huts; they had a long night."

"I'm sure they did," Robin agreed. "I'm surprised Gisbourne even rescued them, but to let them go even after your refusal? What a man wouldn't do for Marian." Robin bent and kissed Marian's cheek with a wink.

Much shook his head, biting his cheek. He couldn't believe this. Sir Guy of Gisbourne, the gang's sworn enemy—a man of no morals who was known to be cruel and ruthless—had rescued innocent children and proposed to Marian. It was true he'd been courting her, but how much must he love her to do such a thing?

"Sir Guy might not be as vile as people say," Dusty commented. Much shot her a glance, wondering if she'd been reading his thoughts in his expression. "Or at the very least, he does have a conscience and does struggle with the choices that he makes."

Allen shook his head. "Don't count on it. He did this for Marian, not for any other reason. His conscience is not getting to him."

"You don't know that," Dusty replied.

Will placed a gentle hand on Dusty's shoulder. "He's evil, Dusty. Don't try to make a saint out of him."

"I don't make saints," Dusty replied. "I am only suggesting he is not fully evil, even as none of us are fully good. Only God can clothe us in any righteousness. We're all the worst of sinners before Him."

Much wished he could be as brave as Dusty and defend his faith in such a way, but he had yet to tell anyone apart from Dusty that he believed in Jesus at all. And more than that, he wasn't sure he liked what she was saying right now, whether he agreed with it or not.

Much shifted on the log, glancing between Robin and Dusty. Was Dusty suggesting that the still small voice that whispered love and acceptance into Much's heart every time he began to feel unworthy was saying the same thing to Sir Guy of Gisbourne? She did speak of the gospel as being for everyone, insisting that all were sinful and fallen from God's glory but through His grace and sacrifice on the cross anyone could be brought back into a relationship with him. But Gisbourne?

Much wasn't sure how he felt about the idea of Gisbourne being forgiven and loved, but he did feel a little guilty for not wishing that peace on him.

"I'd say we're better than Sir Guy of Gisbourne any day," Robin said.

"Robin…" Dusty sighed.

Robin held up his hands to silence her. "Don't start. We all know how you feel. We don't need another lecture."

Little John steered the conversation away from Dusty before the argument could extend further. "Did Gisbourne not speak of anything else, Marian? He knows you are connected to our gang, that could mean trouble for you."

"I know," Marian replied, her gaze turning on Little John. "But he didn't say anything about it after we fought."

"He didn't mention Mark?" Little John pressed.

"Why would he ask about me?" Mark asked.

289

"I'm sure they've noticed you are never home," Little John replied.

"What Gisbourne will do with his information that Marian does, indeed, know who we are remains to be seen," Will said. "It might be too dangerous for her to continue living in Wetherby."

"We'll have to keep watch," Robin said. Much could tell by his expression and the way he shifted closer to Marian and slipped his arm around her waist that he was truly worried, though his voice remained relatively calm. "Gisbourne knows Marian helps us, if he came to her directly in order to get the children to us for safety…"

Marian pushed against his shoulder in a playful manner. "Don't look so grave. I will be fine."

"We'll keep an eye on Wetherby anyway," Robin replied.

"You do that," Marian said, kissing his cheek. "I need to get home anyway. Gisbourne might come back today."

"If he does, we'll be there," Robin said.

Marian gave him a last look and then slipped out of the camp.

"Little John, keep an eye on her today, will you?" Robin said.

Little John rose, grabbing his quarter staff from where he'd set it beside his hut. "Nothing will harm her today."

Much rose from the fire and went to his kitchen, gathering supplies to make a meal for the exhausted gang and the children who were beginning to poke their heads shyly out of the huts to see what the commotion was about.

As Much fried sausages and eggs over the fire, the rest of the gang encouraged the children to join the circle and they hesitantly came over. The sight of James sitting with the rest of the gang made the circle seem more friendly and soon all of the children were gathered around with the adults.

There were six of them in total, making the portions of food Much would be cooking for every meal a bit larger than it had been previously. The older kids seemed in awe of Robin Hood and the rest of the group, watching them with wide eyes. The younger ones merely seemed hungry for attention and affection.

As the gang asked questions of the oldest ones to ascertain who they were, it became clear that the six children were cousins. Seven-year-old Beth, six-year-old John, and four-year-old Peter were the children of one man while ten-year-old William, eight-year old Sarah, and five-year-old Rachel were the children of his brother. It was their fathers who had angered the Sheriff, but he'd arrested them to prove a point and scare the rest of Nottingham.

"Being in the prison was scary," young William said, his brow furrowing. He turned to Will. "Have you been to prison?"

"I haven't…I'm sorry it was scary."

"I didn't like it," William said simply.

"I'd imagine not."

Little Rachel, the five year old, crawled into Will's lap as Much began to scoop eggs and sausages onto plates and hand them out to the gang and the children. "Are you nice?" the little girl asked, staring up at Will.

"I don't know, little lady." Will winked, brushing a wayward curl out of her face. "Am I?"

Rachel tilted her small head to one side, seeming to study his face. "I think so."

Allen shook his head with a laugh. "Don't be fooled, Rachel. You're only five, so maybe you can't see the truth, but Will is a—"

Dusty's elbow connected with Allen's ribs and cut off whatever he'd been about to say as he shied away from her with a wince and nearly dropped his plate of food.

Will raised his eyebrows. "I'm a what, Allen?"

Allen shrugged, glancing at Dusty. "I don't know. Nothing."

Robin laughed. "Don't worry, Rachel. Despite the silliness of our group, we're actually very nice, I promise."

Once everyone had eaten, Robin entrusted James to Much to return him to his family, while the rest of the gang continued to get to know the children who would be living in the camp. or went to keep an eye on Marian in Wetherby.

The ride from Sherwood to Leicester took most of the day, and Much spent the majority of it listening to James recount the adventure of the day before.

"I'm going to be part of Robin Hood's gang someday," he said confidently. "I won't get caught next time, either! I'll help fight the bad men and save people."

"I'm sure you will, but maybe wait until you're a little older."

"I wish I could live in Sherwood with the other kids. It's not fair they get to stay."

"They can't go home without getting in trouble with bad men. You can still go home to your family without being arrested."

James continued to pout. Once they returned to Leicester, however, he gave Much directions to his home and then eagerly ran into the waiting arms of his mother.

"Where have you been? What happened?"

Both James and his mother were crying and embracing while Much explained to his father everything that had happened. Both parents thanked Much profusely, and then he made his way back to Nottingham. It was late in the evening when he rode into camp, and he was relieved to see that Dusty was cooking dinner and he wasn't responsible for feeding everyone that night; he was exhausted enough from the past two days he felt he could fall asleep in the saddle. But he dismounted and moved to the fire ring to partake of Dusty's meal before he retired to his hut and fell asleep.

Chapter 35

THE NEXT MORNING, Robin gave out assignments as Much cooked up breakfast for everyone and the children gathered around the fire— some watching Much intently, while others gathered around Will and pestered him with questions which he gently answered.

"Much, Mark, you'll be with me today," Robin said. "We're keeping an eye on Marian. Dusty, you take Nottingham—pass out food, keep an eye on the Sheriff and Gisbourne, heal the sick…whatever seems necessary while you're there. I trust your judgment. Allen…you get to keep an eye on our small charges for the day."

"I'm playing nursemaid?" Allen crossed his arms, frowning deeply.

"Someone has to," Robin replied. "We'll take turns every day. Today it's you. Deal with it."

Before long, Much, Robin, and Mark were camped out in a clump of bushes not far from Mark's childhood home. They could see Wetherby, and specifically Mark and Marian's home, and they also had a good view of the path that led from Wetherby to the main road that entered the city of Nottingham which they could see some miles in the distance.

They'd barely settled into place when Robin tensed.

"Look! Gisbourne incoming, with soldiers."

Much shivered as he watched as Sir Guy of Gisbourne marched down the path toward Marian's home with a company of soldiers bearing torches. He was dressed in his black tunic and trousers as always, with black-painted leather armor over the top. His dark hair offset his pale, stern face as he marched down the dirt path. The man's arrogant confidence always unsettled Much.

"We weren't here soon enough," Mark hissed. "If we'd been waiting earlier we might have seen his approach sooner and warned Marian!"

"Hush," Robin hissed. "I'm trying to hear them."

Robin leaned forward, and Much did the same as he peered through the bushes toward the group of soldiers. Marian appeared to have come to the front door and was conversing with Gisbourne, but whatever they were saying Much couldn't hear it. All he could make out was the body language: Gisbourne's tense and angry gestures and Marian tossing her head with her usual rebellion. Whatever they were saying, they seemed to be arguing.

Suddenly Marian cried out and Much could hear her clearly. "No, Sir Guy, don't!"

Much leaned forward, trying to see better through the bushes. Gisbourne snatched a torch from one of the soldiers with him, and waved near Marian's face.

"Gisbourne is trying to burn my home!" Mark hissed.

"Be quiet!" Robin glared at Mark and then turned back to the tense scene.

The argument between Gisbourne and Marian wasn't any more clear than it had been before, but suddenly Marian dropped to her knees and appeared to be begging.

"I'm going to kill him," Robin said, his jaw clenching. Much had rarely heard him so angry.

"If he doesn't get away from my sister…" Mark's hands were curled into fists at his side as he watched Marian's begging. Much put a hand on his arm, hoping to calm him. There were far too many soldiers for the three of them to try and take them on just now, and he didn't want Mark to do anything stupid.

All at once, Gisbourne threw his torch into the house and the other soldiers began to do the same with theirs. Marian and Mark's home was soon flickering with flame as Marian cried out. She tried to run for the house, but Gisbourne caught her and pulled Marian away from the growing fire.

Mark reached for the sword at his waist, standing up, but Robin grabbed his arm and jerked him back down behind the bush. "No! There are too many, Mark, even for us!"

Mark scowled, his hand still gripping his blade. "I can't let him have her!"

Robin looked back at Gisbourne, who was now dragging Marian down the path away from Wetherby and towards Nottingham, the rest of the soldiers following them. "She'll be okay…she has to be okay. Come on, as soon as the soldiers are out of view we can get the villagers to help us try and put out that fire! We'll go to Nottingham and find Marian afterward."

"What if the Sheriff harms her before then?" Mark asked, shoving his blade into its sheath and standing up as Gisbourne's party moved off further down the road.

"Marian can take care of herself. And whatever caused this disaster," Robin stood, gesturing toward the burning house, "he was willing to put himself in potential danger to save children for Marian's sake only a few days ago…I doubt he'll let her come to any real harm now."

"You trust Gisbourne?" Mark crossed his arms.

"No. I don't. But I do trust Marian, and I know what it means to love her. If Gisbourne is sincere in his affection, he won't let her be harmed."

"He just burned my house!"

"He pulled her back from the flames," Robin replied. "Now come on, let's get that fire out and then get to Nottingham!"

Robin moved toward the burning house and Much hurried after him, leaving Mark to brood for a moment before he also followed. Widow Mary and other villagers were already running with buckets of water toward the house, but even with help from Much, Robin, and Mark, putting out the flames was a difficult task.

They were too late. Once the fire itself was out, nothing was left but the charred husk of what used to be a house. Marian and Mark's home was gone.

Mark was in a foul mood and wanted to go straight to Nottingham but Robin insisted he return to the camp.

"I'm not abandoning Marian!"

"You're in no frame of mind to come to Nottingham," Robin insisted. "You'll do something reckless and get yourself and possibly others killed. Go to camp. I'll bring news of Marian."

"I'm coming to find my sister," Mark growled, pushing past Robin. Robin sighed heavily and then grabbed Mark, pinning his arms behind his back as he struggled against him.

"You can't fight me, Mark. And you can't fight Much either. I won't let you get yourself killed, or get Marian killed, with your reckless anger. You need to calm down and get control of yourself."

"I'm going to kill Gisbourne!"

"I would like to as well," Robin replied, his voice so full of ice it sent a shiver down Much's spine. "But I have more control over my emotions and I know better than to do something stupid. You are going to camp until you have a level head."

Mark tried to pull himself free of Robin's grasp and failed. "You can't make me."

"I obviously can," Robin replied calmly, keeping his grasp on Mark firm. "And so can Much. We've been training and fighting a great deal longer than you have, you can't beat us."

Robin glanced toward Much, indicating with a jerk of his head that he wanted Much to take over holding onto Mark. Much didn't hesitate, moving over quickly and taking hold of Mark's arms as Robin let go. He wasn't convinced he could actually handle Mark as smoothly and easily as Robin had, but he wasn't going to argue.

Mark tried to pull free as he was transferred from one grip to the next, but Much latched onto his arms tightly and shifted his stance so his legs could bear the burden of Mark's movement in such a way that Much wouldn't lose his balance.

"I'll come to the camp as soon as I know Marian is safe," Robin said, giving Mark a sharp look. "Don't come to Nottingham. I don't trust you and your volatile emotions."

"He burned my house!"

"I know," Robin said, backing away. "But you can't do anything stupid because of it." Robin spun on his heel and marched toward Nottingham and Much reluctantly starting moving, keeping his grip on Mark.

Mark tried one last time to pull free of his captor, and then groaned. "Alright, alright. I'll come to the camp."

Much wished he could trust him and let him go, but he knew Robin was right; Mark was liable to do something stupid. So he kept his firm grip on him and practically dragged him all the way back to camp.

When they entered the clearing he let go, and Mark shoved away from him, turning to glare at Much.

"What's going on?" Allen asked. He and the children eyed the angry Mark and the harried looking Much with curious eyes.

"Gisbourne burned the house in Wetherby and has taken Marian captive," Much said. "Robin said Mark isn't to leave the camp until he comes back, in case he does something stupid in retaliation."

Allen crossed his arms and studied Mark, who glared at him and then in a huff moved toward the fire ring. "If anything happens to Marian because I wasn't there to help her…"

"Robin Hood will keep her safe," young William declared.

Some of the fight seemed to go out of Mark as he settled onto one of the logs that served as benches around the fire. Some of the children resumed their playing in the open area of the meadow, while young William settled onto the log beside Mark and tried to convince him that Robin Hood could do anything.

Mark remained tense, but he stopped verbally lashing out. Much settled onto the log across from him and William, watching him carefully. Allen seated himself next to Much.

"Eventful day, I guess."

"Things just get worse and worse," Much sighed. "First the botched raid and the hostage situation, then the children nearly getting hanged, and now Marian's taken captive and her home is burned to the ground…I feel something terrible is coming."

"Or maybe the disasters have run their course and things will settle down again," Allen said, though the tone of his voice made it clear to Much that he did not believe that any more than Much did.

It was hours before Robin returned, and before he came back to the camp the rest of the gang returned from their various activities.

298

Much and Mark let them in on what had happened in Wetherby, and they all waited for Robin's return with trepidation. Much thought the tension in the air was thick enough to slice like a tough piece of meat. The children were eventually put to bed, and then the gang gathered around the fire ring to wait.

When Robin did entered the camp, Mark was on his feet instantly. "Where's Marian? Why are you so happy?"

Robin came to join the circle around the fire ring. "Sit down, Mark. She's alive, she's fine." Mark sank back onto the log-bench with a sigh as Robin continued, "She's under house arrest and has a personal guard to tail her wherever she goes within the castle. It will be difficult to see her, but not impossible. Her room is, in fact, one of the many that has a door directly into the secret passages."

"That's a relief," Mark said. "Why didn't you get her out as long as there's a passage that leads right to her room?"

"She wants to stay to be near your father, and also to pick up information from the Sheriff and Gisbourne that we might not be able to get simply from the secret passages. They don't connect to every room in the castle; it is possible there are plots and schemes that we miss, that she will now be able to hear about and help us foil."

With the news that Marian was safe, albeit under house arrest, the tension bled from the group around the fire and their usual teasing resumed. Soon enough they were all retiring to their respective huts to sleep.

Because space within each hut was limited, each member of the gang, apart from Robin, bunked with one of the small children. Much's roommate was four-year-old Peter, who was sound asleep when Much crept into the hut and into bed. He'd piled a few blankets on the floor to create a little bed for the toddler, and given the boy's snoring, he was perfectly satisfied with his make-shift bed.

Chapter 36

MUCH AWOKE THE next morning to a small body jumping on his stomach. With a groan he opened his eyes to see Peter sitting on him and smiling brightly. "I'm hungry!"

"Is that why you're jumping on me?" Much laughed.

"You do food," Peter said with a firm nod of his small head.

"Yes, I do food," Much said, sitting up and moving Peter off of himself. "Let me up and I'll start breakfast for you."
Peter clapped his hands. "I like you!"

As Much began preparing breakfast, more children—in various stages of wakefulness—began to exit their tents and gather around him to watch.

"Can I help?" Beth asked softly.

"Of course." Much let her sit beside him on the dew covered ground and held her hand, guiding it to use his spoon to flip one of the eggs he was frying. Young William sat on one of the logs near the fire ring with Peter in his lap and little Rachel sitting beside him.

Rachel seemed to grow bored of watching Much and Beth cook, however, and soon ran toward one of the huts. Much wasn't sure what she was doing until he heard Will groan and Rachel fall into a fit of giggles.

Will soon emerged from his hut with little Rachel in his arms. "Did you tell her to jump on my chest, Much?"

"No!" Much laughed. "I am sorry if she hurt you."

"She didn't."

"Peter woke me in the same fashion this morning."

Will sat beside young William and shook his head with a laugh. "I hope this doesn't become a tradition."

Much watched as Rachel pulled on Will's ear and began to chant in a sing-song voice, "Will, Will, Will..."

"What do you need, Rachel?" Will asked patiently.

Rachel giggled. "Will."

Will commenced tickling the silliness out of young Rachel, which sent her and the other children into squeals of laughter. Soon the rest of the gang and the other children were emerging from their various huts.

"What is all that racket?" Robin asked, stepping out of his hut.

"We have children," Dusty said with a smile as the gang gathered around the fire and Much and Beth began scooping breakfast onto plates for all of them. "What do you expect?"

Allen sighed, rubbing his eyes as he sank onto one of the log-benches. "Are you saying we aren't going to have any peace and quiet anymore?"

"I believe that is what she is saying," Mark said, playfully glowering at the children.

"I think I'd rather go to prison," Allen groaned.

"Allen!" Dusty elbowed him in the ribs. "Don't be ridiculous. I think it was a true joy to wake up to the children's laughter."

Allen rolled his eyes, but Will smiled at Dusty. "I agree. This has been one of the sweetest mornings I've had since all our adventures began."

As they ate breakfast, Robin began to give out assignments to the gang for the day, and Much was given charge of the children for the day. Allen let it be known how grateful he was not to be stuck in the camp this time, which caused Dusty to elbow him again.

As the gang began to adjust to having six children underfoot, Marian was adjusting to being locked inside the castle walls with only the Sheriff, Gisbourne, and their soldiers for company. Robin tried to visit her as often as he could, and Mark often went with him.

To Marian's relief, Mark soon developed a plan to get her out of the castle now and again without being seen—namely, that she be given a matching Hooded Rescuer disguise as his, so she could move about Nottingham helping people without the Sheriff or Gisbourne ever knowing that she'd left the castle at all.

Mark and Dusty, with help from little Sarah and Beth who were eager to participate, took a week to create the new disguise. At the end of the week, Robin took the disguise to Marian late one night. When he returned to camp he was humming to himself.

"Did Marian profess her love again?" Will teased as Robin joined the gang gathered around the fire—the children had been put to bed when the sun went down, but the adults remained gathered around the fire as the stars made their appearance overhead.

"No," Robin said as he sat down. "Why?"

"You're extra cheerful tonight."

"Oh. Well, there was no confession of love made by Marian, although I made one myself."

"You do that constantly," Allen rolled his eyes. "That's nothing new."

"Why are you so cheerful?" Will asked Robin.

"I saw Marian! Do I need another reason? Also, I've convinced her to come to camp every few nights to train with me. She's not nearly as proficient with weapons or hand-to-hand combat as the rest of us, and I would like her to be."

Mark grinned. "I can only imagine how offended my sister must have been when you offered to train her."

"She was not very appreciative," Robin chuckled. "Claimed I didn't believe in her."

Dusty crossed her arms, but said nothing as Robin continued, "But I merely want to help her be the best she can be. I love her."

Allen and others in the gang rolled their eyes at Robin, but Much found himself feeling less amusement toward Robin and more of a rather darker emotion. First he'd taken Mark under his wing, and now Marian…when was he going to offer such attention to Much? Never, was the most obvious answer.

Much bit his lip. He didn't want to be envious. He knew Robin didn't mean anything by it, but it was just one more thing that made it so obvious to Much that though people might say he was an equal in the gang, he was in fact still just the orphan boy in servitude to a nobleman.

The very next night, Marian arrived in the camp and spent an hour training with Robin. Young William and some of the other children gathered around them to watch. Rachel and Peter settled onto Will's lap as the rest of the gang sat around and chatted, occasionally throwing teasing comments toward Robin and Marian—who pointedly ignored them.

Marian had been somewhat downcast when she'd first arrived in camp, and had spoken to Dusty quietly about her father's continued illness. But now she was shooting her bow with Robin standing beside her and giving her pointers, whispering things into her ear that made her throw back her head and laugh.

As the hour drew on, more of the children gathered around the fire ring, most of them sitting as close to Will as they could. As pleasant conversation swirled around him, Much couldn't keep his eyes off of

Robin and Marian. He couldn't explain why it cut so deeply that Robin never bothered to take the time to assist him...but it did.

When Robin and Marian were through training for the night, they joined the group at the fire ring. Will crossed his arms as they approached. "I don't suppose you could come any earlier the next time you visit?"

"I doubt it," Marian replied with a frown. "If I retire too early to my rooms, Andrew will likely take notice. I have to wait for nightfall. Why?"

"Because you are keeping my children up." Will gave a nod to the six children who were now in various positions on and around his person—Peter was sleeping in his arms, Rachel was seated next to him, leaning her head into his arm and nearly asleep as well. Most of the others were also close to nodding off, but apparently the sounds of sword-play had been keeping them awake.

"*Your* children?" Marian laughed. "Have you claimed them?"

Will grinned. "Possibly."

"They have families, you know," Robin said.

"I know. And as soon as we rid ourselves of the Sheriff, or King Richard returns and is able to do so for us, they'll go home. But for now...someone needs to claim them."

"Better you than me," Allen laughed.

"Either way, we do need to get them all to bed," Will said.

He promptly carried the sleeping Peter to Much's hut, while Dusty and Marian moved forward to guide the rest of the children to their own beds. That seemed to be the sign that the evening's activities were over, and the rest of the gang began to retire to their own huts. Robin accompanied Marian back to Nottingham and Much stayed by the dying fire.

305

Much tried to push his jealous thoughts of Robin's attention to Marian and Mark from his mind, but with no success. The sad fact remained that all of them continued to tell Much he was family to them and then treated him as though he was nothing.

And perhaps he was nothing, after all.

Slowly, the flames of the fire began to go out leaving the glowing coals behind. Much grabbed a stick and began poking at the coals, impatient for the last of them to die down so he could go to bed himself.

Robin returned to the camp and moved across the dark meadow to join Much beside the dying embers.

"Why are you brooding, my friend?"

"I am not brooding."

"Please, I know that frown."

"It's…nothing."

"Much."

Much glanced at Robin, his profile barely visible in the darkness. "You…"

Much shook his head. He couldn't tell Robin the truth.

Robin leaned forward, trying to study Much's face despite the darkness.

"Much?"

"It's nothing. I was just thinking about the way you help Marian and Mark with training, that is all."

"Have you been feeling overlooked and mistreated again?" Robin shook his head, playfully pushing his shoulder against Much's. "How could you possibly feel so? You are my best friend. You always have been, and that hasn't changed."

Much jabbed his stick into the leftover coals and bit his cheek.

"I know I help Mark and Marian more than anyone else, but that's because they're amateur, Much. You have never needed my assistance. Don't shake your head at me, it's true. I don't take the time to assist you because you're a capable warrior already. You don't need my help. And yes, I do turn to Marian for advice more than you these days, which I'm sure you've noticed as well…that is something I cannot help. I do value your opinion still, that hasn't changed, it's just that Marian…"

"You love her; I know that." Much was rather impressed Robin had correctly guessed the majority of what Much had been feeling lately. Perhaps he paid more attention than Much gave him credit for.

"Yes, I do love her. And when we are married, things will be different. I will go to Marian for everything because she will be my wife and best friend, also. Yet I cannot have you thinking I will cease to care for you, my friend. Things are changing, and you'll have to deal with that, but you can't think I don't love you, too."

"I don't think you don't care," Much said quickly. "Of course Marian's opinion would be of greater value to you."

Robin shook his head. "You aren't hearing me. Your opinion is valuable to me; more than that, your friendship is. I don't want to break this relationship simply because I am pursuing Marian. And as for the training…you should know you don't need it. You're as good as I am."

"I doubt that."

"You think too little of yourself, Much. I will certainly be more careful in the future to ensure we are on the same page and I am not wounding my dear friend."

"You don't need to worry about me. This seems to be a personal problem of mine and not a fault of yours."

307

"And there you go again," Robin sighed. "I can't promise things won't continue to change—our lives are chaotic these days, and more than that I am hoping to marry Marian someday, in which case I won't be as available as I often have been. But all that aside…you are a man I respect and admire, Much, and I wish you would see yourself how I do."

More to the point, see yourself how **I** *do.*

Much could feel the love and acceptance caressing his heart again as it so often did and he tried to fall into it the way he had the first time he'd felt it while they were still traveling home from the Crusades, but it was harder than he expected.

Robin pushed his shoulder against Much's for a moment. "Go to sleep. And stop being so down on yourself. I'll watch the fire till it dies down."

Much sighed and then nodded. He could appreciate Robin's attempt to cheer him up. And the fact that Robin could so easily read him was in some ways comforting. He did care enough to notice, after all, which lent credibility to the idea that he did actually care for and respect Much as a friend and equal.

Even so, Much's heart was still heavy as he drifted off to sleep.

Chapter 37

ONE BRIGHT, CRISP morning, as Much cleaned off the breakfast dishes and prepared to put them away in his hut, Robin sauntered over with a pouch of coin in his hand.

"Much, can you go to Locksley today?"

"Of course, what do you need?"

"I just want to make sure Sarah and the rest of the manor are being taken care of and aren't in need. And while you're there you could ask her about what we can do with our children…what to feed them, how to entertain them. She's good with little ones."

"Yes, she is." Much couldn't stop the smile that spread across his face remembering how Sarah had looked after him and Robin when they were young. "She'll probably start talking about what we were like as kids…"

"I wish I could hear her reminiscing, but I have other things to do today." Robin held out the money bag and Much took it, tying it to his belt.

"Any messages you want to send to her?"

Robin shrugged. "She knows we love her. Just make sure she's doing alright."

"I will."

Robin strode off as Much finished his chores and then prepared to go visit Locksley. He made sure his sword was strapped to his belt, his bow and quiver were slung over his shoulder, and double-checked that the money bag from Robin was still on his belt.

He hadn't been to Locksley in a while, there was no telling what he might encounter while he was there. Robin and Much had been avoiding visiting to keep suspicion off of Sarah and the rest of the household, but now that Robin had given the approval for the visit Much was eager to go. He missed Sarah.

Much made the long walk through Sherwood forest and then across the open fields to the village of Locksley. As far as Much had been able to tell, after Robin was declared an outlaw his lands were transferred to the Sheriff. The Sheriff didn't live at Locksley, or visit often, which left the running of the village to Robin's senior staff—Sarah and Matthew—with Gisbourne occasionally dropping by to check up on the estate and collect the revenue due to Robin for himself.

The village itself was quiet when he walked through it, not a person in sight. Whether they were hiding in their homes because visitors usually meant Gisbourne and they didn't want to see him, or because they knew it was Much and were too afraid of Gisbourne and the Sheriff to be seen fraternizing with outlaws, Much didn't know. Either way, the result was the same—not a single soul approached him in any way as he passed through the village and then up the winding lane that led to the manor.

On the bright side, it seemed Gisbourne didn't leave a contingent of soldiers at Locksley manor which meant Much likely wasn't going to run into the trouble he'd been worried about.

Much slipped around the back of the manor, choosing not to knock on the front door. Robin might have freed him, but he was not a noble. Entering through the front door without Robin at his side felt wrong, somehow. So he went for the kitchen instead.

He could smell Sarah's creations before he entered, and Much stopped for a moment to breathe in the familiar scents, letting the simple peace of being home flood his being.

As he stood there, the door flew open and Sarah dashed out, dragging him forward into her warm embrace. "You're home! Why are you here? Did something happen to Robin?"

Sarah planted a kiss on his forehead and then pulled back, her eyes darting around his face as though searching for something.

"Robin is doing well, Sarah. I only came to check on you."

Sarah closed her eyes, breathing for a moment, and then nodded. "Well come in, then."

Sarah led him into the kitchen. None of her underlings were bustling about the kitchen, making the space feel empty and quiet in a way Much had never seen it before.

Sarah was baking bread, which Much could smell, and there seemed to be a pot of stew or pottage of some kind over the open fire of the hearth, but there were no preparations laid out across the large table that dominated the center of the room. Much had never seen it empty before.

Sarah pushed Much into a chair at one of the small tables along the wall and then poured him a cup of tea.

"You gave the servants a scare, you know!" Sarah said as she seated herself across from him. "They saw a man wandering up the lane and panicked, thinking Gisbourne was coming back again."

"Does he visit often?"

"Often enough to terrorize us into submission and to steal Robin's wealth. But no, he doesn't come back all that frequently."

"Does he hurt anyone?" Much took a long drink of Sarah's tea as he hesitated with his next question. "Has he killed anyone?"

"No. He shouts a lot, and makes it known he could hurt us if we step out of line. I believe him; Sheriff's right hand, known to be

311

responsible for so many deaths in Nottingham, and now burning our Lady Marian's home to the ground. I believe him, Much."

"I believe him, too. That's why Robin and I wanted to check on you."

"Where's Robin then?"

"Busy."

"Ah, you're so worried about me you don't visit for a year, and when you do it's only one of you."

"Robin is concerned for you. This visit was his idea. It's just that Robin also has an entire country to look after, you know."

"I know. My boys, saving the world." Sarah shook her head. "I remember just yesterday you were playing pirates and would come crying when one or the other of you would whack too hard with your stick…"

"That's another reason I came today, actually."

"To play pirates?" Sarah raised an eyebrow, her eyes dancing with laughter.

"No, to talk about children. Do you remember those kids the Sheriff was going to hang?"

"I do. Terrible thing. Rumor has it Lady Marian got them out somehow."

"She did. And they're living at the camp now, until it is safe for them to return to their families. But…we don't really know what to do with them."

Sarah chuckled at that, shaking her head in a fond sort of way. "How old are they?"

"Young. The oldest is ten, the youngest four."

"Hmmm. Do you have toys at the camp?"

Much sat back in his chair and looked at Sarah. Toys in the

camp at Sherwood, where outlaws were living and planning their schemes against the Sheriff and Gisbourne?

"A silly question, perhaps," Sarah conceded when Much said nothing. "You'll have to take some of your and Robin's old things back to the camp, give them something to entertain themselves. Especially the youngest ones. A ten year old can likely entertain themselves anyway living in a forest. They could be helpful, too. Put them to work a bit."

"Some of the kids do like to help me prepare meals for the gang."

Much listened to Sarah discussing how best to care for the children in the gang for a while, and then he brought the conversation back around to the empty kitchen.

"Where is everyone, Sarah?"

"Hiding. I told you, you gave everyone a scare when they saw you coming. They all scurried off to find work out of sight so Gisbourne couldn't pick on them. Turns out it was just you, though."

"So the staff here…you're all okay?"

"Everyone is still here, just wary of visitors."

Much glanced around the room and the lack of food preparations on the big table. Sarah followed his gaze.

"We don't have a lord to feed every day anymore. Gisbourne is rarely here. When he is, we scramble to put together something, but on the day-to-day it's just us. We don't need the big fancy meals we used to make for the Earl. That, and we don't have nearly as much food to begin with. Pulling off one of the Earl's favorites would be hard to do these days. No complaints though, to be sure. We are far better off than most. I am grateful Gisbourne didn't turn us out into the street when he took over after Robin became 'Robin Hood' and all that."

"I am glad of that as well, but if he had, you know we would have found you and taken care of you."

"Oh, the great Robin Hood would have time for me then, if I was out on the street?"

Much reached across the table and grabbed her hand, giving it a gentle squeeze. "You have to know the reason we didn't visit sooner is simply that we didn't want to arouse suspicion. Everyone associated with Robin Hood and the rest of the outlaws is treated harshly...Lady Marian's home was burned and now she's under house arrest at the castle. I do believe the only reason she wasn't killed outright is that Gisbourne loves her. If the Sheriff and Gisbourne think you know more about Robin and the rest of us than you are letting on, you'll be in danger. They figured out fairly easily that Robin is Robin Hood, so they are probably already keeping an eye on his household and estate for any suspicious behavior..."

Sarah's eyes softened and she nodded. "I see that, little one. Gisbourne has questioned us, extensively, but the fact that we know nothing beyond Robin being gone has proved to be true, so he moved on. I understand your concern, it's just that I miss my boys."

The way Sarah always spoke of her affection for both of them equally without hesitation was a balm to Much's heart.

I have always told you that you are loved precisely as you are.

Much closed his eyes for a moment, letting the overpowering love and acceptance of Christ wash over him. The idea He'd just planted, that he had placed Sarah in Much's life to show him what His love looked like all along, was a comforting one.

"Much?"

Much opened his eyes and smiled at the woman who was his mother in all but blood. "Have I ever thanked you for loving me so

314

completely? You didn't have to. I was just a random orphan boy, but you did anyway."

"Of course I did," Sarah said. "I couldn't let you grow up under the Earl's strict eye without some comfort. You were just a tiny little boy with a big heart; you needed someone. And from the first day you set foot here in my kitchen, you stole my heart. I don't view you as an orphan, you know. Nor Robin either. You're *my* boys."

Much stayed for longer than he probably should have, just chatting with Sarah and relishing in the love she had that reflected the love of his Father in heaven. Before he left he gave her the money Robin had sent, and promised to try and visit again soon.

When Much returned to the camp, he was laden with things Sarah had sent—loaves of her freshly baked bread, fruit from her kitchen, and a bag of toys for the children. Wooden blocks to stack, clay figurines of various animals and people, as well as clay rattles—with grain inside rounded clay to shake and produce a sound. The children eagerly dug through the bag Much brought while he stashed the food in his little kitchen.

As the days continued to pass, the children made good use of the toys that Sarah had sent.

Young William convinced Will to start teaching him archery. Will could also be seen telling the children stories and entertaining the most out of anyone in the gang. Much was glad to see the way Will handled the children; they needed someone to love them in the absence of their parents, and Will certainly did that.

When the gang went on raids they always had to leave someone in the camp to keep an eye on the young ones. Much was often chosen for this job, but he didn't mind. He preferred it to killing soldiers anyway.

The children were fond of Much, but they spent most of their time clambering over Will or begging Dusty to sing for them.

Chapter 38

MUCH PUT ANOTHER log on the fire, watching as the flames from below slowly licked across the bark. It was late, and the children were all sound asleep, but Much was keeping the fire going as he waited for Robin's return.

The camp was empty as the rest of the gang was traveling beyond Nottingham, helping the rest of England in whatever small ways they could, and none of the traveling groups had returned yet. When Marian had visited the camp earlier in the evening, Much and the children had been alone. She hadn't stayed long, but she had spoken to Much of her concern for her father's ongoing illness.

Hearing the soft sounds of footfalls, Much reached for the sword resting against the log bench beside him, but he relaxed when Robin came into view.

"Much? What are you doing still awake?" Robin moved to the fire ring and sank onto the log beside Much. Even in the relative darkness, Much could see the dark circles under Robin's eyes—he looked truly weary.

"How was your journey?"

"There was an execution in Blenthorpe that I failed to get to in time. A woman was beheaded…"

"I am sorry."

"So am I. There are too few of us, Much. We need more help…"

"The people are forming rebellions of their own in some places," Much said. "They are emboldened by our work. Perhaps they'll start to look after themselves."

Robin shook his head, running a hand over his eyes. "That won't help the woman who died today."

They sat in silence for a moment, and then Robin shook himself. "But why are you awake?"

"I was waiting for your return. Marian visited tonight."

"Is she okay?" Robin sat up, his weariness giving way to sharp attention. "What's happened?"

"Marian is fine, nothing has changed with her situation. She's still under house arrest. She is worried for her father though; Sir Godfrey is still sick. It's been worse since her arrest, because now Gisbourne hasn't been helping her; he hasn't sent for a physician for Sir Godfrey since before Marian was taken into custody…"

"I am sorry for Sir Godfrey—he was a sort of uncle to us growing up, after all. And I do grieve for Marian…but I don't know what we can do about it."

"Could we get him out of the castle?"

"It would be risky, and nearly impossible. There is a secret passage that leads to the dungeons, but there are also guards there. Allen and I have been trying to plan for an escape for Sir Godfrey, to be honest, but we're not confident we can pull it off."

"I think he's seriously ill, Robin. He could die."

"I know," Robin sighed. "I'll talk to Dusty, see what we can do…she can give Marian some of her healing concoctions when Marian visits, and then Marian can pass them along to her father."

"That's a start," Much nodded.

In the days and weeks that followed, more soldiers of the Sheriff were seen wandering through Sherwood Forest even when no caravan was expected to come through. Robin believed the Sheriff was doing his best to find the camp and root out the gang. Robin insisted the gang deal with them, so when they came across soldiers searching the forest, the gang began to jump them—killing them quickly—or lead them to the various traps that they had set up and then killing them there. It was dirty work that Much hated, so he avoided it as often as he could, instead informing Allen or Will when he found groups of soldiers wandering about the forest.

In spite of the roving bands of soldiers the Sheriff sent into the forest never coming back out, the caravans of taxes still came through Sherwood. With every passing raid he sent more soldiers, and every now and again he diverted his route to another road—like he had at Leicester. Sometimes the money slipped through the gang's fingers, but such occasions were rare.

One day as Much watched the rest of the gang set off from camp to plan an ambush of a caravan, six children clambered around him eager to be entertained.

"Well…what should we do?" Much asked, scooping up little Peter.

"I'm going to practice my archery!" young William declared. He went to Allen's hut where he bunked and fetched the bow that Will had made specifically for him to fit his size and strength. Then he moved to one side of the meadow and began shooting at a tree that Will had crudely carved a target into. John, who was only six, went to sit near William and watch him shoot, while Sarah, Beth, and little Rachel looked expectantly to Much.

Much pulled out the toys from Locksley and sat down in the grass with Peter on his lap. Rachel came toddling over and squeezed in to sit beside Peter. Much reached around both of them to start building a tower with the wooden blocks, and Sarah and Beth came to join him.

Time passed slowly, but eventually the sounds of voices caught the children's attention and a moment later the gang began to drag themselves into camp. Will's eyes were wide and his movements jerky as he dragged a chest toward the storage hut, Little John following behind with a deep scowl and a wooden chest of his own.

The lack of any carts or horses struck Much as odd as Mark stomped into camp and threw his sword toward his hut.

"Mark! You could hit the children," Dusty scolded as she came along behind him.

"What happened?" Much asked, glancing between his harried looking friends.

"All was going well," Mark said as Robin finally stormed into camp. "Until *he* showed up."

"Who?" Much asked.

"Gisbourne," Robin snapped, kicking a rock and watching it sail across the meadow. The children gathered around Much, seeming to cower around him in the face of the frustrated atmosphere of the camp. "We had nearly completed the raid and were just finishing off the last of the soldiers—"

"And then in rode Sir Guy of Gisbourne like a thief," Will said. "He bolted in on his black stallion, scooped up Allen, and rode off."

His chest constricting, Much looked around the meadow at his friends, realizing with a sinking feeling that one was indeed not present. "Didn't Allen fight him?"

"Of course he did!" Mark said. "But Allen is no bigger than Marian is; he was no match for Gisbourne."

"Gisbourne was riding too fast." Robin shoved a hand through his hair with a sigh. "I was worried I'd hit Allen...my aim wasn't good. I pierced his saddle and did nothing worse."

320

"So Allen is…what? Taken in custody? Killed?"

"Probably in the castle dungeons by now," Robin replied.

"What are we going to do?" Much asked.

"We're going to rescue him," Robin said, crossing his arms and glaring at the members of the gang. "We'll have to plan this carefully. I don't want anyone else being caught by the Sheriff! But Allen and I were already drawing up plans for an attempt to rescue Sir Godfrey, so we can just convert our plan to get Allen out as well."

The rest of the day, Dusty kept the children away from the fire ring while Robin explained his idea to everyone else. That night the majority of the group left the camp, leaving the children in the capable hands of Dusty—who was undoubtedly going to spend the evening praying.

The moon was obscured by clouds, making it easy for the group to sneak around the city of Nottingham without detection. Much kept his hand on the stone wall as they walked, partially because with the moon covered it was a dark night and he didn't want to wander in the wrong direction, and also partially because his legs were shaking beneath him and every crunch of leaves beneath their feet sent his heart rate spiking and Much felt he needed something solid like the wall to keep him steady on his feet.

They were doing something outrageously dangerous tonight and after the mishap during the raid, Much's confidence in their success was shaky.

The group followed the city walls until they were on the far side of Nottingham, where the walls of the castle merged with the wall of the city. There was a little known door in the wall of the castle, barely visible unless you knew what you were looking for—which Robin and Much most certainly did.

Much located the thin cracks on the smooth stone first, and then called Robin over, who deftly slid the door along the track within the stonework, revealing the secret passage beyond.

"Everyone, follow me," Robin whispered. "Much, take up the rear. We know the hallways best, so we're the least likely to get lost..."

"I know these passages!" Mark protested.

Robin ignored him and disappeared into the darkness beyond. Mark followed him, and then Little John and Will did, too.

Much stepped into the cool passageway and carefully moved the sliding slab of stone back into place, shutting out the darkness of the night and being enveloped in the deeper blackness of the secret passageway.

Much began moving down the passage, keeping his hand on the wall out of habit. He could hear Will breathing in front of him, which was a good sign—he didn't want to be responsible for losing a member of the gang on the very night they were trying to rescue one.

As they traversed the winding, twisting passages toward the stairs that led to the level of the dungeon, Much kept his hand on the wall and his ears open to any sounds from beyond their secret hallway. He felt the cracks beneath his hand to indicate various secret doors and peepholes, and his memory was flooded with nostalgia from his childhood even as fear coursed through his bloodstream.

The sound of a voice caused Much to stop breathing momentarily, until he recognized that the woman's voice was coming from inside the castle proper and not the secret passageway. They were passing a guest room, and he was likely hearing a noble woman speaking to her husband or a servant.

The walk to the dungeons felt longer than it ever had before— Much was sure he'd jumped at every odd sound he heard, forgetting to

322

breathe most of the time. But eventually, they arrived. The group paused outside the secret door and waited for Robin to open it.

Much curled his hands into fists, letting his fingernails bite into the palm of his hand. The secret passage opened next to the real door located at the end of the first level of the dungeons, leading down to the second level. There would be a line of cells to their right and the wooden door to their left when they exited the secret passage.

At the far end of the cells would be the door that led out of the dungeons into the castle proper. There would be guards posted outside it —there almost always were. Whether or not there were guards *inside* that door was more pertinent at the moment, or if the door was open and the other guards would see them.

Much assumed Robin was leaning against the smooth stone, listening through the cracks, though he couldn't see anything in the darkness. There was also the question of whether there would be guards at the second door, the one next to the secret door they were now waiting behind.

Much reached for the hilt of his sword, waiting with bated breath as he heard shuffling in front of him—Will was probably moving past Little John and Mark in the crowded space, as the plan was for him and Robin to go in first. Much likely wouldn't be able to do anything at first if they did surprise guards when they opened the secret door. He was at the back of the line.

Light suddenly lit up the passageway and Much could see Robin pushing open the door. Will darted past him and Mark followed. A moment later there was a resounding clank of armor hitting the stone floor.

"You could have caught him!" Little John hissed as he pushed his way out of the secret passageway.

"No, *you* could have caught him," Will shot back. "I did the best I could."

Much stepped out of the secret passage. The wooden door leading into the dungeons at the far end of the cells was open—two soldiers were laying on the floor, both unconscious. Will and Mark had done their job well.

Most of the cells were empty, except for the one Sir Godfrey was laying in, and the one beside him where Allen was leaning against the barred door grinning at the group. Much assumed any other prisoners the Sheriff might currently have were in the cells beyond the door behind him that led to the deeper level of the dungeon.

Robin grabbed the keys from one of the unconscious soldiers and moved toward Allen's cell. "We're getting you out of here."

"Thanks."

"Anytime." Robin winked. "We'll always be here when you need us. Do try not to get kidnapped by Gisbourne again."

"Enough joking around, we need to get out before more guards come or these wake up," Little John said.

Robin moved to unlock Sir Godfrey's cell.

"No." Sir Godfrey waved a weak hand from where he sat on the little bed at the back of his cell. Much's stomach turned to see the strong lord he'd grown up admiring reduced to this thin sack of skin and bones, with his hair falling out. "I'm not going with you."

Robin ignored him and continued to unlock the cell. "Sir Godfrey—"

"Absolutely not." His voice had grown a bit in strength as the old lord straightened in his bed.

"Father!" Mark moved to the cell. "You have to come with us!"

324

"I won't leave here just to die in the forest," Sir Godfrey said. Given the sharp look in his eyes, Much was sure his mind was unlikely to be changed.

"We have a healer in our group," Mark insisted, reaching for the keys from Robin, "if she could just see to you, you'd feel better. I'm sure of it."

"Go," Sir Godfrey said. "I am not leaving, but you must. More soldiers will come eventually. You do not want to be caught, or to have the secret passageways discovered. Get out."

The hesitation was practically palpable, but eventually Robin glanced toward the unconscious soldiers in the doorway and sighed. "If we're going, we have to go. Sir Godfrey, I do wish you would change your mind."

"I won't."

"Father!" Mark started to unlock the cell, but Robin snatched the keys from his hand. "We don't have time to argue, or to drag your father bodily from his cell. Marian will keep looking after him. Now come on."

"Robin—"

"Move!" Robin tossed the keys toward the sleeping soldiers and dragged Mark by his arm back toward the opening of the secret passage. Much glanced between Robin dragging Mark away, and Sir Godfrey slumped against the back wall of his cell watching the departure.

Should they take him, against his will or not? It would certainly be safer in the camp than in the castle...

"Much!" Allen whacked his shoulder. "Come on. Robin says it's time to go, so it's time to go."

"Of course."

Much dutifully followed Allen into the secret passage, checking to make sure everyone else was already inside before he closed the stone door and shut out the sight of the dejected Sir Godfrey.

"Are we making the right choice? Leaving him, I mean?"

"The choice is made, right or wrong," Allen replied. There was something bitter in his voice that Much wasn't expecting, and he stood still in the darkness for a moment trying to understand it.

The soft sounds of retreating footsteps, however, shook him back into reality—the rest of the gang was leaving. Much hurried after, and the gang made their way through the varied passages back to the exit at the back of the castle. They followed their same path around the city walls and then across the fields and into Sherwood Forest to return to the camp.

Dusty greeted Allen with a hug, and the group gathered around the fire ring after putting the children to bed to decompress from their stressful night. Mark, however, stormed off to his hut and didn't say a word to anyone.

Chapter 39

THE NEXT DAY, Much found himself traveling with Robin and Mark and a stranger. They were riding horses provided by Marcus, and headed south of Nottingham. The stranger, Daniel, had come from Fossmere—a village beyond the authority of the Sheriff of Nottingham —and had been asking around Nottingham for someone to get a message to Robin Hood that his son was being executed. Marcus had gotten wind of it and informed the gang, and now Much, Robin, and Mark were following Daniel on their way to save the boy while Allen led the remaining members of the gang in keeping an eye on the Sheriff and Nottingham.

It was a warm autumn day, the landscape brightened by the reds and yellows of the trees and the varied colors of the late blooming flowers. Their pace was quick, but not panicked and Much felt surprisingly comfortable in the saddle. Until the outlaw adventures in Sherwood had begun, he'd had very little experience riding. It was only a month ago that Much's fear had startled his horse when they were attempting to rescue the boy from Leicester, so he was grateful for the feeling of calm and confidence as he rode now.

When they arrived in Fossmere, Daniel led them to his home on the outskirts of the village.

"You can make your plans here," he said as they dismounted.

"Can you show me the gallows meant for your son?" Robin asked. "I'd like to scope out the area and see how we might best rescue him."

Daniel nodded. "Of course…I can take you there…but if we go wandering to the gallows the soldiers will notice…"

"Just me," Robin assured him. "Mark and Much will stay here and wait for further instruction. And you and I can keep out of sight as much as possible. Trust me…we've done this before."

"Make yourselves at home," Daniel gestured toward his house. "It's not much…my wife was executed over a year ago when I couldn't pay taxes…that was before you lot started providing for all of us. Your monetary contributions do far more than keep food on our tables, you know. But my son…he talks back to the soldiers every chance he can get, won't keep silent. I guess they'd had enough of that."

"Don't worry," Robin put his hand on the man's shoulder. "We'll save him."

Daniel soon led Robin down the street, and Mark and Much entered his house to wait after they'd tethered the horses outside. The room they entered was small and dark, lit only by the sunlight filtering through the grimy window. There was a small hearth, a little table, and a couple of roughly-hewn wooden chairs in the room. There were doors leading to other rooms, but Mark and Much settled into a couple of the rickety chairs and waited there.

When Mark realized his chair was uneven he began to shift his weight slightly, back and forth, letting first one wooden leg and then another lift into the air, tapping out a rhythm as the wooden pegs hit the floor again with each shift.

Tick. Tick. Tick.

"It's rare for us to get advance notice of soldiers dealing out their own justice," Much commented. "Usually they just beat and kill at their own discretion, while the sheriffs and those in authority make executions more of a show."

"We're lucky this time," Mark said.

"Or…maybe it's a trap."

Mark rolled his eyes. "Why would it be a trap?"

"Prince John's cronies are getting clever, as evidenced by our Sheriff planning new routes for his caravans of treasure, and Gisbourne successfully kidnapping Allen."

"We got Allen back right away."

"That hardly changes the fact that Gisbourne did take him. We are either getting sloppy, or predictable, because they are definitely getting better."

"You might not be wrong about the predictable part, but if this is a trap, Robin will see it when he scopes out the area. He'll know, and adjust our plans accordingly. Either way, we'll save that kid and then head back to Nottingham."

"What will they do when we leave?"

"What?"

"Daniel and his son. They'll still be targets after we save him."

"They'll do what most people do when we save them from executions; they'll go into hiding, either nearby or by traveling to a new shire, or by going as far as Scotland, or crossing the channel to go abroad."

"Seems sad to have your life saved only to have to pick up and leave everything you know and love."

"If it's that or be killed, I'd do it in a heartbeat, and so do they." Mark stretched his arms over his head for a moment, then attempted to crack his back. Apparently he was bored with the conversation.

"I do wish we could keep track of everyone," Much said softly.

"What?"

"So that once Prince John is out of power—if the king returns, or something else occurs—we could tell them all it was safe to come home."

329

Mark shrugged. "Who knows if that will ever happen. It doesn't seem likely, does it?"

Robin and Daniel soon returned with the report of what they had seen, and Robin pulled a parchment and charcoal from his satchel to draw a map of the area around the gallows and explain how he wanted Much and Mark to approach and hide before the ambush.

"Are we all clear?" he asked when he was done.

Much and Mark nodded.

"Be careful," Daniel said. "And thank you. Thank you for taking a chance on my boy."

"Every subject of King Richard is our concern," Robin replied. "Of course we'd take a chance on him."

The fact that he was a human being on the verge of being killed was more to the point, in Much's opinion, not that he was a subject of the king. But either way, Robin was right; taking this chance was precisely why their gang existed at all.

Robin instructed Daniel to pack a few belongings—necessities and not frivolities—so that once they'd rescued his son, the two could be on the run immediately.

"You can take two of our horses," Robin said. "That will make travel easier."

"I couldn't possibly—"

"Yes, you can," Robin said. "We exist for your benefit, not the other way around. You don't owe us anything. We are only here to help you; so you'll take our horses and the money we brought for you, and you'll run as far as you can until you find somewhere safe to stay."

Daniel bowed deeply, tears in his eyes.

"Go pack," Robin said gently. "We all need to be ready to leave at a moment's notice—particularly if things go wrong."

330

Soon enough, Much was crouched at the edge of an unfamiliar building, his bow in his hand as he peeked around the corner. The gallows stood in the middle of an open area where two streets of the village intersected. A few villagers stood near the edges of the streets, seemingly afraid to openly watch, but somehow unable to stay away. The soldiers were roughly dragging Daniel's son toward the gallows, his hands bound behind his back. There were only four of them—a measly number compared to how many the gang had killed over the last year.

Much raised his bow, waiting for Robin's signal.

When the sharp whistle came, Much's arrow shot through the air and cut through one soldier's neck. Simultaneously, Mark and Robin's arrows sprouted in two more soldiers and they all three fell to the ground while a couple bystanders cried out in surprise.

The last soldier standing spun around, drawing his sword and looking for the culprits, but within seconds Robin had sent a second arrow through his eye and he dropped to the earth with a thud.

Robin moved from his hiding place, running to Daniel's son to untie him and then took off running down the street. Much tucked his bow over his shoulder and sprinted after them.

When they neared Daniel's house, he came running outside and scooped his son into his arms.

"Grab your things," Robin said, interrupting the warm embrace. "You've got to go before any other soldiers come investigating. You may have a head start, but at some point they will come looking for you…"

Daniel and his son were soon riding away on two of Marcus' horses and Robin glanced at the remaining one. "Well…who's walking?"

331

"I'll walk," Much said immediately.

Robin shot him a grin. "How did I know you were going to say that. Mark, you get on the horse…Much and I have walked all over the world, the path back to Nottingham will hardly kill us."

"You don't think I know how to walk long distances, too?" Mark rolled his eyes, but he mounted the horse regardless. The journey back to Nottingham and their camp in Sherwood Forest was uneventful.

"See, Much?" Mark grinned once they were safe at camp. "No disasters. You were a bit paranoid, that's all."

One night, a few days later, Robin returned from his attempt to visit Marian in a temper. He stormed into camp, kicking away a loose stone and flinging himself onto the ground outside his hut.

"What is wrong with you?" Will asked from his place at the fire ring where everyone was gathered. The children had already been put to bed.

"The passageways are being closed up! The Sheriff has discovered the secrets of Nottingham castle. I couldn't get in. He's blocking some off, and having others guarded…"

"So you didn't see Marian?" Mark asked.

"I went in through the stables. It was trickier than the secret passages because I could have been seen at any moment, but I got there."

"Does Marian have any idea about why the Sheriff found the passages?" Little John asked.

Robin picked himself up from ground and came to join the group by the fire. "No…but I do. How could he have learned of them?"

"They have always been there for anyone to run across, Robin," Dusty said. "It should not have taken the Sheriff as long as it did to discover them."

332

It was shocking that their means of spying on the Sheriff was taken from them but there was nothing to be done about it. The gang broke up and went to their huts for the night, though Much found it hard to fall asleep.

Little Peter was snoring softly, and Much's mind was spinning with the possibilities of how they would get information from the Sheriff to stop executions and plan raids on caravans of treasure. The obvious answer was Marian, but she wouldn't be able to leave the castle any longer if the secret passages were being closed up. Her days as the Hooded Rescuer alongside Mark were ending.

Robin would undoubtedly still find ways to sneak into the castle to visit her, and therefore an exchange of information was possible. But it was also going to be more dangerous—and likely less frequent because of that added danger—and Much worried for how many lives they would fail to save. They missed many simply because there were so few of them dealing with an entire country, but now they'd be working with even less information.

They were losing their upper hand on the Sheriff, and that concerned Much a great deal.

Chapter 40

MUCH WATCHED THE gang storm into camp after what should have been a raid on a caravan coming through Sherwood—no one brought carts or chests of treasure with them, and everyone was scowling. They dispersed to their separate huts as soon as they were in the meadow; even Will brushed aside the children when they ran to greet him.

Much moved to Robin's hut and poked his head inside. It was dim inside, but he could see Robin sitting on his bed with his head in his hands.

"Robin?"

"This is not a good time." Robin sighed, glancing up at him.

"What is wrong with everyone?" Much stepped into the hut and sat down beside Robin. "Where is the treasure? What happened out there?"

"They knew we were there. I don't know how, but that caravan —the soldiers—they knew we were there."

"Every caravan goes through Sherwood with a wary eye. They've all come to expect our ambushes. You've seen to that."

"This was different. They *knew* we were there. Exactly where we were. They broke off from the caravan itself and came directly to our hiding places, some of them flanked us from behind, not traveling on the road at all, because they knew precisely where we were hiding before we attacked or moved a muscle. I hadn't given the signal yet… but they knew!"

Was it possible for the Sheriff's men to know where they were hiding? Robin always moved the place of their ambush along the road —the fact that they did ambush the caravans was predictable, but Robin never wanted the act itself to be predictable. Sherwood was a large forest and the stretch of road that passed through it long; there were many places for them to ambush caravans, and they'd rarely used the same stretch of road twice.

"How could they have known?"

"There's only one explanation that I can see." Robin's hands curled into fists as he spoke through his clenched teeth, clearly struggling to maintain his composure. "Someone told them."

"But no one knows about out ambush plans except for us."

"Indeed." Robin gave Much a hard look. Slowly, the truth of Robin's suspicions began to dawn on him...

"No!" Much's back stiffened, a familiar tension in his shoulders cramping. "No one would betray us. We're a family; it isn't possible."

Robin sucked in a long breath and let it out slowly. "And now you know why we're all in a bad mood right now."

"But none of us would ever betray each other."

"I don't like to think anyone would...maybe I am overreacting."

"You have to be. There has to be an explanation."

"I don't know what that explanation would be, Much. No one outside of the gang is privy to our plans. Even Marian doesn't always know the exact details of each ambush, she just knows we will likely be ambushing. If she knew more...I could see it being possible for the Sheriff or Gisbourne to coerce or torture the information out of her. Maybe hold her father's life over her head until she gave us up."

"Marian wouldn't—"

"No, not by choice. Yet she loves her father and I could see it happening through coercion. But it can't be that, because Marian doesn't know the minute details. Only we do."

Much shook his head. "No. It has to be something else."

"I'd like to believe that, but you'll have to find me proof that my suspicions are wrong before I can trust that there isn't a traitor in this camp."

Much noticed the shift in the camp that night. Hardly anyone left their huts that evening, and when they did they kept far from each other. There wasn't a gathering at the fire ring to discuss their day like usual.

When Much cooked up supper with help from Beth and Sarah, Robin came to eat but no one else appeared right away. After Robin ate, Mark came to sit with Much and the children. When Dusty came to join the circle, Mark immediately stood up and returned to his hut. Slowly, one at a time and not speaking to one another, the gang ate as the evening wore on and then returned to their huts. Some sat inside, probably brooding, some sat outside, leaned up against their huts and sharpening their swords while they sent furtive glances at the other members of the gang within sight.

As the days passed, it seemed to get worse. The gang took their meals separately and the camp became as silent as a graveyard. The children could feel the tension in the air, too, and their play was muted —whenever a member of the gang would exit their huts all of the children would stop what they were doing entirely and just sit quietly until the camp was cleared again before they returned to their whispered conversations and suppressed games.

One day, Much went to speak to Robin in his hut after everyone had gone to bed.

"We can't let the gang fall apart like this," Much said, seating himself on the floor across from Robin's bed. "We don't even know for sure that there is an informant."

337

"But the idea that there could be a traitor in our midst has been born, and nothing you say now will dislodge that belief."

"Everyone is so distrustful and frustrated, and we don't even know for sure…"

"I know…everyone seems to believe that everyone *else* is the traitor."

"But if everyone thinks it is someone else, then doesn't that mean there isn't one at all?"

Robin shook his head, running a hand through his hair. "That's hardly proof, Much."

"We can't let everyone suspect each other. Everyone is hurt to be suspected when they are innocent. Despite the suspicion everyone feels, the biggest emotions clouding the camp these days are feeling hurt, betrayed, and angry at being suspected."

"I don't suspect you," Robin said. He stopped pushing his hand through his hair long enough to give Much an open look.

"I'd like to believe *no one* is a traitor and it was just a coincidence that those soldiers knew where to look for you."

"I would like to think that, I really would, but I can't. The evidence is too clear. The ambush plans were leaked…and before that, the Sheriff found the secret passages. All these years, and he suddenly stumbles across them? No. He was told. That's two strikes against whoever is betraying us."

Much held onto his hope that it was all a grave misunderstanding as the days passed. He tried to comfort Robin, though he hardly spoke to anyone else except Dusty.

Dusty alone remained friendly to the rest of the gang. Much could see that she believed Robin—there was a sadness in her eyes and wariness to her interactions with everyone else—but she did talk to everyone, which was more than anyone else could say.

"What are we going to do, Dusty?"

"Pray."

Much and Dusty were sitting at the fire ring, watching the crackling flames as the moon shone down into the empty meadow. Everyone had retired to their huts, as per usual, and the children had been put to bed.

"The gang is fracturing…"

"I know." Dusty placed a hand on Much's forearm. "That is why I've been praying. Our God is the Way, Truth, and Life. I have to believe that He will lead us to the truth—whether or not there is a traitor in our camp—and He will give us wisdom on how to respond. He was betrayed, too, you know, by one of his closest disciples."

"How did He take it?"

"With grace and forgiveness, though Judas killed himself before Jesus was given the chance to show Him that mercy. And in the end, it was all a part of His grand plan to save us from our sins. He will use this, too, Much. I don't know how…but I believe He will."

When Robin heard from Marian about another caravan of treasure coming through Sherwood, he gathered the gang together to plan an ambush. It was a quiet planning session. It was rare to see Will, Allen, and Mark sit quietly without any of their playful banter as they listened to Robin and it broke Much's heart. Dusty volunteered to be the one to stay behind at the camp so that she could pray for their safety.

Later that day, Much's hands were sweaty as he leaned against a large boulder near a curve in the road, waiting for the caravan to come through. He strained to hear Robin's whistle above the pounding of his heart in his ears.

339

A cracking twig behind him sent Much's heart into his throat. He spun around, raising his bow and letting the arrow fly immediately. A soldier standing two feet behind him, sword raised, dropped to the ground with Much's arrow in his throat.

Much searched the trees around him for a second but didn't see anymore approaching soldiers, so he spun to the road.   Everyone was fighting off the Sheriff's men who'd crept up to their position, while the soldiers riding the carts and wagons carrying the chests of treasure continued down the road unharmed.

Much glanced around, trying to decide who might need his help when he saw Little John fall to the ground, struck by the soldier he was fighting. His quarter staff rolled from his hand as the soldier bore down on him.

Much grabbed an arrow from his quiver, but before he'd pulled back his bow, Allen had already shot the soldier and was running to Little John's side. A glance to the left showed the caravan of treasure disappearing around the bend; there were still a few soldiers with swords in hand trying to kill the gang, but Robin was picking them off one by one as he ran toward Little John.

Much sent an arrow sailing into one of the soldiers who was trying to approach Little John and then ran toward his friend still laying on the ground. By the time he got there, Allen, Will, and Robin were all bending over him. He seemed to be conscious, but his shirt was stained a deep crimson along his chest and side.

"I'm going to kill someone," Robin grunted through clenched teeth, pulling Little John to his feet. He draped one arm of Little John's over his shoulders as Will stepped forward and took their injured friend's other arm.

Much turned from them to send another arrow flying at the few remaining soldiers who were creeping closer. Allen stood beside him, fending off the soldiers when they tried to approach as Robin and Will half dragged Little John away from the road and back toward camp. Mark flanked the soldiers from behind, driving his sword first into one and then another.

As they fought, Much ached to run after Robin and Will and see how Little John was doing. Was he dead?

Once the soldiers were dealt with, Much, Allen, and Mark ran to catch up with the others.

When they neared camp, Robin began to shout, "Dusty! We need you!"

They burst through the trees, and Dusty ran forward, her eyes wide with worry. She lifted Little John's shirt and then began issuing orders. "Much, boil me some water! Allen, get my bandages. Robin, take him to my hut, and Will…get this shirt off so I can see what I'm doing."

Much ran to his kitchen to collect a large pot and then sprinted out of the camp toward the stream that ran nearby and supplied the gang with fresh water. He dunked the pot into the icy water and lugged it back out, running toward the camp—and sloshing water along the way —until he was back at the fire ring. He knelt quickly and began putting kindling and logs into the fire ring, then he grabbed his knife and piece of flint he kept tucked under one of the log benches and started striking them together.   Sparks flew, but nothing was catching.

"Hurry up," Much hissed at the kindling as he continued to strike the knife against the rock. He glanced toward Dusty's hut. Little John's shirt had been removed, and Allen was running over with the bandages from the storage hut. Dusty and Robin seemed to be putting pressure on the wound to stop the blood flow, while Mark and Will watched from the doorway.

Much turned back to his flint and struck it again and again until the sparks finally lit the kindling. Then he leaned down and blew softly on them to encourage the flames to grow. In a few more minutes, he had enough heat to put the pot—half full of water at this point—over the flames and heat it to a boil.

As soon as it was hot he carried the pot over to Dusty's hut. Allen had collapsed to his knees outside the hut, and the children had gathered in a tight knot a few feet away, watching with wide eyes.

Much watched from the doorway as Dusty began to clean the wound and apply a mixture of her herbs and spices. From her various lessons on the subject, he knew she started with a mixture that would slow the bleeding, and then added more that would encourage the wound to heal.

"What's the verdict?" Little John asked, his voice lacking its usual strength and timbre.

"You'll live," Dusty replied.

Allen let out a groan from outside the hut. Robin stood up. "Keep an eye on him, Dusty. I'm going to Nottingham to talk to Marian."

As Dusty continued her work and Will sat beside Little John to keep him company, Much went to gather the children on the other side of the meadow.

"Will he be alright?" William asked.

"Dusty says he'll be fine," Much replied. "She knows what she's doing. I've never seen Dusty fail to heal anyone."

The children were subdued as Much brought out their toys, but they were always subdued these days. The tension in the camp was only going rise further now that another caravan had known where their ambush was located.

When Robin returned that evening, he gathered the gang at the fire ring. The children circled up nearby, keeping a distance from the worried and angry grown-ups.

"I have asked Marian to keep an eye on things in Nottingham," Robin said, glaring at everyone around him. "Whoever is informing the Sheriff will be caught, and I will kill him."

"Him," Mark repeated, glancing toward Dusty.

"I do not believe that Dusty would do this to me," Robin said, still glaring.

"None of the rest of us would do this either," Will snapped, his voice ice cold and sending shivers down Much's spine.

"Obviously someone has!" Robin growled. "Little John nearly died today because of the coward who betrayed me! I expect to kill whoever has done this."

Much winced, looking around at his friends. Surely Robin didn't mean that; he loved these people the same way Much did. Yet... one of them was feeding information to the Sheriff, and it had almost cost Little John his life today.

Robin was done with his lecture and stormed out of camp. An awkward silence followed. Much sat in the discomfort for a minute, and then stood and walked to his kitchen to start making preparations for supper.

The rest of the week was quiet in the camp. Hardly anyone spoke at all. The distrust was mounting.

344

Chapter 41

A WEEK LATER, Robin came into the camp in a huff and ordered the gang to gather at the fire ring. Will and Dusty helped Little John—who was recovering but weak—to the log benches as everyone gathered around. Without preamble, Robin said, "I spoke to Marian today."

Robin didn't say anything else for a moment.

Much glanced between Robin and the rest of his friends, his palms suddenly sweaty as his heart rate increased. Had he found out who was leaking information to the Sheriff?

The first one to break the silence was little Rachel who whimpered quietly. Will scooped her up into his lap and said, "What did you find out, Robin?"

"Nothing I didn't already know. Marian followed Gisbourne to a tavern where he apparently meets his informant, and she overheard Gisbourne speaking with the tavern keeper."

"What did they say?" Little John growled, leaning forward.

"Nothing of importance," Robin said.

"Then why are you telling us?" Allen asked, his voice strained. Much understood how he felt; Robin now had real proof that there was a traitor. All hopes that this was some misunderstanding were gone.

"Because Marian said they were speaking of a 'him' which means that I was correct in saying Dusty would never betray me. It's one of you men...and I will never forget this."

With that, Robin rose and disappeared into his hut.

No one spoke after he left. There were a few furtive glances exchanged, and then slowly they dispersed—some wandering through the forest in search of answers they couldn't find, some simply going to their huts and shutting themselves in.   Much set about making dinner while Will and Dusty sat with the children. Cooking was his only comfort at the moment.

Once food was prepared, Much left it in the care of Dusty and Will and went to speak to Robin.

When he poked his head into Robin's hut, he saw him laid out on his bed, his arms draped over his face.

"Robin?"

"Come in. You're the only person I trust, you know."

"You trust Dusty." Much moved to sit on the floor beside Robin's bed. Robin removed his arms from his face and turned his head to look at Much.

"I guess I do."

"What was Marian doing outside the castle? I thought she was on house arrest."

Robin sat up, pushing a hand through his frazzled looking hair. "She is on house arrest…she somehow convinced Gisbourne to let her be free of the soldier—Andrew—and once she was no longer being followed, she snuck out and stalked Gisbourne through Nottingham."

"That could have been dangerous."

"It is, but it's Marian. What do you expect her to do?" A wisp of a smile graced Robin's face.

"What exactly did Marian overhear?"

"If you are trying to find a way for this to all be a misunderstanding, you can't." Robin shook his head, his eyes flashing. "Marian heard Gisbourne ask after his informant. The tavern keeper gave him gold that the traitor had passed along, but he wasn't there today."

"So…someone truly is betraying us."

"Yes."

"But who?" Much's heart squeezed in his chest as a darkness settled over the room. "We've known Mark since childhood...he wouldn't do this to you, to Marian. Allen has been our brother for years now—we've fought wars together and survived so many dangers. The bond between us, and Dusty, is unshakable. Will is a good man—probably one of the best I've ever known. I don't know Little John that well, but Will trusts him and I trust Will."

"It doesn't matter who it is, it will be heartbreaking. But the fact remains, it is one of them, Much. I don't know who, but it is one of them. I've asked Marian to keep a close eye on the Sheriff and Gisbourne and their conversations so she can figure out who it is, and then I'm going to kill him."

"Robin..."

"What? They deserve it after what they've done."

"Maybe they do, but you love every one of those men out there in the camp. You would be devastated if you killed one of them. You'd never forgive yourself."

"I'll never forgive *them*," Robin hissed. "You're right. The bonds that bind this gang together are firm. For someone to break that...it is unforgivable. That's all there is to it."

Days passed, and the gloom within the camp did not dissipate. The gang continued to eat their meals separately. Robin still suggested various missions for people to go on throughout the day, but no one trusted the others in the gang enough to travel beyond Nottingham with them at their side. How could they? They might be traveling with the traitor and end up dead.

Robin stayed on top of the executions in Nottingham and the surrounding villages, but Much was sure the rest of England was

347

suffering in the absence of the gang. How many innocent people were going to die before the traitor was unearthed and the gang could rebuild their trust again?

The time of the Nottingham Fair drew near, but it did not improve anyone's moods.

Much didn't want to go anywhere near Nottingham on the day of the Fair, so when Dusty suggested she needed to collect more plants and herbs for her healing potions he eagerly volunteered to go with her. He followed her in silence as she walked, her eyes searching the forest floor for the plants she desired. Every once in a while she'd bend down and collect a few flowers, weeds, or roots and stuff them into the satchel she'd brought with her.

"I can't believe we've been betrayed," Much said softly as Dusty knelt to pull a flower up by the roots. "I hate to think anyone would do this…and Robin is so angry! He scares me sometimes."

"You have no cause for fear," Dusty said, not pausing in her work or looking up. "Robin would never harm you."

"But he is going to hurt someone, whoever the traitor turns out to be."

"I know." Dusty stuffed a flower into her sachet and brushed the dirt from her fingers. She stood and finally met Much's gaze. "I do wish Robin wouldn't threaten to kill the traitor, yet he does have the right to be angry. This betrayal is no small affair. I'm angry, too."

"But still…aren't we supposed to forgive him, whoever he is? That's what you said before."

"Yes. As hard as that is going to be, we are called to forgiveness. But you have to keep in mind that Robin does not share our faith. He does not have the same conviction that we do, or feel the need to follow in the Lord's footsteps as we might."

348

"Who do you think did it, Dusty?"

"I don't know. I just don't know…"

A week later, Robin went to visit Marian and returned to the camp in a fog. Much tried to greet him, but Robin brushed past him without a word and went to his hut. The gang slowly began to gather at the fire ring. It was becoming a habit for Robin to gather them when he came home from Nottingham—despite how distant and apart they kept themselves normally due to the tension in the camp—so they sat silently on the logs around the fire and waited for him to exit his hut.

It was several hours before he came out. Dusty attempted small talk, which Much tried to participate in, but they both fell silent when no one else picked up the conversation. The children were already sleeping, so they didn't have anything else to distract them from their anxious waiting. It was simply stony silence, and avoiding making eye contact with anyone.

Eventually, however, Robin stormed out of his hut, his face red with anger.

"Allen!"

"Yes, Robin?"

"You better start running now if you expect to live," Robin shouted as he marched toward the group at the fire. Much's heart sank to his toes.

"Robin?" Will looked from Robin to Allen. "What do you mean?"

Robin drew his sword as he came toward the group. "I mean it, Allen."

Little John's brows knitted together like the oncoming of a winter storm. "He's the traitor?"

Several people shifted position as Robin kept his gaze on Allen. "Yes."

Mark spun toward Allen. "I hate you."

"No," Dusty whispered beside Much.

Little John growled and then in one swift motion he stood up, scooped Allen over his shoulder and marched toward the edge of the meadow. Much followed after him, as did the rest of the gang.

When Little John reached the edge of the meadow he chucked Allen as far he could. Allen landed with a thud and the cracking of twigs, and then he scrambled to his feet and took off running as Little John and Robin chased after him.

Much sank to his knees, feeling a sharp stone on the ground press into his knee.

Allen, the traitor? It couldn't be. Not the man who walked beside them though the Crusades and promised to be a brother to Robin.

Much could feel the heat rising in his body as his shock dissipated and anger set in.

He would never forgive Allen for this.

He'd given their secrets to the Sheriff! Little John had almost died; they *all* could have died!

Much felt a hand on his shoulder and turned to see Dusty kneeling beside him, tears in her eyes. "We have to forgive him. We who are the true followers of Jesus here have to set His example."

"Can you forgive him so easily?"

Dusty sighed, looking out at the forest where Allen had run off. "No. I cannot. I am more angry than I could ever say...but we have to, Much. We have to."

Chapter 42

THE EVENING AFTER Allen was thrown from the camp, Robin took Mark and went to Nottingham to sneak into the castle and visit Marian after the children had been put to bed.

"I'm afraid of what he might do," Dusty said softly. She and Will were sitting with Much at the fire ring watching Robin and Mark leave. "He wants to kill Allen."

"He won't be able to kill Allen easily," Will said. "Not without the Sheriff catching him. From what I could gather in Nottingham today, Allen is living in the castle now. He's protected."

"I still can't believe he did this," Much sighed. "After everything we've been through…"

"It is horrible," Dusty agreed.

Much waited anxiously for Robin's return. He was still angry with Allen, but he loved him, too. He couldn't wish him dead no matter what he had done, and he knew that deep down Robin would eventually regret it if he murdered his friend.

When Robin and Mark returned to the camp they were subdued. They came to the fire ring quietly. Noticing their return, Little John joined the group at the fire.

"Did you see the traitor?" Little John asked.

"No," Robin replied. "We only saw Marian. You'd be proud of her, Dusty." The bitterness in Robin's voice was unmistakable.

"Why?" Dusty asked.

"She told me not to kill Allen." Robin pushed a hand through his hair with a sigh. "I can't let this pass though. I have to kill him."

"Marian told us something else," Mark said. "She said…"

"She said what?" Will asked.

"She said Allen did what he did in order to protect my father."

"To protect Sir Godfrey?" Much asked.

"How was hurting us going to protect Sir Godfrey?" Little John crossed his arms and scowled.

"It doesn't," Robin said. "Allen is pathetic."

"He's misguided." Mark sighed, staring at his hands. "That's what Marian said. Misguided. He wanted to protect my father from a plot to kill him in his sleep. I don't know how Allen knew of that plan … but that was apparently the excuse he gave Marian."

"We could have rescued Sir Godfrey," Robin said. "Allen had no reason to betray us."

"I still don't fully understand," Dusty said. "What does that plot have to do with Allen's betrayal?"

"Allen made Gisbourne promise to protect my father," Mark said. "In exchange for that promise, he agreed to give Gisbourne information."

Dusty shook her head. "Marian is right, that is misguided."

"Misguided or an idiot or a downright traitor, whatever he is, I'm going to kill him," Robin said.

Later that week, Much was kneading bread in his kitchen, preparing to bake. Since Allen had been unmasked and thrown out of camp, the gang had begun to lighten up. Everyone was mad at Allen, of course, and Robin was intent on killing him, but the other relationships within the gang began to lose their tension and that made Much happy. And when Much was happy there was no where he'd rather be than in the kitchen back home at Locksley baking bread with Sarah. In the absence of his adoptive mother and the kitchen he grew up in, Much set to work in the make-shift station he'd built for himself in the middle of Sherwood Forest.

It wasn't the same, but it would do.

Suddenly he heard the unmistakable sound of pounding hoofbeats and stepped out of his hut in time to see Will grabbing the halter of a horse Marian was dismounting. She moved across the meadow toward Robin, where he sat in front of his own hut sharpening his sword.

"Marian."

"No time to chat, Robin. Allen is out of control. He's bringing Gisbourne here. Now. With soldiers."

"Allen? Bringing soldiers here?" Dusty asked.

Marian nodded, and Robin sighed. "Get back to Nottingham before you are missed, Marian."

"What will you do? He's bringing soldiers…there's only six of you!"

"We'll do what we're best at," Robin said, standing up and setting aside his sword so he could hold Marian's hand.

"We'll set an ambush," Will said, leading Marian's horse to her.

"Be careful, Robin. And work fast. They're on their way here; I don't know how I beat them here." Marian then reached for her brother. "Be safe, Mark."

"I'm with Robin Hood," Mark grinned as he pulled away from her embrace.

"That's what worries me." To the rest of the gang she called out "good luck!" as she prepared to ride away.

"Pray," Dusty called back. "I've always found it more effective than luck."

Marian didn't respond as she turned her horse around and rode out of the camp.

"Much, stay with the children," Robin said. "The rest of you, get your weapons and follow me. We have a traitor to catch."

The eagerness in Robin's voice concerned Much, but he didn't argue with him. The rest of the gang grabbed their weapons and followed Robin out of the camp. If they successfully ambushed Gisbourne, Allen, and the soldiers, then no one would come to the camp. If, however, they failed…

Much glanced at the children. How was he alone going to protect them.

Remembering Dusty's comment to Marian, Much began to pray.

It was several hours before the gang returned. The moment he saw Robin walking into the meadow he could feel the tension bleeding from his shoulders in a rush.

"We killed a few soldiers," Will reported. "But Gisbourne and Allen got away."

"I almost killed him," Robin said. "Nearly had him. I can't wait any longer. I'm going to Nottingham tomorrow to finish him off."

"Robin, please don't," Much said. "Don't kill Allen. Remember everything he means to you; we're family."

"We stopped being family the day he betrayed me," Robin snapped. "He's nothing to me. I can't forgive him. I trusted him, I cared for him…and look what he did to us!"

Much didn't respond. It wasn't that he didn't agree with Robin, but in this moment, listening to Robin suggest that Allen had gone too far to be loved and forgiven, Much was suddenly aware of the love and grace that he had found in Christ, a love he most certainly did not deserve and could do nothing to earn. If God loved as Robin did, with such conditions…what a dark future Much felt he would have.

"He's still dangerous," Robin continued. "He almost brought Gisbourne right here to our camp! I can't let him live. He'll destroy us all. And it's only a matter of time before he informs Gisbourne and the Sheriff of Marian's involvement! What would I do if Marian was killed because I didn't stop him first?"

Despite Robin's intentions, he was unable to kill Allen as he had hoped. It was difficult to sneak into the castle without the secret passages, and whenever he did, he was unable to locate Allen.

Slowly, the autumn air turned cold as the weeks passed and winter came. With the tension within the gang easing, Robin was able to pair them up and send them out to the rest of England again, yet with the colder weather returning travel was once more difficult.

Much still felt the weight of Allen's betrayal, but between Dusty's encouragement and the still small voice he heard and felt deep inside, he was leaning toward the forgiveness that Robin refused to extend. One thing Dusty had said that stuck out to him the most was that forgiveness was the opposite of giving someone what they deserved or earned. It was a free gift that could only be given willingly.

One cold evening when Robin returned from visiting Nottingham, he was in high spirits. He came into camp with a light step and a smile on his face, striding over to join the gang gathered around the warmth of the fire.

"Mark, I have joyous news!" Robin said as he sat himself between Much and Mark.

"What?" Mark asked.

"Your father is doing better; his health is improving."

"That is good news," Much said.

Mark grinned. "I knew persuading Marian to convince Gisbourne to send for a physician was a good idea."

"She wants your father to come here," Robin said. "She can't stand the thought of him staying in the castle any longer."

"He wouldn't come when we had a chance to rescue him," Mark said.

"Marian is determined this time, whether Sir Godfrey likes it or not."

"Can we even get him here?" Mark asked. "We don't have the secret passages this time."

"He's right," Will said. "You sneaking into the castle through the stables is one thing, but the whole gang wandering in through the stables and courtyard and then traversing the halls down to the dungeons…"

"It would be far more difficult than last time," Dusty said.

"Marian will get him out of his cell," Robin said. "I'm not sure how, but she's forming a plan. She'll get him out and we'll collect him."

"It's a shaky plan at best," Little John commented.

"We don't have details, but we have heart," Robin said, a grin lighting his face. "This is how it used to be, you know. No firm plans, just jumping in and doing the work. It makes it more fun."

"This is serious, Robin," Much chided.

"I am taking it seriously. This is Marian's father we're talking about. All I'm saying is that I have complete confidence in us; we work well in the heat of the moment."

"But without the passageways…" Will leaned forward, resting his elbows on his knees as he studied Robin across the fire.

"We'll be fine," Robin said. "We won't take the whole gang so we attract less suspicion. We just have to sneak in, grab Sir Godfrey—

who will be out of the dungeons thanks to Marian—and sneak back out."

"What will my father do here at camp?" Mark asked. "He's not the outlaw type. He still considers Marian and I foolish dreamers for thinking we could do anything to stop the Sheriff or Prince John."

"He can stay with the children; he loves children," Robin shrugged. "And that way we can all go on raids and rescues and not be down a member because we need a nursemaid."

Much bit his cheek, trying not to sigh. He rather preferred playing nursemaid over the violence of their raids. Yet it would be good to get Sir Godfrey out of the castle. It was true he hadn't wanted to come before, and it was likely he wouldn't like the idea now, but if Marian could convince him—or if they simply dragged him away against his will—he would at least be safe.

If Allen had spoken the truth about the plot to kill Sir Godfrey, then it was best to bring Marian's father to camp. According to Allen— if he could be believed—Gisbourne had promised protection for Sir Godfrey only if Allen provided information on the gang. Now that Allen was no longer privy to that information, one side of the deal wasn't holding up anymore. Would Gisbourne continue to hold up his end?

The next day, Robin took Mark, Will and Dusty to sneak into the castle. Little John didn't want to sit around on his hands and wait for news, so he busied himself distributing food to the poor in the villages around Nottingham while Much sat in the camp with the children.

William practiced his archery while Beth and Sarah entertained the youngest three with the toys from Locksley, all of them wrapped in blankets to ward off the cold air. Much sat by the fire, adding logs every so often to keep it burning.

Much crossed his arms as he watched William struggling to use his bow. The air was frigid and the poor child's hands were stiff.

Had Robin and the others reached the castle yet? Perhaps they'd been caught sneaking through the stables and the courtyard...

Much glanced toward the other children and uncrossed his arms, shifting his position on the bench before grabbing another log and tossing it onto the flames.

Much couldn't sit still and the urge to get up and start pacing the meadow was strong, but he held himself firmly in place.

It was agonizing wondering what might be happening with the attempt to rescue Sir Godfrey. Much closed his eyes and took a deep breath. He knew what Dusty would tell him.

Pray.

"I don't know what's happening," Much whispered, reaching toward that comforting small voice. "But You do...keep everyone safe. Please."

It felt so inadequate in the face of the dangers his friends were facing, but instantly he felt the warmth of love and comfort flood his being. The overwhelming knowledge that the events unfolding were under the watchful gaze of One far more powerful than Much set him at ease as he waited for news.

It was hours before the gang returned. Much entertained the children, kept the fire going, and prepared a meal for himself and the children as he waited.

Time continued to pass. The children seemed hungry again, so Much prepared a large pot of stew to ward off the cold as the sun began to fall and darkness closed over the forest.

Eventually, Much encouraged the children to bed, tucking all of them in with extra blankets and hot rocks he'd placed in the fire to warm their beds.

Finally, as he sat and tended the fire a lone figure walked into camp.

"Robin? Where are the others?" Much rose as Robin trudged toward the fire. Much could see no wounds on Robin as he drew close to the light of the fire, but his face was ashen and wet with tears.

"No..." Much sank onto the bench as Robin slumped to the ground near the fire. Were they all gone? Dusty...

"Will and Dusty stayed in Nottingham," Robin said, his voice subdued. All of his confidence from the day before was gone. "There is going to be a funeral in two days, and when it is over they will bring Marian here."

"A funeral...Mark..."

Robin's eyes darted up toward Much. "No. Mark is alive. The funeral is for Sir Godfrey."

Much closed his eyes and let the news wash over him. He didn't know Sir Godfrey well, but he had been a staple in his childhood. And he loved Mark and Marian—their grief was one he would share.

"He's dead, Much...and it's my fault. We took too long getting into the castle—there were too many soldiers in the courtyard...he was killed just as I reached him."

"I'm sorry."

"I only hope Marian can forgive me."

"You said there's going to be a funeral...are we putting that together?"

"No. Gisbourne is dealing with it. He found Sir Godfrey's body not long after the soldier killed him—and I killed the soldier. I had to

359

duck down the hallway to not be seen by him. Then I went to see Marian…"

Robin shoved his hand through his hair, letting tears course down his cheeks unchecked. "Gisbourne is planning a funeral for Marian's sake, I think…"

"Can we go to the funeral then?"

"It would be risky. I won't stop you if you try to go…but I'm staying here."

Robin stood, glancing up at the night sky for a moment. He seemed on the verge of saying something else, but then he turned and walked slowly to his hut.

Much stared into the darkness of the camp, wondering if he should try and talk to Robin, to comfort him somehow. He would have known Sir Godfrey better than Much did, and he also knew and loved Marian and Mark in a deeper way. This loss was surely devastating for him.

Much felt a hand on his shoulder and spun around to find young William standing there.

"Could we go to the funeral?" he asked.

"You heard all that?"

"Yes."

"No. It would be far too dangerous for you to go. You'll have to stay in the camp as always."

Not long after Much sent young William back to bed, Little John returned to the camp. Much informed him of the tragedy that had occurred that day, and then went to his own hut. He made sure little Peter was still wrapped in several blankets, and then climbed into his own bed.

"You didn't keep everyone safe," Much sighed.

He could instantly feel the warm presence surround him again. It was comforting, but that only served to confuse Much. He made a mental note to discuss the whole experience with Dusty when she returned.

Two days later, Much made his way to Nottingham for Sir Godfrey's funeral. As the procession passed through the city to the abbey where he would be buried, a large crowd gathered. Sir Godfrey had been a beloved sheriff of Nottingham for many years before Prince John had replaced him with the cruel Sheriff who ruled over the shire now. It was easy for Much to slip into the crowd and join the throng gathering for the burial.

He caught sight of Marian at the head of the procession, her eyes swollen and red, tears pouring down her face. Gisbourne stood next to her, his hand on her arm. For once his ruthless face was softened, his dark eyes watching Marian with a gentle expression.

Studying the surrounding crowd of citizens and soldiers alike, Much saw Mark off to one side. Of course he would attend his own father's funeral, but more than that he was going to help Marian sneak away once it was over—how he planned to get her out from under the watchful gaze of Gisbourne Much wasn't sure, but Mark was confident.

It was a short ceremony, no finesse, likely to avoid angering the current Sheriff who—Much had learned from Marcus—disliked that Gisbourne had put it together at all.

Once the funeral was over Much went to Marcus' home where he waited with Will and Dusty until Mark and Marian showed up and they all hurried to Sherwood before she could be missed.

Chapter 43

MUCH WAS IN Nottingham Square, keeping an eye on the market. He leaned against the wooden wall of his favorite bakery, scanning the crowds. There were fewer people in the market today than usual. Still, this was the best place to be. If the Sheriff or Gisbourne were going to do anything nefarious, they often cut through the streets that criss-crossed into the Square as it connected to most major thoroughfares in the city, making it the best place to keep an eye on things—particularly now that the secret passages were out of commission, and Marian was no longer feeding them information from inside the castle.

Two caravans of the Sheriff's taxes had made it to Nottingham in as many weeks. One went through Leicester, the other Sherwood Forest. It didn't matter the route the Sheriff took these days, the gang always got wind of it too late to do anything about it.

They needed some way to keep an eye on things from within the castle itself, but Marian was unlikely to volunteer. She was their best bet, not being declared an outlaw herself and with Gisbourne so fond of her…but she would never go for it, and it seemed unfair to ask her to.

"You are brooding," Robin said, appearing at Much's side.

"I am wondering if we will ever succeed."

"What do you mean?"

"Our life in the woods seems never ending…I cannot help but wonder how long it is going to take us to free King Richard."

"We send a shipment along to Austria every chance we can get; it has to be adding up."

"Assuming the Duke of Austria deals fairly with us, and assuming the king coming home changes things at all."

"I have to believe it will make a difference…otherwise this fight will never be over, and that would be a dark future. I hope it won't be too long before we've payed the ransom and Richard comes home."

"I want peace and quiet again. I hardly remember what they feel like, but I want it."

"We cannot live in peace now, not while the people are suffering under corrupt leadership. How could we live in comfort while the rest of England suffers?"

"I know. I just…I'm tired."

"As am I. But wars don't last forever."

"I suppose not."

"Do not be so negative, my friend. We will succeed, and do so quickly."

"It's already been more than a year since our return from the Crusades."

"Much, trust me. We will get through this; we always do."

A few days later, Much was sitting beside the fire watching the snow drift lazily down from the dark sky above. The camp was mostly empty, apart from himself and Dusty who was on one of the other benches, her dried plants spread out beside her, her mortar and pestle in her hand. Marian had taken the children on a walk through the forest, likely as much to keep her own mind occupied as theirs.

"Dusty?"

"Mhm?" Dusty didn't look up, concentrating on her work.

Much watched her for a moment, debating whether or not to bring up the questions that had been lingering in his mind since the day Sir Godfrey died.

"What is it?" Dusty glanced up at him.

"When you went to Nottingham to free Sir Godfrey…I was worried. I prayed for all of you, and I felt…comforted. Assured."

Dusty nodded, a knowing smile creeping across her face. "He does provide comfort when we need it most."

"But…it didn't work. I mean, He didn't answer that prayer."

Dusty's hands stilled. For a moment, she stared down at her plants, and then she set aside the pestle and mortar and looked at Much, leaning forward. The snowfall was catching in her dark hair, covering it in a powdery white.

"He did. He gave you that feeling of comfort and assurance."

"But Sir Godfrey died anyway."

"I know." Dusty sighed. "Sometimes He works miracles. Sometimes terrible things happens."

"But why?" Much pressed.

"Why?" Dusty mused, looking up into the sky and letting snowflakes catch on her lashes. "We live in a fallen world, Much. It was perfect once, long ago, but that changed when man rebelled. Now it is broken. Tragedy happens because of the broken nature of our world. It wasn't how God intended the world to be, yet He loved us enough to give us free will. Sometimes that means people choose to do bad things. It's sin, Much. It isn't our Savior."

"But you say He's all-powerful. He could stop tragedies from occurring, stop evil men from abusing their power…He could stop all of it."

"Could He? Yes. Does He sometimes? Also yes. Why doesn't He always? I imagine there are a great many reasons." Dusty leaned forward, studying Much intently. "If He always dictated our lives, that would make free will a moot point. There's also the fact that He uses

365

our lives—the horrible, the ugly, the beautiful—to grow and teach us, and sometimes to use us as examples and teachers to others facing similar tragedies. I don't always understand His plan or why He does what He does, but I can tell you with absolute certainty that I trust Him regardless."

"Why, though?"

"That still small voice, Much. You've felt Him; there's nothing that compares."

Much couldn't argue with that.

"Even when tragedies strike, I can trust Him because I know He is a good God. Scriptures teaches that He is good, that He is loving. And if I believe that, then I can rest in it when everything else seems to be falling apart. I won't always understand why, but I can trust that *He* knows why, and He's working it all out for the good of those who love and trust Him."

Dusty spoke with such conviction, Much couldn't argue with her. And she was right; he had felt that wonderful, overwhelming, peace, love, comfort, grace. All of it. And he'd heard the words spoken to his heart that he was loved, he was worthy, he was forgiven. Much couldn't deny any of that. He wasn't sure he could rest so completely in faith the way that Dusty did, but he could see why she did.

A few weeks later, the gang caught wind of a caravan passing through Sherwood before it arrived for once, so Robin hurriedly threw together a plan and the gang rushed to the road to ambush the Sheriff's men.

Much was soon in place, though breathing heavily from all the rushing, before the caravan came in sight. He leaned against the bark of the tree behind him, closing his eyes and breathing deeply. His job today was simple: jump on a cart and drive it away.

They'd missed enough caravans that their store of money in the camp was running thin and their contributions both to King Richard's ransom and to the people of England were growing smaller. Therefore, Robin had decided that getting any of the gathered taxes at all was paramount.

When Robin's whistle pierced the air, Much waited half a second for an arrow from one of his friends to remove a soldier from the front of a cart weighed down by chests of treasure, then he sprinted forward and leaped onto the cart, grabbing the reins of the horse drawing it and turning it off the road.

There were soldiers scattered about the road, some running to engage in combat with the members of the gang they could see, and some moving protectively closer to the other carts. Much spared a glance to see if Dusty had grabbed her wagon as Robin had instructed and then he froze.

In the space of a moment he saw an arrow flying through the air toward Dusty's chest.

Much closed his eyes, unwilling to see the inevitable.

A cry of pain rent the air, but it wasn't Dusty.

Much's eyes snapped open. He saw Will collapsed on the ground with an arrow in his chest. Dusty was running to him.

Much hesitated, pulling his horse to a stop. Should he help Will and Dusty? Take the treasure, as he'd been ordered to?

"Little John!" Robin's shout echoed over the sounds of sword fighting along the road. "Get Will back to camp! We'll be there soon. Much! I need your help!"

Much leaped down from his cart, turning back to the soldiers. He saw Little John tuck his quarter staff into the loop of rope on his back and then scoop up Will and run from the fight.   The next thing he saw was a soldier's sword swinging toward him. Much whipped out his own sword in time to block the blow. He shoved his weight into his sword, causing his opponent to stumble backward. Two more soldiers joined the first and the three began to close in on Much.

Much blocked an incoming blow of one sword, sidestepping while their swords were still connected to get out of the reach of a second blade. Suddenly a dagger appeared in the neck of the third soldier and when he dropped to the ground, Dusty was standing there.

"You're supposed to be helping Will!"

"I couldn't let you die first."

Dusty darted away as Much focused on the two soldiers still flanking him, and then for several minutes it was blocking, parrying, slicing, alongside Mark and Robin until the immediate danger had passed.

Much could feel his heart pounding in his ears and a headache was building in his temples even as a familiar tension began to run through his shoulders. Will had taken an arrow to the chest. Much hadn't had a good view of it, but he was likely dying.

He'd died to save Dusty.

Once the fighting was through, Robin insisted they bury the dead, as they always did. Much tried not to picture digging a similar grave for Will as he worked. It was some time before they returned to camp with the treasure in tow.

Much glanced around eagerly and to his relief he saw Will laying in his hut, the door open, with Dusty kneeling at his side and several of the children sitting outside looking in.

"How is he?" Robin asked as they approached.

"He will live," Dusty said. "He will need plenty of rest. He must stay in bed for several weeks."

Will groaned, turning to look at them. "I am going to die from lack of exercise if you keep me here day and night."

"You will *not* die," Dusty said. "Though I have no doubt you will complain profusely."

Robin laughed. "I believe that. Much, I think you're going to have another friend to watch over in the camp."

"Nonsense," Marian said, coming up behind them. "I'll look after him. I stay in the camp anyway. There's no reason for another member of the gang to stay behind as well, particularly since you'll already be down a man."

"I don't want you to always be stuck in camp either," Robin said, taking Marian's hand. "You aren't under 'camp arrest,' always stuck here the way that you were in the castle."

"I'll be fine, Robin. I want to do this. Besides, it will take someone with a lot of stubbornness and strength of will to keep Will Scarlett in bed. Much is too soft, he'd easily give in to Will's demands."

"Now, Will..." Robin crossed his arms and grinned down at him. "You have to be a good patient."

"I'm a saint, Robin."

"We shall see."

As the weeks passed and the weather grew ever colder—snow falling every other day it felt like—Much and the rest of the gang began to notice they were not alone in their endeavors. Every so often they would hear of a family getting rescued from soldiers' brutality, or a hanging in a village some miles away that had been stopped but none of the gang had been there.

In the meantime, Will remained confined to his bed. He did his best not to complain and to follow Dusty's instructions but it was easy to see how unsatisfied he was as an invalid. The children often tried to ease his discomfort; Much had seen Beth sit by his bed for hours, ready to run for anything he should ask for while Sarah would tell him stories —as Will had once done for the children—and William practiced his archery every day in the hopes of raising Will's spirits.

Much noticed Dusty was also by Will's bedside every chance she could get. At first glance this did not strike Much—she was, after all, the healer and he the injured. Yet sometimes Much would catch a look in her eyes or a smile on her lips that reminded him of someone else.

It reminded him of how Robin looked at Marian.

Chapter 44

EVERY DAY IN the camp would begin the same, with Much cooking breakfast for everyone while Robin gave out assignments for the day to everyone who was still in the camp—sometimes a handful of the gang would still be gone, traveling to various places in England to distribute money and food. Once breakfast was eaten and assignments were given, the gang would disperse, going about their business until the evening.

On one particular day, Robin had brought Much and Mark along to Nottingham to keep an eye on things because he was worried about the calm—the Sheriff hadn't tried to hang anyone in a while and it worried him.

Robin, Much, and Mark settled along the edge of Nottingham Square, wedged between a booth selling blankets and the baker's cart of fresh bread.

"Is all well, Robin Hood?" the baker asked, his voice low and quiet.

"As far as I know," Robin replied, his eyes scanning the relatively empty square. "You haven't heard of anything I should know about, I assume?"

"No, sir."

For a while, nothing of interest happened and Robin, Much, and Mark simply chatted with the baker and the seller of blankets while they watched people moving about the Square. The market was not particularly busy and only a handful of people moved between the booths.

As the sun began to dip towards the horizon, however, two soldiers came galloping through the Square and passed into the street that would take them to the castle.

"Come on," Robin stood and pulled Much to his feet as well. "We should see what they're up to."

Much followed Robin and Mark as they jogged across the Square and then entered the street the soldiers had raced down. When the castle wall came into view, Robin veered course to the left, instead of continuing straight through the gate to the courtyard of the castle. There was a stretch of stone wall on either side of the gate, and then there were shops that backed up against the wall. One particular shop— a bakery—had been frequented by the gang because it afforded a view into the castle courtyard and it also held one of the secret doors into the passages that the Sheriff had now blocked off.

Much had many memories of the place, savoring the smells and tastes as he often did in any kitchen, but also playing with Marian, Mark, and Robin as they explored the different passages of the castle, sometimes running in and out of the bakery, much to the baker's amusement.

Robin followed a woman with a basket over her arm into the shop, a servant running an errand for a noble by the looks of her, and Much and Mark hurried after him.

The woman began speaking to the baker as the smells of breads and pastries wafted into Much's grateful nose.

The baker looked over to the woman's head, caught Robin's eyes, and then deftly took the woman's arm and led her to another part of his shop, expertly maintaining his conversation with her as he guided her away so that her back was to the group as Robin moved to the back where the staircase led up to the baker's apartments above the shop.

Much noticed the longing look he cast toward the back wall, where there was a loose slab of wood that could be slid to one side to enter the stone wall that surrounded the courtyard and follow it to the secret passages inside the castle itself. The Sheriff had filled in the doorway with a large stone, and interrogated the baker himself for weeks after Allen had fed the Sheriff information about the secrets of the castle.

Robin led Much and Mark upstairs and to a room at the back where another loose slab of wood could be slid to one side. The Sheriff hadn't found this one because it wasn't a secret passage: it was a window.

Robin pushed the wood away, revealing the chink in the stone wall through which he could see down into the castle courtyard. Mark crowded next to him, leaving no space for Much to see anything. He stood back, waiting to be told what was going on.

Suddenly he heard the Sheriff's voice drifting up from the courtyard beyond. "I was sorry to miss it, I do so love to see feet dangling."

"I'm sorry, Sheriff," another voice said, "but there was no hanging today."

"What?!"

Much winced at the sharp change in the Sheriff's voice.

"One of the outlaws was there!" the soldier continued. "He stopped the hanging."

"One outlaw?"

"Yes, Sheriff. He kept his hood up, as they often do. Couldn't see his face…"

"One! Only one? How could one single pathetic outlaw stop you from killing that traitorous disgrace of a man who couldn't pay my taxes?"

"Please, Sheriff, you must understand…he was a remarkable archer. I've never seen anyone shoot so sure before—"

"Excuses!"

"And he was fast and nimble, once he stopped shooting and engaged in close combat—"

"I don't care."

"There was nothing we could do! If we'd stayed we'd surely be dead, too."

"Well there is plenty that *I* can do," the Sheriff said. "Gisbourne!"

Much noticed Robin's back stiffening as the Sheriff yelled for Sir Guy of Gisbourne.

"We have two more men who deserve to be hanged! Robin Hood has foiled me again and I can't stand for it. Something must be done!"

Robin straightened, sliding the wood back over the hidden window. "We need to get back to camp."

As they left Nottingham and walked toward Sherwood Forest, the sun sank below the trees and darkness began to creep over the land. Much couldn't enjoy the sunset spilling over the treetops however, as he was preoccupied with watching Robin. Something about the encounter in the castle courtyard had caught his attention, and Much didn't know what it was. Robin offered no hints either, remaining relatively silent and thoughtful on their walk to Sherwood.

Once they'd returned to camp, Robin gathered everyone at the fire ring.

"Who didn't follow my orders?"

"Didn't follow orders?" Will called from his hut, where he was laying in bed with the door open, still healing from his wounds. "We all did our jobs, I assume. Even me, though my job was just to lie here. Marian was here in camp with me and the children all day."

"We were all busy as usual," Dusty said. "What is this about, Robin?"

"There's someone else foiling the Sheriff's plans," Much said. "We heard about a rescue they did today that none of us helped with."

After that day, they heard more and more instances of the mysterious someone who was a remarkable archer and foiled the Sheriff's plans when the gang couldn't. They also started to notice the renowned archery themselves in various raids and ambushes. Every time it became clear that someone was in the woods with them, shooting down the Sheriff's men—it was most obvious because they always wounded rather than killed as the gang would have done— Robin would becomes thoroughly distracted from the task at hand as his eyes roamed the trees around the road, searching for their unknown helper. Much worked extra hard to ensure Robin didn't get himself killed in their ambushes on the Sheriff's treasure when he grew so distracted.

Despite his curiosity, however, Robin and the rest of the gang couldn't find the person who seemed to be stalking their raids and helping to save the innocents that they could not.

Chapter 45

A COUPLE OF weeks after the discovery of the mysterious archer, Robin caught wind that the Sheriff was traveling to the town of Abingdon in order to personally collect the caravan of taxes collected in his shire, as he could hardly trust his soldiers with the job.

The gang gathered their weapons, fetched their horses from Marcus, and then set out for Abingdon. It was the first real outing Will was allowed to go on. He'd been allowed out of bed some days before, with Dusty watching his every move as he set about training with his sword and bow to recover his previous skill, but this was the first time he'd left the camp since he was wounded. Marian remained in the camp with the children.

When the gang arrived in the town of Abingdon, Robin had them leave their horses at the livery on the edge of town, asking around to ascertain where the Sheriff was. When the stable hand pointed him in the right direction, Much and the rest of the gang followed slowly as Robin moved down the streets of the town until they came to an open area—probably a market of some kind.

Robin paused the group before they entered the area, pressing himself into the wall of a nearby building.

Much stood next to him, and could see very little around Robin and the building. Will was beside him, and the rest of the group behind; all of them moving to stand against the building as Robin had.

From the little Much could see, there appeared to be carts and wagons with the same chests of treasure that usually carried the Sheriff's taxes in the open space between the buildings, with a variety of soldiers guarding them.

A horse galloped into the area from another street, pulling to a sudden stop and kicking up dust.

Much leaned forward. "Who is that?"

"I don't know," Robin hissed. "Hush, so I can hear."

It wasn't hard to make out the rider's words as he called out, "I have an urgent message from Sir Guy of Gisbourne!"

"Well, what is it?" the Sheriff's voice snapped back.

"Sir Guy of Gisbourne said to tell you that he's caught the Hooded Rescuer and will hang him at dawn tomorrow. He desires your presence at such an event."

Much whipped around, his wide eyes catching Mark's horrified expression.

"Marian…" Robin breathed out, sounding equally horrified. He turned toward the group. "Weapons at the ready, we're taking that treasure now and then beating the Sheriff back to Nottingham! We can't let Marian hang."

"Then let's go!" Mark said, shoving off the wall.

Much unsheathed his sword and followed as Mark ran into the open area, while Robin whipped out his bow and started picking off the soldiers one by one.

They had the element of surprise, which certainly worked in their favor. The soldiers weren't expecting their ambush and it took them a moment to get their bearings as the gang bore down on them with swords and Robin shot them down. The Sheriff leapt upon his horse and ran from the fight the moment he caught sight of the outlaws.

As Much parried a blow from an opponent, he watched as the soldier's face blanched for a moment, then his eyes went blank and he slumped to the ground, dropping his sword. Much stepped back surprised. He hadn't struck him.

Much glanced around and then noticed that the people of Abingdon had gathered in the open area, some with make-shift weapons such as pitchforks, and others throwing large stones at the Sheriff's men. It appeared that one such stone had struck the back of the head of Much's opponent. The bloodied stone was lying a few paces away.

When the Sheriff's men were dead—both from the gang's weapons and the villagers'—Robin called a thanks to the people who'd stepped in to help while he and the rest of the gang jumped into the wagons and began leading the treasure away. They stopped by the livery to collect Marcus' horses and then began their trip from Abingdon to Nottingham.

They were miles away, and had to travel through the night. With every passing hour Robin's scowl increased and Mark's restlessness became more obvious. As the morning light began to creep into the air, Much could feel his shoulders tensing. It was nearly dawn. Marian was being executed soon!

The minute they were close enough that they'd have to choose between traveling to Sherwood or Nottingham, Robin called for a halt.

"Little John, Will, take the treasure to camp. Much, Dusty, Mark, come with me."

"We'll never get there in time," Mark said, moving from the wagon he'd been on to one of Marcus' horses while Little John began lashing all the wagons together. "She's going to die."

"I won't give up that easily. I won't lose her! Not to the Sheriff."

Much pulled himself into the saddle of one of Marcus' horses and prepared to follow Robin. His heart had settled in his throat, and he didn't dare speak for fear of breaking down entirely. It was hard enough to keep the tears from his eyes as it was.

Robin, for his part, set off at a gallop towards Nottingham without waiting for anyone else. Much kicked his horse into a run, as Mark and Dusty did the same. When they came close to Nottingham gate, Robin didn't slow down. The guards at the city gate definitely saw them this time but the group on horseback galloped right past them before they could raise an alarm or shut the gates.

It would likely be harder to get back out now that the Sheriff's men would be on alert and watching for them, but that was a problem for another time. Right now the only goal was getting to Nottingham castle. What Robin intended to do once they were there, Much couldn't fathom. They'd be outnumbered, and they'd probably die trying to save Marian, if they even arrived before her execution at all.

As they barreled down the streets of Nottingham, people were forced to jump out of their way, crying out in shock and surprise. The sounds of the horses' hoofs pounding against the cobblestone streets rang in Much's ears as he tried not to think about what they might find.

As they neared the castle wall they heard shouts from inside. Mark pulled his horse to a sharp stop before they exited the street into the one that ran along the castle wall. "Robin! Look, up there!"

Robin, Much, and Dusty came to a sudden stop beside Mark, looking up at the castle wall where he was pointing. Just over the courtyard, high up on the battlements, was the Hooded Rescuer. It was the disguise Dusty had made for Marian, though how Marian had ended up on the castle wall was anyone's guess.

"Look at how that person is moving," Robin said, his brow creasing. "That's not Marian's grace."

A moment later, the figure jumped down and hit the pavement with a thud and a gasp of air, then they were up and running down the street to the right, away from the castle.

Much moved his horse to the side of the street closer to one of the shops, hoping to stay out of sight as Sir Guy of Gisbourne came running out the gate with a band of soldiers, they looked along the wall for a moment before Gisbourne commended, "Search the city! Find him!"

The soldiers dispersed quickly, though one remained at his side—Andrew, the soldier who had been Marian's guard during her house arrest.

"What do we do?" Mark hissed, glancing at Robin. They were in plain view; if Gisbourne turned around to look down the side street they'd stopped at the edge of, though he hadn't yet, he'd certainly see them. The group remained on horse back, though they shifted closer to Much. The castle wall was directly in front of the end of their street, the gate into the courtyard further to the left and nearly out of sight if they stayed closer to the side of the street.

"Look!" Dusty whispered.

Much's confusion at the whole ordeal was heightened by the sudden appearance of Allen, a sack slung over his shoulder. He and Gisbourne began a whispered conversation that Much could only catch the barest pieces of.

"…done…work…wait until…straight to…"

"What are they saying?" Dusty leaned forward over her horse's head, straining to hear.

"I'm not sure," Robin said.

Gisbourne and Andrew soon returned to the castle courtyard and Allen leaned against the wall, waiting. Robin backed up his horse just a bit, and Much followed suit, trying to keep out of sight while still remaining close enough to the cross street to be able to see the castle wall and Allen.

The unmistakable resounding crack of a hand striking a face came echoing out of the courtyard and then Much heard the Sheriff yelling.

"You have failed me one too many times!"

Allen shoved off the wall with his sack and moved toward the gate into the courtyard. Robin urged his horse into a slow walk and as Allen disappeared into the courtyard Robin entered the street to follow him. Much and his companions followed, inching along the wall to get a view inside the open gate without being seen by the soldiers within.

Gisbourne was leading Allen toward the stables, and Much caught sight of Andrew leading lady Marian inside the castle itself.

"There she is, Robin!"

"I see her. I don't know what to make of all of this…"

"It appears Allen and Gisbourne saved Marian," Dusty said. "Which is remarkable. But on more pressing matters, perhaps we shouldn't sit right here under the castle wall where we can be seen."

Robin reluctantly led the group to Marcus' house where they stowed the horses and then gathered at Marcus' table while his wife Lillian brought them a bite to eat.

"I could almost forgive Allen after this," Mark said, staring into his mug of ale. "He betrayed us for my father's sake, to keep him safe from the Sheriff's plots. And now he's saved my sister…I can't hate him."

Dusty nodded her agreement, but Much looked to Robin. He was leaning back in his chair, arms crossed, his brows knitted together as he stared at the wall across the room.

Much touched his arm. "Robin?

Robin shifted, his gaze coming into focus. "Mark and I will sneak into the castle to visit Marian. She might be in the dungeons, but given what occurred today, it seems more likely Gisbourne would have put her back in her own room. You and Dusty go back to camp, if you can get out of Nottingham safely."

As it turned out, the city guards were more invested in finding the Hooded Rescuer who they'd been told was running around Nottingham than in keeping an eye out for Robin Hood's gang returning after their hurried entrance into Nottingham, so it was easy for Dusty and Much to fall into stride beside a couple of merchants leaving the city and get outside the city walls without being detected. From there they made their way easily to camp, and informed Little John and Will what had happened.

"I'm glad Marian wasn't hanged," Will said. "Though now that she's alive, I do have a bone to pick with her. She left the children here alone! So bored by being the camp, she just left them..."

"William is nearly a young man," Dusty said, placing a gentle hand on his arm. "I'm sure she thought he could handle taking care of the others."

"That's no excuse," Will replied.

Much quietly made dinner for everyone while they waited for Mark and Robin to return from their attempt to visit Marian.

"I wonder why he did it?" young William asked as everyone began to dig into Much's meal. "Why would Gisbourne help the good side?"

"He cares for Marian," Dusty replied.

"But to rescue her in such a manner," Much said, "making it seem like someone else entirely was the Hooded Rescuer...I can hardly believe it happened."

"And Allen helping," Will said. "Let's not forget that. It must have hit Robin hard, he has been so set on hating Allen, threatening to kill him every chance he can get. And now Allen saved Marian."

"I thought Allen was bad," Beth commented, her seven-year-old face scrunched up in confusion.

"He's not bad," Dusty said. "He has made regrettable choices."

"What will we do with him?" Will asked.

"Why must we do anything?" Little John growled. "He is with the Sheriff. He is nothing to us."

"Little John!" Dusty scolded. "Allen is a brother to us. He always has been. Even brothers make terrible mistakes sometimes, but that doesn't make him nothing to us."

"And how can he be nothing after saving Marian's life?" Much asked.

"He was never my brother," Little John said. "He was a stranger Robin Hood brought home from the Crusades, whom none of us got to know well before he betrayed us. I have no love of him."

"You'll have to get over that," Robin's voice called out from the darkness.

Will leaned forward, peering into the woods as three figures approached the fire. "Robin?"

Robin, Mark, and Allen came into view. Little John leaped to his feet with a growl, while Much's heart leaped to his throat and the children instinctively cowered closer to Will.

Robin calmly sat on one of the logs, reaching forward to grab a bowl from the stack near Much's feet so he could scoop some of Much's pottage out of the pot near the fire. "Allen is once more a part of the gang. You'll have to try and not hold it against him too much."

Little John cursed softly as he sat back down.

"You're accepting him back just like that?" Dusty asked, reaching around Much to scoop some of the pottage into a bowl and handing it to Allen.

"After what he did today…" Robin shrugged. "Besides, Marian told me I had no choice."

"Where is Marian?" Will asked.

"She promised Gisbourne she would stay in the castle."

"Why would she do that?"

"Out of gratitude, I suppose," Robin said. "But also for us. We need someone on the inside getting information from the Sheriff. Too many people have died because we didn't know what he was planning."

Later that night after the gang had dispersed to bed, Robin came knocking on Much's door. Much stepped out into the chill air, keeping a blanket wrapped around his shoulders to ward off the wintry weather. "What's up?"

"Sorry if I woke you…I have news I wanted to share."

"What news?"

"Marian agreed to marry me."

"That's not news, Robin. We all know you love each other."

"Yes, but she actually said yes when I proposed this time, unlike every other time."

Much grinned. "You proposed today of all days? When's the wedding?"

"We didn't set a day. Not until after Richard is back though… life in too much upheaval right now."

"Robin…about Allen…" Much glanced around the darkened camp, unsure what he wanted to ask. Dusty and the still small voice inside he attributed to Jesus had been leading him toward forgiveness ever since Allen had first betrayed the group, and Much was willing to do so. But he somehow doubted Robin was so generous.

"It will be strange having him back," Robin sighed.

"I am glad you let him come home."

"Are you?"

"Yes. It wasn't the same with you being so angry and bitter. We are a family, but we were divided and that was painful to watch, and live through."

"I don't think of Allen as family anymore," Robin replied.

"I know. But I do, and so does Dusty."

"You two are far too trusting and forgiving. I'm not sure why, but you are."

Much bit his cheek. He wished he had the courage to tell Robin exactly why. The only reason was his faith in Jesus. But he said nothing.

"You did let him back into camp, though…" Much finally said.

"Marian insisted...he does seem contrite, and more than that he did save her life today at the risk of his own. Perhaps I was too caught up in those emotions to think clearly, but he's here now, so we'll just have to make the best of it."

"Are you certain? You aren't going to try and kill him?"

"I've considered it." Robin shrugged, glancing toward the starry sky. "But Marian asked me to let him back—not just because he saved her, but because she believes him to be remorseful. I can't trust him, but for her sake I'll let him live here and help in our work. We can always use more hands, you know that."

"But if you don't trust him, will you be able to assign him missions to carry out? Will you allow him to have your back in a fight against the Sheriff's men?"

"I don't know, Much. I didn't think all of this through. Marian asked, and I agreed. Yesterday I thought I'd lost her; today, as the sun rose and we weren't there to save her I thought..." Robin shoved a hand through his hair. "I was overwhelmed. I would have done anything Marian asked today."

Chapter 46

MUCH STRETCHED HIS arms over his head for a moment, cracking his neck to one side and then the other. It had been a long day, traveling with Dusty and distributing food to various villages and farms around the Nottingham area. His muscles ached from the physical labor, and his feet were sore from walking. He'd made a quick supper for everyone once he and Dusty returned to camp, and now everyone lounged around the camp, waiting for Robin to return. The children had been put to bed, but there was little conversation between the group as everyone was exhausted.

As Much finished stretching he grabbed a log from the nearby stack and tossed it onto the fire. He wondered if perhaps the silence could also be attributed to Allen's presence.

Robin had let Allen back into the gang, so no one could argue with him being there, but apart from Dusty no one seemed comfortable with him around. He'd been back for a couple weeks now, but still the children went out of their way to stay clear of him, Little John never spoke to him except to cast insults at him, and Will seemed perturbed by his presence.

It was into this calm that Robin crashed into the camp, stumbling over his own feet as he ran into the meadow.

"What's wrong?" Will sat up, instantly on alert and reaching for his sword.

"We have to go. Now!"

"What is it?" Dusty asked, half rising from her place on the log bench.

"The Sheriff is leaving Nottingham," Robin said as he hurried over to the group.

"Where is he going this time?" Mark asked.

"To Austria!"

"Austria?" Much's heart began to race. The king was still imprisoned in Austria…

"I just spoke to Marian," Robin said as he hastily moved around the camp, throwing provisions from the kitchen and weapons from storage hut into small piles. "We have to pack. He's going to Austria to kill King Richard!"

"No!"

Will, Allen, and Mark were on their feet the next moment.

"When is he leaving?" Allen asked.

"Tomorrow morning. Hurry up, all of you. We have to get there first, we have to leave tonight."

"What is our plan?" Will asked.

"I don't know yet…" Robin paused in his work to shove a hand through his blond hair. "All I know is that we have to beat the Sheriff to Austria and rescue King Richard from Durnstein castle."

"Perhaps the Duke will hand him over if we explain the situation," Dusty said. "After all, we have been paying the ransom all this while."

Robin snorted. "I doubt the Duke will do any such thing."

Much joined the frenzied packing, taking over the provisions portion of Robin's chaos so that he could properly prepare for their long journey. They would be gone for weeks, traveling to the coast, and then across the channel, and then across the rest of Europe. It had taken them two months after their escape from prison, but they were less well stocked back then.

Once Much was satisfied with the food store, he went over to where Robin and Will were sorting through weaponry.

"Robin…what are we going to do about the children?"

Will paused, looking back at Much, and then glancing toward the huts where the children slept. "We can't leave them alone."

"We have no choice, Will," Robin said. "We have to go *now*. I don't have time to make arrangements for the children; the King of England is in danger!"

"I can ride to Nottingham," Allen spoke up from behind them.

Robin whirled around, fire flashing in his eyes. "And what exactly do you plan to do there?"

"Speak to Marcus." Allen took a step away from the group gathered at the storage hut, putting his hands up in a placating manner. "He can look after the children while we're gone."

Robin eyed Allen suspiciously in the darkness until Dusty moved over and placed a hand on Allen's arm. "That is a good idea, Allen." She glanced at Robin and then continued, "Set up a place where young William can meet Marcus in the woods, not far from here but not in the camp either. No one can know the location of our hideout."

"I'm aware of that; I'd never bring anyone here."

"You did before," Robin snapped, crossing his arms.

"I *didn't* though. Maybe you didn't notice as you were too busy hating me, but I did not lead Gisbourne here. I told him and the Sheriff I would in order keep my own life, but I was leading him to a different part of the forest when you ambushed us."

"Fine." Robin continued to glare at Allen. "Go to Nottingham, speak to Marcus. But if you aren't back soon enough, we'll just leave without you. You can watch the children yourself."

Much's heart sank. The trip they were about to embark on could potentially be a dangerous one—all his travels abroad had been up to this point—and on top of that, the tension between Allen and the rest of the gang was building once more.

Will reminded Robin that their quickest way of traveling was by using Marcus' horses, so Allen was given a second task when he left for

Nottingham, that of retrieving the horses. Little John went with him, and Much was sure it was because he, of all the members of the gang, trusted Allen the least.

Will woke young William to tell him what was happening so he wouldn't be confused when he and the other children awoke in the morning.

When Allen and Little John returned with their horses, everyone loaded their packs swiftly and Robin urged them into a gallop.

Their travel to the coast was hurried and stressful, but surprisingly uneventful. They did catch sight of the Sheriff's party behind them on more than one occasion, and Robin had snuck back to the Sheriff's camp to scope out the possibility of merely ambushing them on English soil—but they were too heavily guarded. He did discover, however, that Marian was with them.

"Why would they bring Marian?" Mark asked when Robin reported what he'd found to the gang. The moon and stars were shining brightly overhead, illuminating the worried look on Mark's face.

"They likely didn't *choose* to bring her," Robin said. "This is Marian we're talking about."

"That's true," Mark said. "She must have found a way to make them bring her along, which means she's up to something. Maybe she has a plan."

"But how will we know what that plan is?" Much asked.

"We won't," Robin said. "We'll just have to keep an eye out for anything. I just hope she doesn't do anything reckless."

They crossed the channel without trouble, finding a stable in Dover to keep their exhausted horses. Once on the other side, Robin paid for more horses and the race to Durnstein castle began.

As they drew ever closer to Austria and the place where Much, Robin, Allen, and Dusty had been imprisoned for a year, Much's whole body seemed to be reacting poorly to their environment and the stress of the situation. There wasn't a day that passed when his shoulders weren't tense, his stomach wasn't nauseous, and his palms weren't sweaty. His heart was beating a constant and loud rhythm in his ears matching the pounding of his horse's hoofbeats on the ground as he galloped after Robin and the rest of the gang.

Chapter 47

EARLY ONE MORNING just as the sun was beginning to cast its warm glow across the sky, the group crested a hill and came in sight of a familiar town in a small valley, nestled against the back of another hill across the way.

"Do you think Lord Isenbern might be of assistance to us?" Allen called out as they continued their furious gallop forward.

"Doubtful!" Robin shouted back. "He was loyal to the Duke last time; if he'd known we'd escaped imprisonment he probably would have sent us back."

"Who's Lord Isenbern?" Will asked.

"An old friend from our travels," Dusty replied.

In the grey light of dawn, the town looked sleepy, still in shadow from the surrounding hills. The gang skirted wildly around the city to keep racing toward their destination.

It was still early in the morning when the castle came into sight on the horizon. Robin had the group come to a halt as soon as he saw the castle, leading the group over to a clump of trees.

"What's the plan?" Allen asked.

"We'll just have to go in the way we came out," Robin said.

"Right past the guard house?" Much asked.

"It's fool-hardly, but I've got no other options."

"What if they've moved the king?" Allen asked. "What if he's not in the same cell, or they blocked up the hole we created? What if—"

"I know it's not a plan!" Robin shoved a hand through his hair. "But I've got nothing else. We get in there, we hope to find him, and we get out before the Sheriff arrives."

As they crept forward on foot, leaving the horses in the outcropping of trees, Much's heart beat an erratic dance inside his chest.

Much kept his eyes on the castle ramparts, carefully timing the marching of the soldiers on guard up there. When he and Robin felt there was an opening, they sent the gang running forward to press up again the castle wall and hopefully be out of sight.

Much pushed his back into the wall as well as he could, breathing heavily from the sprint to the castle wall and the terror of sneaking back into the place where he had been imprisoned for so long.

Without a word, Robin moved toward the gate leading into the castle courtyard, Will close on his heels. Much took a deep breath, trying to steady his heart that had now lodged itself into his throat.

Will and Robin pounced on the two soldiers stationed at the gate, cutting them down swiftly as Dusty and Mark rushed into the guardhouse beside the gate to finish off the three soldiers in there.

Much moved a step into the courtyard where he could see up on the ramparts—from there, he began to shoot down the soldiers stationed above as they became aware of the sounds of the fight below. One by one they dropped, some falling off the rampart altogether to crash onto the ground below.

As soon as it seemed the way was clear, the group darted across the open space of the courtyard to the front door. Much wasn't entirely sure he was breathing as he followed Robin into the familiar and yet foreign castle. He'd only been in this portion once before, during their reckless escape. Robin, however, seemed to remember where they were.

The fact that it was so early worked to their advantage, as few nobles were awake and Robin remembered where soldiers were stationed in various parts of the castle. How he remembered all of that, Much didn't know, but he dutifully followed along behind.

As they turned a corner, however, they came across a group of noblemen.

Robin came to an abrupt halt, and the conversation that had been taking place in the hallway did so as well as each of the men turned to study the strange group that had stumbled across their path. Much wondered how strange they must look, all armed to the teeth and sneaking into the castle as they were.

"Gentlemen…" one of the nobles, tilted his head to one side, as another's hand twitched toward his belt.

"Don't kill them," Dusty spoke to the gang in Arabic rather than English.

"What is your business here?" the noble who'd spoken before stepped forward.

"We are here to visit a friend," Robin said smoothly, stepping forward as well and straightening as he spoke, suddenly looking every bit the young lord that he was. How he managed to slip into that intimidating persona with ease always astounded Much.

"If we don't kill them, they will alert the Duke and other soldiers to our presence," Allen hissed behind Dusty, speaking Arabic as she had done.

"They are innocents."

"More so than the soldiers we killed?"

Much was distracted by the Arabic conversation as Robin continued to speak to the nobles.

"If we don't kill them, word of us being here will spread," Allen said, still in Arabic.

"We can knock them out," Much said, joining the conversation.

Robin turned slightly toward the gang. "I agree."

He'd spoken in Arabic as well, which seemed to unnerve the gentlemen he'd just been speaking with.

Robin darted forward suddenly, and in an instant had his arm around the man's neck, stopping his breathing so he would pass out.

The other nobles cried out in alarm, some reaching for weapons while others moved to run down the hall. The rest of the gang sprang into action, and Much ran forward, ducking under the dagger blade of one of the nobles and punching him in the face. He grabbed the wrist of the hand with the blade while he brought his knee forward into a harsh kick in the side. The man slumped slightly in pain, his grip on his blade loosening. That was all Much needed to slip the dagger into his own hand and slam the pommel down on the man's head.

He collapsed to the floor. Either unconscious or dead, Much wasn't sure. He spun around to see who else he could help, but it seemed each of the gang members had successfully knocked out their own nobles and the hallway was now full of sleeping men.

"Let's go." Robin marched away from the mess they'd just made, and Much hurried after him. The rest of the group followed.

Robin led the group to the small chamber that led them into the tunnels below the castle.

Unfortunately, when Robin opened the door to the small chamber, two soldiers stood there.

Much raised his bow and shot down one in the same moment Robin rushed forward with his sword to fight the other. The struggle was brief, as Will and Allen squeezed into the room to assist Robin and soon the soldier was dead.

Robin pushed past the dead soldiers, and Much began to wonder how the Duke might retaliate now that they were killing so many of his men. Given that he had imprisoned the King of England—despite him being both a king and a protected crusader that the Duke had no right to capture at all—merely because King Richard had offended him by taking down his standard at Acre, it was likely he would have a strong reaction to a group of vagabonds from England killing his men.

Robin grabbed a torch off a sconce in the wall as he entered the tunnels, and hurried down the passages. Much and the rest of the gang followed him.

Much tried not to think about the body count they were leaving behind them as he hurried down the dark tunnels.

"I think we're getting close," Robin said.

"How can you tell?" Allen asked. "There's so many branches and passages, I'm not convinced we're on the right one."

"I remember the tunnels," Robin said. "I'm not worried about that. I do think we're close. Keep an eye out along the wall for our hole."

"Which likely isn't there anymore," Allen said.

Robin swung around, the torch in his hand flickering and the shadows on the wall recoiling from the light of the flames. "If you don't want to save King Richard, go home. I didn't want to bring you at all."

"I want to be here, Robin. I only meant it might be harder than you let on."

"I don't need your negativity."

"Enough." Will stepped between Allen and Robin. "We have likely attracted attention with all the soldiers we have killed. We don't have time for arguing. Let's keep an eye on the wall for any sign of a hole, whether it is open or plugged up in some fashion. Let's move."

Robin spun on his heel, marching down the hallway while Allen remained still. The rest of the gang moved past him to follow after Robin, but Much paused.

"Are you okay?'

"He hates me."

"You aren't being helpful, that's all. He's stressed and your comments added to that. If he hated you, you would be dead and certainly not a part of the gang again."

Allen sighed.

"Come on. Let's keep going."

Allen nodded, allowing Much to pull him along the tunnel after the others.

"I think I found it!" Dusty's voice called through the relative darkness. The rest of the gang hurried to gather around her. The wall of the tunnel was dirt and rock, seemingly carved directly from the ground and not built, yet there was a large portion of the wall that was discolored.

Much leaned forward, running his hand along it. "It's clay."

"That's it," Robin said. "They filled it in, but that's it."

"The other side is our cell," Dusty agreed.

Robin kicked at the clay, but nothing happened. He passed his torch to Much and began to shove his weight against the wall.

Will crossed his arms, watching. "Should we have a plan before we break that down?"

"We're getting the king before the Sheriff does," Robin grunted.

"What if the king is not in that cell?" Will asked. "What if he is, but so are a bunch of soldiers. What if it is only soldiers, lying in wait for us?"

"Now you sound like Allen."

"Allen has a point." Will stepped closer to Robin, laying a hand on his shoulder. "Before we rush in, we need to think this through."

"We've already rushed in."

"Robin."

Robin sighed, straightening and crossing his arms. "Okay. Okay. Get your weapons at the ready. Little John, smash this in and then duck out of the way—you're too large to fit through quickly. Dusty and I will dive in, Will and Much can cover us at the hole. Mark, stay clear for your own safety."

"You don't have to be protective of me," Mark snapped.

"There's not space for everyone around the small hole we created the last time. I doubt when they plugged it up they made it any larger! Just stand aside, please."

Mark grumbled under his breath, but he moved to one side. Allen moved to stand with him as Robin hadn't given him any direction, which was not a fact that escaped Much.

Much grabbed an arrow from his quiver and held it at the ready as Little John took Robin's place and began to kick at the clay. At first, nothing seemed to happen, but then it caved inward.

The resounding thud sent shudders running through Much. He was sure soldiers would soon come running at any second.

Robin and Dusty disappeared into the relative darkness of the hole and Much leaned close, bow raised, squinting to see if there were soldiers.

He saw the vague outline of his friends, and a third person.

"Robin?!"

"Richard. We've got to get you out."

"You're supposed to be in England dealing with my brother!"

"And so we have been," Robin replied, pulling King Richard to his feet and shoving him out of the hole.

Much moved aside as Robin clambered out as well.

"Right now we have to run because we've undoubtedly attracted attention in here, and because the Sheriff of Nottingham has brought his own batch of vile men to kill you here in Austria. So let's *move*."

As Robin spoke and Dusty dove back out of the hole, Much caught sight of more shadows within the dungeon. It was dark in there, made darker still to Much's eyes by the presence of Robin's torch in the tunnel, but he let his arrow fly as best as he could, shooting down soldiers with Will at his side.

Robin pushed the king and began moving back down the tunnel, and the others hurried after them. Much and Will remained by the hole a moment longer, shooting down the last of the shadow within sight of the cell.

Shouts sounded from further within the dungeon.

"Time to go." Will grabbed Much's arm for a second to tug him along and then they both ran after the rest of the gang.

Little John took up the rear as they joined the group, brandishing his quarter staff at the few soldiers who were pushing their way out of the hole in the dungeon wall.

Robin led the group back to the castle itself. Much held his breath as they traversed the hallways for the third time in his life. Shouts followed behind and Will and Dusty spun around to shoot at any followers as Little John continued to look threatening but was mostly useless at a distance.

Somehow, they made it out without the soldiers catching up, which was nothing short of a miracle.

Much began to breathe again.

Chapter 48

"ROBIN!" THE KING drew him into an embrace.

"We cannot have a reunion here, Your Majesty," Robin said as he pulled away. "We must be on our way."

Robin hurried everyone away from the castle, to their horses in the nearby cropping of trees where they'd left them. "We ride to Vienna!"

"Why the city?" Allen asked.

"In order to get lost in the city crowds," Much said, spurring his horse after Robin. "If we flee over the open knolls it would be far easier for the Duke's men to follow."

"We lose them in the city crowds," Robin said.

The group galloped across the countryside toward the city of Vienna. They hadn't visited Vienna when they fled the castle the last time, and despite the fear of pursuit, Much couldn't help but feel fascinated as they drew close to the city. It was well-known for both trade and culture—the Earl had once suggested that he might send Robin (and therefore, Much) to Vienna to study music but that had never happened.

Robin slowed his horse as they entered the city streets, hoping not to draw too much attention to their group.

As they rode as inconspicuously as they could, Much heard the distinctive sound of a bow twanging. His heart fell to his toes as he saw King Richard, riding in front of him, slump out of his saddle with an arrow in his shoulder.

Robin swung his horse around, searching for the culprit. "Dusty, help him!"

Dusty dismounted and ran for the king, but before she could reach him, soldiers came pouring out of nearby buildings, the Sheriff and Gisbourne among them.

Much jumped down from his horse and grabbed his sword as the soldiers swarmed their group.

Much blocked and parried, his sword moving quickly first one way and then another as more and more soldiers approached him.

Over the din of swords clashing and men crying out in pain, Much heard Gisbourne shouting Marian's name. He turned swiftly in the direction of his voice and saw Marian standing near the king—who was still prone on the ground—her arms held out, as though she could stop him from hurting the king by her mere presence. They were speaking to each other in an animated fashion, but Much could not hear what they were saying.

Footsteps approaching from behind brought Much's attention back to his own predicament and he swung around, raising his sword in time to block the incoming blade. A few more blocks and parries, and he'd disarmed the soldier and lopped off his head.

Much swung around, searching for Marian and Gisbourne once more. When his eyes landed on Marian, he saw that Mark was standing beside her, one hand on her arm, the other brandishing his sword.

Without warning, Gisbourne's sword flashed forward and emerged out the back of Marian, blood spurting out with it.

The edges of Much's vision narrowed darkly as he watched Marian fall. Dimly, he could hear cries and shouts coming from Robin and others as Marian's body slammed into the hard dirt, Gisbourne's sword still sticking out of her.

Everything faded to blackness and silence…

Much blinked up into the gentle eyes of Little John. "You need to get up. Marian needs all of us, my friend."

Much sat up, rubbing the back of his head where he could feel a welt growing. He must have fainted. "Is she alright? What happened?"

Little John pulled Much to his feet. "Come."

Little John led him over to where the gang was gathered in a circle around a group gathered on the ground. Marian was still stretched out on the ground where Much had seen her fall, her head now in Mark's lap as he bent over her, weeping. Robin knelt beside her, tears pouring down his own cheeks as he held her hand.

Dusty was rising to her feet as Much and Little John came to stand beside Allen, Will, and the king. There was no sign of the Sheriff or Gisbourne, and all the soldiers in the vicinity were clearly dead. Much had obviously missed the end of the battle, whatever it had looked like.

Much watched as Dusty buried her face in Will's shoulder, and then he looked back down at the three people he'd grown up with. His earliest understanding of what family could and should be came from Robin, Mark, and Marian.

Much's vision blurred once more, this time with tears. The fact that Dusty wasn't working away at Marian's wound meant she didn't believe she could do anything to help—Dusty, who healed everything, had given up.

"Stay with me, Marian," Robin moaned, stroking her hair. "Stay with me."

"Marry…me…Robin…"

Much brushed his tears aside in an attempt to see as Marian pleaded with Robin to marry her before she died. Mark moaned in agony and turned his face away.

Much could see dark spots dancing across his vision again. This was so wrong, so messed up. Marian couldn't die, she belonged with Robin…

"Not now," Allen hissed in his ear, grabbing Much's hand. "Stay with us."

Much turned to him with wide, tear-filled eyes.

Allen's eyes were red from crying as well, but he held firm to Much's hand. "She needs all of us right now. Don't faint again."

Much took a shaky breath, turning back to Robin, Marian, and Mark.

Robin began to comply to Marian's pleas, repeating the oft-used words of the sacred vow to love and cherish his wife in sickness and health.

Marian struggled to repeat the vow back to him, but couldn't get past "I…I…" as her strength waned.

"She needs a wedding band, Robin," the king said, bending down and pulling a ring from his finger and handing it to Robin.

Much's knees went weak and he felt himself begin to wobble.

"Steady," Allen's quiet voice beside him gave Much a moment of clarity.

"Robin," Marian's weak voice cracked. "Promise me…you'll keep fighting."

"Marian…"

"Please…England…needs…."

The king nodded. "England does need you, Robin. Especially since I am not going back yet. I have unfinished business here. You must take care of my people."

Robin shook his head, bringing Marian's hands to his lips as tears cascaded down his cheeks, splashing onto her face.

Much looked to the king, wondering how he could possibly stay in Austria now. He was free; his people in England were suffering, and now on top of everything else the one person looking after England

and leading the gang was going to be devastated and in no state to lead anyone. How could the king abandon England, abandon Robin, in such a way? Much could not fathom what the king could possibly want to do here in Austria, his 'unfinished business' could hardly be more important than his people.

"Robin…" Marian's voice was weak. "Promise…me…"

Finally, Robin sighed. "I promise. For you, my darling Marian."

Marian's eyes suddenly filled with a vacant, distant look and Robin's shoulders shook with his sobs, as Mark let out a howl of anguish. Dusty reached down to carefully close Marian's eyes.

The silence that followed Mark's wail was unbearable. Much shuddered, his heart squeezing inside his chest.

"She can't be gone," Much whispered.

Allen let go of Much's hand, his shoulders shaking with silent sobs.

"She can't!" Much looked around at the group, all of them weeping. How could this be happening? Nothing but sobs met Much's outburst.

Much closed his eyes, searching for that still small voice. "Why? Why did this have to happen?"

And then once more, Much fainted.

Chapter 49

THE RETURN TO England was a blur to Much. He had the vague notion that they'd buried Marian in Austria at Dusty's insistence, but otherwise it was all a jumble of pain, tears, and the sound of hoofbeats as they rode across Europe. Where they stayed, what they ate, Much hadn't the slightest idea. But one day, they finally were back at the camp and everyone was shutting themselves into their own huts.

Much sank onto his bed, staring up at the wooden ceiling of his hut.

Marian was dead.

An ache had lodged itself in Much's chest as soon as Marian died, and it grew with every passing day, the tightness in his limbs and shoulders adding to his discomfort every time he thought about what happened.

Much was exhausted from his trip and his grief, and found relief in sleep sooner than he had expected.

Much was the first to appear from his hut the next morning, as per usual. The children soon came entering the camp; apparently Marcus had learned of the gang's return and had sent them home from wherever he'd been keeping an eye on them. The older ones helped Much cook up breakfast while the younger ones played with the toys from Locksley. Soon both Dusty and Allen came to sit around the warm fire.

Winter had given way to spring on their long journey to and from Austria, so though the morning air was chill, Much knew the fire wouldn't be necessary later in the day any longer.

No one spoke as Much finished frying up some bacon and eggs and mushrooms and began scooping it onto plates for the children and for Allen and Dusty.

Much scooped out a bit of food for himself, although he didn't feel like eating. None of them spoke for several minutes, the only sounds in the camp were that of the youngest children playing and the first of the spring birds chirping in the trees nearby.

When he'd finished eating, Allen stood. "I'll wash up the dishes, Much."

"You don't have to do that."

"I know. But you have been working to keep us all fed this whole journey, though I know you haven't been entirely present. You are grieving and you deserve a chance to do so properly. You've known Marian as long as Robin and Mark; this has to be hard on you more than some of the rest of us."

Much didn't fight Allen as he took over his kitchen. He stood and wandered to the edge of camp. He didn't know where his feet would lead him, but it didn't matter at the moment.

He wandered off toward the stream nearby, following its path through the trees.

Much remembered this stream; not right here, in the forest, but where it exited Sherwood and traversed the countryside toward Wetherby. He had played there with Marian, Mark, and Robin as a child. They'd made mud pies together, and listened to Robin propose to Marian even when he was a child, while Marian would turn up her nose and stomp off. They'd skipped stones up the stream as far as they could, getting their toes wet and imagining their futures—Robin, of course, assuming he'd be married to Marian and bringing his children to skip stones along with them someday.

Much sat down hard, pulling his knees up to his chest and wrapping his arms around them, dropping his head onto his arms and shaking with sobs.

Marian was gone.

Much could still see the point of Gisbourne's sword emerging from her back every time he closed his eyes. He shuddered, letting his pain expand in his chest until he could scarcely breathe.

When his sobs eventually subsided, Much slowly made his way back to camp.

Allen, Will, and Dusty were sitting close together around the fire speaking softly, and all three of them were crying. The children had gathered a distance away to play, though William, Beth, and Sarah kept casting glances toward the weeping grown-ups.

Much seated himself beside Dusty. "Are you alright?"

"No one is alright anymore," Will said from the other side of Dusty.

"But we will be," Dusty said. "Grief is no small thing, but I know the Lord is in control of this situation as with any other. He knows the pain we feel now, and He is my greatest comfort."

Allen shook his head. "I see no reason to turn to him for comfort. If he is all that you say he is, you could have saved her, if he really cared."

"Oh, Allen! He does care," Dusty leaned forward around Will to see Allen's face more clearly. "He loved Marian more than you or I—or even Robin—ever could. Much like the story of Lazarus, I do believe Jesus is weeping now."

Allen sighed and said nothing.

Will took Dusty's hand in his own. "I am glad that you can find comfort at this time. I feel no comfort, from any quarter."

"If you'd only turn to Jesus. He'd comfort you; He's so willing and ready to do so."

Will smiled at Dusty, but shook his head. Much, on the other hand, closed his eyes and reached out to God. The warmth and love spread over his being to his very bones, as it always did. He knew Christ was present with him and grieving alongside him.

"We will need to put up a brave front for the children," Will said. "They will have a hard enough time with the grief that has settled over the camp, without seeing so many grown men and women crying all the time."

"That's a tall order," Allen said.

Much glanced toward the circle of children not far away, casting furtive glances toward the adults around the fire. Will was right, this was going to be hard on them.

The next few days were quiet. The gang tried to settle back into their routines; Much was busy taking care of everyone's physical needs while Will took Allen and Little John into Nottingham every day to keep an eye on things. The children did their best to stay out from underfoot, and particularly to steer clear of Robin—who was always in a fowl mood and prone to lash out and snap at anyone at any given moment—and Mark, who never said a word but carried a great darkness with him wherever he went.

And then there was Dusty, trying to offer comfort and encouragement and for the most part being met with rejection.

While Will tried to keep the gang in some semblance of order, Robin would often wander through Sherwood Forest aimlessly, while Mark stayed holed up in his hut for most of the day. Much would take food to Mark every day, and wait to be sure Mark would eat some of it. Though he reluctantly ate, Mark never said a word.

410

Will soon learned of a caravan of treasure passing through Sherwood and eagerly told Robin. Robin showed no interest in the news.

"We will be running low on money to hand out to the people of England," Will said. He, along with the rest of the gang, was sitting by the fire while Robin sat in front of his hut a short distance from them. Will wasn't deterred by Robin's disinterest or failure to get up and move to the fire. "This is how we replenish our supplies. We need to do this ambush."

Robin shrugged.

"When does the caravan pass through Sherwood?" Much asked.

"Two days from now," Will said.

"Then we have time to truly plan an ambush," Allen said.

"I don't care," Robin said calmly from his position by his hut. From the apathetic look on his face, he certainly seemed to mean it.

"Robin," Will stood up and took a step toward him. "The people of England still need us."

Robin didn't respond.

"Okay." Will crossed his arms. "You don't have to help. But we are going to do this; we're confiscating this treasure and continuing to help the people of England survive Prince John's reign and the Sheriff's cruelty."

Will led the rest of the group in a discussion of how best to ambush this caravan, while Robin pointedly ignored the group. They hadn't been discussing the potential raid for long when Mark exited his hut.

A hush fell over the group. Much watched Mark carefully as he walked toward the rest of them. He didn't say anything, he simply walked over to the fire and sat beside Will.

411

Will greeted him and was met with no response, so the group went back to planning.

Much studied Mark even as Mark sullenly watched Will. His shoulders were drooping, his eyes were red and puffy, and held a vacant look not unlike Marian's when she died. He never spoke, and yet he stayed by Will's side throughout the planning session. And when the time came for the actual ambush two days later, he silently followed along, his weapons in hand, to help with the raid.

It was a successful endeavor, as they so often were, but Robin was still disinterested when they returned to camp with the carts full of treasure. Allen set to work putting the chests of gold and jewels into the storage hut while Little John and Will set off with the new batch of horses and mules to gift them to farmers in the area.

Days began to pass with a sort of cloud hanging over the camp. Robin was vacant, Mark was worse. Will took charge and gave out assignments in the mornings to Little John, Dusty, and Much. Mark only helped if they were attacking a caravan of treasure and otherwise spent all of his time in his hut and not saying a word to anyone.

There were also the reports of rescues of innocents from the brutality of the Sheriff's soldiers that the gang heard about but took no part in, and the archer they could never see who shot down and wounded soldiers during their ambushes. It seemed the mysterious archer was still at work, and many in the gang were eager to find him.

With Marian dead, Robin out of commission, and Mark only half there, bringing new members into the gang seemed imperative. Particularly this archer who was already helping them in so many ways. Will insisted working in tandem with the mysterious archer would be best, if they could ever find him.

412

One morning, after the gang had been fed and Will had sent everyone off on their missions for the day distributing food and money and the like, Much went to speak with Robin, who was sitting outside his hut casually sharpening his sword. The children were playing across the meadow, and Mark was still in his hut. Much had taken food to him that morning, but he still hadn't said a word.

Much seated himself beside Robin, who made no sign that he was aware Much was there at all.

"Robin."

Robin drew his whetstone slowly down the edge of his sword in a long methodical motion.

"We are all hurting from…what happened. But we have each other to lean on and get through the pain, if you'll only let the rest of us help you."

"I don't need your help."

Much studied Robin carefully as he continued to sharpen his sword, taking his whetstone down the blade in slow, smooth strokes. There was a fire burning in his eyes, Much realized, and with a shudder he wondered if Robin was picturing doing to Gisbourne what had been done to Marian.

"Mark won't let anyone in," Much commented, hoping to draw Robin into conversation and away from his dark thoughts, whatever they might be. "He's shutting us out; he's going to be bitter before too long."

"I know…" Robin's hand paused mid-stroke and he glanced at Much. "I'm just…heartbroken, and angry with Gisbourne." Robin nearly snarled as he spat the name.

"I know. But you can't shut us out. And we have to help Mark."

"Do what you will, Much. I don't have the strength for it. I just...I just want to kill Gisbourne and then myself."

"Robin!"

"There's nothing left for me."

"Your friends here? Mark? Sarah, the woman who is in nearly every way your mother? I understand you are hurting. So am I. We all are. Marian didn't deserve what happened to her, and now that she's gone...it's all wrong. But giving up isn't an option."

"Help Mark if you will, but stop bothering me." Robin stood, grabbing his sword and whetstone and moving inside his hut. "I don't want your help."

Before Much could respond, Robin slammed his door shut.

Much wished there was something he could say to ease Robin's pain. He knew what Dusty would say, but Robin had no interest in getting to know the God that Dusty and Much followed so it was unlikely he would find comfort there.

Much also knew that on some level forgiving Gisbourne was as encouraged as forgiving Allen, but he wasn't ready to face that himself so there was no chance Robin would.

Much continued to take meals to Mark every day and try to coax him into speaking about his grief—or speaking of anything at all —but Mark refused to say a single word. He barely glanced at Much at all.

Despite the lack of Robin's leadership, the gang was getting back into the swing of things. They didn't hear of every caravan of treasure, or every execution, and so the Sheriff got his money and people died; but as much as they could, they did what they had been doing before Marian died. Will led them on raids and rescues—some of which Mark would participate in—and Dusty continued to try and urge everyone to find solace in the only true Comforter, though no one apart from Much seemed to take her up on that offer.

Chapter 50

SPRING WAS IN the air, making travel to further cities to help distribute food or money easier—there was, of course, still the risk of muddy roads due to the spring rains, but those weren't nearly as bad as trying to travel through a blizzard. The trees of Sherwood bloomed green, and those with buds flowered pink and white while the ground was covered in many different colors as flowers sprouted across the forest floor.

One day, Dusty gave Much a list of herbs she was running low on as she had taken up healing the sick in Nottingham and the surrounding villages once more.

"You should be able to find them easily enough in the woods. If you can't, come back and I will help you."

"I am glad to be of service to you, but can I ask why you don't want to go yourself?"

"Will is especially depressed today; I cannot leave his side."

Much glanced toward Robin, sitting outside his hut and sharpening his sword as he was wont to do these days. He wished he could do something for his brother—if Dusty could do something to comfort Will, Much wasn't going to get in the way of that. "Of course. I'll be back soon."

"Thank you, little mouse. I am grateful for you."

Much took Dusty's list and one of her satchels and wandered through the woods collecting the different plants she had requested. After a time, he heard the unmistakable sound of thudding hoofbeats. Looking up, Much's heart leaped to his throat. Riding toward him was a group of soldiers.

Much backed away, moving closer to the nearest tree, his heart pounding. What was he supposed to do? He was one man, against the whole group; he couldn't fight them.

As soon as he was spotted, shouts filled the air and Much's blood turned to ice. He had the terrifying notion he was going to die.

Much shook himself as the group drew near, grabbing the knife he'd been using to cut plant stocks and chucking it at the nearest horse as the group drew near. The horse shrieked as the knife found purchase in its neck, and Much spun on his heel and ran. The crash behind him seemed to indicate that the horse had fallen.

One down.

Much heard the continued hoofbeats behind him, gaining on him. Much spun around, leaping in front of the nearest horse. It reared back to avoid hitting him, throwing its rider, and Much turned on his heel and took off sprinting again.

He heard heavy footfalls behind him and then was tackled to the ground.

"Did you get him?"

"Nearly."

Much struggled against his captor as the soldier tried to pull him upright.

Suddenly the soldier let go of him, and Much scrambled away on his hands and knees, spinning around and seeing an arrow protruding from the soldier's shoulder.

Robin had apparently followed him into the woods, for which Much was grateful.

"Where'd that come from?" one of the soldiers asked.

More arrows began to fly, first from one direction and then shortly after that from another. The soldiers dropped to the ground, their eyes wandering the trees searching for the source, but Robin kept them guessing as his arrows flew from a new spot each time.

Much got to his feet and slowly backed away from the soldiers in the chaos. He glanced around, wondering whether to bolt for it or hide. Suddenly a hand clamped over his mouth and he was hauled behind a tree just as another soldier came running toward the injured ones.

"What happened?" the soldier asked.

"Get us back to Nottingham," one of the injured soldiers snapped. "We need a healer."

"What happened?" the soldier demanded again.

"Robin Hood," one of them grunted in response, pain and annoyance coating his voice.

Robin was pulling him backwards, away from the injured soldiers. It was unusual for him to leave survivors, but perhaps he was so sore over Marian's death he couldn't bring himself to kill them.

Once they were a good distance away from the soldiers, the hand left his mouth and Much breathed a deep sigh of relief. He was safe.

"Thank you, Robin."

A musical laugh sounded behind him. "You're welcome. But I'm not Robin."

Much spun around and beheld a young woman with sparkling eyes. Where had she come from? He took in the bow and quiver over her shoulder, and glanced back the way they'd come. The arrows that had flown from one place and then another so swiftly to save him…

"Sorry to startle you," the woman said.

"You're the mysterious archer, aren't you?"

A smile graced her face. "I don't know about mysterious."

"But you are the archer who has been helping us?" Much insisted. "We've seen your work, though we could never seem to see you. It has been you, hasn't it?"

"Yes, it has been me."

"You have to come to the camp." Robin might at last take interest in the present if Much brought her to camp, and Will had been saying all along that they should find the archer and bring them into the gang so they could all work together.

"I can't." Something in the woman's eyes shifted and Much had the distinct feeling she was nervous.

"Why not?"

"Will Robin allow it?"

Much waved his hand nonchalantly. "Robin's been trying to locate you for some time. He said you would be a great addition to our team."

"Oh."

"We should leave here in any case. Those men might wander this way and notice us in a moment, and no doubt more will come from Nottingham after they report what happened."

The woman was still hesitant, but Much grinned at her and gestured behind her. "Come on, it's this way. You'll love the gang."

He started walking, glancing over his shoulder to be sure she'd follow.

"Don't you...I mean, shouldn't you be sure you can trust me before you let me inside your camp?"

"We've never seen you do anything except help people," Much said as the woman fell into step beside him. "And besides, we let Allen back in..."

"Ah, yes, I did notice that."

Much stopped walking and turned to look at her. "You... noticed?"

"I...I've been watching the gang from a distance since coming to Nottingham."

"Trying to decide if we're worth joining forces with?" Much asked, resuming his brisk walk and grinning over at Lucy.

"Something like that."

420

"We're definitely worth it."

As they neared the camp, Much pointed out the traps on the ground to avoid.

"I don't use the ground as often as the trees," Lucy replied.

Much grinned. "And Marian thought *we* might be dryads."

Marian.

Much's smile faded. He glanced at Lucy, then away into the trees. Marian was dead and here Much was being all glib about her. It hardly seemed appropriate.

Much silently began walking again. The woman followed quietly behind.

When they walked into the clearing, Will, Little John, and Allen jumped to their feet from where they'd been sitting near the fire pit. Dusty was nearby with the children gathered around her, and they all turned to look at Much and the newcomer. Robin, however, barely glanced up from the bow he was restringing, and Mark was nowhere to be seen.

"Much!" Will came over, eyeing the woman with him with evident curiosity. "Who's this?"

"I've found the mysterious archer!"

Robin did look up then, though he didn't approach.

"Are you really the mysterious archer?" Little John asked as Much led the woman and Will over toward the fire.

"Yes," the woman said.

Dusty stood, leaving the children as they continued to gawk at the newcomer, and came to sit beside the woman as the gang—apart from Robin who stayed by his hut and Mark who was nowhere to be seen—all settled down on the logs around the fire.

"Are you planning on joining us?" Dusty asked.

"Well...I hadn't planned on..."

"But you must!" Allen said.

Much nodded. "You have to. All the people fighting for England have to work together."

"It does seem we can do more good when we all work in tandem," Little John agreed.

The woman looked around the group and then she glanced to the side where Robin leaned against his hut, nonchalantly ignoring the conversation.

"I…I'll pray about it," she finally said.

Dusty grinned. "Now that is a wonderful idea!"

Robin rose slowly to his feet and Will turned to him. "Robin? What do you say to another gang member?"

Robin studied the woman for a minute and then shrugged. "What we really need is a way to get information."

"You need someone on the inside," the woman said.

Much glanced at Robin, seeing a darkness brewing on his face. Marian had been their way to get information from the Sheriff and Gisbourne prior to the trip to Austria. And now she was dead.

"Yes," Robin said. "We need someone with the Sheriff and… Gisbourne." The latter name came out in a strangled sort of manner, and Robin turned away from the group.

"I don't know that I want to be on the Sheriff's good side…but I'll see what I can do."

Robin nodded curtly and then proceeded to introduce the gang to her. Much did not miss the hesitation before Robin introduced Allen, and a glance toward Allen's face suggested he didn't miss it either.

"I'm Lucy. I've…well, to be honest, I've seen all of you in Nottingham before, and recently I've been stalking your ambushes, so I know who you are."

"We've noticed your presence in our raids," Will said. "You've definitely saved a few of us more than once. The more raids we have, the more soldiers the Sheriff and other lords send with their caravans, the more trouble we have successfully ambushing without falling to harm." Will absentmindedly rubbed his chest where his own wound had once been, and Dusty reached over to take his hand.

422

"We do appreciate what you've been doing," Little John said. "And it will be good to have eyes and ears in Nottingham again."

"I guess we'll have to build you your own hut as soon as we can," Will said.

"And you should meet the children," Dusty said. "Come over here…" Dusty led Lucy away from the group by the fire ring to introduce her to the children and Robin returned to his mindless stringing of his bow, paying no more attention to what was happening in the camp.

It had been short-lived, perhaps, but he had come to speak to her and shown a brief hint of interest so maybe that was a good sign. Much was going to take it as a good sign, at any rate.

Chapter 51

WILL TOOK LUCY to Nottingham the very next day to introduce her to Marcus and his wife to make a plan for Lucy to live with them for a while. When they returned to the camp Will gathered the gang together—with the exception of Mark who was brooding in his hut. Robin joined the group around the fire ring, but seemed mostly disinterested in the conversation.

"The next step will be spreading the word that you're here," Will said. "We want everyone, especially the Sheriff, to know."

"We have to find a way for him to take notice of you," Dusty said.

"I know," Lucy said. "I'll have to earn his trust so I can get into the castle and start feeding you information."

"I don't think it will be a hard task," Will said. "He'll be desirous to have you stay in the castle once he knows you are a nobleman's daughter. He is rather fond of his reputation. He won't risk snubbing a nobility."

"That's the hope anyway."

"It might be best if you didn't let on to the Sheriff that your father is dead," Robin said. Lucy had told them about her parents' deaths earlier that day. "Especially the part where he was killed by Prince John."

"I won't lie, Robin."

"If the Sheriff knows your father was loyal to King Richard and killed because of it then he won't trust you. He'll probably kill you."

Much watched Lucy's spine stiffen as Robin spoke, but was unsure what to say to ease her discomfort. It seemed lying was beyond the scope of what she was willing to do.

Will must have sensed her displeasure as well for he said, "We'll simply omit any information about your parents at all. You don't have to lie. As long as he doesn't ask about details, it doesn't matter."

So Lucy moved in with Marcus and Lillian. Will was right; Lucy hadn't lived with Marcus and Lillian long before the Sheriff heard of the nobleman's daughter in Nottingham and invited her to stay in the castle.

Lucy visited the camp the day after she moved into Nottingham castle.

"We did it. I'm in."

"We're going to need you to start being incredibly observant," Will said as Lucy, Will, and Much sat around the fire. Dusty was playing with the children not far away. "You are our eyes and ears now. If we don't want to miss any more executions, you will have to be the one to inform us."

"I will do my best."

"Will you be missed in Nottingham?" Much asked.

"Not yet. For now I am an honored guest, and so far the Sheriff has suggested I can do whatever I please. As long as I don't do anything to arouse suspicion, I should be free to roam as I will."

"Good. Then we won't have trouble exchanging information."

A week later, Will assigned Much and Allen to food distribution duty, so once everyone within the camp had eaten and Much had washed up his pots and plates they set out with large baskets of food from Much's kitchen.

They made their way first to Locksley at Much's request.

426

"How long has it been since you've visited Sarah?"

"Nearly eight months," Much said.

The people of Locksley village kept to their homes, much as they had the last time Much had visited, so they left parcels of food on people's doorsteps. When they arrived at the manor's backdoor, Sarah was already waiting with the kitchen door open.

"I saw you coming!" She moved forward, pulling Much into an awkward hug around his basket of food. "Usually our village gets the big fellow…"

"Little John," Allen said.

"That's the one," Sarah nodded. "Come inside, come inside."

"Has Gisbourne been frightening the village more?" Much asked as he and Allen followed Sarah into the kitchen. It was as empty as it had been the last time he visited.

"No. We haven't seen him since before…" Sarah looked at Much and suddenly there were tears welling in her eyes. "Not since before you came back from your trip abroad."

Much nodded, setting down his basket on the large table in the center of the kitchen and not meeting Sarah's gaze.

So Gisbourne had let them be after he murdered Marian. What did that mean exactly?

"I miss seeing her, you know," Sarah said, seating herself in a chair. "She was always so vibrant. And poor master Robin…how is my boy doing?"

"He's grieving," Much said.

"Oh, and her brother…the poor baby. How is he?"

"Not well. He's…he won't talk to anyone."

Sarah nodded. "Poor dears. They'll have to grieve in their own time, in their own way, I imagine. I just want to wrap them both up in a

427

hug, you know? Poor young Mark has lost everyone now, with both parents dead, and now Marian…"

"We're trying to keep an eye on him," Allen said.

Sarah turned toward him, seeming to take notice of him for the first time. "Ah, Allen. You came home from the Crusades with my boys, and you are one of the outlaws, too. The one who can't decide which side he is on, yes?"

Allen flushed and looked down at his boots.

"He's with us," Much said.

Sarah stood, moving toward Allen and lifting his chin until he made eye contact with her. "You better be. If I hear you've put my boys in danger again, you'll have me to answer to. Do you understand?"

"Yes, ma'am."

Sarah nodded, seeming satisfied with whatever she saw in Allen's eyes. "Right, you should both have a bite to eat before you head out again. And I can refill your baskets so you've plenty of food to hand out to those who can't afford to buy it. Where are you headed next? Wetherby?"

Much's heart constricted for a moment and then he took a deep breath and nodded. "Yes."

Sarah fed them, replenished their baskets with food, and then sent them on their way. Much expected visiting Wetherby to be traumatic in some fashion, but as they entered the little village his eye was drawn to the charred remains of Marian's home and he didn't feel any great sadness from it. The burned out home didn't reflect the woman they'd lost.

When Much and Allen returned from distributing money to various villages around Nottingham they found the rest of the gang scurrying about the camp making preparations.

"Hurry!" Will called as they walked into camp. "We must be on our way."

"Lucy informed us of a caravan coming through Sherwood," Dusty said, throwing her bow over her shoulder.

"And Gisbourne will be there," Robin said, shoving his freshly sharpened sword through his sheath and buckling his belt around his waist in a tense manner. "I have a chance to avenge Marian. Let's *move*."

Much hurried to his hut to collect his bow and quiver—his sword was already swinging at his hip as he rarely went anywhere without a weapon.

Robin was joining them on one of their ambushes. It was the first time he'd been active in the group since the return from Austria. And yet, he wasn't helping because he was their leader or because it was the right thing to do to keep fighting to save the innocent people of England. No, all he wanted was to kill Gisbourne.

Much could understand why Robin felt that way, but it still irked him that Robin's only motivation was revenge when the rest of the gang were actually trying to make a difference in people's lives. Robin had abandoned them for his grief and now the first time he joined them again it was out of hatred and Much felt an uncharacteristically strong annoyance toward his old master.

The raid was successful in the sense that the treasure was confiscated from the Sheriff, but Robin was unable to kill Sir Guy of Gisbourne and when they returned to camp he was in a sour mood.

Much lifted a chest off of one of the carts and carried it to the storage hut as Little John and Dusty unhitched the horses and prepared to lead them away from the camp to find deserving owners for them.

Allen assisted Much carrying the treasure into the storage hut while Robin tossed aside his sword by his hut, kicking the ground.

Much lifted a chest onto the top of a stack and grinned. "We're getting rich again.

"And we'll give it all away again," Allen replied, dropping his own chest into the hut with a thud.

"I like helping people," Much replied, walking back to the carts to grab another large chest.

"So do I, Much. I wasn't meaning to complain."

"Oh."

"Has Mark spoken to you today?" Allen asked as they brought their last load to the storage hut.

"Did he talk to you?" Much spun toward Allen, his heart leaping in his chest. Was Mark finally going to open up and start healing?

"No, no. Don't get your hopes up. He hasn't spoken a word to me or to anyone as far as I can tell. I simply thought if anyone was going to get him to talk again it would be you...or Robin, but he's too bitter himself these days to be much help."

"No, I haven't broken through to Mark either." Much shut the storage hut's door and leaned against it, surveying the camp around them. "I think the sight of Robin closes Mark up even more, because of his connection to Marian."

"I hadn't thought of that, but you may be right. Robin always says you are the most observant little mouse and I am beginning to agree with him. You see everything, don't you?"

"I don't think I do, Allen."

"Regardless of what any of us do or do not see...we have to break Mark from this silence. It can't be healthy."

A few days later, Much was sitting on his bed watching little Peter sleeping. The toddler seemed so serene in his rest. It was a feeling Much envied. It was late, and Much ought to be sleeping himself but his mind was too full.

Mark was bitter and speaking to no one, Robin was consumed with his vengeance and cared nought for anything else. Much didn't know what to do about either situation.

A knock on his door interrupted what would have been a solid brooding session. Much reluctantly got up to open the door.

The camp was dark. They didn't try to keep a fire burning now that it was no longer winter. The starlight cast a dim glow from above, however, and was partially blocked out by the unmistakable shadow of Robin.

"Sorry to wake you." Robin pushed past Much and sat down in the cramped space between the wall and the sleeping form of little Peter, his knees pulled up to his chest.

Much sat down on his bed, peering through the darkness toward his oldest friend. "What's wrong?"

"Everything. The whole world is wrong since Mar—since we came back."

"I know."

"Lucy came to the camp today, while you were out…doing whatever it was Will sent you to do."

"I was in Nottingham Square most of the day. Did Lucy have information for us?"

"No. She merely came for a visit, to be free of the Sheriff's company. But no one was here."

"Except you and the children."

"Yes."

431

"Did she say something to upset you?" Much asked, trying to decipher what Lucy's visit must have been like in order to bring Robin knocking on his door so late at night.

"Yes."

"Tell me."

"She told me I can't kill Gisbourne; that I have to forgive him." Robin was clearly tying to keep his voice down so as not to wake little Peter, but the anger lacing every word was obvious despite his hushed tones. "That I'm as bad as he is, a murderer and all that!"

"She called you a murderer?"

"Well...no. She didn't say that. She said that if I killed Gisbourne I'd be no better than he is. But it's different!"

Much didn't know what to say. He leaned back against the wall next to his bed, lifting his legs up off the floor and criss-crossing them on the bed. Lucy was right; forgiveness was the better course of action. Anger and bitterness and revenge would consume Robin and turn him into something that he was not. Marian would not have wanted to see him rot in such a way. Although Marian probably would have been on board with killing Gisbourne.

"Was there anything else she said?"

"You agree with her."

"I didn't say that."

"You don't have to!"

Much sighed, wishing he could see Robin better in the darkness. "You haven't been yourself, and if it is your hatred of Gisbourne that has made you this way then...yes, I do agree that you shouldn't pursue it."

Robin was silent for a moment before he spoke again. "When she arrived today…I was crying. It felt…violating for her to find me in my grief like that."

"We're all grieving. We've all been crying. Crying is a natural response—"

"It wasn't that I was crying, Much. It was…I mean…she *saw* me like that. So…vulnerable."

"And that bothers you?"

"Yes!"

"I've seen you at your worst before…"

"That's different. You're my brother, my closest and oldest friend. It's different. She's already so high and mighty and above us all…and…"

"And?"

Much stared through the darkness toward the shadow of his friend. He wasn't sure what to make of Robin's outburst. Much had only known Lucy a short time, but he'd never seen her acting arrogantly.

"Don't look at me like that, Much."

"You can't see how I'm looking at you."

"I just don't want her to see me crying."

"There's more than that."

Robin sighed, the sound reaching across the darkness and breaking Much's heart. "How do you always know?"

"What is it?"

"I wanted to quit. I still want to."

"I know."

"I gave up…I abandoned all of you. I know Will has done a fine job taking over and keeping people as safe as any of us can, but I shouldn't have left you alone."

"You never left; you were right here."

"I wasn't though. You know I wasn't. I was wallowing in my own pain and left you and the others to fend for yourselves. I'm your leader. I should be leading, not cowering in camp crying. I haven't helped in our fight against the Sheriff and Prince John…I've just been…"

"Grieving. You've been grieving."

"So have you. That didn't stop you from taking care of everyone, as usual."

"No one blames you—"

"I blame myself. Lucy does, too. She told me today that I can't keep ignoring the fight against evil and cruelty, and I was so frustrated with her for saying it. I know it's true, but I didn't want to hear it."

"And that's what's been bothering you."

"Yes."

"It's okay. We all understand you are in pain. You and Mark knew Marian best, loved her the most. The fact that you took her death the hardest is not a surprise. We understand."

"I know…but it's going to change. I will be Robin Hood again, leader of this gang and savior of England."

Much bit his cheek. As much as he wanted Robin to be his old self again, he also didn't feel Robin was actually ready for it. He needed to take the time to heal more.

As the days passed, Much was hopeful that Robin was, indeed, healing.

One day Lucy came to the camp on an afternoon when only Much and Dusty were present.

"Where's Robin?"

"Everyone is busy," Dusty replied. "Little John and Will are on a trip to the west, distributing our wealth beyond the sphere of Nottingham. Robin heard there was a particularly blood-thirsty sheriff a few shires over and went to investigate, and see if there was anything to be done about it. Mark tagged along, I believe."

"What's wrong?" Much asked.

"The Sheriff, as always," Lucy replied. She relayed the Sheriff's plot to hang a man, and then asked Dusty to pray for Gisbourne.

"Pray for Gisbourne?"

"God loves him too, Dusty."

Dusty sighed. "I suppose He does."

"He's horrible," young William piped up. "And so angry all the time."

Lucy didn't respond to that and soon changed the subject to archery. William and Beth eagerly took her up on her suggestion of a lesson. Lucy moved to one side of the open meadow to help them shoot, while Dusty stayed beside Much, with the smaller children still gathered around them.

"Do you think you can?"

Dusty turned toward Much. "Pray for Gisbourne? She's right; God does love him, too. So yes, I believe I will."

"Have you forgiven him?"

"No."

"Neither have I."

"I am trying."

"So am I."

"Well it seems we are in the same predicament then. Perhaps we should take the time to pray together about all the aspects of this disastrous situation."

435

Chapter 52

SPRING SLOWLY GAVE way to summer. Robin came out of his shell. The darkness and despair behind his eyes didn't entirely leave, but he was more active in the gang, leading alongside Will once more. Mark remained reclusive, participating in raids and clearly relishing the chance to take out his anger through the act of killing the Sheriff's men, but he still hardly spoke to anyone at all.

One day, Lucy rode into camp with urgent news that the Sheriff was preparing to hang someone in Nottingham.

"Get back to Nottingham before you are missed," Robin said, catching the reins of her horse—a mighty black stallion that looked vaguely familiar to Much. "We'll be there."

As soon as Lucy was gone, Robin began issuing orders for everyone to gather their weapons. "We'll sneak into Nottingham in pairs, and meet in Nottingham Square, by the bakery. The execution will be there, and I can get a feel for where we'll need to station ourselves in order to successfully stop it without being caught."

Much grabbed his sword and his bow, slinging his quiver over his shoulder. Much knew in that moment, listening to Robin issue his orders as the gang jumped to follow them that Robin was on the mend. He was going to be okay.

They hurried through the forest and then across the hills toward Nottingham. Robin split them into pairs before they came in sight of the city, sending Dusty and Will in first.

"Little John, Mark, you can go next. Much, you're on your own until you get to Nottingham Square. Allen and I will bring up the rear."

When it was his turn, Much walked toward the city carefully, keeping his pace steady so he wouldn't attract attention simply by looking as though he were suspicious. He held his head high, falling in line behind a group of villagers heading into Nottingham. News of the execution had spread and people were coming to watch—either from morbid curiosity, or to see if Robin Hood and his gang would actually stop this one.

Much slipped past the guards unnoticed, and hurried along the streets until he came to Nottingham Square, at which point he headed straight for his favorite bakery. He could see the gallows that had been constructed over the heads of the crowd that pressed around it. Much skirted around them and slipped into the bakery.

"That's almost everyone," Little John commented. He, Mark, Dusty, and Will were lined up along the front wall peering out the window.

"No sign of Robin yet," Will said.

Much joined them, waiting for the last of the gang to arrive. When Robin and Allen slipped into the bakery, Robin immediately started issuing orders again.

"Will, Much, Allen, and I will take up positions in buildings on every side of the Square and use our archery to cut down soldiers and keep the prisoner alive when he or she is brought out. Little John, you're on snatch and run duty. Marcus is already ready with horses for the escape, Allen and I stopped there on our way here. We all know this Square and have done this sort of thing a hundred times. You can find the best position; you don't need me to hold your hand."

Robin put a hand on Dusty's shoulder. "Keep an eye on the crowd. If the soldiers start harming innocents, I expect you to find and heal them. Mark, you can either work with Little John or be an archer. Any preference?"

Mark lifted his bow but said nothing.

Robin nodded. "Very well. You'll be with me. Let's go."

Robin sent Much to the southern side of the Square, and he had to thread his way through the ever growing mass of people gathered around the gallows to get to the other side.

He slipped into the shop of a tailor he knew and hurried up the stairs to a window that overlooked the Square. He'd used this spot before during other rescues, so the view was familiar and he was fairly confident he could protect whoever the innocent victim turned out to be.

Much leaned against the wall, away from the window, keeping the gallows in view but himself as out of sight as he could, and lifted his bow with an arrow at the ready.

Much held his breath, waiting.

Soon the crowd grew more restless as a group of soldiers dragged a woman toward the gallows. Much could see several people crying and heard others yelling insults at the soldiers, but still they all parted and let them pass. The soldiers dragged the woman up the step leading to the gallows.

Suddenly one fell with an arrow in his chest. Robin's signal.

Much let his own arrow fly and quickly grabbed another.

The soldiers in the Square began searching for the source of the arrows as Robin, Will, Allen, and Mark dropped the soldiers one by one. Much saw Little John barreling through the crowd to snatch up the woman.

The crowd cheered and then formed a human wall behind him so that the soldiers chasing him couldn't immediately follow him. It was good that Robin had put Dusty on healing duty, for the soldiers had no qualms cutting down the unarmed citizens of Nottingham.

Little John disappeared down a side street. With the woman out of the Square, Much's job was done. He hurried down the steps of the shop and slipped out the back door onto a street not connected to the Square itself, bolting away and toward Marcus' home where horses would be waiting to carry the gang to safety.

439

At Marcus' home, Much ran to the back where the horses were all saddled and waiting. He pulled himself into one just as Will ran up. Much didn't wait to speak to him. They had to get out of Nottingham and to the forest where they could send the woman on her way with food and money before they returned to the camp.

Much was concerned, as always, for the safety of his friends but soon enough everyone but Dusty was gathered at the edge of the woods. They'd all made it out—Dusty had likely stayed in Nottingham to continue her healing work.

Robin made sure the woman had provisions and a purse full of coin, giving her directions to the nearest safe haven—a tavern they'd often used to send refugees on their way toward Scotland. The tavern keeper would send her to the next spot, and so on until she was far enough from the Sheriff of Nottingham to be safe.

Much watched Robin with satisfaction. He was back.

In the weeks that followed, the Sheriff tried many times to hang various persons and Lucy always informed Robin. Robin then led his valiant followers to save the innocents who had run foul of the Sheriff —which wasn't hard to do given his temper.

Round and round they went, the Sheriff plotting, Lucy informing Robin, Robin and the gang saving the innocent. It was just like the early days of Sherwood, except the woman with all the information had changed.

Not many days later, Lucy came riding into camp in the evening and dismounted before her horse had even come to a stop. Much had finally realized why he found the horse she rode so familiar—the black stallion was Sir Guy of Gisbourne's horse.

"Lucy!" Dusty moved to greet her. "Any news from Nottingham?"

"Who is the Sheriff hanging now?" Allen asked from where he lounged against one of the log benches by the fire pit.

440

"The Sheriff isn't hanging anyone." She spoke softly, glancing toward where Robin sat by his hut with a look Much recognized. Whatever she had to say, she was worried it would upset Robin.

"Is there anything of interest happening in Nottingham?" Will asked from his place on one of the benches by the fire.

"Well…" Again, Lucy shot a glance toward Robin, this time glancing toward Mark who sat by the fire next to Much. "Sir Guy confronted me today, about helping the outlaws. He suspects I am an informant."

"Oh no!" Dusty's face mirrored the concern in her voice as she and Lucy joined the group at the fire ring.

"What happened?" Will asked, leaning forward with interest.

"Nothing happened. I told him he was right."

"You did what?!" Robin snapped, jumping up to move closer to the conversation.

"It's alright," Lucy said, throwing up her hands in a placating manner. "He didn't tell the Sheriff. He didn't do anything at all."

"You've blown your cover! Now who is going to be our informant?"

"I am," Lucy said. "Nothing has changed. Guy won't betray me."

"Guy?" Robin's eyebrows shot to his hairline and Much resisted the urge to cower from the anger radiating from his old friend. "Since when are you so familiar?"

Lucy crossed her arms. "For your information, Sir Guy of Gisbourne and I have been sort of friends for nearly two months."

Robin rolled his eyes. "Oh, splendid. Now our informant hasn't only blown her cover she's also fraternizing with the enemy."

"I live with them, Robin! How can I not?"

"She has a point," Will said.

"I need to get back to Nottingham," Lucy said, standing up. "I only came to let you know what had happened. I am quite thrilled that Guy…Sir Guy…Gisbourne, that is, didn't turn me in."

"Go on then," Robin said. "Run back to Nottingham."

Much frowned, biting his cheek. He knew why Robin's sarcastic tone was present—anything to do with Gisbourne set him on edge—but Much didn't appreciate how rude he was to Lucy.

As Lucy mounted Gisbourne's horse, however, Robin took hold of his halter. "Lucy…be careful."

"Don't worry. I'm no safer at camp than I am in Nottingham."

Much hoped she was right, and that Gisbourne would, indeed, keep her secret. It seemed doubtful however.

"Will, you are keeping an eye on Nottingham tonight," Robin said as Lucy rode out of camp. "We'll take turns watching out for any news of Lucy being arrested until we're entirely sure this has blown over. I don't trust Gisbourne."

In the days that followed, various members of the gang spent the night in Nottingham keeping an eye on the castle and any news of Lucy. She wandered the streets of Nottingham passing out food from the castle and visiting the sick much as she had always done, and rode to the camp on occasion as well. It seemed Gisbourne had kept her secret after all.

A week later, Lucy visited late one evening and joined the circle at the fire ring with an announcement. "I'm going to test Guy, I think," she said as she seated herself between Robin and Much.

"Don't," Will said. "Please, don't do anything foolish. He's unpredictable and dangerous."

"I'm not afraid of Guy. I trust him."

Robin snorted. "You are foolish if you trust Gisbourne."

Lucy shrugged her shoulders. "Then I'm foolish. Regardless, I'm going to ask him to let the children go."

"What?" Much glanced from Lucy to the children playing across the meadow.

"I'm going to ask him to speak to the Sheriff to see if we can get the children pardoned so they can go home to their families."

"That will never work," Robin said.

"Besides, what would camp life be like without them?" Will said. "I'd miss them."

"They belong with their parents, Will," Lucy said. "They need to go home."

"Gisbourne won't help you," Robin said, crossing his arms.

"He might," Allen piped up from across the fire. "I think he is capable of great kindness."

"Says the man who betrayed my trust," Robin said. "I should have expected you to defend my enemy."

Allen's face flushed and he lowered his head.

"Great kindness from the man who murdered my wife? What nonsense."

Lucy sighed. "I need to go. I'm causing more rifts in this camp than anything else I think."

"It's hardly your fault, Lucy," Will said quietly.

A few days later, Lucy came to the camp with the news that the Sheriff was pardoning the children. She delivered the news and then with Dusty's help gathered up the children and their belongings to take them back to their families.

"How in the world did you convince the Sheriff to leave them be?" Will asked.

"I didn't," Lucy said. "Sir Guy did."

Much flinched as Robin threw a stick into the fire, glaring at Lucy.

"There is good in him," Allen said. "I saw it brought out by Marian."

443

"And that good she brought out is, I suppose, the reason he killed her!" Robin stood and stomped away from the circle around the fire, leaving a pained silence behind him.

There were a few tearful farewells once the children were ready to leave, particularly when the children hugged Will, and then they were gone. Lucy enlisted the help of Will and Dusty to walk the children to their home in Nottingham.

"Peace and quiet at last," Allen said, though from the look on his face Much knew he'd probably miss them as much as anyone else would. The children had been living in the camp for a year; it would be strange to have the camp to themselves once more.

Will suggested the gang take turns keeping guard near the homes of the children's families for a few weeks to be certain the Sheriff would leave them alone, and so the gang made a schedule to keep watch over them. But in the days and weeks that followed, the Sheriff never so much as looked at their house.

Chapter 53

MUCH WIPED THE sweat from his brow as he pulled another loaf of bread from his little oven on a particularly sunny summer day. Much was alone in the camp. There were no children to mind any longer, but he wanted to get ahead on baking so there would be plenty of food to continue to pass out to the various families in need.

Much set the loaf aside and grabbed one that had been rising nearby to put it into the small oven next. Hearing hoofbeats entering the camp, he hurriedly finished his work and stepped out of his sweltering hut to see Lucy dismounting.

"What brings you to the camp today?" Much asked, walking toward her.

"I need your help…but what have you been doing in this heat to look so rough?"

"Baking bread."

"In this heat? Much."

"Don't scold, I'm already feeling the consequences of it. Now, I am willing to help you, my lady. What do you need?"

"Just Lucy, if you don't mind. None of this 'my lady' nonsense."

Her comment reminded him of Marian saying something similar to him once, and his heart squeezed. "What did you need, Lucy?"

"I spoke to Allen recently." Lucy seated herself on one of the log benches and Much joined her. "He's feeling depressed. He knows none of you fully trust him, and it hurts him."

"I'm sure it does," Much said. "But he did make his choices."

"I know what he did was terrible, but he is trying to do right now. I think if some of us would treat him normally the others would follow."

"Robin will never trust him."

"Perhaps not, but we can at least try."

Much nodded. "Dusty has forgiven him, if that's any consolation."

"And yet at times she is still as suspicious of him as Little John. You all are. I wasn't a part of the gang when Allen betrayed you, so me treating him with respect and friendship doesn't have an impact. But if you and some of the others would forgive him and trust him as you did before…"

"I doubt me trusting him will change anyone's mind."

"But you will try, won't you?"

"I have forgiven him," Much said. "Dusty and I talked of it often, before…Austria. I think Will might come around, given his relationship with Dusty, but you will be hard-pressed to erase Little John's suspicions and Robin's inability to trust Allen."

"We can still try. And I don't think you give Robin enough credit, or yourself for that matter."

"What do you mean?"

"Robin is a good man. His grief has led to a great deal of bitterness right now, but underneath it all he's still a good man; he's compassionate and caring and open. He is more than capable of seeing Allen's remorse and responding to it with kindness. And you, well… you underestimate how great your influence over Robin is, I think. He trusts you implicitly. The longer he sees you treating Allen with grace and respect, the more it will have an impact on him."

"Perhaps." Much didn't think Robin was half as interested in what Much did as Lucy seemed to think, but it was a nice thought. "The more pressing forgiveness Dusty and I have been ignoring of late is Gisbourne himself…you are building a friendship with him, which is horrifying. Yet regardless of whether there is good in him or not, it is our duty to follow our Lord's example and extend forgiveness to those who don't deserve it."

"No one deserves it. That's the very nature of being forgiven, Much."

"He killed Marian."

"I know. It's…*awful*. I don't know how I'm able to see past that, except by the grace of God. I know He loves him, just as He loves us, so I lean into that."

"I don't know that I could, or that Dusty can."

"I can't on my own. Only through relying on God's own strength and compassion…"

"Every time I see him, I just think 'he killed Marian' and I can't move past that."

"I know. I don't think forgiving Guy in this lifetime will be feasible for most people, if any."

"But you've done it."

"I've always found grace to be my strongest virtue, if I have any."

"I'm trying."

"I know. With both Guy and Allen. I've seen your patience and grace, Much. I respect you for both, and that is why I wanted to ask you to help me change the minds of the gang…at least in regards to Allen. I doubt they'll ever come around to Guy…"

Much couldn't help but agree with her. What Guy had done was the most unforgivable, and the prospect of Robin ever getting over it was nonexistent. Still, she had a point about Allen; he did regret what had happened and he was trying to do better. And Robin had let him come home to camp, so perhaps Lucy was right and he would eventually stop harassing him or being suspicious of him.

A week or so later, the gang foiled an execution of the Sheriff's after a tip from Lucy and that night, Dusty pulled Much aside from the group to speak to him.

"Did Lucy tell you how she came by her information today?"

"No?"

"She told Allen and I…and it's remarkable. A miracle, you might say."

"A miracle? What happened?"

"Sir Guy told her about the hanging."

"He…told her?"

"Yes! Lucy said he told her what the Sheriff was planning in order for her to stop it. He had no other reason to inform her."

"Unless it was a trap?"

"But he didn't ambush our rescue today, so how could it have been? He's intentionally helping us, Much."

"If he is, that truly is remarkable. Why didn't she tell everyone?"

"She knows it would upset Robin and Mark."

"What of Will and Little John?"

"Will is Robin's right hand; Lucy wasn't sure how he'd react either. But I've told him since then. He's not nearly as bitter as Robin and Mark."

"But what about—"

448

"If you must know, the reason she told Allen and I is because Allen is Sir Guy's only ally within the gang, and she is under the impression I am the only person apart from her who cares about Sir Guy at all."

"Oh."

"You were intimately connected to Marian. She was worried that telling you Marian's murderer was now helping us would only upset you."

"But you told me."

"I have more confidence in you it seems, little mouse. More than that, I know you are pursuing the grace and forgiveness Christ would bestow, despite how difficult it is."

"Lucy and I talked about that recently…" Much wondered if something he'd said in that conversation had made Lucy hesitant to share this news about Gisbourne. It was true that he was finding it difficult to extend grace to Gisbourne; he was a murderer! But if he was willing to help them against the Sheriff, Much wouldn't complain about it.

The next time Lucy visited the camp it was still early in the day. She came riding in on Gisbourne's black stallion with a smile on her face. Much and Dusty were alone in the camp, having finished their rounds in Nottingham visiting the sick and passing out food.

Lucy hurried to the log benches around the fire ring where Much and Dusty were sitting.

"I've been hoping to catch the two of you at some point!"

"Do you need something?" Dusty asked.

"I merely wanted you both to know that Mark spoke to me the other day."

"He spoke?" Much leaned forward eagerly.

449

"What did he say?" Dusty asked.

"He was blaming himself for Marian's death. He broke down and cried, actually." Lucy's usually bright eyes were suddenly shadowed, dark clouds swirling within them.

"Crying is good," Dusty said. "He needs to let it out. He's bottled up his grief all this time, and it can't be healthy for him."

"But he shouldn't blame himself," Much said. "We were all there…none of us could have stopped Gisbourne."

Lucy winced as Much spoke, but it was slight and he wondered if he'd imagined it.

"No," Dusty said. "He should not be blaming himself. We will continue to pray for him and his healing."

"I think he's made the first step," Lucy said. "He's talking at long last. He might come around after all."

Sometime later, Lucy came to camp in a harried state, her eyes wild with worry.

"The Sheriff knows!" she called out as she was dismounting, before she hurried over to where the gang was lounging around the fire.

"The Sheriff knows what?" Will asked.

"That I informed you of the hanging. He is convinced Sir Guy would never betray him, so he's accusing me."

"Oh no," Dusty said, shooting a glance toward Much. Maybe it had been a trap after all.

"You've blown your cover *again*?" Robin asked.

Lucy shook her head. "Not exactly. It was this morning that the Sheriff accused me, and as of yet he has done nothing about it."

"You can't go back to Nottingham," Allen said. "He'll likely have you executed."

"Sir Guy will see to it that I am rescued if the Sheriff tries anything, and I'll come to live in the camp with the rest of you. That is if, indeed, the Sheriff decides to harm me at all. I thought he would throw me into prison immediately, but he hasn't."

"I would stay here, if I were you," Little John said.

"I have considered it, but I cannot. I must return to Nottingham. I am greatly needed there. You won't have an informant without me, and…"

"And?" Robin raised an eyebrow.

"And I am simply needed, that's all."

In the days that followed the gang spent more time in Nottingham, worriedly waiting for any news of the Sheriff arresting Lucy, but none came. Lucy continued to visit the camp when she could, and moved around the city helping the poor and needy the same as always.

One night when she came to camp Allen remarked on the Sheriff's lack of action while the group—save for Robin who was still in Nottingham and Mark who was holed up in his hut—were gathered around the fire. "It's good that he isn't going to harm you, but it is also strange."

"I wonder why he let you off so easily?" Will mused. "When he knew Marian was helping us he put her under house arrest."

"Lucy seems to find herself well-loved in whatever circle she moves in," Dusty commented. "Perhaps she won over the Sheriff, too."

"You think the Sheriff is too fond of me to harm me?" Lucy asked, laughing. "That is ridiculous. He's an insane man; I believe he simply forgot."

451

"That is impossible," Will said. "His entire mind is wrapped around destroying us, destroying Robin Hood. He would not forget if he knew you were helping us."

"But he must have," Lucy said. "There is no other explanation for leaving me be."

"Unless he is fond of you," Dusty said. "And couldn't bring himself to harm you."

Lucy rolled her eyes. "I don't believe that."

Some time later, Allen and Will returned from Nottingham where they'd been keeping an eye on the Sheriff's men as Much was cooking up supper for everyone.

"There's a caravan going through Sherwood tomorrow," Will said without preamble.

"And Lucy wasn't the one to give us that information," Allen added.

Robin frowned, accepting a plate of Much's meat pie and tilting his head toward Allen. "Where did you get the information?"

"From Sir Guy," Allen said. "I met him in Nottingham Square."

"Why?" Dusty asked. "Why didn't he simply tell Lucy and have her inform us as he did before?"

"Perhaps he is simply trying to get close to the gang," Little John said. "Get our guards down so he can kill us, too."

"Lucy knew of the caravan," Will said. "She is the one who came to us and sent Allen to Sir Guy."

"Why?" Robin's frown deepened.

"Because she made a promise to the Sheriff that she wouldn't tell anyone about it," Allen said.

"She did what?" Much asked. How could she promise such a thing? And why was the Sheriff telling her secrets anyway?

452

"She promised the Sheriff she wouldn't tell us," Will said. "So she had us meet with Sir Guy to hear it from him instead."

"That is ridiculous!" Robin said.

"I agree," Will said. "But it's done now, so it hardly matters where we came by the information. We know there's a caravan of unfairly collected taxes coming through Sherwood, so let's plan where we'll ambush it."

Robin and Will discussed the best places along the road to set up an ambush until Lucy came riding into camp. Much chewed on his lower lip, concerned how Robin would react. Lucy took her place beside Dusty and Robin sullenly threw a stick into the fire.

"We didn't have to go to him. You could have told us."

Lucy stiffened and Much bit his cheek, waiting for the outburst of anger that was sure to come.

"Not after I promised I wouldn't."

"You're playing games with us, Lucy."

"I am not. But seriously, Robin, the Sheriff might decide to get rid of me at any moment—he's certainly suspicious—and then you never would get information from inside the castle."

"I still say you could have delivered it. We don't need Gisbourne! He's entirely untrustworthy. He. Murdered. My. Wife."

"And he's as tormented by it as you are! More, probably, considering…"

Robin stood and Much flinched. Robin didn't do anything to Lucy however, he simply stormed off.

"You didn't expect that to go any differently I hope," Mark said, his voice full of venom as he too glared at Lucy. "You can't trust Gisbourne."

"I know you all think that, and I perfectly understand why—"

"Then why are you so insistent?"

"Sir Guy has helped us in the past," Dusty said. "He's made mistakes; massive, unforgivable mistakes one might argue. Yet somehow, he still helps us."

"Even so," Little John piped up, "in this scenario, Lucy could have simply told us herself, using Gisbourne was superfluous. And more than that, if this is a test, a trap, she should have been much more careful and perhaps not told us at all."

"Well next time I'll just keep my information to myself," Lucy huffed.

"If you are going to do something as stupid as tell us you can't talk to us about whatever you find out, you might as well," Mark snapped.

"Well unlike some people, I keep my promises."

Robin came fuming back toward the circle as Lucy lashed out at Mark, and Much kept his eyes on him.

"You're asking me to break my word like it's no big deal. But it is a big deal to me."

Robin jumped back into the argument immediately. "A promise that was forced out of you—"

"It wasn't forced."

"What?"

"It wasn't forced. I didn't have to promise. I only did because I knew you could still get the information without me telling you."

"Lucy—"

"You still got the information you needed, so why does it matter?"

Robin threw up his hands in disgust and stomped away again, and Mark withdrew to his hut as a silence settled over the gang.

"That…went about as expected," Will sighed.

"Guy did give me the news without hesitation," Allen said. "Lucy's right. He is helping us."

"I almost believe it myself," Dusty agreed. "He hasn't given any indication he'd turn on Lucy."

"*Yet*," Little John growled. "There is, however, the glaring truth that he murdered Marian."

The gang continued to argue the merits of Sir Guy and the potential danger for Lucy if the Sheriff was truly using this particular caravan as a trap to ensnare her. Lucy left the camp in a sour mood. Much left the circle as they argued the point back and forth, and went in search of Robin.

He found him not far outside the perimeter of camp, leaning against a tree. It was darker under the canopy of trees and away from the fire, but the moonlight trickled through the branches enough for Much to make out his form.

"Are you okay?"

"No."

Much leaned against the tree beside Robin, not saying anything. He could hear the voices of the rest of the gang by the fire, though from this distance couldn't make out what was being said.

"Why does she have to use him?"

Much turned toward Robin, though he couldn't see his face clearly in the darkness. "We did get the information we needed."

"That's hardly the point."

"Is it that working with him brings Marian's death to the forefront of your mind again?"

"How could it not? He killed her! And she acts like it's no big deal."

"I don't think she believes that it doesn't matter."

"She's friends with him! *Him*. Marian used his affection, but she was smart enough to know not to trust him, not to form any real attachment to him. But Lucy? No, she's insistent on seeing good in him where there clearly isn't any! She's going to get herself killed."

Much wondered if mingled within his grief over Marian and hatred for Gisbourne there was also now a concern for the welfare of this new friend they'd made.

"Allen seems to think—"

"I don't care what Allen thinks about anything."

Much bit his cheek. He'd been on the verge of saying Allen saw good in Gisbourne, too, and maybe there was some. Obscured by his worst impulses perhaps, but buried there somewhere. He'd rescued the children who had then lived in the camp—saved them from being hanged. He'd done it for Marian, but perhaps there was something more under his cruel exterior than just a desire to get on Marian's good side. Surely if he'd been purely evil even his proclaimed love for Marian wouldn't have led him to do such an act of mercy.

Apart from Gisbourne's merits, or lack of them, there was also the simple fact that grace and forgiveness were the prescribed order of the day. For Lucy, Dusty, Much, and anyone else who wanted to follow Christ and His example, grace had to be the answer. Forgiveness wasn't about what one deserved, it was a free gift. Gisbourne had done something truly horrendous when he'd murdered Marian, something beyond ordinary forgiveness. But the thing about Christ was that He had *extraordinary* grace.

"I miss her," Robin whispered.

"I know. I'm sorry."

Chapter 54

MUCH CAREFULLY CUT the block of cheese in his hand into thick slices, laying them atop the chunks of bread he'd already cut from a fresh loaf he had baked. He had been the first to return to the camp that day after spending time passing out food in Nottingham, Wetherby, Locksley, and a few other villages, and now he was preparing supper for the rest of the gang to eat when they arrived from their own activities.

Dusty was the first to arrive, coming to sit beside Much and prop her feet up on the stones that formed a boundary circle around the fire pit. There was no fire tonight for it was a warm evening—another reason why Much had chosen to prepare a simple meal tonight, one that didn't require cooking over the heat of a fire.

"How was your day?"

"Nothing of interest to report," Much replied "Yours?"

"It was a calm day."

At that moment Lucy came hurrying into camp, her face as pale as the full-moon that was sure to grace the sky that night.

"Lucy?" Dusty sat up straight. "Are you okay?"

Lucy seated herself across from Much and Dusty, her hands shaking slightly. "The Sheriff almost killed me."

"What happened?" Dusty asked.

"He was upset that you knew about the caravan and he was sure I must have told you so he tried to kill me."

"But he didn't," Much said. "I mean…you're alive."

"Yes. Guy saved me. I don't know how he got there so quickly, but he was there and he and the Sheriff had a moment of altercation and then…"

"Guy and the Sheriff fought?"

Lucy shook her head. "Not exactly. After Guy blocked the Sheriff's initial blow that was meant for me, they glared at each other and argued for a bit…and then the Sheriff left me alone."

"You aren't safe going back," Dusty said. "The Sheriff is sure to punish you this time."

"I don't think so. Guy convinced him in the moment that I wasn't the one who told you, which is the truth. I wasn't."

"You are walking a rather delicate line with the Sheriff."

"It is the path I must take if I want to be an informant for all of you—and therefore help stop some of the cruelty in Nottingham, and help the people—while also maintaining my integrity as an honest woman."

"Do be careful, Lucy," Dusty said.

Much wasn't sure what to think of Lucy. He was worried about her safety given how close the Sheriff had come now to harming her. Could she truly trust Gisbourne to keep her safe from the Sheriff? Gisbourne, the man who'd murdered Marian? It seemed unlikely.

And yet she had such implicit faith in him. Was it naivety? She was simply seeing good where there was none, as Robin thought, because it was just how she viewed the world. Or perhaps she knew Gisbourne better than they did and knew the truth, one they couldn't see from their prejudiced opinion of him.

On top of everything else, there was her strange adherence to being honest while also living the life of an informant. It seemed entirely contradictory, but perhaps that was the very reason why she was such a stickler for keeping her promises—to assuage her own conscience.

One evening as the gang was gathered around the fire Lucy came walking into camp with a withered old man.

Robin was on his feet instantly. "Lucy, who is this?"

"Friar Tuck, a very dear friend of mine. He was a father to me when I was growing up in London."

Robin sat back down as Lucy and Friar Tuck joined the group.

"What brought you to Nottinghamshire?" Will asked.

"Lucy did," Friar Tuck replied. "I have been anxious to see her since she left home so many years ago."

"I told him he could live in the camp, if that's okay, Robin," Lucy said. "I think he'd be safer here."

Robin studied her for a moment. "You don't trust Gisbourne then?"

"I—"

"That's fine. Friar Tuck, you are more than welcome here."

Over the next several days Will enlisted help from Little John and Allen in order to gather material to build a hut for Friar Tuck to use while he lived in the camp with the rest of the gang. The little man sat peacefully near the fire watching the manual labor with interest.

One day, as Much was preparing supper for everyone, Friar Tuck offered to help him so Much set him to work peeling potatoes while Much cut up carrots to put in the stew he was making.

"It's an interesting little village you all have been creating here," Friar Tuck commented.

"It has been strange to live here," Much said. "But no stranger than living in prison for a year, or wandering the Holy Land before that. Most of my adult life has been spent living in strange places."

"Do you miss the comfort of a real home?"

"This place is my home," Much said. "The people I want to be around are here, with the exception of the woman who raised me."

"And yet…"

Much's hands stilled at Friar Tuck's gentle prodding, the knife pressed partially through the carrot in his hand. "And yet."

Friar Tuck waited, continuing to peel the potato in his hand.

Much hesitated for a moment and then sighed. "I do miss living at Locksley, and I miss the stability of living life as anything other than an outlaw."

"Lucy tells me you are the peaceful one here," Friar Tuck said, still peeling his potatoes. "I do not mean to interrogate. I am merely trying to form my own judgments on the people I will be living with."

"Lucy says I'm peaceful?"

"You are peaceful, Mark is tortured, Dusty is sure in her faith and convictions. Are any of her comments false, do you think?"

"Not those ones, no. Mark is definitely the most broken over Marian's death. Not that we aren't all grieving, and of course Robin suffers but…we're healing—Robin's healing—and Mark isn't."

"And apart from Dusty and Lucy, how many here would you say share our faith?"

Much started chopping his carrots again, listening to the sounds of them plop, plop, plopping into the pot. "Just me, I think."

Friar Tuck tilted his head to one side as he continued peeling the potato in his hand. "You are not as outspoken as Dusty and Lucy, I take it."

Much shook his head.

"Are you afraid of admitting the faith you hold?"

"Not exactly. It's…no one would care what I have to say about it, sir."

"I doubt that."

Friar Tuck handed Much his peeled potatoes and Much began to chop them into the pot with the carrots, silently contemplating Friar Tuck's line of questioning.

Was he afraid to tell Robin about his faith and the still small voice who brought him comfort? Given how Robin often reacted to Dusty—with casual and calm disinterest—it was possible he was harboring some fear there. Robin, above all else, was the one person Much had always desired respect from.

But why should his faith in a loving God lose Robin's respect? And more than that, should Robin's opinion hold so much sway over him at all?

These were questions Much didn't particularly enjoy contemplating.

As the weeks passed, Friar Tuck's hut was finished, and the time of the Nottingham Fair drew close once more.

A year ago they'd found out Allen was the traitor and it had devastated the group. Now Allen was once more living in the camp and working alongside the rest of them to free the people of England from tyranny.

The day of the Fair, Dusty, Will, and Much wandered through the busy and crowded streets, hoping to stay out of the way of the Sheriff's men while also wanting to keep an eye on things.

Robin was in town as well, setting up careful meetings with various merchants who had traveled to Nottingham for the Fair so that once they traveled home again they could continue the gang's work in their own towns. Robin was always trying to grow the network of

461

people whom they could reach either as informants who could send for the gang when trouble arrived—always through Marcus, of course, as Robin never gave the camp's whereabouts away—or could be used as places to send the fugitives rescued from executions.

The Sheriff's men patrolled the streets in groups, and most of the people ignored them. But when Gisbourne walked through the crowds, the conversations around him would fall silent and people would send furtive glances his way, probably fearing any outbursts he might have. For his part, Gisbourne looked as tormented as he ever did, scowling at everyone in his path.

"I don't see whatever good Lucy does," Will commented.

"I don't think it's about whether or not he is good," Dusty replied as she, Will, and Much moved through the jostling crowd in Nottingham Square, moving around the extra merchant booths set up for the Fair and pushing past street performers to find a place to stand along the edge of the Square and watch the events unfolding around them. "Lucy chooses to forgive his past, and hope in his future whether or not he deserves such."

"I do think at the very least he is conflicted," Much said as they approached the familiar bakery and leaned up against the wall. "He does vile things like murder Lady Marian; he does decent things like let the children go and not turn Lucy in, and such. He wavers back and forth…"

"You're right," Will said. "It might be less of a good or bad question and more that he simply lacks the conviction to stick with one or the other. I don't have the same problem…when I know what I believe and what I want, nothing will sway me."

Will slipped his arm around Dusty's waist and winked at her. Much turned away from them to watch the busy Square.

He'd suspected for a while that Dusty and Will were in love—starting that day Will had been injured and Dusty had so carefully cared for him in the weeks that followed. It seemed they were finally willing to be open about it.

It was only a handful of days later when Dusty and Will announced to the group that they were engaged to be married.   Robin and Lucy had just returned to camp after rescuing a farmer and his family when Dusty eagerly shared the news.

He sat watching the fire as the gang slowly began to head to bed for the night. Little John was the first to leave, soon followed by Allen. Much didn't miss the longing and pained expression Allen shot toward Will and Dusty before he retired, but he wasn't sure what it meant.

Lucy and Dusty were discussing wedding plans across the fire, convincing Friar Tuck to perform the ceremony and choosing all the other minute details while Will sat beside Dusty, an arm around her shoulders, listening with a smile on his face.

Robin was the next to get up, shooting Dusty and Will the same sort of pained expression Allen had before he moved toward his hut. That one Much thought he could comprehend. Robin was undoubtedly thinking of Marian and the life they could have had together but were robbed of. He'd wanted a grand wedding, wanted to show Lady Marian off proudly, ever since he was a small boy. Instead he'd gotten a hurried profession of love as she died a horribly painful death.

Much glanced toward Allen's hut. Did he have some lost love in his past, too? He had always carried a darkness with him that Much had noticed from the very beginning, the first day they met in Dover.

Two weeks later, Friar Tuck married Dusty and Will under a canopy of golds, reds, and yellows as the last of the autumn colors graced the trees of Sherwood Forest. It was a surprisingly pleasant and peaceful day, and Much wished that more of their lives could be such.

The next morning Robin was handing out assignments again and Much was sent with Allen on a two week trip to the south of England to look for any cruelty they could assuage as they passed out food and money to the needy.

Chapter 55

"COME ON, WE'RE nearly there." Allen reached down a hand to pull Much back up to his feet.

"If I never have to walk anywhere again, I'll die a happy man," Much said, sighing as he allowed himself to be pulled upright.

It had been a long couple of weeks wandering the countryside trying to distribute food and money to the needy without catching the eyes of any soldiers or sheriffs of the shires they wandered through. And it was disheartening as well.

As much as they tried to visit other parts of England frequently, it was never enough. As bad as Nottingham seemed to be sometimes, Much was under the impression it was the most well off of anywhere because the gang was constantly watching over the city and the surrounding villages and the rest of England only saw them occasionally.

Much followed Allen as they continued their walk along the edge of Sherwood. They only had a few more miles before they would turn inward and head toward the camp, but after their long journey those last few miles seemed insurmountable to Much.

"One foot in front of the other," Allen encouraged.

"Remember when you were the biggest complainer of the group?"

"Well I haven't heard you complain yet, Much, so that title may well still be mine."

Much grinned. "I was thinking about marching through Palestine."

"Ah, when it rained." Allen rolled his eyes and clutched his chest dramatically. "All that mud to slosh through…nothing could be worse."

The last few miles might have felt long, but they were eventually over. Allen and Much made it to camp just as others were arriving from their own travels. A tear-streaked Lucy came to greet them all.

"You were gone…I had no way to tell you…"

"Tell us what?" Robin asked, striding into camp behind them.

"The Sheriff went off to burn a village to the ground—barring the inhabitants inside!"

"Oh no…" Dusty closed her eyes, clutching Will's arm as the gang gathered around Lucy near the log benches. Much knelt to start a fire in the empty ring.

"I had no way to tell you…and I couldn't stop the Sheriff alone. So I went to Guy but…I don't think he's going to help."

Allen touched Lucy's arm. "Sir Guy won't let it happen."

"He gave me no assurance of that."

"Perhaps the Sheriff was watching?" Dusty offered.

"Or perhaps," Robin said. "He really is evil."

Allen shook his head. "He is not."

"He is." Mark said quietly.

Much got the fire going as the gang settled on the benches, each of them considering the possibilities.

"He's done so much…for both sides," Will said. "How can you even tell one way or the other?"

Allen shook his head. "But for Lucy—"

"People said he'd do anything for Marian," Robin snapped. "And he *killed* her."

Mark winced and Much fervently hoped another argument was not about to arise.

466

"I can't believe he'd let them die," Lucy said, wringing her hands. "I don't want to believe it…"

"He won't," Allen said firmly.

"He most definitely will," Robin said. "Where was the village? We can ride there tonight, see if there are any survivors."

"I don't want to see that," Lucy said with a sigh, but she gave Robin directions nonetheless.

"Let's go, everyone. Much…keep an eye on Lucy."

As the rest of the gang prepared to leave, Much began preparations for a small meal for himself, Lucy, and Friar Tuck. Lucy didn't seem to have much of an appetite, however.

"What if Guy does let them die? Or worse, what if he does want to help but what can one man do against the Sheriff and his company of soldiers?"

"Do you trust him?"

Lucy stared into the fire for a long time before she responded. "I want to. I really do. But…he was so rough when he rejected my pleas to help the village or to stop the Sheriff somehow. And he has been cruel and evil in the past. I know I've only been seeing the better half of him since I moved to the castle, but I'm not ignorant of who he has been…"

"Regardless of his past before you knew him," Friar Tuck joined the conversation, "what do you know of him in the months that you have been becoming friends."

"He…" Lucy shook her head, a few tears escaping her lashes and sliding down her cheeks.

"From the beginning," Friar Tuck said gently.

"He was tormented when I first met him—he still is sometimes, but not like then. He was always angry and snapped at the slightest provocation, trying to hide so much pain and remorse. But now…now he's still remorseful, but he's lighter, almost. He can laugh, he can be playful. And he's capable of doing good. I've seen it."

"Before today, would you have said you trusted his friendship?"

467

"Yes, but today he was different…I think I might be wrong."

Friar Tuck let her be, but Much tried to keep her spirits up that night, though his own heart weighed heavy. He didn't trust Gisbourne. Not even a little. Forgiveness, undeserved but unrestrained, was one thing. Trust something else entirely.

Lucy returned to Nottingham in low spirits, and Much waited anxiously in the camp for any word from the rest of the gang.

It was early in the morning when Robin and the others returned; Much was still sitting up, tending the fire.

"It's alright," Dusty called, hurrying over. "We found the village empty, but we soon discovered the refugees. The people are unharmed and we've sent them along the route to Scotland with our line of inns and merchants who help fugitives to safety. They're okay."

"How?"

"I don't know, but they must have had wind of the Sheriff's schemes. Did you stay up all night waiting for us?"

"I couldn't sleep until I heard…"

"Well sleep now, Much. We might have a lazier day than normal as I imagine we're all a bit tired from the excitement of last night."

Much did sleep for most of the day. When he awoke it seemed most of the gang was waiting for Lucy to come and tell them any news of what had gone down with the village the Sheriff had wanted to burn, but she never showed.

"I do hope nothing happened to her," Robin said darkly that night once he and Much were the last two by the fire.

"She knows how to use as many weapons as you do, as well as you do, too. She can take care of herself if something were to happen with the Sheriff."

"Maybe…"

The next day, as Much was finishing up making breakfast and handing it out to the gang, Lucy came riding into camp, a smile on her face.

468

"He did it!"

She dismounted and hurried toward them where they were all gathered around the fire enjoying Much's breakfast.

"Who did what?" Little John asked.

"I imagine she means the village," Dusty said, then turned to Lucy, "We found it empty, and later discovered the refugees. We helped them start their travel toward a safer place to live, for now at least."

"That's good," Lucy said, sitting down between Dusty and Much.

"How did they know to evacuate?" Much asked.

"Sir Guy. He sent Andrew ahead. He rescued the villagers."

Robin frowned while Allen sighed in relief. "I knew he would. Well...I hoped he would."

"I wish he hadn't," Robin said.

"Robin!" Dusty scolded. "You wish those people had died?"

"No. Of course not. But I wish someone else had rescued them."

"It's much easier to hate him when he's always doing evil," Friar Tuck observed. "If he was evil you would perhaps have grounds to hate him."

"I have perfect grounds to hate that man!"

"Hatred is never the answer, my son. And if you gave up this foolish hatred it would not sting so when he proves his worth."

"He isn't worth anything!" Robin stormed away.

Allen sighed. "He'll never change his mind."

"He shouldn't," Mark snapped. "Gisbourne isn't worth anything. He's a murderer."

Lucy didn't stay long at the camp, and Much understood why. Her presence, and particularly her friendship with Gisbourne, always caused strife with Robin and Mark, and sometimes Little John. Lucy didn't seem to like being around the conflict anymore than Much did.

Later that night, Robin came to Much's hut after he'd doused the fire and was preparing to go to bed.

469

"Do you need something?" Much asked, swinging his door wide open. Usually when Robin dropped by for a late night chat he had something weighing on his mind.

"I think I'm going to try and sneak into Nottingham castle."

"Robin! It's dangerous."

"It's always been dangerous, but I used to visit Marian anyway."

"Why do you feel the need to go now? You haven't tried to sneak into the castle since before—well, for nine months or so."

"You mean since before Marian died. I know. I just feel I need to apologize to Lucy. She's doing so much for us, and somehow changing Gisbourne for the better..."

"She's not the one changing Gisbourne..." Much wanted to explain about Lucy's faith in Christ, and His overwhelming love and mercy, but instead he bit his cheek as usual.

"It doesn't matter," Robin said. "He's helping us and I should not be upset by it. I said some rude things to her tonight and I am sorry for it."

"You weren't as harsh as you sometimes are..."

"Perhaps not with the group, but I did speak with Lucy just before we left...anyway, I think I should apologize. I wanted you to know where I was going in case..."

"You think something will happen?"

"Well, as you pointed out, I've grown out of the habit of sneaking into the castle. If I don't come back, you can assume I've been caught. Lucy will let you know, I imagine, and then you and Will can plan my rescue."

"Be careful, please."

"I am always careful."

"You most definitely are not."

After Robin left, Much couldn't sleep so he sat beside the fire ring—it was nothing but cold ash but he didn't light a new one. He just waited in the darkness for Robin to return. He didn't have to wait too long.

"Much, why are you awake?"

"I had to know if you would come back or not, so I could plan your rescue and all that."

"I appreciate that, but I'm fine."

"How did Lucy take your apology?"

"Fine." Robin grinned, throwing Much a wink before he went to his hut. Much wasn't sure what to make of that. Robin had been slowly coming out of his rage-filled darkness over the weeks and months since the return to Austria, but tonight he suddenly seemed almost like his old self again.

A few days later Robin, Will, and Mark returned to camp from distributing money in the village of Wetherby with news from Lucy. The Sheriff was going to hang a woman in Nottingham Square. It was apparently going to be a big event, and the Sheriff wanted all the citizens of Nottingham to attend.

"She did her usual run-around with who she could tell and who she couldn't based on silly promises made to the Sheriff," Robin said with a sigh. "But at least we have the information and we can plan a rescue. We'll have to leave now, however. She was urgent that it was happening today, within a few hours' time."

The gang gathered their weapons, and on the walk to Nottingham Robin and Will gave out orders and assignments. Much's job was to wait at the edge of one of the streets that led into the Square with Marcus' horses.

Running all the way to Marcus had been growing dangerous, and Robin didn't want Marcus and his wife to fall under suspicion so he had Much fetch the horses and wait with them just beyond the Square.

Much had a handful of reins in each hand as he waited in the street. He could hear the hum of the crowd, their voices mingling together as they waited for the execution. He heard the shouts that indicated the rest of the gang were shooting down soldiers and causing general mayhem and chaos within the crowd to distract the soldiers so that Allen could get the intended victim out of harm's way.

His heart rate increasing, Much did his best not to rush down the street to see what was happening. He had to stay put, well out of sight of any soldiers.

Soon enough, Allen came running around the corner from the direction of the Square, a woman beside him. They sprinted toward Much.

"Get on a horse and follow me!" Allen said, jumping onto one of the horses and pulling the reins from Much's grasp. The woman did as Allen suggested and the two were soon galloping down the street as more the gang appeared and jumped on horses of their own.

Once the last of them had arrived, Much swung himself into a saddle as well.

"Behind you!" Robin called.

Much turned in the saddle to see two soldiers turning the corner and rushing toward him. Much whipped his bow from his back as soon as he saw them; they didn't get far before arrows sprouted in both of their chests and they fell.

Much spurred his horse forward and followed after Robin.

Before too long the gang was out of Nottingham and riding toward Sherwood Forest. When they were out of sight of the city itself, Robin slowed their pace and introduced everyone to the woman they had rescued—Ida.

"Lucy and I met her before, when we saved her family from a few of the Sheriff's men. Do you remember the farmer I mentioned not so long ago? That was Ida's family."

"I do appreciate you saving my life today," Ida said.

"It was our pleasure," Robin replied. "This is what we do, after all."

"Yes, and I'd like to be a part of that, as I mentioned the last time we met."

472

Robin grinned. "I can't say no. You don't have a choice this time; you can't go home."

The next morning when Much exited his hut to light a fire for breakfast he found Ida already sitting before a dancing flame.

"Good morning."

"Good morning. I was hoping I could help you with breakfast. I hear you are the one to ask about such things."

"You want to cook breakfast?"

"If it isn't too much trouble. I want…well, to be honest, I just want to do something normal. I almost died yesterday, and not too many weeks ago the rest of my family was being tormented by the Sheriff's men. I'd like to do something to remind me that there is still a bit of normalcy here…even though I am now living in the forest with a bunch of outlaws."

Her eyes were dancing with mischief as she spoke, and Much couldn't deny her the opportunity. He showed her around his little kitchen and then sat back and watched as she cooked up breakfast for everyone.

"Do you have family, Much?"

"What?"

"Just trying to get to know the gang, as I've only heard rumors you know. We've all heard the whispers of Robin Hood and his crew… but I've only met Robin and Lucy, and Allen sort of, when he rescued me yesterday."

"Oh. Well…no. I don't have siblings or parents. But I grew up with Robin and he is my brother in every way that counts."

Ida smiled. "I wish I could say the great Robin Hood was my brother. Mine is a little disaster." Ida rolled her eyes, but there was a fond smile on her face.

"You have a little brother?"

"I do. It's just him and me, along with our parents. They're good people…but they don't speak out against the Sheriff's tyranny enough. I do…that's partly why I ended up on that chopping block, I think."

In the days that followed, Ida seemed to fit into the gang as if she'd always been there. She was playful and outspoken which resonated well with Robin, Will, and Allen. Little John admired her efficiency with daggers, and she eagerly pitched in with the distributing of food and money to the needy, so Much could find nothing to fault her with. She seemed like a good woman who wanted to help people as much as the rest of them did, although she did so with a bit more brashness than Much would have done.

Robin, Will, Little John, and Allen gathered supplies and built another hut in the clearing for Ida. Much thought Friar Tuck might have been right—they were building quite the village in Sherwood Forest.

Only a week after Ida had joined the camp, Lucy visited in a distressed state, running into camp and crying out, "Ida!"

"What's wrong?"

"The Sheriff…Sir Guy…"

"What?" Ida asked again.

Everyone began to move toward Lucy as she stood before Ida, her eyes filling with tears. "Sir Guy didn't know what the Sheriff was planning or he would have told me…"

"What did the Sheriff do?" Robin asked, crossing his arms. Much glanced between the tear-streaked Lucy and Ida, whom Lucy seemed intent on telling her news to.

"He burned Ida's farm!" Lucy finally said.

Much's eyes darted to Ida, his heart falling to his feet.

"Where is her family?" Allen asked. "We can give them money to rebuild, we can—"

Lucy shook her head. "You can't."

"Why not?" Much asked, though he knew the answer she was going to give.

"Because the Sheriff burned them with the farm…Ida, I am so sorry!"

There was a long silence, and then Ida asked, "How do you know?"

Lucy tentatively reached out to touch her shoulder. "When Sir Guy found out what had happened, he came to me—"

"A little late," Little John said.

"Yes, but he didn't know sooner," Lucy said. "He was distraught, Ida, believe me. If he'd known he would have told me."

"I don't believe it," Ida snapped, jerking away from Lucy's touch.

"But he was! And so am I, Ida. Your mother and little brother…" Lucy shook herself, seeming to remember something. "Your father. Your father is alive, he's in the castle dungeon right now, set to be executed later this week."

"You could have led with that," Little John said.

"My father!" Ida turned her desperate eyes toward Robin. "We have to save him!"

"Of course we will," Robin said. "Ida, don't worry. We can handle this."

"Why did he do it?" Will asked.

"That hardly matters," Ida said. "The Sheriff is vile."

"He was frustrated," Lucy said. "He's angry that he can't find Ida after her failed execution and he needed a way to retaliate…"

"So he killed my mother and baby brother." Ida shook her head, tears beginning to fall from her eyes. She jerked away when Dusty reached out to hug her. "We need to get my father out of the Sheriff's clutches as soon as possible, Robin."

"Let's go to Nottingham and see what we can do," Robin agreed.

Though the gang loitered in Nottingham for the day, they learned nothing of when or where Ida's father might be executed. They returned to the camp in low spirits.

The next day Robin sent them all out on their usual assignments, suggesting he'd stay at the camp in case Lucy visited with news of Ida's father.

When the gang returned to the camp that evening, Robin informed them that Ida's father was already in the camp.

"He's here!" Ida asked, looking around eagerly.

"He's sleeping in my hut right now," Robin said. "I think he was exhausted from his near execution today."

"You saved him?" Ida asked. Robin nodded and Ida threw her arms around his neck. "Thank you!"

As Much and Ida set about cooking up dinner for the group as the gang gathered around the fire, Robin shot Much a look and then wandered off toward the other side of the meadow.

"I'll be right back," Much said, getting up to follow Robin. As soon as they were far enough away from Ida to be out of earshot Much asked, "What's wrong?"

"I went to see him." Robin was pacing in tight circles, clenching and unclenching his fists.

"Who?"

"Gisbourne."

"You...went to see him? Why?"

"Because Lucy had discovered the Sheriff's plans for killing Ida's father, but he'd made her promise not to tell me. Specifically, *me*. But when she came to the camp, none of the rest of you were here

476

because I'd sent you out this morning…so it was tell me, and break her word, or…"

"She asked you to get the information from Gisbourne."

Robin stopped pacing and looked at Much in the most forlorn manner. "Yes."

"And you went?"

"Not at first." Robin shook his head. "We had an argument… but Ida's father was being executed and I couldn't let that happen simply to prove a point to Lucy about how dumb her promises are. So I went. I spoke to him…"

"And he's still breathing?" Much asked.

Robin gave him a wry grin in response.

"Are you okay, though?" Much asked.

"I hated every second of it. I hate him." Robin pushed a hand through his hair and sighed, closing his eyes for a moment before looking at Much again. "I do think I'm okay though."

"You aren't going to kill him?"

"Some part of me would still like to, but no. He did give me the information to save Ida's father, without hesitation. And he's been helping Lucy for weeks now…I don't understand or even *like* the trust she has in him, but at the end of the day I guess I trust Lucy. So, by proxy, I have to at the very least tolerate Gisbourne's existence."

Ida's father Robert was a restless man. Much couldn't blame him; the man had just lost his beloved wife and young son, had his farm and all his worldly possession burned to the ground, and nearly been executed himself before being forced to live as a fugitive in the forest.

Robert spent his days pacing the camp or lying listlessly in Ida's hut. He hardly talked to anyone apart from his daughter Ida.

477

"I wish there was something I could do for him," Much said softly as he and Ida prepared a meal for the gang one night.

Ida glanced toward her hut where the open door showed her father lying in bed and seemingly staring into nothingness.

"What did you do for Robin and Mark?"

"Nothing, really. I mean…I tried to talk to them sometimes after Marian died, but for the most part they didn't respond well to interference."

"I imagine just knowing they had someone to rely on if they wanted to was enough," Ida said.

"How are you?"

Ida glanced toward Much and then away. "I'm ignoring the pain for now."

"Is that wise?"

"Probably not, but it's working at the moment."

After a week had gone by, Robert disappeared.

"He left me a note," Ida said quietly one night when the gang was gathered around the fire after a hard day's work looking after England. "He's gone to find the king."

"What good will that do?" Lucy asked.

"None," Ida said with a sigh. "I expect he won't find the king; he'll perish on the journey."

"Do not think such gloomy thoughts," Dusty chided. "He merely needs some time to himself. He is grieving, as are you. Let him do so in the way that he needs. He'll come back to you."

"How can you be certain?"

"Because Robin and Mark came back to us," Will said.

Winter winds blew in the frost and snow, and traveling beyond Nottingham became less frequent once more.

478

One day Lucy came into the camp despite the snow drifts and the icy wind, with a request for Friar Tuck.

The gang was huddled close together around the fire as Lucy joined them, and Robin adjusted the blanket draped over his knees so that it could cover Lucy as well. Much was wedged between Will and Dusty, hoping the warmth from his friends would find a way to seep into his own body as he felt chilled to his very bones as he watched the air in front of his face crystallize every time he breathed out. Fat, fluffy flakes of snow were drifting down around the group and sizzling out when they got too close to the fire.

"I have spoken to the Sheriff to let him know a friend of mine is in town, and he's agreed to give you a room at the castle."

"I was under the impression you wanted me here," Friar Tuck said.

"I do," Lucy said. "But I would like you to spend time in Nottingham."

"Why?"

"Because…" Lucy glanced at Robin for a moment. "Well, because Guy knows Jesus now, as Dusty and I do, and I believe it would be best to put him in the wise hands of Friar Tuck rather than leave him alone, adrift in a stormy sea."

Much held his breath, watching the frosty air in front of him disappear entirely. Sir Guy of Gisbourne knew Christ? It was remarkable news, and yet complicated to process. And Much knew Robin would not understand or appreciate it.

Robin crossed his arms but he said nothing. Dusty, however, smiled brightly. "That's wonderful news for Gisbourne!"

"Wonderful?" Little John asked. "Gisbourne? I do not think those two words belong together."

"Little John…" Lucy started to say something and then shut her mouth again.

"What is it, Lucy?" Robin asked.

"It's just that…no one is perfect. We all deserve to be judged harshly, but you reserve your judgment for a few."

"We didn't kill anyone," Little John replied.

"I beg to differ," Lucy said. "What about all the soldiers you've been killing?"

"But they deserved it."

"One could easily argue we all deserve death and judgment," Dusty said.

"And why would you assume they deserve it?" Lucy asked. "Because they work for the Sheriff? First of all, that doesn't make them evil. You don't know their stories, why they work for him or what desperate circumstances drove them to do what they do. And secondly, you might have noticed I never shoot to kill because I do believe Scripture when it tells us not to. Death is death, regardless of *why* you choose to kill someone."

Ida rolled her eyes. "This is absurd. We aren't discussing the philosophical questions behind our morality within the gang. We're discussing Gisbourne. He's evil."

"No," Allen shook his head. "I don't think he is."

"Regardless of what any of you think about Sir Guy…" Lucy turned away from the group in her exasperation, turning instead to Friar Tuck. "You will come to Nottingham, won't you?"

Friar Tuck smiled at her. "Of course, my daughter. You need only ask."

"Thank you."

Half the gang was still flabbergasted that Gisbourne could possibly have any good in him at all. Much wondered at his sincerity, having not spoken to the man himself. But he trusted Lucy, and Friar Tuck, and if they both believed what Gisbourne said of his own newfound faith...Much would have to accept it.

Gisbourne—the man who murdered Marian—was not a brother in Christ. Much wasn't sure how he felt about that, but he'd been trying to pursue forgiveness even before Gisbourne's apparent conversion, so this was only more reason to continue in that endeavor.

Nearly a week later, Friar Tuck visited from Nottingham with news.

"Sir Guy has asked Lucy to marry him," he said without preamble as the gang was gathering close to Much's fire for warmth and food.

"What?" Will and Robin both exclaimed as Much nearly dropped the plate of food he'd been handing to Allen.

"I said—"

"They heard what you said," Allen laughed. "They just can't believe it."

"What did she say?" Robin asked. "Did she agree to marry him?"

"I do not know. She would scarcely speak to me about it, despite having brought it up herself."

"She wouldn't marry Gisbourne," Ida said. "She's foolish enough, but she's not stupid."

"Lucy isn't foolish," Robin snapped, though his eyes stayed glued to Friar Tuck's face.

Much was curious about how interested Robin was in Friar Tuck's news. Was it simply because Lucy was a member of the gang

481

and therefore their friend, and he was concerned for her? Marrying Gisbourne would certainly be an interesting choice, given his past, but Lucy had always been his friend when the rest of them had not.

"You're certain you don't know her answer?" Will asked.

"Yes," Friar Tuck said. "I do not know what she told him. We will have to wait for Lucy to tell us herself."

"How soon do you think that will be?" Dusty asked. "Her visits to the camp aren't exactly on a strict schedule."

"I do not know," Friar Tuck replied.

It was two days before Lucy came to the camp. Robin immediately asked her to take a walk with him and they wandered out of the camp. Much watched them until they were out of sight.

"What is wrong, little mouse?" Dusty asked, coming to stand beside him.

"Nothing."

"Oh come, you can speak to me openly."

"I am not sure I'm ready for Robin to love someone again."

"You are not the only one having a hard time accepting that." Dusty's gaze landed on Mark, sitting across the meadow in front of his hut sharpening his sword. He was staring at the trees Robin and Lucy had disappeared through.

"It's not the same for me as for Mark," Much said. "His hesitancy, if he has any, is because he still grieves his sister and thinks Robin should be doing so as well, yes?"

"Something like that."

"I haven't talked to Mark about it recently, but I can see why he would be upset. Marian's only been gone for almost ten months. It hasn't even been a full year."

"I know."

"But that's not what is bothering me," Much said. "It's just… odd, I guess, to see him with anyone other than Marian."

"They have been thrust together by the evil doings of the Sheriff and Prince John. And though it has only been a few months, it has been a *full* few months; so busy, in fact, that it feels to me as though we've been home from Austria far longer than a year. So much has been happening every week feels like a month of its own."

"I know what you mean," Much said. "I like Lucy. I'm happy for both of them if they do love each other, or if they are headed that direction. But it does feel odd to see Robin with anyone apart from Marian. You know he asked Marian to marry him when he was ten… and twelve…and basically every year, all the time, as soon as he was old enough to know what marriage was."

"Did he?" Dusty asked, her eyes dancing. "That is rather adorable."

"Marian hated it. She'd always turn up her nose and ignore him when he would talk about their future…" Much shook his head, his chest filling with the warmth of fond memories. "She used to tell him to stop acting so grown up and silly."

"I wish I could have known Marian better," Dusty said. "I only knew her a handful of years, and even then…she didn't like me when we came home from the Crusades. I think in the beginning she felt threatened by me, thinking perhaps I had stolen Robin's heart. Of course that was ridiculous, I never felt that way for Robin at all."

"I think she knew that by the end."

"I believe she did," Dusty said, "but she died before we could truly get to know one another."

Much glanced toward Mark again and then sighed. "Sir Guy proposed to Marian once…"

483

"I remember."

"What if…" Much shook his head, wondering if Gisbourne was going to end up killing Lucy in a flash of temper, too.

"Sir Guy would never hurt Lucy, not now. He has given his heart to Christ—the same as you and me—and is trying to do the right thing now, to live a life in subjection to Christ, a life of purity and righteousness."

"I know, but I can't help worrying sometimes."

"Unjustly. Sir Guy would never hurt Lucy."

"He's always been so changeable, so unstable…He proposed to Marian and the very next day he burned her house to the ground. He said he loved her and then he put a sword through her…"

"That was before Christ, Much."

"I know, I know…"

"It is a lot to wrap one's head around," Dusty conceded, "but I have to trust in the power of Christ working in his life."

"What if he wasn't honest about that?"

"What do you mean?"

"Lucy is the only one who has any real contact with him, and he must know he has influence over her—she cares for him. What if he lied?"

"Do you think he would?"

"The old Gisbourne, probably…I don't know. Lucy knows him, Friar Tuck has been speaking with him, it all seems real and I should stop being pessimistic. It was just a thought."

Chapter 56

MUCH PUTTERED ABOUT his little kitchen, arranging his pots and pans as he waited for Robin to come find him. It was late—most of the gang had already retired to their various huts and Lucy had returned to Nottingham. Much knew without a doubt that Robin would eventually come looking for him to tell him what he and Lucy had spoken of— namely, whether or not Lucy had agreed to marry Sir Guy of Gisbourne.

As Much picked up his largest pot for the tenth time and moved it to another stack of cooking supplies, Robin stepped into the small space. It was illuminated by a small fire Much had lit in the stove to keep the hut warm, so Much had a good view of Robin's face. He seemed content.

"So…is she marrying Gisbourne?"

"No. She was surprised by his proposal." Robin sat on Much's bed on the opposite end of the hut from the kitchen area. "Seemed completely dumbfounded he'd proposed at all, and was adamant she felt only friendship for him."

"I suppose that was a relief to you."

"Of course. I wouldn't want anyone I cared for spending more time with Gisbourne than absolutely necessary."

Much joined Robin on the bed, studying his face. "So you aren't relieved for any other reason?"

Robin gave him a blank look and Much stared right back at him. Finally, Robin's mouth quirked into a grin. "Okay, so I might be interested in Lucy and I'd rather she didn't marry anyone just yet. You don't miss a beat, do you?"

"So I've been told."

Robin grew serious, though his face didn't bear the darkness it once had. "I still miss Marian. I still long for the days that can never be, of having her as my wife—not on her deathbed, but truly my wife. I love her, Much."

Robin took a shaky breath. "But she's gone, and I'm here, and life is short. If I wait too long with Lucy, who's to say some tragedy won't befall her, too, and I'll be alone again."

"Do you love her?"

"I don't know. Not yet, perhaps…but I know I'm starting to. I know I *could*. I don't want to miss that chance because that's what it is, Much, a mere chance and then it will be gone. She could be gone."

"I understand. Does this means you are going to court her?"

"I am going to pursue our friendship and see where it leads, so yes, I guess I am."

"Have you spoken to Mark about that?"

"No…" Robin shoved a hand through his hair. "I haven't. He won't be happy about it, I know. He's…well, to be honest, he's taking longer to grieve Marian. He's still bitter and angry in ways that I was not too long ago, but he doesn't seem to be coming out of it any time soon."

A fortnight passed in relative tranquility. Friar Tuck and Lucy split their time between Nottingham and the camp, the gang passed out food, blankets, and money to the needy so they could survive the harsh winter months, with Lucy and Dusty visiting those who were sick to facilitate healing.

One day, Lucy came to the camp searching for Friar Tuck—having promised the Sheriff she wouldn't inform 'Robin Hood's gang' of whatever he was planning.

Ida protested the absurdity of the promise while Will pointed Lucy in the direction Friar Tuck had gone walking with Robin.

"Whatever is happening that she won't tell us," Will said, "we should be ready. Grab your weapons, and let's be prepared for anything when Robin and Lucy get back."

Much hurried to his hut to grab his sword and bow as the rest of the gang did the same. When Robin came into the camp with Friar Tuck, everyone was ready to leave for Nottingham at a moment's notice.

"The Sheriff is planning to hang a man and his daughter who were visiting Nottingham," Friar Tuck said to the gathered group. "They haven't done anything wrong, as far as Lucy can tell."

"When?" Will asked.

"Tomorrow morning."

"Do we know them?" Ida asked. "Where are they from?"

"They are not from around here according to Lucy," Friar Tuck said.

"But they are loyal to King Richard," Robin said. "And that is enough for the Sheriff to hang them. We'll need to go to Nottingham tonight so that we can coordinate a rescue plan with Andrew— Gisbourne's lackey."

"Why use Gisbourne at all?" Ida asked. "Oh, right," she rolled her eyes before Robin could answer, "Lucy won't help us because we're Robin Hood's gang so she sends us to the very men who caused this rebellion to start in the first place. So. Helpful."

Robin frowned. "Regardless of how we are getting the information, we need to be at Marcus' home so that we can be ready for anything."

It wasn't long before the group was gathered around Marcus' house, sitting at the table or leaning against the walls in his front room. A knock sounded at the door and Marcus reluctantly opened it to find Andrew standing there. Little John gripped his quarter staff tighter, and Ida fingered a dagger, but Much moved forward to greet him with Allen at his side as Marcus and Robin ushered him into the room.

"The Sheriff has planned a hanging for Faith and her father," Andrew said without preamble. "The gallows are being constructed in the Square this very night, and they will be hanged in the morning. The Sheriff has set a heavy guard on them in the dungeon to ensure that you all don't rescue them there as you sometimes have in the past, and Guy is there now keeping an eye on them. I'm not sure how you want to pull off the rescue, but I imagine it will be much like the other ones you have done."

"Is that all the information you have?" Little John asked. "How many guards will be accompanying them as they are escorted to the gallows? How many soldiers stationed in the Square, and where precisely? Will the Sheriff be there? How is Gisbourne planning on assisting with this endeavor?"

Andrew clasped his hands behind his back, turning to Little John with a slight bow of deference. "I do have the military reports you will require to station yourselves around the soldiers of the Sheriff."

Andrew relayed the bulk of his information, and Robin and Will planned the rescue as they so often did. In the end, Much's job was simple—shoot down soldiers as he generally did during such rescues.

Everything ran as smoothly as it often did, and soon the gang had brought the prisoners—a woman named Faith, and her father—to the camp.

Once the gang had gathered, Robin began introductions. "Now that we are quite safe from any pursuit, I'm Robin Hood. This is my gang; Will, Dusty, Much, Mark, Little John, Ida, and Allen."

The young woman smiled. "I assumed that you were Robin Hood. Sir Guy told us last night while we were in the dungeons that you would not fail to rescue us."

"Gisbourne told you that?" Ida asked.

"Yes, he did. I'm Faith, and this is my father Thomas."

"You are welcome to live with us," Robin said. "Or we can send you on your way to Scotland via our secret route of loyal subjects."

"Thank you," Thomas said. "But tell me, this Gisbourne fellow, is he not as bad as people say? My daughter and Gisbourne spoke much during our stay in the Sheriff's dungeon. I had been under the impression based off of the many tales told among the inhabitants of this country that he is a wretched man and your mortal enemy. How can it be that he would assure us, calm our fears, as though he were helping you?"

Robin sighed before he spoke. "It is complicated. He was a wretched man, and most definitely my bitter enemy, but…things have changed. He has changed; I have changed. We are working together to save England, though I don't particularly like him."

Faith suggested that she and her father stay with the gang at the camp, and so Robin led them all there. Much was surprised at how open Robin had become to letting strangers into the camp—it had started when Much brought Lucy, and then there was Friar Tuck, and then Ida. Now Faith and her father. Much didn't mind—he enjoyed getting to know the new additions to their strange little family, but he was surprised Robin had become so accommodating, when there had been a time when telling anyone the location of the camp would have brought all of Robin's wrath down upon the unfortunate head who had dared to do such a thing.

That night, and for many nights afterward, the gang told outrageous stories of their exploits during their years in Sherwood to the captivated audience that was Thomas and Faith. Even Ida listened with eagerness and delight. Thomas would listen with shining eyes, though more often than not Faith would laugh.

"You know I don't believe half of what you tell me," Faith said one night as the fire began to fade to coals and the gang's stories were winding down. "You all seem to enjoy exaggeration."

"Accusing us of lying, my lady?" Little John asked, a twinkle in his eye.

"No," Faith said, laughing. "Merely suggesting you like to embellish your stories."

Will laughed. "There's no denying that."

"The only one among you that hasn't told me unbelievable tales is Much," Faith continued. "So henceforth, he shall be the only person I believe. If he does not corroborate your tales, I will assume you have embellished your story in some fashion, even if the truth of what happened does lie somewhere in the middle of it."

"You're going to make the mouse your authority on what we say?" Allen asked.

"The mouse?" Faith turned toward Much with questions in her eyes.

"It is a name that Dusty gave me, long ago," Much said. "I haven't always loved it, but it grew on me."

"But why a mouse?" Faith asked.

Dusty shook her head with a laugh. "I don't remember why I chose that particular nickname…but it's stuck."

"Tell me, Much," Faith turned back to him. "Everyone else has shared their grand tales of outrageous proportions…what is your story?"

"I have nothing interesting to tell you," Much said. "I hardly do anything to influence what the rest of the gang accomplish in Sherwood, and it was the same during the Crusades."

"Oh, Much!" Dusty objected. "You were a brave and loyal soldier during our time in the Holy Land."

"And you've been a great help to me in Sherwood," Robin added.

Much shook his head, though he smiled. He was grateful for their support.

One morning as Much and Ida were preparing breakfast together, Faith approached them.

"I wouldn't want to intrude in your kitchen…"

490

"It's not my kitchen to intrude," Ida said with a laugh. "This is Much's domain. But he let me bully him into allowing me space in his sanctuary. Being the sweet thing that he is, he will be unlikely to object to having your help as well, if that is what you came to ask."

"It is," Faith said.

Much smiled. "Of course, you are most welcome." He'd grown accustomed to Ida being in his kitchen and somehow found he didn't balk at the idea of one more person invading his sacred space.

"Thank you, both. I have been feeling rather helpless and useless since coming here. I have nothing to occupy my time."

"You could help in the raids on the caravans," Ida said. "That's what most of us do, save for Friar Tuck when he's visiting."

"I could never do that," Faith said with a quick shake of her head. "I have never used a bow or sword or any other weapon. And I do not wish to. It…it would frighten me."

Ida rolled her eyes. "Don't be ridiculous."

Faith shrugged, her gentle smile still in place. "Ridiculous or not, it is the truth."

"I would not know the use of arms if it was not for Robin," Much said. "I do not particularly enjoy them, but I have come to see their usefulness in certain situations."

"I was raised with the knowledge of how to defend myself," Ida said.

"I was raised with the knowledge of the consequences of violence," Faith replied, "and how diplomacy and peace are better prizes one might pursue."

Ida rolled her eyes at that, but she didn't press the issue further, for which Much was grateful. He didn't need another taboo topic within the gang. Lucy caused enough unintentional strife every time she brought up Gisbourne, Much would prefer Faith and Ida didn't also get into an argument every time the gang went on a raid or rescue with their weapons in hand.

He could see Faith's point of view, however, and in an ideal life he would wish to abide by it himself. But with men like the Sheriff causing such pain and suffering it was impossible, Much felt, to be a pacifist. How could he have lived with himself if he had simply stood by and silently watched all the death and destruction and heartbreak?

Chapter 57

WINTER PASSED AWAY and spring came once more. The flowers blossomed, the trees donned their green leaves once more, and life in the camp continued in a simple manner. Lucy or Gisbourne would inform the gang when the Sheriff began to plot something, and they would stop it. Ida fit in with the group easily, fighting with a relish in every raid and rescue and earning the respect of most of the gang. Faith, on the other hand, was quiet and peaceful and preferred wandering through Sherwood Forest collecting flowers to braid through her hair. Ida found her distasteful, Much thought she was sweet. Her father Thomas was more than willing to be made of use, however, and was put to work distributing money and food along with the rest of the gang.

And so the year wore on.

One day as Much was washing out his pots, pans, and other cooking utensils in a tub he'd set up just outside his hut, Little John came crashing into the camp with a frenzied look in his eye.

"Robin!"

"Robin isn't here," Will said from where he sat by the fire.

Allen perked up from where he sat beside his hut sharpening his sword. "Actually...wasn't Robin with you distributing money in Nottingham?"

Little John hurried over to him, his hands shaking and his eyes darting around in a panicked manner as he tried to catch his breath. "Robin was caught!"

Much dropped the pot he'd been holding and it landed in his soapy water with a splash, soaking his legs as Will stood up.

"How?" Will asked. "When?"

"We were separated in Nottingham, in order to reach more families today. He was caught by the Sheriff's men...I don't know how. I wasn't there. One of the citizens of Nottingham came running to tell me. I saw Robin being dragged into the castle courtyard..."

"We have to rescue him," Allen said, jumping up and moving toward Will and Little John as Much stayed frozen in place. He wasn't entirely sure his heart was beating at all.

Robin had been caught.

Much could feel a darkness encroaching on his vision in the same sort of way it had when Marian died.

"Don't faint," he whispered to himself, closing his eyes as the sound of Little John's worried voice drifted across the clearing toward him.

"He's being beheaded...at dawn."

"Beheaded!" Much gasped. He began to rock slightly back and forth, his eyes still closed. "Oh no, no, no…"

"Much, calm down." Dusty's gentle voice was beside him and he felt her hand on his arm. "We must all remain calm or we will be of no use to Robin. Little John! Return to Nottingham and keep watch. We will meet at Marcus' once the whole gang is aware of what has happened, and we will figure out what to do."

Much heard movements and footsteps in the camp, along with whispered conversations, and then all was quiet. Dusty's comforting hand was still on his arm.

"Much?"

He opened his eyes and looked at Dusty.

"We've stopped plenty of executions; Robin will be okay."

"We haven't saved everyone," Much said. "And if Robin himself can get caught, how could anything the rest of us try to do make any difference."

"Much," Dusty chided, shaking her head. "He's just a man."

"He's Robin! If he dies...if we lose him…"

"We won't."

"Dusty, I don't even know who I am without Robin. We can't let him die, we can't…"

"We aren't going to let him die…" Dusty studied Much, a look of concern on her face. Much thought it was in relation to Robin's

494

predicament until she spoke again. "You put too much of your faith in Robin. How can you say 'who am I without Robin' when Robin is not the one who defines your worth?"

Much lowered his gaze to the sudsy tub of water in front of him.

"Come on. Let's get to Nottingham so we can figure out what we're doing next."

Dusty dragged Much to his feet and walked with him through the forest and then across the open fields toward the city. Much was hardly aware of his surroundings at all.

Robin was going to die.

As the evening wore on, the rest of the gang began to appear at Marcus house, gathering at his table. Faith, however, had said she would be of no use to the gang in their plans and so was staying at the camp to pray.

"This execution will be more heavily guarded," Ida said. "It's *Robin Hood*. The Sheriff will not be willing to let him go so easily."

"We will have to be extra careful," Dusty said.

"What if he doesn't execute him in the Square?" Little John asked. "What if he takes into account how often and easily we stop his executions, and he chooses to do it inside the castle courtyard? We can't get in there like we used to…"

"There's always the stable," Allen said.

Much couldn't keep his mind on the conversation as they discussed various ways they might save Robin.

As darkness began to fall, Marcus' wife Lillian brought food to the group. Some of the gang began to eat, but Much simply stared at his plate.

Robin was going to die.

How could he exist without Robin? His sole purpose in life since he was a small child was to serve Robin. Robin's approval and respect were all he craved for satisfaction and fulfillment.

Is he more satisfying than I am?

Much closed his eyes, taking in the warmth of the still small voice of Christ.

A knock sounded on the door and Much jumped, knocking over the mug of ale Lillian had put before him. She came hurrying over with a towel as Marcus opened the front door a crack.

"Can…can I help you?" Marcus asked, his voice cracking slightly. Around Much, his friends reached for their weapons. He glanced toward the door, wondering why they had reacted that way.

Marcus was opening the door and stepping aside as Gisbourne and Andrew entered the room.

"You have no need for fear," Gisbourne said. "We're here because we need your help."

Silence greeted his words. Much noticed Allen wasn't holding his weapon, but the rest of the gang had their swords held at the ready and were watching Gisbourne warily. Even Dusty and Will were armed.

Gisbourne sighed. "Please. You can trust us. We aren't just doing this for Robin Hood. Lady Lucy has been thrown in the dungeon with Robin and is going to be executed with him at dawn. We need your help if we are going to rescue them."

"Lucy!" Dusty lowered her sword at her side.

"Whatever you are going to do, do it quickly," Gisbourne said. "We only have one night to plan this rescue."

Gisbourne stepped forward, causing Little John and Ida to swing their weapons forward in a defensive stance. "I know we haven't had the best dealings between us in the past, but I need the gang's help. We have to save Robin and Lucy."

Will stepped in front of Ida and Little John. "We are rather good at that. But this execution is going to be more heavily guarded is it not?"

Gisbourne nodded.

"We'll need to know all the details, where guards are stationed and so forth. And to get away, we're going to need fast horses."

Marcus spoke up. "You can borrow mine, as usual."

"I can supply the rest," Gisbourne said. "The Sheriff will expect me to be with him for the most part so Andrew will have to be our messenger."

Will nodded. "We'll be here; Andrew can bring us whatever information you think will help."

Andrew nodded. "I'll do what I can."

Little John stepped up behind Will, glowering at Gisbourne. "I don't trust you."

"But Lucy believes in him," Will said, giving Little John a sharp look, "and that is enough for us."

Will turned back to Gisbourne, "You should definitely stay in the castle. With Lucy coming to the camp after this we're going to need someone on the inside collecting the information she has been. That would be you now, I assume, so it would be best if you didn't draw suspicion now."

Gisbourne nodded. "I am willing to gather information for you. Andrew and I will go back to the castle for now and learn all we can about the execution. Don't fail."

With that, he turned on his heel and marched out, Andrew following after him. Marcus closed his door and the gang's weapons finally lowered, Ida slumping into her seat at the table with a sigh.

"Gisbourne wants to save Robin?" Ida shook her head. "Now that is remarkable."

"It's not Robin," Little John said, starting to pace, "It's Lucy."

Much moved to a corner of the room, sinking down to the floor and drawing his knees close to his chest. The rest of the gang sat or stood around Marcus' table, discussing the plans to rescue Robin. As the hours passed, Andrew visited to relay news. The gang shared their ideas, and he returned to Gisbourne to relate them.

"What happens if Gisbourne really has been playing Lucy all this time?" Little John asked. "He has all of us in one spot tonight and could easily siege Marcus' home and kill us tonight. And now he knows

497

about Marcus, too, whose involvement we've been trying to keep secret all this time."

No one had an answer for him. Andrew returned a short while later with more information from Gisbourne, and so the night progressed with Andrew going back and forth many times between the castle and Marcus's home carrying information.

Dusty came and sat beside Much as the conversation around the table continued.

"Are you alright?"

Much shook his head. He couldn't seem to focus on anything this evening.

"I need you to remember something, Much." She grabbed his chin and turned his face so she could look him square in the eye. Much felt like cowering beneath the weight of her keen gaze. "We all want to feel significant, and we search for things that will do that for us. But the only person who can fulfill that need is Christ."

"I know."

"You do know, and yet you aren't living as though you believe that. He chose *you*, He loves *you*, and He says that you are enough. And for His part…" Dusty grinned at Much. "He is far more than enough."

Much could feel the love and mercy swirling around him, could hear the small voice whispering that Dusty was speaking the truth.

Do you believe me?

Much closed his eyes, sinking into the comfort and strength he always found in Christ. He did believe Him.

"If we lose Robin, it will be horrible," Dusty said. "But you will not lose your worth if tragedy strikes, because Robin is not the one who defines who you are."

Much nodded, and then straightened his shoulders, feeling the power and purpose within him coming from the only source that could ever satisfy him.

Dusty pulled him to his feet and Much willingly followed her to the table.

"Where are we at with the plan?" Much asked.

"The execution will be in the Square," Will said. "The Sheriff wants to make a big deal out of it."

"We'll deal with it as we have all the others," Little John said. "Will and Ida will shoot down those who attempt to kill Robin and Lucy while the rest of you deal with the other soldiers and Andrew and I will get Robin and Lucy out of harm's way."

Much shook his head. "I'll shoot down the executioners with Will."

"You've been a wreck," Ida said. "No offense, but we don't need shaky hands and violent emotions attempting to save Robin Hood."

"I'm a better shot than you are," Much said, his voice calm and confident. "Will and I are the best options for archers with both Lucy and Robin out of commission."

"You been brooding in that corner--"

"I have years of experience as an outlaw that you do not, having only recently joined our crew. I was a soldier for more years before that, seeing real combat in the Holy Land while you were still mucking out your father's stalls. I can do this."

Will nodded. "He's right; he is the next best archer, and we need the best focused on saving Robin and Lucy."

Early the next morning the gang positioned themselves around Nottingham Square as a crowd began to gather. The Square was more packed than normal, leaving only inches of room between each body so it was difficult to move around. Apparently all of Nottingham was coming to see Robin Hood's execution. Much stood among the chaos, his bow strapped to his back and his hood over his head.

There were soldiers in every direction Much looked, causing his heart to pound loudly in his ears as his palms grew sweaty. Was this going to work?

Two platforms were erected in the center of the Square facing each other. On one, several chairs had been placed for the Sheriff and his invited guests to watch the execution, on the other were two chopping blocks for the beheadings that were meant to take place that morning.

The Sheriff's soldiers soon formed a line and began shoving the people of Nottingham back to open a path for the Sheriff to parade up to his platform with his guests in all their finery. The crowd was furious, shouting insults at the Sheriff, yelling at the soldiers who shoved them aside.

In another moment, more soldiers lined the pathway that had been created, separating the people from the soldiers who dragged Robin and Lucy toward their execution.

Much could scarcely breathe. He stood on his tip toes to see over the heads of people and soldiers in front of him. Robin and Lucy appeared to be speaking to one another as they were led up the stairs of the platform and forced to their knees in front of their execution blocks, with two men standing beside them with axes ready in their hands.

The Sheriff called for silence and an eerie quiet settled over Nottingham Square.

"The Great Robin Hood is about to die…does he have any last words?" the Sheriff called across the Square to Robin.

Much watched as Robin lifted his head from his execution block, wondering at Robin's audacity as he spoke to the Sheriff. "A few."

Much closed his eyes briefly, thinking this was hardly the time for Robin to be his usual sarcastic self.

"Do tell," the Sheriff laughed. "If you want to plead for your life, I'm listening."

"Sorry to disappoint you, Sheriff. But I don't want to plead for my life."

"Then what do you want to say, you dirty, terrible, outrageous, traitorous…"

"Alright, Sheriff. You win. You can do what you like with me. But let Lucy go. She's just an innocent girl."

"Proceed with the execution!" the Sheriff bellowed.

The guards pushed Robin's head back down over the wooden block. Much raised his bow, the people in front of him moving as well as they could to give him space, watching him with wide eyes. He ignored them, training his eye on the guard who was raising his axe over Robin's head.

He took a deep breath, watching the axe arc backwards through the air and then he let his arrow loose. His target dropped the axe as Much's arrow pierced his heart and he stumbled backwards and fell off of the platform.

Will's arrow had done much the same to the other guard who'd been set to kill Lucy.

Andrew was on the platform the next moment, untying Lucy's bonds and Much pushed through the crowd, who parted for him as best they could, as he and the rest of the gang rushed for the soldiers to keep them distracted while Robin and Lucy got away. The frantic crowd set to work as well, as they so often did, hindering the advancing soldiers in every way they could think of.

As soon as it was clear Robin and Lucy were free of the Square, Much disengaged from his fight with one of the Sheriff's men and ducked through the crowd, fleeing the Square. He heard footsteps behind him and swung around, sword raised, but saw Gisbourne sprinting after him.

Gisbourne slowed as he approached, glancing over his shoulder. "I was merely putting up a show of chasing you, get out of here."

Gisbourne began heading back down the street toward the Square and Much ducked down an alleyway and ran for Marcus' home where he mounted a horse and hurried to the camp, praying all the way that everyone would make it out alive.

He crashed into the forest, racing through Sherwood until he reached the camp.

Faith ran forward as the rest of the gang rode into camp as well. "Is everyone alright?"

Much looked around, his heartbeat slowly settling back to normal as he counted heads. He began to breathe properly at last. Everyone was accounted for.

"Thank you," Lucy said as she dismounted.

Will hugged her. "We couldn't live without you."

"But you would have left me to the wolves I suppose," Robin laughed.

Much swung his arm over Robin's shoulders. "Oh no. We would have rescued you either way."

"I know you would have, Much."

"How did you plan our rescue?" Lucy asked. "How did you even know I was going to be executed at all? That wasn't a part of the Sheriff's plan until late last night."

"Sir Guy helped us, of course," Allen said.

The group began to move toward the benches around the fire ring as they answered Lucy's questions and discuss the planning of the rescue.

"I suppose we will have to go directly to Gisbourne now," Much said, looking to Robin with wide eyes, and then to Mark.

"It's alright, Much," Robin said. "Gisbourne may be a great help. And we can go through Andrew as well; that would be more to my personal liking."

"Andrew will be more than willing to help," Lucy said. "He has already been acting as a middle man for Sir Guy, myself, and the gang when he needed to."

Mark placed a hand on her arm. "I'm glad you're safe, Lucy. I was so worried for both of you. You're like family to me; everyone in the gang is like family to me."

"That's true enough," Will grinned at the group. "Let's avoid more executions though, shall we? It's becoming rather an old trick, I'd say."

Much agreed whole-heartedly.

That night after the gang had retired to bed for the evening, Robin and Much sat together outside of Much's hut watching the fire slowly die down. The stars were twinkling overhead, and Much heard the distinct hooting of several owls nearby.

"I was so worried, Robin."

"I'm sure you were, but the danger is passed. You don't have to fret any longer."

"I know. Actually…after the initial panic, I did find some peace last night."

"Did you?"

"I've been…well, ever since we were small I've been relying on you, you know. I look to you for guidance on everything. As kids it was because you were the Earl's son and I was your servant, and once we were older it was habit to let you make all the decisions about… well, everything. I had put most of my identity as a person on you. And when I realized you might die today I nearly broke."

"Much…"

"But Dusty helped me remember that my worth isn't defined by you. So…I'm glad you're alive, and yes I would have grieved you as a friend if you died—but I wouldn't have lost who I was."

"I'm glad to hear it. I am proud of you, you know. You've been growing so much over the last few years, truly coming into your own in ways I never thought you would. I'm not sure Dusty could keep calling you the little mouse; you hardly are anymore."

"Thank you."

"On another subject," Robin grinned and winked at Much, "I asked Lucy to marry me."

"When?"

"While we were being executed. She laughed at me."

"She laughed at you?"

"At the absurdity of it, I suppose. Being beheaded and proposing marriage."

"It is a bit odd."

"It was absolutely ridiculous," Robin agreed, laughing.

"Did she answer your question, or just laugh at you?"

"She did not say one way or the other, but I do not have any cause for worry. I know she loves me."

"And you love her?"

"Dearly."

"I'm glad."

"Are you? I imagine Mark will find it hard to forgive."

"Mark will be okay. It is strange to see you loving someone other than Marian, but I am not upset by it. You deserve to be happy and I think you are both good for each other."

"I have more news, as well."

"You had a busy night, it seems."

"The prospect of me being beheaded led to as much introspection for me as it did for you, it seems," Robin said. "I came to an understanding with Christ."

"What?!"

"I accepted Him. I have many questions which I will no doubt pester you, and Dusty, and Lucy, and Friar Tuck with as time goes on, but…I realized my own depravity and my need of a Savior and, well, here we are."

"That is the best news you could have given me."

"I knew you'd think so," Robin said with a grin. "But why did you never tell me about your faith before? Dusty and Lucy are open enough about it, even Faith is, and she rarely holds a strong opinion about anything."

"I was always afraid you would disapprove."

"Your relationship with Jesus is of far greater value than your relationship with me."

"I know. And I realized last night the truth of it, so I probably would have told you now anyway."

"Well?" Robin grinned, slinging his arm around Much's shoulders and watching him with twinkling eyes.

504

"Well. I am a sinner saved by grace, with a loving Savior who has given me a new identity."

Epilogue

"LIFE SETTLED INTO a calm routine," Aunt Lucy said, stroking Mari-Lu's hair. Mari-Lu was still seated at her feet, her head resting in Aunt Lucy's lap. She felt more than content as she listened to Aunt Lucy finish her story—this has been the perfect end to her birthday.

"I helped in several raids now that I lived in the camp but there were few of those to be had anymore," Aunt Lucy said. "Faith and I would often wander the woods together, braiding flowers in each other's hair and living in a rather carefree and peaceful manner. Ida was disturbed by it, but Much would sometimes join us. He understood where our joy came from and was not surprised by it."

"You mean from your relationship with Christ?" Mari-Lu asked.

"Exactly. Soon after all this, King Richard came home. He rewarded the gang, pardoned Gisbourne, we cleared out the camp, and you know the rest."

"You and Robin got married."

"We did."

"What happened to Much?"

"When Robin and I took up residence in Locksley manor we told Much he was more than welcome to stay with us—and Sarah, of course, echoed that sentiment. But Much felt it was time he truly stood as his own person apart from Robin, so he took up residence in Nottingham instead."

"And we all lived happily ever after," Mari-Lu said, sighing contently.

"We lived happily, for sure. Though life was never perfect. It wasn't too long after my marriage to Robin that King Richard died and Prince John became the King of England."

"Oh no!" Mari-Lu's eyes widened. "He probably didn't like any of you very much!"

507

"He most certainly did not."

"What happened?"

"That, my love, is another story entirely…"

Acknowledgments

As always, I have many people to thank for their assistance, encouragement, and insight as they helped me bring Much's story to life. Below are a few of the people who participated in this endeavor both with *The Journey of the Peacekeeper* and with *Always in Shadow*, without which there never would have been a *Journey of the Peacekeeper.*

My parents support means the world to me.

The accountability of the hedgie house (Quill and Cup writing community) is 100% what made this rewrite possible, especially in so short a time. If I had enough page space to thank each and every one of you, I would! I'll limit myself to Mama Hedgie Ania who brought us all together in the first place and made the magic happen.

Also, my BFF (Best Feedback Friend)/critique partner Ellie W: your love for Much carried me through when I lost my own love for this story in the midst of edits. Your comments and suggestions definitely shaped his story to be stronger than I could have made it alone.

My sister Susannah for editing the OG book for me.

My sister Rebekah, my greatest encourager and my greatest critic rolled into one.

Jesus—my constant companion, my inspiration, and the mastermind behind all my stories. Oh, yeah, and my Savior and King. He's pretty cool.